D1796851

Sexuality and Gender in Fictions of Espionage

Sexuality and Gender in Fictions of Espionage

Spying Undercover(s)

Edited by
Ann Rea

BLOOMSBURY ACADEMIC
LONDON • NEW YORK • OXFORD • NEW DELHI • SYDNEY

BLOOMSBURY ACADEMIC
Bloomsbury Publishing Plc
50 Bedford Square, London, WC1B 3DP, UK
1385 Broadway, New York, NY 10018, USA
29 Earlsfort Terrace, Dublin 2, IRL

BLOOMSBURY, BLOOMSBURY ACADEMIC and the Diana logo are trademarks of Bloomsbury
Publishing Plc

First published in Great Britain 2024

Copyright © Ann Rea and Contributors, 2024

Ann Rea and Contributors have asserted their right under the Copyright, Designs and Patents Act, 1988,
to be identified as Authors of this work.

For legal purposes the Acknowledgments on p. xiii constitute an extension of this copyright page.

Cover design: Eleanor Rose
Cover image © Andrei Kobylko/iStock

All rights reserved. No part of this publication may be reproduced or transmitted in any form or by any
means, electronic or mechanical, including photocopying, recording, or any information storage or
retrieval system, without prior permission in writing from the publishers.

Bloomsbury Publishing Plc does not have any control over, or responsibility for, any third-party websites
referred to or in this book. All internet addresses given in this book were correct at the time of going
to press. The author and publisher regret any inconvenience caused if addresses have changed or sites
have ceased to exist, but can accept no responsibility for any such changes.

The author and publisher gratefully acknowledge the permission granted to reproduce copyrighted
material in this book. The third-party copyrighted material displayed this book is done so on the basis of fair
use for the purposes of teaching, criticism, scholarship or research only in accordance with international
copyright laws. It is not intended to infringe upon the ownership rights of the original owners.

Every effort has been made to trace copyright holders and to obtain their permission for the use of
copyright material. However, if any have been inadvertently overlooked, the publishers will be pleased, if
notified of any omissions, to make the necessary arrangement at the first opportunity.

A catalogue record for this book is available from the British Library.

Library of Congress Cataloging-in-Publication Data
Names: Rea, Ann, editor.
Title: Sexuality and gender in fictions of espionage : spying undercover(s) / edited by Ann Rea.
Description: London; New York: Bloomsbury Academic, 2023. | Includes bibliographical
references and index.
Identifiers: LCCN 2023020482 (print) | LCCN 2023020483 (ebook) | ISBN 9781350271364 (hardback) |
ISBN 9781350271401 (paperback) | ISBN 9781350271371 (pdf) | ISBN 9781350271388 (epub)
Subjects: LCSH: Spy stories, English–History and criticism. | Gender identity in literature. |
Sex in literature. | Espionage in literature. | Spies in literature. | LCGFT: Literary criticism. | Essays.
Classification: LCC PR830.S65 S49 2023 (print) | LCC PR830.S65 (ebook) |
DDC 823/.087209–dc23/eng/20230808
LC record available at https://lccn.loc.gov/2023020482
LC ebook record available at https://lccn.loc.gov/2023020483

ISBN: HB: 978-1-3502-7136-4
ePDF: 978-1-3502-7137-1
eBook: 978-1-3502-7138-8

Typeset by Deanta Global Publishing Services, Chennai, India

To find out more about our authors and books visit www.bloomsbury.com and sign up for our
newsletters.

For Mike, Jacob, Leo, and Cian, with all my love.

Contents

Notes on Contributors

Christine Berberich is Reader/ Associate Professor in Literature at the University of Portsmouth, UK. Her research focuses on national identity construction and Englishness and on literary commemorations of the Holocaust. She is the author of numerous articles and book chapters as well as the following books: *The Image of the English Gentleman in Twentieth-Century Literature*; co-editor of *Land & Identity: Memory, Theory, Practice*; *These Englands: Conversations on National Identity*; and *Affective Landscapes in Literature, Art & Everyday Life*; and editor of *The Bloomsbury Introduction to Popular Fiction*; *Trauma & Memory: The Holocaust in Contemporary Culture*; and *Brexit and the Migrant Voice: EU Citizens in post-Brexit Literature & Culture*. She is currently working on a monograph on *Nazi Noir* and a public-facing book on PG Wodehouse and the internment camp of Tost.

Oliver Buckton is Professor and Chair of English at Florida Atlantic University, Boca Raton. He specializes in spy fiction and intelligence history, modern British literature and culture, and film. He is the author of *Espionage in British Fiction and Film Since 1900: The Changing Enemy* (2015) and *The World is Not Enough: A Biography of Ian Fleming* (2021). In addition, he edited *The Many Facets of Diamonds Are Forever: James Bond on Page and Screen* (2017). His current project explores the impact of real-world espionage operations in the Second World War on postwar spy novelists, including Ian Fleming, Graham Greene, and Helen MacInnes. In 2021 Buckton was Fulbright Senior Fellow at the University of Málaga, Spain, where he researched and taught undergraduate and doctoral seminars on his project "Counterfeit Spies: The Arts of Deception in Wartime Espionage and Post-war Spy Fiction." Oliver Buckton has been a visiting research fellow at Indiana University, Yale University, and Churchill College, Cambridge. On a recent James Bond tour of Jamaica, he visited Ian Fleming's home Goldeneye where the James Bond novels were written.

Llewella Chapman is a visiting scholar at the University of East Anglia. Her research interests include British cinema, videogames, production histories, gender, and costume. She is the author of *Fashioning James Bond: Costume, Gender and Identity in the World of 007* (2022) and the BFI Film Classic *From Russia With Love* (2022).

Megan Faragher is a Professor at Wright State University, Lake Campus in Celina, OH (USA). Her research interests focus on propaganda, information studies, and group psychology as it relates to twentieth-century literature. She has also published articles in *Textual Practice*, *Literature & History*, and *The Space Between Journal*. She is the author of *Public Opinion Polling in Mid-Century British Literature: The Psychographic Turn* (2021).

Rachel Hoag received her doctorate in contemporary British literature from West Virginia University in 2023. Her dissertation focuses on the intersections of new economic criticism, globalization, and nostalgia in popular fiction, particularly the post–Cold War spy narrative. Her current research project explores how the rhetoric of Euroscepticism suffuses popular culture in the years prior to the Brexit vote. She works as an instructor of English and Information Literacy at Central Penn College near Harrisburg, Pennsylvania.

Paul Lohneis is Head of the London School of Film, Media & Design at the University of West London, and currently a PhD candidate in Creative and Critical Writing at the University of East Anglia. His background is in film and TV advertising as a writer-producer, and since moving into HE administrative management has broadened his fields of interest to include *inter alia* writing about gender, narrative, and form in the spy story.

Ann Rea is Professor and Director of English Literature at the University of Pittsburgh at Johnstown, USA, where she teaches twentieth-century British and Irish literature. Her research interests include middlebrow culture, both in Britain and Ireland, including a present project about the Irish feminine middlebrow novel. She published an edited collection, *Middlebrow Wodehouse: P. G. Wodehouse's Work in Context*, in 2016, followed by articles about the modern fashioning of the postcolonial mythology surrounding Aran sweaters, a study of spiritualism in Rachel Ferguson's *The Brontës Went to Woolworths*, the 1930s aviatrix and colonial femininity, and an exploration of orphans in Elizabeth Bowen's novels. Her study of internationalism and the Irish spy protagonist appeared in *Pennsylvania English* in 2019.

Kyle Smith is Programme Leader in Literature in the Faculty of Humanities, Education and Gaelic at the University of the Highlands and Islands, UK. His research interests focus on Thomas Pynchon, genre fiction, science fiction, cinema, and popular culture.

Rosie White is Senior Lecturer in Contemporary Literature, Theory and Popular Culture at Northumbria University, in Newcastle-Upon-Tyne, northeast England. She is the author of *Violent Femmes: Women as Spies in Popular Culture* (2008) and *Television Comedy and Femininity: Queering Gender* (2018).

Michael T. Williamson earned a PhD in 1996 from Rutgers University. He is Professor of English at Indiana University of Pennsylvania, where he serves as Director of the Literature and Criticism Doctoral Program. He teaches poetry, spy fiction, British literature, and Global Literature for the Graduate Program in Literature and Criticism and for the Robert E. Cook Honors College. He has published essays on nineteenth-century British women poets, early twentieth-century Yiddish poetry, Holocaust literature, and the comic writing of P. G. Wodehouse. He is editor of *Pennsylvania English*, a multidisciplinary literary journal, and *ARISTEIA: Myth, Literature, and Culture*.

Veronica A. Wilson received her PhD in American History and Women's History at Rutgers University in 2002. She has published several essays on communist and anticommunist spies in book anthologies and journals such as *Twentieth-Century Communism, American Communist History,* and *Diplomatic History.* Her interests in gender and political subversion during the Second World War and the Cold War have led to a book manuscript in progress—a study of Soviet spies-turned-anticommunist activists Hede and Paul Massing. On a less grim note, Wilson's love of space opera and popular culture occasionally moves her to write scholarly analyses of gender and sexuality in the *Star Wars* movie saga.

Acknowledgments

Sincere thanks to "Sisters in Crime" for their financial support of this project, as well as to the College Research Council at the University of Pittsburgh at Johnstown.

Thank you, as always, to Mike, whose love, support, and companionship means everything.

Introduction

Ann Rea

Why Examine Genders and Sexualities in Fiction of Espionage?

Like any form of narrative, spy fiction performs a variety of ideological tasks,[1] many of which literary critics have explored.[2] In spite of important studies that examine genders and sexualities[3] in these fictions, however, the genre's instrumentality in the shaping and scrutiny of gender roles and sexualities deserves more attention.[4] Certainly, although we might seek to debunk the perception that fiction of espionage is a masculine genre,[5] in the United Kingdom in the 1970s everyone's dad was reading John le Carré and Len Deighton, and most people will think first of James Bond on hearing the words "spy fiction," which might suggest that the fiction of espionage constitutes a later iteration of what Kate Macdonald identifies as the "masculine middlebrow."[6] Yet even though many of its writers and spy-protagonists are men, women do write spy fiction with women as protagonists, and male writers portray women in thought-provoking ways that merit analysis. And, of course, men are gendered too: gender does not only apply to women. In addition, spy fiction not only portrays but also frequently engages with the cultural production of masculine identity, as well as sexual identities, as has been the focus of several recent studies.[7] Heaving spy fiction out of the conceptual framework of masculine heteronormativity exposes it as not only potentially engaging with women's identities and with women exerting agency as spies but also engaging with queer identities, including sites where the secrecy of espionage and queer sexuality have historically overlapped. Effectively, a potential analysis of genders and sexualities in the fiction removes the distorting norms that have surrounded the genre, and espionage itself. So, when Rosie White notes that the Scarlet Pimpernel "cross-dresses in terms of gender, class and race" she points to an intersection between narratives of espionage, with their frequent representations of disguise or, perhaps more subtly, cover, and depictions of gender identity which can be performative, deceptive, "fluid," or offer concealment (White 2007: 13).

In case there might persist a perception that a volume of essays about gender and fiction will focus only on the work of women or on women as protagonists, this collection will make clear that the term "gender" now is used, as Wiegman argues, "both to describe the constraints of heteropatriarchal social formation and to figure subversion, disidentification, and dissidence in identity attachments and everyday life" (Wiegman 2012: 38–9).[8] And a genre of fiction that has been concerned with the exploration of national, political, and existential subjectivity—identity on many levels—can allow exploration of the many possible presentations of gender and sexualities. But, of course, literary criticism has paid less attention to spy fiction even than to other kinds of genre fiction, doubtless because of the "thriller's" lowbrow connotations. Criticism that looks past the lowbrow taint,[9] however, rewardingly finds espionage fiction to be deeply concerned with the political and historical narration of, particularly, Britain,[10] and its place in the world in the early half of the twentieth century, complicating and challenging literary-historical narratives about that country's inward turn after the Second World War and the demise of the British Empire.[11]

Spying itself, often involving the erasure of identity or the creation of expedient identities—what is known as "cover"—provides opportunities to alternatively erase or fabricate identity in a kind of performance that John le Carré compares to the work of an actor,[12] and espionage can attract those who seek to camouflage or manipulate certain aspects of their identity, notably their gender or sexual orientation. The contributors to this volume of essays find that the presentation of gender functions in similar ways to the spy's cover. Spy fiction also frequently reveals our culture's preconceptions and biases about gender and sexual identity. When Allan Hepburn observes, "narratives of intrigue, especially after 1945, represent gay men as protean, effeminate, deviant, enigmatic, unstable, leaky," we might note that while many of these stereotypes have historically been used to express male anxieties about women, they also reveal anxieties about the position of male homosexuals and their citizenship (Hepburn 2005: 187). Amid a plethora of beliefs about citizenship and identity, in which heterosexual men were seen to represent a monolith of reliable and acceptable national agency, it is helpful nevertheless to note that women and gay men have often been spies, even if the publishing practices that constructed the genre of fiction overlooked them because of its own distorting masculine heteronormative lens. Phyllis Lassner asserts that "the neglect of espionage fiction by women writers is also a matter of the marketplace: having been out of print for decades, their novels have been invisible" (Lassner 2016: 69).[13] This invisibility creates a dominant narrative that erroneously portrays spies and espionage as masculine, even while it attributes negative feminine or homosexual traits to those who practice espionage! The dominant narrative also perceives women and gay men as lacking in public and private agency and as suspect in their loyalties, and has at times asserted that effective public servants needed to be masculine and heterosexual.[14] Variously, then, women and male homosexual spies might conceal their identities to create camouflage or cover, or alternatively their gender and sexual identities might divert attention from the fact that they are spies, casting them as being above suspicion.

While several critical analyses of spy fiction examine the place of women in the genre, both as writers and protagonists, and several critics examine the complex relationship between homosexuality and espionage fiction, no study to date considers them *together*. The shadow of a scandal involving moles in the Service who happened to be queer drives many spy novels of the 1950s and 1960s. Twentieth-century British espionage, historically and in the fiction, consisted of Establishment men with public school, Oxbridge educations: Michael Denning even notes, "it has been claimed that the word ['Establishment'] was first used during the Burgess and Maclean revelations in September 1955" (Denning 1987: 120). The exposure of Guy Burgess and Donald

Maclean as double agents created the public perception in Britain that the ruling class of *haut-bourgeois* men was unfit to rule. In turn, this contributed to what Eric Carlston describes as "the evolution of a conservative populism in Great Britain and the United States and in the post-war ascendancy of previously excluded classes to political power" (Carlston 2013: 210).[15] So, when Len Deighton's *The Ipcress File*, the subject of a chapter in this collection, asserts a new middle-class masculinity in as-yet-unnamed Harry Palmer, he defines this against Establishment men, portrayed as unreliable in part because of their homosexuality. Increasingly, in the 1960s, social change and the growing meritocracy, accompanied by increasing bureaucratization, create a social climate in which the spy-protagonist pushes back against "superiors." This fiction reasserts spying as a man's game and spy fiction a masculine genre, representing a new, more "virile" man, albeit somewhat anxiously. Several chapters in this collection (Buckton, Berberich, Chapman, Rea) consider spy fiction from the 1960s that assert a variety of masculinities that effectively contradict the perception, at home and abroad, that "British political scandal is associated with British effeminacy," as Carlston posits (Carlston 2013: 210). Historical contexts are crucial, then, not only for explorations of espionage as it functioned in the period under scrutiny in this collection, across the period from 1930s Berlin to contemporary London, but these contexts, in turn, influence perceptions of masculinity and are accompanied by a growth in women's social authority and therefore in women's potential roles as agents.

Gender and Sexualities in Espionage Fiction's Critical Narrative

A critical narrative focused on male spies and writers dominates the earliest studies of spy fiction, and these exclude considerations of women,[16] either as writers or spies, as well, largely, as the consideration of homosexuality.[17] Robert Snyder devotes one chapter to a consideration of a woman spy novelist, Stella Rimington, but faults her mimetic representation of counterterrorism amid *jihad* because Rimington's novels do not fit his model of rhetorical analysis. Allan Hepburn (2005) observes, "Bond has to learn over and over again that agents can be women too," but Hepburn primarily explores fiction of espionage's engagement with ideologies of masculinity especially as they might be observed as queer (Hepburn 2005: 14).[18] Hepburn's chapter about John Banville's *The Untouchable*'s depiction of Anthony Blunt argues that the "narrative of intrigue, especially after 1945, represents gay men as protean, effeminate, deviant, enigmatic, unstable, *leaky*" (Hepburn 2005: 187). Intriguingly, he notes, "As the Cold War progressed, all spies proved to be, in some degree, a bit queer" (Hepburn 2005: 187). He explains, "homosexuality trumps identifiers of manliness, such as Etonian suaveness, fascination with gadgetry, ordinariness, and rigidity of convictions. Invisible when not out, the queer spy takes refuge in the double closets of sexuality and political affiliation" (Hepburn 2005: 188).

Rosie White (2007) begins her consideration of women in spy fiction, *Violent Femmes: Women Spies in Popular Culture* by asserting, "Spying is an appropriate trope to employ when discussing gender, as femininity, like masculinity, is always undercover—a covert operation with far-reaching effects" (White 2007: 1). She argues in her focus on popular culture that the spy destabilizes fixed gender identities, noting, "The *good* female spy offers a powerfully ambivalent account of the nation-state and the status quo because of the discrepancy between femininity and public forms of power in the history of Britain and the USA" (White 2007: 3). Spy fictions, then, she argues, "offer women readers [a] fantasy of individual agency," since, "[w]omen as spies in fiction, film and television map shifts in the politics of gender across the twentieth century and into the twenty-first, disturbing the equilibrium of popular culture" (White 2007: 2). White's book has a chapter about male spies in popular fiction that explores John Buchan's Richard Hannay as well as the Scarlet Pimpernel, James Bond, and Alec Leamas, and explores representations of the "girl" and the anxieties inherent in James Bond's particular version of masculinity in the novels and films.

Phyllis Lassner's *Espionage and Exile* (2016) has one chapter that examines women writers of espionage fiction, noting the proliferating critical examinations of *detective* fiction written by women but continued neglect of women writers of spy fiction. Analyzing novels by Pamela Frankau, Ann Bridges, and Helen MacInnes, she argues that they "trouble and revise the gendered conventions and perhaps the reader's expectations [by] reconfigure[ing] suspense as the development of individual agency" (Lassner 2016: 70). This "double agency" Lassner locates in the fact that the "women spies exile themselves from the domestic sphere and their private roles" (Lassner 2016: 70). Ultimately Lassner characterizes this fiction as "interrogat[ing] women's domestic and political relationships to the meanings of citizenship and activism" in their experience of espionage that moves them from "insular privilege and protection to worlds of political danger" (Lassner 2016: 81). Moreover, as fiction by Helen MacInnes, Pamela Frankau, and Ann Bridge shows, according to Lassner, "the transformation of women's social and economic security into political consciousness also criticizes political isolationism" (Lassner 2016: 82). As polemical fiction, cast in gripping adventure narratives, the "women's writing grants the epistemological perspectives to a woman's empirical and inductive talents and challenges the boundaries between the genre's assigned role for women as follower," and thus Frances in MacInnes's *Above Suspicion* "performs the work of political analysis and critical propaganda" (Lassner 2016: 83). If Hepburn posits the reader's role as one in which a citizen engages in a narrative of national identity made complex by the espionage narrative, Lassner posits that MacInnes, Frankau, and Bridge portray women protagonists in narratives that "encourage their audiences to identify with protagonists who like themselves gain political consciousness as a pathway to resistance," and who, in many cases, are women (Lassner 2016: 88).

Erin Carlston confines her study to male subjects, especially gay men and Jews, not because of "indifference" to the intersections of gender with other facets of culture, as she explains, but because she construes a serious difference between women's and men's relationships to nationhood. She asserts, "I am primarily interested [...] in the question of citizenship, and women have not been citizens of most nations on equal terms with men. Jewish and homosexual men—but only rarely lesbians or Jewish women—have consistently been associated both literally and figuratively with themes of treason and espionage" (Carlston 2013: 5). Focusing on citizenship and difference, particularly, "the potential *invisible* alterity of the Jew and the homosexual, which, at least as early as the Renaissance, had begun to provoke fears that the nation could be surreptitiously undermined by 'moles' whose true loyalties might turn out to lie with their clan, race, or biological type rather than with their country," Carlston explores these ideological constructs in literature (Carlston 2013: 5). She reads cultural texts for a history of homosexuals and Jews in their relationships to nation states, including an exploration of W. H. Auden and his contemporaries' representations of themselves as "upper-middle-class, left-wing, British homosexual[s] as both emblem of, and traitor to, an empire [they were] bred to rule" (Carlston 2013: 7). Consideration of homosexuality and Jewishness then exposes the "ideological requirements for full citizenship," which she argues, "far exceed the limited criteria of formal enfranchisement" (Carlston 2013: 9). And, furthermore, the fictional spy can be "secretly really something else, dangerous, threatening, perhaps reviled or hunted but also intriguing, attractive, even glamorous," which helps to explain how espionage lends itself to narration (Carlston 2013: 6). Carlston's study, in particular, explores the impact of Burgess and Maclean's defections, which appeared to confirm the stereotype of the homosexual or the Jew, or both, as traitor. Subsequently, McCarthyism in the United States equated "national integrity and the impenetrable body of the normatively sexed man" (Carlston 2013: 8). Carlston asserts that fictions of espionage and the cultures from which they emerge portray the citizen as masculine, leaving women with the task of ideological negotiation of nationality.

With a focus on political secrecy, in its relationship to loyalty and treason and the circulation of knowledge, Eva Horn's epistemological study *The Secret War: Treason, Espionage, and Modern Fiction* considers the role fiction plays in our understanding of secrecy and betrayal, and asserts that fictions "expose the fictionality of the political itself" (Horn 2013: 41).[19] Horn argues that women "become figures of disguise and deception precisely *as women*, that is, as seemingly apolitical agents while actually being highly political. Women become the embodiment of the *secret* side of war and politics," according to Horn, who argues that the woman spy represents "a fundamental disturbance of the relationship between the sexes" and was variously invented by women who actually spied, or by men who tell these women's stories as "adventurous, demonic, and highly eroticized narratives" (Horn 2013: 171). Horn observes that the persistent roles for women in espionage are the *femme fatale* or the "invisible functionary or silent organizer," or "secretary," a type which Paul Lohneis's chapter explores in John le Carré's Connie Sachs and Molly Doran, the archivist in "Slow Horses" fiction.

With the exception of Hepburn, White, Lassner, Horn, and Carlston, critical assumptions about spy fiction have accepted the belief that Establishment male figures have sustained espionage. These critics have created a shift in focus that allows attention to genders and sexualities, albeit separately, that change our perspective of the masculine British Establishment. The canon of British spy fiction has been constructed as masculine, upper middle class, and heterosexual. Fiction energized by the perceived need to counteract an effeminate Service, then, came to constitute the canon of British spy fiction, even though women continued to write novels that depicted espionage quite differently. And including understanding of the role spy fiction has played in creating a public sense of masculinity, of women's roles as citizens, and of the exploitation of ideas about homosexuality in a revision of the history of the genre allows us to tell a more accurate story. Women writers' portrayals of espionage do not seek to assert British virility in the face of a British global emasculation, unsurprisingly. While more critical work remains to be done and this collection of essays unfortunately does not include studies of Pamela Frankau and Ann Bridges, or even a full study of Stella Rimington, and is limited to studies of British fiction and one example of internal espionage in the United States, it will begin the work of creating a critical context for further study. And Pamela Frankau,[20] Ann Bridge,[21] and Helen MacInnes each used their knowledge of international affairs, the result of their extensive travel as wives of diplomats and military officers, to publish throughout the 1930s and 1940s, throughout the Second World War and past the 1970s. This fiction by women with international sensibilities— not "mere" domestic fiction—constitutes a strand of espionage fiction in its own right.[22] Publishers of the genre have been guided, and misguided, by assumptions, which the critical lens of New Modernist studies allows us to see and helps us to understand. A consideration of the evolution and readership of genre fiction, especially in Britain from the 1930s onwards, deepens our understanding of how changes in the literary market resulting from increasing literacy are inflected by assumptions about gender. We now recognize that efforts to assert certain types of middle-class cultural authority led to beliefs about literary quality that depended upon evaluations of readers according to their gender and social class.[23]

The Social and Political Context

The end of the Second World War changed Britain's place in the world. In spite of the perception that British resistance to Nazism and fascism was central to the defeat of the Axis powers, Britain emerged from the war deeply indebted to the United States and facing an era of rapid decline as a colonial power. The Empire constituted an economic drain on a country that continued food rationing until 1954.[24] Economically and militarily weakened, Britain confronted the Suez Crisis in 1956 with the recognition of its need to "cleave loyally to US positions," a dependence that also illustrated Britain's "fundamental weakness and isolation," as Tony Judt observes (Judt 2005: 299, 302).[25] Vis-à-vis the postwar superpowers, Britain occupied a mere third place, especially when Moscow assumed the role of protector of the colonized nations after Suez, further diminishing Britain's Cold War authority. As Judt notes, "The country could no longer afford to pretend to power and influence across the oceans" (Judt 2005: 299). Early 1950s optimism about the booming economy gave way to a sense of instability characterized by fiction, film, and theater that, Judt argues, portrayed England as "divided, embittered, cynical, jaundiced and hard-faced [. . .], its illusions shattered" (Judt 2005: 301). Britain appeared to have lost its sense of national direction.

The defections of Guy Burgess and Donald Maclean, and later Kim Philby, traumatized Britain's sense of potency in international affairs, a malaise that persisted into the 1980s. Male homosexuality, both historical and fictional, works in complex ways. On the one hand, as Erin G. Carlston observes, the director of MI5 from 1909 until 1940, Sir Vernon Kell, sought intelligence officers "of good character—which ruled out homosexuals, Catholics and men who had not been to public school. Homosexuals, Kell thought, were disgusting and unreliable and Catholics were habitual intriguers with loyalties that extended beyond Britain" (Carlston 2013: 177). Nevertheless, many homosexual men evaded detection when they applied to the Service, including Guy Burgess, one of the Cambridge spies, who was flagrantly gay, and also openly a communist.[26] Carlston asserts that Andrew Boyle blamed "the right academic and social background, and evidence of clubbability and good fellowship" for the fact that Burgess, Maclean, and Blunt found jobs with the War Office before being recruited as double agents by the Russians (Carlston 2013: 177). Effectively, their public school and Oxbridge ties trumped their communist sympathies, while, astonishingly perhaps, their sexual orientation remained somewhat invisible. Carlston contests the usual assumption that the Soviets sought what they would have regarded as "sexually deviant recruits" because these men could be susceptible to blackmail, arguing instead that Russians believed these men would provide them access to the elite stratum of English society (Carlston 2013: 178). The outcome was that gay spies like Burgess could "sow confusion about the causes of deception and illicit behavior [so that] homosexuality seems at times to have constituted a convenient smokescreen for espionage" (Carlston 2013: 178). This "fungibility of sexuality and spying," as Carlston terms the coincidence of two forms of clandestinity among three of the Cambridge Spies, might be construed in different ways, however (Carlston 2013: 180). Conveying the news of the identities of these men, the British press saw their "deviant" sexuality as the reason for their disloyalty to Britain. Carlston points to "the idea that Communism and sexual deviance are mutually constitutive aberrations that dispose men to treachery" that dominated news coverage, or the belief that "deviation in one direction may indicate deviation in another" (Carlston 2013: 180, 181). We should remember, though, that in spite of their communism and homosexuality, Burgess, Maclean, and Blunt were Establishment figures, or, as Cyril Connolly noted, "members of the governing class, of the high bureaucracy, the 'they' who rule the 'we'" (quoted in Carlston 2013: 183).

An important counterpoint to the view that homosexual men represent treachery because of their supposed innate deviance is the view, expressed by members of the Auden group and also in John Banville's fictional account of Anthony Blunt, that these gay men spy, as Carlston says of *The Untouchable*, "as a response to a social and political climate that engaged them in an obligatory relationship to both duplicity and criminality [in which] rather than being swayed to Communism by homophobic oppression, Banville's protagonist, Victor Maskell, uses his experience of being a double agent as the libidinal testing ground for his eventual exploration of homosex" (Carlston 2013: 185). In Carlston's reading of *The Untouchable*, "the causal relation between homosexuality and espionage on which commentators had insisted for decades is cleverly inverted; homosexuality does not necessarily lead to spying [. . .], but spying can be a rehearsal for homosexuality" (Carlston 2013: 185). The queer spy's propensity for clandestinity becomes the outcome of his closeting. That Banville compounds Maskell as both Anthony Blunt and Louis MacNeice, turning him into the "queer *Irish* spy," intensifies his portrayal as a figure suspected of having a tendency to betray.

Critical accounts of espionage fiction effectively closeted narratives about gay men; in turn, spy fiction, particularly in the late 1950s and early 1960s, anxiously sought to resist the appearance that spies were queer, for example in the portrayal of James Bond. Rosie White reads the Bond stories as needing to repeatedly refute any implication that Bond is gay. She argues that the narratives require the girl in order to confirm compulsively that Bond is "fully heterosexual" (White 2007: 27). To White, this indicates that "Bond's hetero-masculinity is dysfunctional," and that his "gender identity [. . .] is inseparable in these fictions from his sexual performance" (White 2007: 26). Hypermasculine fictions then seek to affirm the idea of Britain's international virility, even as they express anxiety about their hero's masculinity. The canon of espionage fiction can construct and defend acceptable versions of masculinity as a masculine stronghold, which, in turn, explains why women writers and women spy-protagonists have been rendered invisible.

The Scope of This Book

The chapters in this book consider intersections of gender and sexualities with spy narratives in a variety of ways, appearing in chronological order according to the historical periods they study. The first chapter, by Megan Faragher, considers how a strategy of camouflaging and simultaneously expressing queer identities—camp— became a dangerously volatile tool for enemy exploitation during Nazism's rise to power in Berlin. Camp is a double-edged sword in 1930s Berlin's shifting sexual politics, from the tolerance and openness of the Weimar Republic to the increasing oppressiveness of Nazi Germany. While it serves as camouflage, like cover, camp also potentially allows dangerous deception and betrayal.

Several chapters examine women in spy fiction, with three (by Smith, Williamson, and White, respectively) examining narratives in which women spy-protagonists either exploit derogatory perceptions of women to their advantage or take agency to define their politics, regardless of how their gender might be used to restrict them. Helen MacInnes's fiction, Williamson and Smith show, depicts Nazism in late 1930s Germany and 1940s Poland, in which the role of academic wife and tourist provides cover, as Kyle Smith shows, in her 1939 novel, *Above Suspicion*. Women's invisibility, Kyle Smith and Rosie White argue, can be valuable for a spy. Williamson examines how MacInnes's 1944 novel, *While Still We Live*, depicts a woman agent developing meaningful political engagement when she joins the Polish Resistance and develops an understanding of the Polish experience of war. White, Wilson, Smith, and Hoag examine women spies placed precisely because their gender, which, in combination with other factors such as their race or age, camouflages the fact that they are spies. For Rosie White, negative perceptions of the ageing woman provide cover, both historically and in le Carré's fiction. Veronica Wilson narrates the history of the same period, the early 1960s, showing the infiltration of the civil rights movement by two Black women planted by the FBI, in an exploitation of race and gender together as cover. In America, the enemy agent is feared to be within. Lohneis and Hoag explore how women can endure severe restrictions in their agency in espionage work, again when their gender is combined with, for example, disability or youth and attractiveness. For Hoag, conventional femininity serves as cover, in John le Carré's unusual, if unwitting, focus on women's agency in *The Little Drummer Girl* (1983). Amid the Arab-Israeli conflict in the 1970s and 1980s, its protagonist both capitulates to and exploits regressive ideas about women's agency. Paul Lohneis's chapter examines le Carré's Cold War *Tinker, Tailor, Soldier, Spy* (1974) alongside Mick Herron's very contemporary "Slow Horses" fiction (2010–2022), a study that spans a publication period of about fifty years of depictions of women maintaining institutional memory. Abject because of the combination of their age, disability, and femininity, these women are marginalized as much because they embody their institutions' truths. After setting up his examination of women spies' exploitation of their social and civic invisibility, Kyle Smith links this strategy to recent portrayals of women-as-spies in fiction by Natasha Walter, Manda Scott, and Laura Wilkinson.

Four chapters (by Christine Berberich, Oliver Buckton, Ann Rea, and Llewella Chapman, respectively) consider portrayals of masculinity after the Burgess and Maclean defections of 1951, and spy fiction's efforts to reassert British spies' virility. James Bond (Berberich and Buckton), Alec Leamas, and the as-yet-unnamed Harry Palmer (Rea) assert new forms of postwar masculinity in gendered narratives about Britain's recalibrated global-political role after the war and decolonization. Llewella Chapman explores tailoring as part of the depiction of "gentlemanly" heterosexuality in le Carré's post–Cold War novel *The Tailor of Panama* (1996), and the film adaptation (2001), in 1980s Panama before the American invasion.

One of the important findings that emerges in this collection is that in narratives of espionage, gender presentation and sexual identities sometimes function in the same way in which "cover" functions for spies. In other words, spies create fictional identities for themselves to evade detection, or exaggerate their femininity, for example, in order to render themselves invisible, or create other versions of masculinity to defend against the charge of effeminacy. Therefore, fictions of espionage are firmly located in the gender-politics and history of the era that they depict; moreover, these narratives do not just explore but also influence their cultural moments, even by intervening in the gender and sexual politics of their time. A careful examination of spy fiction reveals that, at any given cultural moment, the narratives' portrayals of sexualities and gender not only inhere to the politics of national identity, but these narratives also actively intervene in producing the culture's ideology, as the following chapters will show.

This volume is concerned primarily with British spy fiction, which emerged from the imperial adventure narrative and narrated Britain's political role during the decades leading to the First and Second World Wars, its wartime political engagements, and of course its declining influence during the Cold War and its aftermath in international terrorism. One chapter, however, examines an example of espionage in the United States, revealing the American concern, specifically, with the threat of spies *within* more than with international espionage, although the threat of international communism always loomed. Espionage fiction continues to engage with international politics and has adapted to the prevailing historical conditions of the twenty first century. Even though it appeared moribund after the end of the Cold War, a resurgence of stories concerned with counterintelligence and international politics in the last ten to fifteen years, as well as with Russia's totalitarian resurgence, has coincided with a growing number of serious studies of spy fiction from a variety of critical perspectives.

The Chapters

The book opens with a consideration of espionage and camp as cover in 1930s Berlin, Megan Faragher's chapter, "Camp Camouflage: The Art of Espionage in *Mr. Norris Changes Trains.*" Any consideration of espionage in the 1930s to the 1950s in Britain should include consideration of the Auden group, members of which, although they were not spies, were nevertheless in proximity with the Cambridge spies, and also used espionage as a recurring trope in their work.[27] Faragher examines the representation of camp as camouflage for gay men and spies in Christopher Isherwood's 1935 novel, set at the moment of intersection between Weimar Berlin's sexual liberation and the dangers of Nazism. Nazi criminalization of homosexuality increased sharply between 1932 and 1934, increasing the political dangers to the queer community, and its members were forced into hiding, like spies. She notes that Auden was writing *The Orators* while Isherwood wrote *Mr. Norris Changes Trains*, and although Auden's highbrow text seems dissimilar to Isherwood's middlebrow and apparently frivolous novel, they nevertheless shared the concern of emergent fascism and with the difficulties of identifying an enemy. Fascism, Auden posited, threatened artistic autonomy and, as Faragher argues, queer aesthetics appeared to threaten the fascist state. To the fascist, the homosexual and the spy shared the characteristic of looking like any other heterosexual man, so sexual orientation and political affinity required decoding. Camp figures in this process because, as Faragher notes, it allows a "performative self-presentation [that] simultaneously veils and unmasks queer identification." As the originator of the term "camp," Isherwood characterized it as, in Faragher's words, a "conspicuous, unconventional aesthetic approach to identification and definition." Faragher takes issue with Susan Sontag's definition of camp as apolitical, arguing that "camp camouflage" can either appear frivolous or politically dangerous, which Faragher argues applies equally to Isherwood's novel. While camp can expose the performative nature of gender presentation, and offer a safe queer space, it also represents "a liminal, besieged space, permeable by those weaponizing camp as political camouflage," and becomes dangerous. Camp can be appropriated, Faragher contends, which marks Isherwood's use of camp as inherently political.

Chapter 2, by Kyle Smith, and Chapter 3, by Michael T. Williamson, examine the fiction of Helen MacInnes, deeply important in understanding the political forces at work in twentieth-century Europe, and Chapter 4, by Oliver Buckton, makes reference to her work. First, Kyle Smith's chapter, "Vanished Ladies: Helen MacInnes's *Above Suspicion* and Women in Spy Fiction," examines women's public invisibility. Smith and Rosie White, in Chapter 8, argue that this invisibility can be exploited by the woman spy. Smith argues that a middle-class woman's respectability and inconspicuousness can provide cover, as MacInnes explores in *Above Suspicion*, set in Germany in 1939. He creates an interpretative context provided by historical accounts of the invisibility of many women in the fight against Nazism as well as the critical and publication invisibility of spy fiction by women. Smith also offers an analysis of tourism, an inherent recurring trope in spy fiction since its earliest iterations. As a tourist, Frances observes Nazi Germany, comparing it both to her experience of travel there before Hitler's rise and to the England for which she yearns. Smith explores the trope of tourism for its ties to concepts of mobility and immobility and the figure of the refugee as an unwilling traveler. His reading of MacInnes's early fiction alerts us to tourism's potential opportunities to provide cover and reshape identity in *Assignment in Brittany*, as well as MacInnes's exploitation of her protagonist Frances's invisibility. Frances exploits this invisibility in a text which, Smith argues, also hides her for periods of time, although his chapter also asserts, importantly, that Frances reveals how women-as-spies can be both "confined (or released) by their invisibility." In spite of this invisibility, however, Smith argues that MacInnes depicts Frances as a protagonist who articulates the Allies' anti-Nazi political ideology and in so doing "repudiate[s] the genre's restrictive roles for its women characters," as Smith quotes Phyllis Lassner as saying (Lassner 2016: 234).

Michael Williamson's Chapter 3, "Helen MacInnes's *While Still We Live*: Gender, Secret Agents, and National Ethics," posits that representations of Poland in historical fiction by women inform MacInnes's 1944 novel about the complexities of Polish nationalism and resistance to both Nazism and the Soviets. Williamson's chapter argues that MacInnes "uses the already ethically engaged genre of the romantic historical novel" to "transform" the witnessing of suffering in war narratives into "politically and ethically aware knowledge of geopolitical history." Williamson asserts that the novel argues for "gendered partnership" instead of depicting a woman agent who will merely restore Polish masculinity or serve as a witness to Polish suffering, a partnership which works on a broader level as the novel engages its British and American readers in sympathy with Poles enduring German occupation. Exploring the concept urged by Adam Piette and Mark Rawlinson in their introduction to *The Edinburgh Companion to Twentieth-Century British and American War Literature*, Williamson notes, "war tends to alter the genres it inhabits" (Piette and Rawlinson 2016: 6). Williamson explores the alterations MacInnes's spy fiction makes to the romantic historical novel, a disparaged feminine genre, under the pressure of women's experience of war. National identity, Williamson asserts that MacInnes shows, consists of a multiplicity of affiliations and identities, many informed by the experience of history. This process, according to Williamson, has been written out of the history of the Cold War, and out of the history of the genre of espionage fiction. The protagonist of *While Still We Live* develops an ethical response to the people of occupied Poland as the result of her confrontation with their suffering. On a larger level, this metonymizes what Phyllis Lassner identified as "Britain's moral consciousness," and criticizes "privileged isolationism" (Lassner 2016: 82, 93).

Chapter 4, Oliver Buckton's "'Some Other Man Who Would Have to be Set Aside': Burgess, Maclean, and the Adversarial Spy in Ian Fleming's *From Russia with Love*," considers Ian Fleming's anomalous 1957 novel in its historical and political context in the aftermath of the scandalous defections of Establishment figures, Guy Burgess and Donald Maclean. Fleming's novel's opening reveals a male body that resembles James Bond, but belongs instead to "Red" Grant, a figure who becomes Bond's double as his

Soviet counterpart. As a British (although with Irish parentage) defector to the Soviet Union, Grant suggests Burgess and Maclean, who defected in 1951, and the narrative establishes Bond as, in Buckton's words, "the virile British spy hero needed to counteract the damaging effects of the notorious episode." Bond will simultaneously correct the image of the British secret agent as a traitor and queer, restoring Britain's manhood and correcting American loss of faith in Britain as an ally, and assuage British anxiety about the country's emasculation on the global-political stage. As Buckton argues, the perception was that queer men, already seen as prone to blackmail, might react to the sense of their surrounding society as alien and hostile by becoming spies. But Bond is not an uncomplicated figure, as the hypermasculine savior of Britain's manhood, but shares Burgess's promiscuity, if not his orientation, and in this, Fleming's fifth Bond novel appears "soft," pampered by inactivity, and in comparison, as Buckton argues, "Grant is the sociopath, driven by bloodlust not ideology." Serving as Bond's double, then, Grant also stands as what Emma Grundy Haigh describes as "the adversarial spy," and a recurring figure in espionage fiction as "both that which the spy-hero seeks to define himself against, and that which the spy-hero desires to become." While Grant exceeds Bond in his ruthlessness and brutality, Bond also recognizes in him his own boredom and sense of futility which for each will be appeased by having a worthy opponent. The resulting duel, Buckton argues, also serves as a duel between east and west, but with the risk that Bond, as the west, might lose.

Buckton notes that Helen MacInnes's 1958 novel *North from Rome* also alludes to the Cambridge spy scandal in featuring a double agent, Luigi Pirotta, described as "a friend of [Donald] Maclean's" (MacInnes 2012: 114). The rivalry between Pirotta and the novel's protagonist, American writer, William Lammiter, is characterized as sexual, and results in another struggle between east and west which, Buckton argues, promotes the union between Britain and America against an aristocratic figure who threatens violence against women. Both *From Russia with Love* and *North from Rome* depict a woman as the mediator between the adversarial spies, so that "the Cold War adversarial spy relationship is fought over the body and mind of a beautiful woman." But ironically, Buckton argues, instead of reinforcing the image of Britain's Secret Intelligence Service in response to the Burgess-Maclean scandal, *From Russia with Love* portrays Bond as weak and incompetent, and even prone to queer proclivities in his quasi-monogamous relationship with M. The novel suggests the British Service's Establishment ties create inherent weaknesses that are no match for SMERSH's ruthlessness and discipline, with Bond only emerging alive as a matter of luck

Christine Berberich's chapter, "Bond, Colonialism, and 'the Other'" shares Rosie White's objective of examining portrayals of women in spy fiction written by men, by exploring the "Bond girl" in the context of Britain's post–Second World War economic hardship and subsequent imperial decline. As part of what Berberich terms Fleming's "reactionary, nostalgic notion of national identity," the Bond films simultaneously feminize the racially disparaged enemies of Britain's Secret Service who hail, variously, from Russia, China, Korea, Japan, the Caribbean, Africa, and even France. Portrayals of women—the "Bond girls"—simultaneously exoticize Bond's sexual conquests and also offer portrayals of women characters of racial diversity that shore up a mythical British racial and political superiority. This takes place in a period of rapid change for Britain in a racially diverse world, as well as amid the increase in immigration from former colonies into Britain. Ultimately, Berberich argues, the reactionary Bond novels pervert history in their clinging to myths and symbols of white superiority, embodied in their portrayals of women, as much as of men.

One chapter, by historian Veronica Wilson, addresses a significant American example of espionage and its representation, both revealing the extent of American suspicion of spies *within* the country, a preoccupation with domestic instead of international espionage. Wilson's chapter, "'Learn, Babies, Learn': Race, Representation, and the John Birch Society Activists Julia Brown and Lola Belle Holmes," examines the role of two Cold War, African American anticommunist informants. Embedded in the Communist Party of the USA by the FBI, as well as in groups advocating for civil rights, Brown later testified to the House Un-American Activities Committee, to which she described herself as an "undercover agent." When members of the CPUSA discovered her embeddedness in their organization, she became a speaker on a lecture circuit devised by right-wing groups, particularly the John Birch Society, which directly challenged the civil rights movement and sought to undermine Dr. Martin Luther King's credibility. Brown and Holmes, with the support of the FBI and HUAC, became prominent anticommunist campaigners who undermined the civil rights movement and the National Association for the Advancement of Colored People, arguing that they had been infiltrated by communism and that they manipulated African Americans in order to foment civil unrest. Both women carved lucrative careers that exploited the anxieties of white Americans who feared the civil rights movement, student protests, the Cold War, and growing social welfare programs, during an era when racial politics were at the forefront. Brown and Holmes told these conservative white people what they wanted to hear, while effectively eliding their own identity politics as African American women. But Wilson self-reflexively scrutinizes her own role as a historical researcher and narrator of Brown's and Holmes's stories. Not only does Wilson point to a scarcity of accounts of their lives by Brown and Holmes themselves, which she had to overcome, but this also presents the risk that anyone narrating their stories might misrepresent or unwillingly appropriate their stories, with fragmentary evidence about them. Wilson affirms the importance of research such as this, however, that enables our increased understanding of the intersections of race, gender, and the political and historical moment in which people live, even while she urges sensitivity and the commitment to respectful interpretation of their meanings.

Chapter 7, Ann Rea's "A New Class of Domesticity: Home, Abroad, Foreignness, and Masculinity in Len Deighton's *The Ipcress File* and John le Carré's *The Spy Who Came in from the Cold*," explores the opposition between home and abroad and the safety and comforts of the domestic space against the exigencies of the field, in these two novels from the early sixties. Le Carré's novel shows Leamas yearning for the emotional and physical comforts of the home that stands as a metaphor for the purpose of a spy's work, carried out so that "ordinary people here and elsewhere can sleep safely in their beds at night" (le Carré 1962: 15). Deighton's Harry Palmer displays a surprisingly domestic competence and epicurean knowledge when he cooks sophisticated continental food, fashionable in the early 1960s as Elizabeth David's cookery books began to influence tastes. This chapter argues that Palmer serves as a model for a new English virility, open to foreign influences, and resistant to the masculine Establishment that emerged as untrustworthy, to the British public, as a result of the Burgess, Maclean, and Philby defections. The awareness of Mediterranean gastronomy in turn challenges Jed Esty's formulation of the "shrinking island" and an inward-turning, conservative English modernity.[28] Although Deighton's novel was published in 1963, a year later than le Carré's *The Spy Who Came in from the Cold*, the earlier novel exhibits a domestic awareness characterized by postwar austerity, whereas Deighton's protagonist, the as-yet-unnamed Harry Palmer, evinces the food tastes of Britain's emergence from austerity and embrace of Mediterranean food that connoted sunshine and flavour. This allows Palmer to impudently defy his "superiors" in the Service, portrayed as effete and effeminized, as the younger, classless spy asserts his modern *chic*, in food, domestic interiors and clothing that amount to a new meritocratic masculinity. In comparison, le Carré's Alec Leamas inhabits a domestic impoverishment and professional disempowerment, with a concomitant emotional deprivation even though Leamas yearns to finish his assignment and "come in from the cold," to ordinary domestic life. Although neither novel fully assuages British readers' anxieties about their country's place in the world, especially in comparison with the United States, except to assert Britain's moral superiority to America, both texts offer domesticity as an alternative, showing that spy fiction has developed from the imperial adventure novel's repudiation of home for the spy.

Rosie White's chapter, "A Queer Thing? The Older Woman Spy," argues that in depicting the ageing woman in fiction, spy novelists "queer" her gender identity. Indeed, White astutely observes "the extent to which espionage in the West is embedded in discourses of class, colonialism and illicit sexuality," most notably in the continuation of the legend of Mata Hari in "the fantasy of women spies as *femmes fatales*" which older women escape by being, according to White, "more akin to what Eva Horn calls 'the invisible functionary, the secretary and silent organizer'" (Horn 2013: 171). White urges that the older woman spy evades detection because of her invisibility and simultaneously "disturbs masculine mythologies around espionage and at the same time challenges dominant discourses about ageing femininity," even as she offers a critique of the functioning of power. Like other contributors to the collection, White considers both historical and fictional spies, although she primarily focuses on John le Carré's Connie Sachs as a stark alternative to James Bond's hypermasculinity. Connie combines the cultural rejection of both femininity and ageing and offers a figure of abject "ridicule and disgust," an argument that Lohneis's chapter reiterates. White argues that society has such low expectations of older women's abilities that they become doubly invisible, so their ageing femininity offers "a fantastic cover story." As examples of what Eva Horn calls "the invisible functionary, the secretary and silent organizer," these women queer our understanding of the nature of ageing itself, in its necessitation for confrontation of the "mutability of identity" but also its potential to "remake it" (Horn 2013: 171). Connie Sachs is a striking example of the potential of the ageing woman to render the reader uncomfortable in the detailed physical description of her divergence from the norms surrounding women's appearance. As the "human memory" of the Service, White argues, Connie serves as "a synecdoche for the thousands of women who have worked in the British secret services since their inception, not as agents but as researchers, administrators, archivists, and typists" whose work remains invisible. But Connie's knowledge of the mole in the Service stands as a threat, so she is a discredited figure in her inability to limit herself to the roles ascribed to her by gender norms. White asserts, "Connie is a leaky parcel of nostalgia, despair and rage," and offers, then, a contradictory conflation of authoritative, indispensable knowledge and the inability to discreetly contain it. White explores both le Carré's portrayal of Connie in the George Smiley novels, and Beryl Reid's performance in the role in the BBC productions, as well as the real-life Melita Norwood, a Soviet agent who was exposed—but not prosecuted—in 1999, after forty years undercover in the British nuclear industries, as well as her fictional precursor, Dorothy Gilman's Mrs. Emily Pollifax, a retired widow who appeared in many of Gilman's popular novels.

Rachel Hoag's chapter examines both John le Carré's 1983 novel *The Little Drummer Girl* and Park Chan-wook's 2018 television adaptation of the novel. The highly improvisational role Charlie, the protagonist, plays in infiltrating a Palestinian terror cell prompts her to explore questions of identity that begin as being operational but become increasingly personal. In both texts, the protagonist, Charlie, takes a supposed acting job as an agent in the center of the Arab-Israeli conflict. While choosing her as much for the absence of her opinions on that conflict, her spymaster seeks to exploit her as a young Western woman whom he can control, although as Hoag argues, the Park adaptation grants Charlie more agency. Both narratives suggest that, as a woman, Charlie cannot be expected to influence the political conflict. Treated as an object, then, as a young woman she lacks national agency, and Hoag quotes Erin Carlston saying that women "have different relationships to the nation state" than men, and have generally "not been citizens of most nations on equal terms with men" (Carlston 2013: 5). When Hoag quotes Carlston as saying that women historically were seen as "lack[ing] the mature rationality necessary to form a true social contract," Hoag explains the perspective that allows Kurtz to deprive Charlie of agency (Carlston 2013: 5). Drawing upon Eva Horn's definition of women spies, across history, as being either seductresses or "secretaries, the latter of which do the silent organizing of intelligence," Hoag advances a similar theoretical perspective as White and Lohneis do, in acknowledging the less glamourous side of women's espionage, the work of the unseen (Horn 2013: 171). As Smith and White have argued in this volume, women become invisible in war and in espionage.

Noting that le Carré portrays the Arab-Israeli conflict as intractable without taking a side, Hoag argues that this typifies his other fiction, which records the toll taken on people living in the midst of conflict. In particular, though, Hoag examines Charlie as being, "a protagonist without agency. She is a woman being run by men." Hoag notes that her political naivete places Charlie as at "odds with Hepburn's assertion that 'ideology produces spies'" (Hepburn 2005: xiv). But performing as an object, without true subjectivity, she has little control over her visibility to others. Unlike this volume's many invisible women-as-spies, Charlie's act depends on her appearance, which belies her interiority. Park's adaptation allows Charlie to push back against Kurtz's efforts to define and control her and allows her to scrutinize her performance and its relationship to her sense of herself. Hoag quotes Eva Horn who said that the woman spy "is first of all an actress" who often performs in front of the curtain while the men direct from behind (Horn 2013: 177). Nevertheless, in Park's adaptation, Charlie attempts to influence her own performance instead of submitting to Kurtz's handling of her, even as her performance points to gender roles functioning not only as performance, but as cover. The novel offers the interesting possibility, Hoag suggests, that le Carré has offered an exploration of a version of a feminine spy who differs sharply from Connie Sachs.

In examining another, and again very different novel by John le Carré, Llewella Chapman's chapter, "'Extolling the Virtues of Alpaca Cloth or Buttons Made of Tagua Nut': The Influence of Douglas Hayward, Tailoring, and James Bond on *The Tailor of Panama*," explores tailoring as a plot motif, whose protagonist, Harry Pendel, has a bespoke tailoring business which allows him access to his clients' confidences, and thereby to intelligence. The novel, like Graham Green's *Our Man in Havana*, ironically portrays an ineffectual spy working for the British Secret Service. Pierce Brosnan, cast as MI6 operative Osnard, makes visible the film adaptation's allusions to James Bond's characterization. Chapman argues that the Bond films and tailoring carry significant meaning in both the film and the novel, with well-tailored suits being endemic to the role of the "gentleman spy," and that they place tailoring as a facet of the production of Bond's masculinity and his social class. Chapman defines these in terms of the new meritocracy, with Bond occupying a position as a "middle-grade civil servant" in the rising professional society. Pendel, the tailor, uses the appearance of being gentlemanly in part to hide his criminal past. Chapman reveals, "Brosnan's Osnard is presented in character and costume as the antithesis of Brosnan's Bond, as well as a twist on the perception promoted in other films relating to spying and suits in that they exemplify the 'gentleman hero.'" Tailoring functions visually too, in the films' costume designs.

Paul Lohneis's chapter, like Rosie White's, also considers Connie Sachs, seen by George Smiley in *Tinker, Tailor, Soldier, Spy* as he undergoes "currents of alarm and anger and disgust," and whom Lohneis places alongside another disabled woman figure of institutional memory, Molly Doran, the archivist in Mick Herron's "Slow Horses" spy novels (le Carré 1999a: 130). In the Karla trilogy, at various points, George Smiley depends on Connie's memory, just as Jackson Lamb needs access to what Molly knows, a recurring piece of the "Slow Horses" narratives in which Lamb vacillates between perturbation and sympathy for Doran. Lohneis considers how the women's ageing and somatic representation mark them as abject and grotesque: Molly Doran is handicapped and dependent on a wheelchair; Sachs is alcoholic and crippled with arthritis. Lohneis asserts, "Although both are seen as paragons of competence, their characterisation suggests that there is an underlying fragility to institutional memory, one that their respective male protagonists ultimately must control and remediate." George Smiley and Jackson Lamb intermittently depend on these women for their knowledge that simultaneously contains the potential to threaten the institutions it appears to uphold: they can both be expended as a means of occluding their knowledge. As Lohneis observes, the records that Molly Doran maintains have already been discarded and will someday be replaced by computerization. Sachs's marginalization is also a strategic effort to repress the information that she contains. Embodying the "truth as subjective and unknowable unless it is somehow controlled or managed," these figures represent "the notion of the archive as a flawed symbol of intellectual freedom and a postmodernist metaphor for truth," in Lohneis's words, even as the archive can also hide the truth. In each case, the male spy exhibits empathy for the expendable woman repository for institutional knowledge, even as her precarious embodiment of that knowledge appears to threaten the Service.

What These Chapters Reveal

To consider masculinity and heteronormativity, as well as femininity, in the study of immensely popular spy fiction, and to engage with other ways in which spy fiction foregrounds the "queering" of groups of people or social phenomena in culture, is to engage with historical shifts in thinking about gender and sexuality, as well as to consider how popular cultural forms might influence gendered or sexual behavior in their readers, and the concomitant roles of the citizen. So, spy novels might offer consolations for the loss of the British Empire experienced as emasculation, for example, offering heavily sexualized racial "others" as compensation and harshly repudiating male homosexuality, as Christine Berberich shows that the Bond novels do, and as le Carré portrays spies doing. Increasingly the fiction of espionage portrays men made powerless by the postwar bureaucratization of society that appeared to promise social mobility in its new meritocracy and even helps to usher in a new adaptable version of masculinity.

Emerging from these chapters, the concept that espionage requires the creation of cover identities, leads to the concept that the presentation of genders and sexualities, in and of itself, functions as a kind of cover. This, in turn, complicates the long-accepted notion that gender entails performance. Faragher's term "camouflage" raises this concept in asserting that queer characters in Weimar Berlin would mobilize camp as a tool to obscure their identities. The "camouflage" provided by camp safely empowers while also creating danger in changing circumstances. Similarly, Charlie, le Carré's protagonist in *The Little Drummer Girl*, Rachel Hoag argues, appears to create versions of femininity that serve her purposes as an agent, but perhaps begins to take charge of these identities in developing agency, at least in the television adaptation. That le Carré, wittingly or unwittingly, questions whether these performances undermine Charlie's own sense of *agency* allows us to see further complications in her gendered presentation as cover.

For White, these women spies capitalize on perceptions of ageing women and perform according to the expectations those perceptions might create. Thinking of gender performance as cover extends our concept of this performance so that it becomes disguise, an appearance that we create not merely to express our sense of our own identities or orientations, but to camouflage them. Accordingly, then, a consideration of the functioning of sexualities and genders in fictions of espionage can allow us to see that gender identities consist of forms of cover which can work as lies, as approximations of the truth, as Leamas's cover does, or as camouflages that distract the eye from identity. These revelations of and challenges to the existing hetero-masculine canon of spy fiction, and histories of the genre that portray fictions of espionage as masculine, explain the invisibility of women's espionage and queer spying and intervene in the places where acceptable versions of masculinity and femininity are constructed and defended, rendering women visible in this masculine stronghold, and preventing easy assumptions about gay men and their assumed unreliability.

Notes

1   Spy fiction, seen through a historical lens, expresses the anxieties produced by its cultural and historical moments and, particularly in the case of James Bond, seeks to assuage them. This context of geopolitical analysis context helps us to understand why, since the end of the Cold War, spy fiction might have been regarded as an obsolete genre, but increasingly, international terrorism and counterterrorism as well as Russia's resurging dominance as a world power and its propensity for engagement in the political concerns of other countries have led to a corresponding resurgence in espionage fiction.

2   Michael Denning (1987) describes spy fictions as "cover stories" that tell other, ideological, stories about our culture. Denning urges that we "move beyond the manifest politics to their characteristic narrative structures in order to re-emerge with a sense of the ideologies of the forms themselves" (2). He advances his book's aim as to "explore the relation between narrative structures and ideology" for which he draws on Marxist and structuralist theories (2). By placing the spy novel in the narrative of Britain's loss of its Empire and the "crisis in Britain's world hegemony, and the compensatory ideologies of amateurism, popular imperialism and nationalism," Denning argues, these "cover stories facilitate the exploration of the fact that, [. . .] the secret services were the only real measure of a nation's political health, the only real expression of its subconscious," and endorses le Carré's description of the services as "microcosms of the British condition, of our social attitudes and vanities" (5, 143).

   Allan Hepburn (2005) describes his focus as, "theories of psychoanalysis, trauma, gender, narratology, and the representation of death [and examining] codes and conducts of behavior in intrigue narratives" (xiv).

   Robert Lance Snyder's *The Art of Indirection in British Spy Fiction: A Critical Study of Six Novelists* (2011) focuses on a rhetorical analysis in which he describes his objective as the disentanglement of "veracity" and "narrativity," or mimesis and diegesis (19). Even so, ideological questions arise as the result of Snyder's examination of rhetorical strategies.

   Phyllis Lassner's *Espionage and Exile: Fascism and Anti-Fascism in British Spy Fiction and Film* explores the figure of the "exiled Jew and other refugees" (2), contesting Denning's claim that "although spy fiction is one of the most 'political' of pop fiction genres," dealing with "the Empire, fascism, communism, the Cold War, terrorism," its "political subject is only a pretext to the adventure formulas and the plots of betrayal, disguise and doubles [. . .]" (2). Lassner argues instead that

> political crisis demanded art that could represent the documented experiences of displacement, incarceration, torture and the threat of state-sponsored murder. As Ambler, MacInnes and [Leslie] Howard assert and Frankau and Bridge strongly suggest, their remit was to alert their British and North American audiences to the imminent threat of Fascism to human rights and national sovereignty in Europe and beyond. The warning would take the form of dystopian espionage fiction. (5)

Lassner argues, "these writers also distinguish and relate the journeys of characters into political and ethical consciousness and the narratives' political trajectory," a growing consciousness that attests to the predicament of the stateless refugee, which the spy comes to represent, as "inherently disjunctive and displaced" (5, 9). Even when the figure of the exile or Jew is minor, or "killed off early on," Lassner asserts, "each of these writers situates exile as a political condition and state of being and identity. Whether enforced or voluntary, exile is endemic to the secret worlds of espionage and to the character of spies" (3).

Toby Manning construes le Carré's novels as offering an anticommunist ideology beneath their overt critique of the English Establishment's role in the Service.

Eva Horn's *The Secret War: Treason, Espionage, and Modern Fiction,* translated from the German by Geoffrey Wintrop-Young (2013) examines "fictions: literature and film" and their portrayals of treason. The book focuses on fictions because, as Horn says,

> Fictions illuminate secrecy's structure because they reconstruct its logic, its subtle and mysterious economy of light and dark, truths and lies, presence and absence. Unlike memoirs or historical accounts, fiction is able to circumvent the legal interdictions that necessarily surround state secrets, whether gag orders, and secrecy clauses imposed on insiders or the classification of certain types of information. "Invention" has always been a mask to reveal otherwise unspeakable truths. [. . .] T]he literary narrative can make the secret "readable," decipherable without explicitly solving it, thereby rendering visible the structure of a type of knowledge inextricably entangled with nonknowledge, truth blended with lie. (25)

In explaining why she "resort[s]" to literary representations of espionage, Horn observes, "faced with the double-edged epistemology of the political secret in the modern age, fiction comes with the advantage of being able to reflect these difficulties in its very structure," not unlike Snyder's construction of spy fiction's diegetic mode. Horn argues, "Fiction alone can *narrate something* and at the same time *hint at something else to be deciphered* underneath the obvious plot. Even more so, literature is able to make the narrative's unstable basis a part of the narrative" (39). The result is that "By speaking of things whereof one cannot speak, literature touches on—and even interferes in—the very structure of political secrecy" (40).

Beginning with the narrative of Judas and betrayal, Horn observes, "the traitor is the emblem of a society that observes its inner mechanisms—its circulation of knowledge, use of media, and social and communicative interconnectedness—with a maximum degree of ambivalence and suspicion" (37). But her book, as she makes clear, is not the history of a genre, but is rather "a literary epistemology of state secrets" and therefore "concerned not with the history of secret operations and their administrative reorganizations but with the internal logic that structured this secret at a given historical moment [with] the goal of a detailed analysis of the constellations of enmity, secret, and treason in these highly diverse fictions [. . .] to expose their eminently political foundation" (43-4).

Erin G. Carlston's *Double Agents: Espionage, Literature, and Liminal Citizens* (2013) also takes up the term "double agent," as does Lassner, but in order to consider male spies against the abstract construction of the nation and as people who

> are supposed to lie and deceive, to perform loyalties that they do not actually feel. So a spy's capacity for dissimulation, which makes him useful, also makes him irremediably dangerous, since his employer—his country, usually—can never be sure that even the most apparently patriotic and dependable spy is not really a double agent, working for the interests of a foreign power. (4)

3 Rosie White begins her consideration of women in spy fiction, *Violent Femmes: Women Spies in Popular Culture* by asserting, "spying is an appropriate trope to employ when discussing gender, as femininity, like masculinity, is always undercover—a covert operation with far-reaching effects" (1). She argues that the spy "destabilis[es] unitary formulations of gender identity" (2). Focusing on popular culture, White notes that, "The *good* female spy offers a powerfully ambivalent account of the nation-state and the status quo because of the discrepancy between femininity and public forms of power in the history of Britain and the USA" (3). Spy fictions, she argues, "offer women readers [a] fantasy of individual agency," since, "[w]omen as spies in fiction, film and television map shifts in the politics of gender across the twentieth century and into the twenty-first, disturbing the equilibrium of popular culture" (2, 7). White's book has a chapter about male spies in popular fiction that explores Richard Hannay in Buchan's novels as well as the Scarlet Pimpernel, James Bond and Alec Leamas, as well as exploring representations of the "girl" and the anxieties inherent in James Bond's particular version of masculinity in the novels and films.

   Allan Hepburn observes, "Bond has to learn over and over again that agents can be women too," but primarily Hepburn explores fiction of espionage's engagement with ideologies of masculinity especially as they might be observed as queer. *Intrigue* has two chapters about spy novels written by women, Joan Didion's *Democracy* (1984), and Elizabeth Bowen's *The Heat of the Day* (1949) which he reads as portraying a woman's second-hand experience of war and of espionage, even though he argues that Bowen "situate[es] a female character at the center of a spy story, reversing our expectations of a conventional genre which usually places female characters on the periphery" (14). Hepburn's chapter that analyses John Banville's *The Untouchable's* depiction of Anthony Blunt as a queer spy posits, "narratives of intrigue, especially after 1945, represent gay men as protean, effeminate, deviant, enigmatic, unstable, *leaky*" (187). Furthermore, he argues, "As the Cold War progressed, all spies proved to be, in some degree, a bit queer (187)." He explains, "homosexuality trumps identifiers of manliness, such as Etonian suaveness, fascination with gadgetry, ordinariness, and rigidity of convictions. Invisible when not out, the queer spy takes refuge in the double closets of sexuality and political affiliation" (188).

   Phyllis Lassner's *Espionage and Exile* has one chapter that examines women writers of espionage fiction, noting the proliferating critical examinations of detective fiction written by women and the continued neglect of women writers of spy fiction. Analysing novels by Pamela Frankau, Ann Bridges and Helen MacInnes, she argues that they "trouble and revise the gendered conventions and perhaps the reader's expectations," and posits that these novels do this by "reconfigure[ing] suspense as the *development* of individual agency" (70). The "double agency" Lassner locates in narratives about women and espionage arises from the fact that the "women spies exile themselves from the domestic sphere and their private roles" (70). Lassner's *Espionage and Exile* denotes the women spy protagonists in her study as performing a "double agency" because they "exile themselves from the domestic sphere and their private roles" (70).

4 Rosie White has examined depictions of women gaining agency as spies in television and film, and Allan Hepburn has examined masculinity as a facet of male spies' identities, noting that the fiction carries "encoded messages" about "masculinity and sexuality" (21). Erin Carlston focuses her study on male homosexuals and espionage and has very valuable insights about male homosexuality and espionage, in particular how homophobia becomes tied with fear of Communism. Eva Horn's

book devotes a section to "Spies, Male and Female: The First World War and the War of the Sexes" which considers the gendering of espionage and examines the various types of the woman spy, the seductress, the "female secretary," and "the medium."

5 Robert Lance Snyder observes, "Virtually any roster of major British contributors to this popular mode indicates that it is a gender-imbalanced preserve" (148).

6 See Kate Macdonald, *The Masculine Middlebrow: What Mr. Miniver Read* (2011), in which collected essays examine the various texts consumed by middle-class men in the period between 1880 and 1950.

7 In particular, Rosie White, Allan Hepburn, Eva Horn, and Erin Carlston examine male homosexuality and espionage.

8 As Robyn Wiegman (2012) has observed, "While many academic feminists [. . .] remember when *gender* was a synonym for women, the term has come to collate much of what the category of *women* is said to exclude: from men, masculinity, and queer sexualities to trans and intersex identities and analysis" (Wiegman 2012: 38).

9 Allan Hepburn notes the intention in his study to "migrate between literary and mass-market fiction" and finds equal value at either end of the scale of literary quality. *Intrigue* explores the meaning that spies carry in British and American culture and the epistemological and hermeneutical work that spy fiction performs. Lassner observes, "The literary value of spy fiction has now been firmly established by Allan Hepburn, Erin Carlston, Robert L. Snyder, Michael Denning and Eva Horn" (13n).

10 Work remains to be done on the spy fiction of many other cultures, for example Eileen Chang's spy novels about occupied Shanghai and Hong Kong, and this will yield important insights.

11 For a history of British spy fiction's development from the Empire narrative of adventure, see John Atkins, *The British Spy Novel* (1984) and John Cawelti and Bruce A. Rosenberg, *The Spy Story* (1987). See also Ann Rea, "Subtle Covenants" (2019). Michael Denning noted that espionage fiction narrated the British Empire and its decline and Cold War spy fiction takes place amid a postcolonial Britain in the process of redefinition.

12 In *The Spy who Came in from the Cold*, le Carré explores the psychological complexities of the practice of cover for spies. Alec Leamas, his protagonist, has apparently defected to the east, having created the impression that he has become increasingly dissipated and disenchanted with the Circus, by performing anger and dissolution. During the first stage of his interrogation by east German officials, we read this:

> A man who lives apart, not to others but alone, is exposed to obvious psychological dangers. In itself the practice of deception is not particularly exacting; it is a matter of experience, of professional expertise, it is a facility most of us can acquire. But while a confidence trickster, a play-actor or a gambler can return from his performance to the ranks of his admirers, the secret agent enjoys no such relief. For him, deception is first a matter of self-defence. He must protect himself not only from without but from within, and against the most natural of impulses; though he earn a fortune, his role may forbid him the purchase of a razor, though he be erudite, it can befall him to mumble nothing but banalities; though he be an affectionate husband and father, he must under all circumstances withhold himself from those in whom he should naturally confide.
>
> Aware of the overwhelming temptations which assail a man permanently isolated in his deceit, Leamas resorted to the course which armed him best; even when he was alone, he compelled himself to live with the personality he had assumed. [. . .]
>
> Only very rarely, as now going to bed that evening, did he allow himself the dangerous luxury of admitting the great lie he lived. (129–30)

In this description of cover, the fictional identity the spy creates consumes his identity, even as it protects him. To allow momentary lapses in that identity is dangerous; yet, to perpetuate the "lie" damages the spy's own identity. Not only does the creation of cover resemble the performance gender or the camouflage of sexual orientation, but, when Helen MacInnes portrays her spies as tourists, or when Martin Hearne assumes the identity of Bernard Corlay in *Assignment in Brittany*, they assume cover, as do the ageing women spies whom Rosie White investigates in her chapter.

13   Several literary critical histories of the Cold War devote no attention to spy fiction, strangely, and Adam Piette even refers in the introduction to his book, *The Literary Cold War: 1945 to Vietnam* (2009) to "literary studies [as being] sometimes bafflingly indifferent to the importance of the Cold War in shaping cultures in the postwar," although he includes a discussion of Graham Greene's *The Third Man* (5). Andrew Hammond's *Cold War Literature: Writing the Global Conflict* also excludes all fiction of espionage except for Brian Diemart's chapter about Graham Greene's novels, although, after observing that most postwar fiction turned inwards, Diemart remarks on "another side of British fiction that exploited international concerns" (213). He continues by observing that "increasingly popular" spy novels "tended to affirm readers' beliefs in a secret world existing beneath ordinary reality," evoking SPECTRE and SMERSH, Fleming's James Bond novels (213). He notes that "for many observers, [. . .] Cold War fiction" means espionage fiction and then lists Elizabeth Bowen's *The Heat of the Day* (1949) and C. P. Snow's *The New Men* (1954). Like Piette, Hammond appears to see spy fiction as undeserving of attention.

14   Allan Hepburn notes that when President Eisenhower took office in 1953, he ruled that homosexuals should be excluded from federal employment (194).

15   Carlston points to the press's denunciation of "the intellectual, Eton-educated, aesthete cabal that allegedly controlled British foreign policy" (211). She quotes the *Daily Mirror* on the "intellectuals, the Old School tie brigade [. . . who took] a mighty drop in the estimation of the very ordinary men and women of Britain who are armed with just a little bit of commonsense and caution" (211). She cites the emergence of the new Conservative party under Margaret Thatcher that "identified more with the nonconformist petty bourgeoisie than with the aristocratic or upper-middle-class Anglican establishment" (211). Notably, her denunciation of Anthony Blunt took place soon after her ascension to power.

16   Atkins, Cawelti, and Denning, all published in 1987, mention Helen MacInnes briefly. Robert Lance Snyder (2011) has a chapter on Stella Rimington.

17   Atkins makes a few references to the Cambridge Spies' homosexuality in reference to the decline in the significance of the British Service. Cawelti mentions Kim Philby's treachery, but none of the other Cambridge spies. Denning argues that John le Carré and Graham Greene wrote in an era of growing cynicism about the role of the Service in the wake of the exposure of Philby, Maclean, Burgess and Blunt. Interestingly, he mentions that Philby "assumed the characteristics of a recognizable type: the gentleman eccentric with his epicureanism, his associations with homosexuals, and his heavy drinking," suggesting that these characteristics of his membership of the Establishment at least formed part a form of cover (119).

18   In examining the thrill excited by the fiction in examining "Fear and Catharsis," Hepburn points to Victor Maskell's sense of the homoerotic charge of danger, and "the pleasures of being caught." Convincing for Banville's Maskell, this pleasure in danger

appears very different for the woman spy in Helen MacInnes's *Above Suspicion*, when Frances fears the sexual dangers of captivity in Nazi Germany.

19 Carlston's study ranges internationally, often considering German history and texts, although she also considers British and American fiction, film and television, although no British novels by women or depictions of British women spies in fiction.

20 Except for Virago's reprint of *The Willow Cabin* (1989) Pamela Frankau's novels have been allowed to go out of print. A free Kindle edition of that title and *A Wreath for the Enemy* are available, with the latter sporting the blurb, "An ideal novel for summer reading."

21 Ann Bridge's novels largely have been out of print until in 2012 Bloomsbury Reader reprinted the Julia Probyn series of detective novels involving international intrigue.

22 Notably, some recent retrospective fictions have appeared, that portray women Cold War spy protagonists, such as John Boyd's *Restless*, Ian MacEwan's *Sweet Tooth* and Sebastian Faulks's *Charlotte Gray* as well as American Adam Brookes, *The Spy's Daughter*. Alongside publishing retrievals of spy novels by women, biographies of women spies have appeared on the market.

23 For analysis of constructions of literary quality according to assumptions about social class and gender, see in particular Mary Grover, also Ann Ardis, Erica Brown, and Faye Hammill.

24 David Kynaston's *Austerity Britain, 1945–51* provides a detailed examination of Britain's postwar economic condition.

25 Tony Judt, *Postwar: A History of Europe Since 1945* (2005) explains how Prime Minister Anthony Eden's handling of the crisis simultaneously increased Nasser's anti-colonial prestige, gave the Soviets a propaganda tool in Africa and the Middle East, and offended the Americans who resented Eden's deceptive handling, and that he managed to divert international attention from the Soviets' invasion of Hungary.

26 Of the other three Cambridge spies, Anthony Blunt was homosexual, and Donald Maclean was, according to Carlston, "conflictedly bisexual, or perhaps simply a repressed, and alcoholic, homosexual" (177). Kim Philby's heterosexual "philandering," however, appears to have been acceptable (Carlston 2013: 177).

27 See Erin Carlston for a detailed consideration of the Auden group's proximity to the Cambridge spies. Carlston notes Auden's own awareness of his position:

> That of a homosexual man who, like Burgess and the other Cambridge spies, had been drawn to Communism in the early 1930s and later left England—we perceive that it is informed by homologies between male homosexuality, espionage and treason that were already circulating widely in the work of Auden and his literary contemporaries in the late 1920s and the 1930s. Long before Burgess, Donald Maclean, and Kim Philby defected, even longer before Anthony Blunt was unmasked as the fourth man in the spy ring in 1979, British writers had helped fashion an image of the left-wing intellectual—particularly the homosexual intellectual—as a subject exceptionally inclined to disloyalty and alienated from the dominant national culture; these writers both responded to and helped invent the context within which they, and the Cambridge spies, would be understood as traitors. (Carlston 2013: 142)

Auden saw affinities between himself and Guy Burgess, his friend, regarding his own transplantation to America in 1939 as akin to Burgess's defection to the Soviet Union as an act of treachery.

28 Spy fiction's awareness and perhaps exploitation of tourism generally challenges any argument that British culture showed a completely inward turn in this era.

References

Ardis, Ann (2008), *Modernism and Cultural Conflict*, Cambridge: Cambridge University Press.

Atkins, John (1984), *The British Spy Novel: Styles in Treachery*, London: John Calder.

Carlston, Erin G. (2013), *Double Agents: Espionage, Literature, and Liminal Citizens*, New York: Columbia University Press.

Cawelti, John G. and Bruce A. Rosenberg (1987), *The Spy Story*, Chicago: University of Chicago.

Denning, Michael (1987), *Cover Stories: Narrative and Ideology in the British Spy Thriller*, London: Routledge and Kegan Paul.

Esty, Jed (2004), *A Shrinking Island: Modernism and National Culture in England*, Princeton: Princeton University Press.

Grover, Mary (2009), *The Ordeal of Warwick Deeping: Middlebrow Authorship and Cultural Embarrassment*, Madison: Fairleigh Dickinson University Press.

Hammond, Andrew (2006), *Cold War Literature: Writing the Global Conflict*, London: Routledge.

Hepburn, Allan (2005), *Intrigue: Espionage and Culture*, New Haven: Yale University Press.

Horn, Eva (2013), *The Secret War: Treason, Espionage, and Modern Fiction*, Evanston: Northwestern University Press.

Judt, Tony (2005), *Postwar: A History of Europe since 1945*, New York: Penguin Books.

Kynaston, David (2007), *Austerity Britain, 1945–51*, London: Bloomsbury Press.

Lassner, Phyllis (2016), *Espionage and Exile: Fascism and Anti-Fascism in British Spy Fiction and Film*, Edinburgh: Edinburgh University Press.

Le Carré, John (1999a), *Tinker, Tailor, Soldier, Spy, [1974]*, London: Sceptre.

Macdonald, Kate (2011), *The Masculine Middlebrow: What Mr. Miniver Read*, Middlesex: Palgrave Macmillan.

MacInnes, H. (2012), *Above Suspicion*, New York: Titan.

Maugham, Somerset (1928), *Ashenden*, Middlesex: Penguin.

Piette, Adam (2009), *The Literary Cold War: 1945 to Vietnam*, Edinburgh: Edinburgh University Press.

Piette, A. and M. Rawlinson, eds. (2016), *The Edinburgh Companion to Twentieth-Century British and American War Literature*, Edinburgh: Edinburgh University Press.

Rea, Ann (2019), "'Subtle Covenants': Dispossession, Frontiers, and the Internationalist Education of Fiction's Spies," *Pennsylvania English*, 40, no. 1 (Winter): 54.

Snyder, Robert Lance (2011), *The Art of Indirection in British Espionage Fiction: A Critical Study of Six Novelists*, Jefferson: McFarland and Company.

White, Rosie (2007), *Violent Femmes: Women as Spies in Popular Culture*, Abingdon: Routledge.

Wiegman, Robyn (2012), *Object Lessons*, Durham: Duke.

1

Camp Camouflage

The Art of Espionage in *Mr. Norris Changes Trains*

Megan Faragher

Introduction: The Two Sides of the Rügen Summer

When W. H. Auden and Christopher Isherwood vacationed with Stephen Spender and Otto Nowak off the north German coast in the summer of 1931, it might have seemed an unlikely place for both to explore the ramifications of espionage.[1] And yet, it was here where both would conceive of works that dealt—either obliquely or overtly—with the subject. Auden, for one, joined the group "rather unwillingly," "shut[ting] himself up in his bedroom with the blinds pulled down," writing what the former imagined to be *The Orators* (Isherwood 1976: 81). Before this trip, both Isherwood and Auden spent part of the final years of the 1920s in Germany, sometimes together and sometimes not, inspired by its "richly deserved reputation for sexual permissiveness and for the diversity of its sexual underworld"; Norman Page even presents a convincing argument that it was Isherwood's "spiritual homeland" (Page 1998: 8). But, as Page argues, "with sex and money went politics," and reflections on sexuality—particularly sexual expression—in the works of Isherwood and Auden (both gay men) were often haunted by the potentiality of violence as a tool to suppress political expression (Page 1998: 30). Auden witnessed a violent clash between communists and police in 1930 that not only anticipated the violence to come but also reinforced the cost of being either political or social outsiders. In response, *The Orators* understandably centered on "the rhetorical subjugation of humanity's sexual, group and survival instincts" (Gay 1968: 129). It also, arguably, set the tone for his collection *Poems* (1933), where Monroe Spears argues that one of his main tropes becomes "the Spy" or "the Secret Agent" (Spears 1963: 129). And while Auden began to explore the relationship between politics, espionage, and sexuality through production of *The Orators* at Rügen, Isherwood contemplated his own middlebrow homage to the sexual and political milieu of Weimar: the novel *Mr. Norris Changes Trains* (Harker 2013: 181). And, while I will here primarily argue that Isherwood's contribution is a uniquely proficient example of the phenomenon, *The Orators* provides another small exemplar of the importance espionage as a trope would offer for exploring the political risks of self-expression.

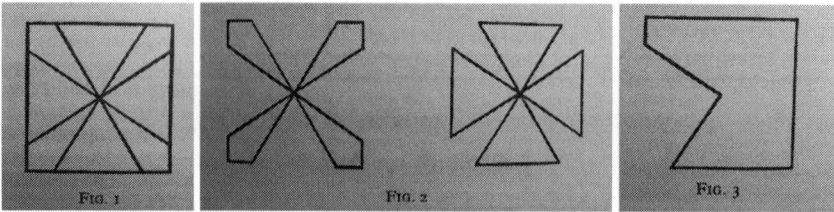

Figures 1–3 W. H. Auden. *The English Auden: Poems, Essays, and Dramatic Writing: 1927-1939.* Ed. Edward *Mendelson.* Random House, 1977: 74. *Copyright © 1932 by W.H. Auden, renewed Reprinted by permission of Curtis Brown, Ltd. All rights reserved.*

The Orators' ironical tone, one that it shares with Isherwood's *Norris*, finds its most crystallized form in the section titled "Journal of an Airman," which centers on the surveillance of expression to identify outsiders, like the spy (Isherwood 1976: 81). In this section, the airman describes a politicized Rorschach test he facetiously calls "The Sure Test," wherein the inquisitor presents the subject with three images.

The airman instructs the reader how to use the images to find a hidden enemy: "Give the party you suspect the above figure and ask him to pick out a form from it. If he picks out either of the two crosses below" (Figure 2) "you may keep him as a friend, but if he chooses (Figure 3)" it is wiser to shoot at once (Auden 1977: 74). While "The Sure Test" intends to mock the aesthetic litmus test's value in determining hidden or opaque ideological commitment, the joke all the same reveals, presciently and ominously, the way in which aesthetic taste was continually intertwined with politics. Several years after publication of *The Orators*, the *Entarte Kunst* exhibition of 1937 posited aesthetics to identify fascism's ideological enemies. Equal parts comic and tragic, "The Sure Test" cautions readers of the complex connections between politics and representation.

As many scholars have rightly identified, themes of espionage merge with those of sexuality in *The Orators* as, I would argue, they do in *Mr. Norris Changes Trains*; the third figure in "The Sure Test" clearly represents not just avant-garde but also queer aesthetics as a threat to any dominating state ideology. Figure 3 not only symbolizes high-modernist abstraction as a threat, but this notably asymmetrical form also signals non-normative sexual orientation; the unconventional shape syntactically delineates insiders from outsiders. Both Erin Carlston and Richard Bozorth draw connections between queerness and espionage in the 1930s, both citing "The Sure Test" as exemplifying this intersectionality.[2] Auden's obfuscation regarding his own sexuality, according to Bozorth, led him to insinuate sexual orientation through "figurative valences" like the "Sure Test" (Bozorth 2001: 170). The test covertly reveals the queerness of the airman's test subject, and it is this that enables the masked political enemy to be unveiled. As Carlston reminds us, the overlap between espionage and queerness is pervasive in the genre of spy fiction. And while Carlston writes that both spies and gay men "[appear] to be just like everyone else—that is, just like all other adult white heterosexual male citizens," the airman's test proves that one might unmask normativity as performative if the proper cipher is at hand (Carlston 2013: 6). The case of the "Sure Test" performs this function. The discovery of Mr. Norris's true sexual and political allegiances in Isherwood's *Mr. Norris Changes Trains* requires the protagonist

William Bradshaw to deploy, I would argue, similar modes of decryption. Like in *The Orators*, the oft-comic tone of this novel lacks the severity of an Eric Ambler or Ian Fleming. But Bradshaw's wild times in Berlin, tracking the quirky Norris, unveils the latter to be a spy for the highest bidder, selling the secrets of his political allies and friends for his own benefit. The series of tragedies that end the novel, including exile and murder, fall on Norris's head. Bradshaw is no political agent; he is not actively trying to uncover a spy. But the convergence between Norris's flamboyant style and his duplicity recalls all too distinctly the sardonic commentary of Auden's that conflates queerness and espionage.

The interpolation of the camouflaged enemy is the core of most espionage fiction; at the same time allusions to homosociality and homosexual panic are persistent tropes in mid-century spy fiction, suggesting anxieties over the power of camouflage can and must intersect with questions of sexuality. In Allan Hepburn's taxonomy of espionage and sexuality, he argues that many critical spy novels—including John le Carré's *The Spy Who Came in from the Cold*—position sexuality itself as a sort of performance: an ersatz self-presentation that is essential in the work of the spy for purposes of secrecy. In this analysis, he also suggests what he calls an "ideological queering" of the spy, not dissimilar from Erin Carlston's later argument in *Double Agents* (Hepburn 2005: 201). Like other novels which must grapple with the characteristically deceptive self-presentation of the spy, Isherwood's *Mr. Norris Changes Trains* must also assess the repercussions of masking one's identity amid the political and social turmoil of the 1930s. But, in choosing his "spy" the ultimate bon vivant, Arthur Norris, who mixes seamlessly into a permissive, socialist milieu, Isherwood allows us to ask a more nuanced question, tailored to communities at risk under rising fascism: To what extent does the manifestation of style provide camouflage for *any* politics, and how can this style be weaponized by the right? While other novels might theorize the obfuscation of espionage as a threat to heteronormativity—fearful, above all, that queerness would challenge hegemony—Isherwood instead chooses to imagine the threat of camouflage to queer communities and those of the oppressed. The case of Arthur Norris demands attention to the way all performance may be a tool of oppression, even if that camouflage is, recognizably, queer.

Norris's Disguises

Arthur Norris's ostentatious sexuality and vivacious persona crystallize the political ramifications of camp and its relationship to espionage, and the story came from Isherwood's personal experience. As the narrator William Bradshaw records Norris's exploits, Norris transforms from a bumbling man with sexual peccadillos to one who undermines major political parties for financial gain. Isherwood underwent this same process of disillusionment in his experiences with Gerald Hamilton, the inspiration for the eponymous character. Isherwood recounts meeting Hamilton about six months before his summer on Rügen Island; Hamilton marketed himself as the sales representative for Germany's *Times*, a position gained under false pretenses.[3] Of course, it is risky to assert Norris as a mere representation of Hamilton. As Isherwood writes in his preface to Hamilton's autobiography *Mr. Norris and I*, "How, indeed, *can a fictional character 'be' a live person?*" (Hamilton 1956: 10). Isherwood makes clear that the more sexually explicit aspects of Hamilton's personality are hyperbolized in *Norris*. On the one hand, Gerald Hamilton never gave Isherwood a self-authored book of pornography like *Mrs. Smith's Torture Chamber*, which Norris gives to Bradshaw; on the other hand, Gerald Hamilton's biographer, Tom Cullen, records that Hamilton did show a school friend a self-authored "pornographic essay on Rugby caning" (Cullen 2015: 44). And while Gerald never participated in a scene like the one written in *Norris*, where Bradshaw finds Arthur in a compromising position subject to a woman's whip, Hamilton and Isherwood certainly spent time together at the boy bar Cosy Corner at Zossenerstrasse 7 (Cullen 2014: 138). The two also did not meet on a train; all the same, Isherwood recognized, from the second of their meeting, that Hamilton had the raw materials of a true "character." Isherwood claims the first sentences of *Norris* come directly from his first conversation with Hamilton (Isherwood 1976: 74). And so, despite any reasonable hesitation at seeing Hamilton as too closely mirrored in the fictional Norris, enough aspects of Hamilton's experience, as Isherwood knew them at the time, make a comparison worth pursuing. From biographical and autobiographical records, a more holistic image of Hamilton develops. As it turned out, Hamilton's charisma masked a variety of problematic political dealings, some of which would harm Isherwood and those he cared for. If the traumatic ending of *Mr. Norris Changes Trains*—with many of its characters "disappeared" and presumed dead—warns us of nefarious figures appropriating the freedom camp provides for purposes of political espionage, Hamilton's life demonstrates the harrowing consequences of such deception.

Among the qualities of camouflage that disarm vulnerable communities, Hamilton and Norris certainly shared one: disarming charm. Isherwood describes this quality in the first pages of *Mr. Norris Changes Trains*. When William Bradshaw meets a hapless Norris on a train, he almost immediately pegs him as "engaged in a little innocent private smuggling" (Isherwood 1935: 6). Norris, sweaty and nervous, too frightened to engage in high-stakes duplicity, is barely able to get past the border without falling to pieces. Isherwood depicts Norris as "innocently naughty," immediately reminding Bradshaw of a "schoolboy surprised in the act of breaking the rules" (Isherwood 1935: 6). Far from being a stealthy thief, Norris stands out as the pettiest and most obvious of criminals. When Norris asks for a match, Bradshaw describes Norris wearing an "expensive-looking soft grey suit," carrying a "gold spirit-lighter," and having "white, small and beautifully manicured" hands (Isherwood 1935: 4). Here Norris's ostentatious aestheticism signals both his effeminacy and failed criminality. A schoolboy and a dandy, Norris is not to be taken seriously.

In real life, Isherwood never took Hamilton too seriously either, though arguably Hamilton was more suave than his fictional counterpart. In *Christopher and His Kind*, Isherwood describes Hamilton as being more like a piece of art deco furniture than as a man who would facilitate the conscription of his lover, Heinz Neddermeyer. Even in 1976, Isherwood playfully dismissed Hamilton's antics: "Good old, bad old Gerald!" (Isherwood 1976: 73). Isherwood preserves a residual nostalgia for Hamilton, continuing to regard him in purely aesthetic terms. Writing in the third person, Isherwood recalls that "Gerald was enchantingly period." He introduced Wystan,

Stephen, and other friends to him, and soon they were all treating him like "an absurd but nostalgic artwork which has been rediscovered by a later generation" (Isherwood 1976: 75). The aestheticization of Hamilton's behavior, like Norris's, assuages concerns about his duplicity; the interpretation of him as an aestheticized and, thus, apolitical agent mirrors the propensity for viewing camp through the same lens—as an apolitical practice that revives a nostalgic aestheticism; those in Isherwood's milieu welcomed Hamilton "*because* of his shady past, not in spite of it" (Isherwood 1976: 75).

In the novel, upon meeting Norris, Bradshaw absolves him of serious crimes due to his overtly suspicious behavior. At best, Norris presents himself as a disheveled outsider, whose physical characteristics mirror his messy interior. Norris's physical depiction suggests an outlandishly conspicuous presence equal parts incongruous and endearing:

> He had a large blunt fleshy nose and a chin which seemed to have slipped sideways. It was like a broken concertina. When he spoke, it jerked crooked in the most curious fashion and a deep cleft dimple like a wound surprisingly appeared in the side of it. Above his ripe red cheeks, his forehead was sculpturally white, like marble. A queerly cut fringe of dark grey hair lay across it, compact, thick and heavy. After a moment's examination, I realized, with extreme interest, that he was wearing a wig. (Isherwood 1935: 3)

Each part of Norris's body is evaluated as a discrete aesthetic artifact. The description, piecemeal and disjointed, disrupts the desire to see Norris as a holistic character with conjoining features. The fragmentation of Norris's appearance—cleft dimple, red cheeks, sculpturally white forehead—likens Norris to a Cubist painting in the *Entarte Kunst*, or "Figure Three" in "The Airman's Journal." To an extent one could argue that the disjointed description reifies a regressive "medical stereotype of homosexuality," where his "so-called abnormality was no longer confined to individual sexual acts, but was part of his psychological makeup, his looks and bodily structure" (Mosse 1985: 37). But, for Bradshaw (also an outsider in Berlin), his disjointed sketch only corroborates his theory that Norris does not pose a threat. In part, Bradshaw internalizes the medical stereotypes around sexual deviancy, perhaps ironically and unwittingly, and assumes that precisely *because* Norris presents as a deviant, he is incapable of any serious crime. A man this messy, so goes the logic, could never conduct a plot with any success; a hapless grifter would be incapable of traumatizing political duplicity.

Norris's wig is crucial to this disguise; the wig metonymizes duplicity but, like his other conspicuous characteristics, its detectability underscores Norris's apparent benignity. Like Norris, Hamilton also had a wig; in fact, Isherwood makes a point about their physical identicality. Hamilton likewise wore it as a conspicuous, though innocuous, coiffure, suggesting a performativity sans substance, failing to perform its function by accentuating, not masking, the subject's baldness (cited in Page 1998: 140). The wig's obtuse angles and occasional misalignment continually suggest Norris's lack of credibility, ironically disarming those who suspect him as a political operative. On New Year's Eve, the loosened atmosphere is reflected in Norris's wig, described in a similarly abstract fashion: "I caught a sudden startling glimpse of Arthur's head, its mouth open, the wig jammed down over its left eye" (Page 1998: 29). As time passes, Arthur's wig is removed; the disguise is undone. And yet, no one suspects what Bradshaw would later discover—that Norris had done the "dirty on the [Communist] Party" (Page 1998: 171). It seems impossible that a man, both flashy and inept at maintaining any disguise, is capable of the political duplicity revealed by the novel's end. In the end, the internalization of assumptions about queerness's separation from politics is the very thing that facilitates the betrayal of those very communities.

Camp as Camouflage in *Mr. Norris Changes Trains*

As the detailed descriptions of Norris might prefigure, Christopher Isherwood is a key contributor to our contemporary understanding of performance and sexuality, though seldom has this been understood in light of *Mr. Norris Changes Trains*, where the revelation of Norris's political double-dealing with communists and fascists lies at the center of the plot. But Isherwood was the first to use "camp" to describe the practice of conspicuously concealing queerness on stage and screen. Much like in Auden's airman's test, Isherwood defines "camp" through aesthetic exemplars, identifying both the "swishy little boy with peroxided hair" dressing as Marlene Dietrich and "the whole emotional basis of the ballet" as models (Isherwood 1954: 110). Defining camp by description, Isherwood mirrors Auden's "Sure Test" in his elevation of conspicuous, unconventional aesthetics as core to the performance of both ideology and sexuality. But Isherwood's citation of ballet alludes to the fact that even if camp "contains a large element of artifice," it can do so in a way that is *inconspicuous* and unthreatening (Sontag 1961: 279). Likewise, the enemy's aesthetic preferences in the "Sure Test" *might* mark him as an innocuous eccentric, implying—like Sontag—that camp aesthetics are largely apolitical.[4] Sontag argued that camp resisted politicization because it did not take itself too seriously. But if we return to "The Sure Test" as an allegory for camp aesthetics, Auden's imposition of a serious hermeneutic value on aesthetic choice contradicts this de-politicization in the 1930s context. Rather, the test takes such conspicuous but benign choices seriously. In doing so, the test suggests how a brand of campy camouflage might be the most nefarious of all.

Scholarly work on camp in *Mr. Norris Changes Trains* concentrates on its positive political efficacy for queer communities, identifying camp's humor as an avenue for resistance and empowerment.[5] As true as this is, particularly given the novel's many comedic scenes, Norris's espionage into leftist communities also reveals alternative visions of camp's importance. While camp's artifice exposes gender as constructed and performative, spies appropriate the same pathways of performativity cleared by revolutionary camp aesthetics to trek down problematic political corridors. Arthur Norris, representing sexual and political deviance, reveals artifice as a troubled political praxis; camp thus becomes a liminal, besieged space, permeable by those weaponizing camp as political camouflage. Isherwood's early camp is therefore couched in anxiety about its appropriation, a truth attested to both in the novel's depiction of Norris and

Isherwood's experiences with Gerald Hamilton, the person who inspired the Norris character.

While camp in *Mr. Norris Changes Trains* inextricably ties it to its politicization, the tendency to depoliticize camp partly derives from Isherwood's rather opaque efforts to define the term in the 1950s. Sontag's own style in "Notes on Camp" takes inspiration from Isherwood's aphoristic form; beginning with Isherwood's scant definition-by-exemplar, Sontag outlines the aesthetic parameters of camp but emphasizes its relationship to aesthetics. But reading camp as apolitical and purely aesthetic explains why *Norris*, too, has been read as *either* a novel about camp *or* a novel about political betrayal, with the twain seldom meeting. What remains valuable in "Notes on Camp," and relevant for readers of *Norris*, is the suggestion that camp's importance derives from its stylization of secrecy. On the one hand, Sontag assesses camp as "a private code"; on the other, she defines it through its "degree of artifice," "mode of aestheticization," and "stylization" (Sontag 1961: 277). Isherwood's description of Marlene Dietrich, similarly bifurcated, positions her as both public celebrity and iconographic shorthand for clandestine queerness. But this duality should incite more, not less, exploration of the relationship between the private and public natures of camp. If camp emphasizes "texture, sensuous surface and style," the assumption that it does so "at the expense of content" derives from an insistence that camp's sensationalism occludes its relationship with secrecy (Sontag 1961: 278). But camp aesthetics are *both* conspicuous *and* concealing; camp camouflages—and codes—queer identification. While Sontag relies on camp's conspicuity to present it as "disengaged" and "depoliticized," Isherwood would imply that it is neither (Sontag 1961: 277).

Some scholarship on camp's relationship to Isherwood falls into similar traps. Such readings suggest that taking *Norris* seriously means focusing on the titular character's style, thus deemphasizing his political commitments and espionage.[6] This aligns with Sontag's assertions about camp by suggesting that "camp clearly values style above all else," and interprets Arthur Norris as a "[c]amp version of the corruptor of innocent youth . . . and a means of escape into Art whenever Life makes too many demands" (Thomas 1976: 122, 124). This analysis is useful and pragmatic, but needlessly restrictive on two fronts. First, it fails to identify camp's political ramifications as a coded practice within an ostracized community that aids in its security. Second, this reading of Arthur Norris omits the bulk of the narrative arc, which traces Norris's political double-dealing; one could argue that the focus on social and sexual exploits is the novel's red herring. It, secondly, ignores political ramifications of the life of Gerald Hamilton, on whom Isherwood based the Norris character. To ignore the content of Norris's character forecloses a political reading of Isherwood's interwar novel. It likewise casts aside work on the political praxis of 1930s aesthetics to reify characterizations of Norris as a benign *bon vivant*. Finally, reading Norris through this lens ignores the novel's dramatic arc, which rests on Norris's betrayal of communism.

Others recognize camp in *Mr. Norris Changes Trains* as codifying a queer community against the oppressive forces. Dennis Denisoff, challenging the misreading of camp as a de-politicized stylistic form, argues that camp in *Norris* fosters readerly sympathy with queer communities: "the novel's camp is an attempt to locate the points where private desires and public demands interact and to construct from them a workable model of respect based on inclusion through diversity" (Denissoff 1998: 82). Readings like Denissoff's build on the work of queer theory around camp, particularly that of Eve Sedgwick and Judith Butler, who see camp as a performative gesture aestheticizing the desires of straight audiences and presenting camp as imbricated in a coded, queer self-presentation. But Norris's political deviance complicates matters. The irony of Norris's campy self-presentation serves two distinct narrative functions. Firstly, Norris's performativity emulates the homoeroticized aestheticism of the Wildean *fin de siècle*. But performance also enables Norris to mask subversive practices that would upend the sympathetic relationship between audience and performer; Norris's political double-dealing, benefiting both the Nazi State and the French Secret Service, undermines camp's ability to make audiences sympathetic to queer communities when the risks to those communities increased daily. By betraying his political allies, Norris also betrays his compatriots in sexual libertinism, leaving many to suffer from inevitable violence of Nazi aggression. While Norris's charm enchants the public, his political calculations undermine these gains substantially.

Norris's iconic and campy performativity, including the wig and affinity for leather boots, is so vital to the text that both are featured on the cover of the first Hogarth edition. The original cover (see figure 4) reads as a collection of disjointed symbols, not dissimilar to physical descriptions of Norris himself: a wig, some boots, currency symbols, and political emblems. The cover presents them all as a heterodoxy, the visual cacophony suggesting little significance and even less correlation. But the John Banting cover subtly connotes a tie between Norris's campy eroticism and his shifting political allegiances. The cover displays artifacts of gender performativity—the wig, boots, gloves, and whip—alongside the Swastika and hammer and sickle. These items stand in for the "trains" that Norris "changes," transgressing political as well as sexual boundaries. But money also provides the *modus operandi* for political and sexual practices in the novel. Money gives Norris his excuse to betray both the communists and the Nazis. It also lies at the heart of camp aesthetics; part of camp's potential for criticism lies in its ability to navigate between high and low culture, using hyperbolized heteronormativity to both denigrate high culture and make it (and queerness, by extension) salable to the masses. Put another way, camp performers maintain economic subsistence through the dramatization of bourgeois affectations. Norris's political speeches about the working classes may seem sincere, but he holds his financial interests above all others, centralizing his subsistence at the hands of hoodwinked benefactors. Norris suggests as much when he tells Bradshaw, "what a lot of good money is lying about, waiting to be picked up. Even nowadays. Only one must have the eyes to see it. And capital. A certain amount of capital is absolutely essential" (Isherwood 1935: 43).

What Norris seems to understand—and what perhaps Bradshaw is foolish to ignore—is the political ramifications of the relationship between, as Klaus Theweleit describes it, "the flowing of desire" and "the flowing of money," which lies at the heart of Norris's betrayal (Theweleit 1987: 270). It is this fungibility—between sexual and economic desire—that motivates Norris's political betrayal, not a conscious instinct toward fascism or violence. But, perhaps because of the relative economic power of foreigners like Isherwood (or Bradshaw) who benefited from that "flow of money," the prospect of others' petty larcenies, which frequently emerged in Isherwood's

Figure 4 John Banting, Cover Art, *Mr. Norris Changes Trains* (London: Hogarth Press, 1935). Tate.org.

discussion of Berlin prostitutes, is hardly seen as threatening; they were "greedy but not calculating" (Isherwood 1976: 30). "What they stole," he writes, "they stole stupidly and got caught" (Isherwood 1976: 30). Similarly, in *Norris*, Bradshaw describes a boy picking his pocket during a debauched New Year party. Far from feeling like an injured party, Bradshaw allows the pilfering, thinking, "Why make a scene at the end of such an enjoyable evening? He was welcome to my money . . . The Baron would pay for everything, anyhow" (Isherwood 1976: 32). But not all grifting is harmless, Hearing Norris's screams from down the hallway later that night, Bradshaw immediately assumes it a violent mugging, imagining that "[t]hey had got Arthur in there, and were robbing him and knocking him about, I might have known it" (Isherwood 1976: 33). Opening the door, Bradshaw instead finds Olga and Norris *in flagrante*; Olga, having donned the black boots of the book's cover, whips Norris, prostrate on the floor. The latter, playing the exhibitionist, seems happy to see Bradshaw, playfully begging for relief while Olga screams after the fleeing Bradshaw, "It's your turn next. I'll make you cry for Mummy!" (Isherwood 1976: 34). While Bradshaw does not uncover the violent robbery he anticipates, the passage underscores the thin line between desire and violence, pilfering and theft. While Bradshaw expects the passive, blundering robbery of his own person, and while unconcerned by consensual masochism, the scene reveals why Norris's political underhandedness, fueled by his greed, remains such a threat to the community Bradshaw describes in *Norris*; it carries with it the possibility of inciting and abetting violence. Just like the underground boys' clubs of Weimar Germany, eventually choked out of existence by the electoral victory of the Nazis in 1932, the liminal spaces facilitated by camp suggest the potentiality of a safe community; however, in this scene, capital makes every enemy potentially one from within.

The threat of violence in *Norris* reverses the age-old Marxist maxim; it first presents itself as farce, but later emerges as tragedy. While some instances of dishonesty in the text remain harmless, the specter of non-consensual violence becomes increasingly prevalent in the later pages of *Norris*, suggesting Norris's duplicity has significant political ramifications. But this first necessitates viewing Norris as a political animal, something the novel unveils unexpectedly. In fact, the revelation of Norris's party "loyalties" stands as the second biggest shock to Bradshaw in the entire novel, only bested by the exposure of his political duplicity. Bradshaw remains convinced that Norris's dealings amount to a series of sexual trysts and some petty scamming. Unconvinced that Norris has any political ideology at all, Bradshaw attends a Communist Party meeting with him on a lark. Bradshaw stands shocked when Norris takes the stage and delivers a rousing Communist lecture. Bradshaw records that, "It seemed so absurd to me to see him standing there that I could hardly keep a straight face" (Isherwood 1976: 54). Bradshaw is shocked, finally, by Norris's seeming political earnestness. Bradshaw eventually learns that Norris's speeches were performative. The speechifier turns into a double-agent and Norris, taking money to betray the local Communist Party to Nazi leadership, also betrays Nazi high command to the French Secret Service. The revelation of Norris's true duplicity enables Isherwood to assert the importance of camp as a political tool, however precarious and dangerous. Up to this point, Bradshaw maintains the illusion that Norris represents the frivolous figure of the arrière-garde aesthete. This changes drastically when Bradshaw blends the language of serious political oratory with the sensationalist language of Berlin's erotic underworld during Norris's moving political speech. Bradshaw describes Norris's oratory in terms of the sexual act as he "exchang[ed] his graceful bantering tone for an oratorical seriousness," and was "approaching his climax" when describing the struggles of Chinese peasants (Isherwood 1976: 55). No longer a caricature, but a political actor, Norris is subject to Bradshaw's radical reinterpretation, and becomes an actor of political consequence. Framing Norris as the speaker of the Party, Isherwood undercuts the reading of camp as an apolitical aesthetic positioning, devoid of content. In so doing, he also counters abstract readings understanding Norris's benignity.

Norris Exposed

Peter Thomas, discussing the ramifications of camp in *Mr. Norris Changes Trains*, argues that "the failure of the left was to ignore the implications of style and fantasy and their potential potency" (Thomas 1976: 124). Indeed, the best lesson readers learn from an example like *Norris* is that the fantasy provided by camp blinds one to the spy in your midst. But while Norris's duplicity confronts all who read about him, his real-life counterpart's fame partially derived from a very similar duplicitous quality. Gerald Hamilton records a charming satiric poem Auden wrote in his honor, playfully referencing the widespread recognition of his political duplicity:

> Uncle Gerald, your charm is a mystery
> I shall not attempt to define;
> It concerns your appearance, your history,
> And your knowledge of servants and wine;
> Do you think if I summoned the waiter,
> He could tell us instantly why
> [*The Embassy thinks you a traitor,*
> *And Olive [Mangeot] thinks you a spy?*]
> Now it's you that I raise my cup to,
> Though I haven't the slightest idea
> What on earth it is that you're up to,
> I wish you a happy New Year. (Cullen 2014: 166)

Hamilton quotes this poem in his autobiography but, always the unreliable narrator, leaves out the two pertinent lines about espionage, italicized here. Despite his efforts to obfuscate this history, Hamilton's friends knew of his duplicity; Isherwood and others made offhanded jokes about his grifting and shady contacts. As Isherwood described it, "If you wanted to sell a stolen painting to a collector who didn't mind enjoying it in private, to smuggle arms into a foreign country, to steal a contract away from a rival firm, to be decorated with a medal of honor which you had done nothing to deserve, to get your criminal dossier extracted from the archive, then Gerald was delighted to try to help you," if you paid the right price (Isherwood 1976: 76).

Hamilton had an exquisite skill at folding into the surrounding community, masquerading as an established gentleman. Hamilton's privileged background led his acquaintances and friends to overlook his criminality, never seeing themselves as prospective targets for his double-dealing (2004). In the novel, Norris never damages Bradshaw personally, though he puts him at risk. But in real life, Hamilton left collateral damage. While Isherwood attempted to get Heinz Neddermeyer, his lover, out of Germany to escape persecution, evidence points to Hamilton as the cause for his eventual arrest and conscription, having failed to secure him appropriate passage on forged papers. Various accounts suggest Isherwood was disappointed, but not surprised; as he wrote, "Gerald was *capable* of this crime. Gerald's dishonesty [. . .] was pathological" (Isherwood 1976: 285). Failing to provide Heinz an appropriate disguise, leading to his conscription, Hamilton attempted to use his selective skills of camouflage to earn money and seek a policy of German appeasement.

Like Norris, Hamilton weaponized camp aesthetics toward personal and political gain; one instance, in particular, got the bon vivant arrested under clause 18B in the Defense of the Realm Act, which applied to the detention of suspected Nazi

Figure 5 Ronald Searle, "Sister Hamilton," in *Mr Norris and I* (London: Wingate, 1956).

sympathizers.[7] Hamilton tried to personally proctor peace between England and Germany through mutual alliance against Russia. Arranging negotiations in neutral Ireland, Hamilton appropriated the most camp of disguises: that of a nun from Sudberry Hill (Cullen 2014: 281). Police arrested Hamilton before his departure, but the evocative Ron Searle illustration of Hamilton as a nun captures the farce exquisitely (Figure 5).

Hamilton's July 1941 arrest as a Nazi sympathizer postdates Isherwood's *Norris*, but there are striking similarities between Norris's espionage and that his of counterpart Hamilton, whose boondoggle was coincident with wide-scale concerns over espionage. In the same year, during the BBC broadcast *Answering You*, Mass-Observation's Tom Harrisson cited one significant rumor about the war: a story of "two nuns traveling in a railway carriage, who were noticed to have hair on the back of their hands and boots under their skirts and turned out to be parachutists."[8] Harrisson's testimony over Nazis cross-dressing as nuns suggests that Hamilton was not alone in thinking of this audacious disguise. It also recognizes the well-known contemporaneous concern over gender performance and espionage; far from a harmless lark, the disguise threatened to strengthen the Nazi state, even as Hamilton fled Germany fearing sexual persecution.

Norris's political scheming and its impacts uncannily mirror Hamilton's. Playing on Bradshaw's sympathy, Norris draws him into political schemes bound to break their bond. Norris makes Bradshaw an accomplice to treason against the Nazi Party, subject to imprisonment, when he asks him to take on a business deal on his behalf. Baron von Pregnitz, a Nazi attracted to Bradshaw, first exchanges coded messages with a figure named "Margot." Von Pregnitz then plans to transmit this coded information to the French Secret Service, with Bradshaw serving as an unwitting accomplice. Norris, using Bradshaw to do the heavy lifting, looks forward to payment when the mission is complete. While planning the scheme, Norris also receives a series of coded messages, which landlady Fräulein Schroeder and Bradshaw read. We find later that the French Secret Service sent these messages, seeking out information on German operations. Notably, such messages use the language of sexual indiscretion as a cipher for political information. One such cipher reads, "Tea you sent no good at all cannot understand why believe you have another girl no kisses. Margot" (Isherwood 1935/1939: 128). Schroeder interprets the message literally, imagining "Margot" to be a lover reporting about the ineffectiveness of an abortifacient tea. Bradshaw recognizes the messages as code but does not think them to be about political espionage but, rather, about sexual deviance. The Margot letters, followed closely by the revelation of Norris's espionage, remind readers of the slippage between an interpretation of camp as purely performative (as in Schroeder's misinterpretation) and one that views camp as a political tool.

When Bradshaw learns of Norris's duplicity from communist leader Bayer, he is, at last, unsettled by Norris's actions. Bayer claims that Norris relayed communist plans to the Germans without consequence as, according to Bayer, "We act openly. It is easy for all to know what we do" (Isherwood 1935/1939: 167). But the betrayal also involved German intelligence; in his plot to introduce von Pregnitz to the French affiliate "Margot," Norris insinuates Bradshaw in an act that could have significant impact on the latter's safety. Bradshaw's reaction is visceral; shaking and panicked, Bradshaw confronts Norris, even telling him, "My God, I wish you'd go away somewhere where I'll never see you again" (Isherwood 1935/1939: 172). Norris's efforts to use his charm and duplicity for financial gain hit a snag just when his espionage exposes his aestheticized veneer as a fraudulent cover for political duplicity.

While the nun masquerade sent Gerald Hamilton to prison, Norris's bumbling efforts at espionage sentence him to a different form of entrapment, as he circles the globe to escape from his former secretary Schmidt, similarly grifted by Norris. But, traipsing from city to city, Norris's ostentatious self-presentation makes hiding impossible. Schmidt embodies Norris's ultimate punishment, the former acting as a haunting witness to Norris's misdeeds. The final line of the novel comes from Norris, who writes to Bradshaw asking, "Tell me William . . . *what* have I done to deserve this?" (Isherwood 1935/1939: 203). The superlatively ironical line (by this point we know very well what he has done to deserve this) belies a distancing of Isherwood from both the real-life Hamilton and the fictional Norris. And stories about the increasing violence against Norris and Bradshaw's former associates in Germany give Norris his answer. Bayer, the Communist leader, is dead; one woman recalls that "his left ear was torn right off" (Isherwood 1935/1939: 192). Bradshaw also describes a morning when their friend Otto arrives at his doorstep with "a stain of dirty blood down the side of his face from a scratch on the temples" (Isherwood 1935/1939: 194). Otto had barely escaped imprisonment by storm troopers. After wistfully telling Bradshaw, "Don't worry. . . Our time will come," Otto leaves and Bradshaw never hears from him again (Isherwood 1935/1939: 197).

Arthur Norris's duplicity and espionage in Isherwood's novel challenge any vision of camp as a depoliticized aesthetic form. That Isherwood follows this barrage of horrors by recalling Norris's self-pitying letter acts as a final act of abnegation. Of all the characters in *Norris*, Norris is the *only* one deserving of his subsequent treatment. While Norris continues to run from Schmidt, his former friends find themselves defenseless and suffer immeasurably thanks to his scheming. When he boards his train out of Germany, Norris hopes Bradshaw will fall for his well-worn disguise one more time, pleading for William to ignore his treason: "This life is so very complex. If my behaviour hasn't always been quite consistent, I can truly say that I am and always shall be loyal to the party. . . . Say you believe that, please!" (Isherwood 1935/1939: 189). Bradshaw retorts, "Yes, Arthur, I do believe it," though narrative commentary suggests otherwise: "He was outrageous, grotesque, entirely without shame. But what was I to answer?" (Isherwood 1935/1939: 189). Bradshaw identifies Norris's disguise for what it is; no longer just an outrageous and campy cover, Norris's persona is recognized for its inherent grotesquery. Norris may first present as a whimsical anachronism, bound to a Wildean aesthetic veneer, with little to offer in terms of his political positioning. But Norris's espionage and Bradshaw's recording of its violent aftermath remind readers of the dialectic between Norris's campy persona and his political duplicity. Analyzing Norris via his links to espionage re-politicizes camp and gives camp a novel position in spy fiction. At the same time, it places *Mr. Norris Changes Trains* firmly within the discourse of 1930s political writing, without ignoring the entertaining, whimsical nature of Arthur Norris's cunning performance.

Notes

1   Davenport-Hines (1995: 106). Richard Davenport-Hines partially corroborates Isherwood's account, placing the writing of *The Orators* in the summer and autumn of 1931, though stipulating that most of this time was spent teaching at Larchfield.
2   Carlston (2013: 165); Bozorth (2001: 170). Both Carlston and Bozorth connect the "Airman's Journal" to queer aesthetics. Carlston parenthetically suggests that we might read the "oblique, crooked" diagram as "queer," linking the enemy to homosexuality. Less directly, Bozorth looks at the airman's analysis as a version of "crooked geometry" and sees the airman's perspective as analogous to Auden's on the topic of sexuality: "Its semiserious obliquities, which capitalize on innuendo and public image, seek to derive community from comic recognition of difference in an age of lowest-common-denominator politics" (Bozorth 2001: 170)."
3   Isherwood (1976: 72–3). Isherwood further details the fact that Hamilton felt himself unsuited for the position, and uses the fact as a means to attack *The Times* for its low standards in his autobiography *Mr. Norris and I*. Tom Cullen has recorded some faults in this account, as "in his letter of application to *The Times* . . . he passes himself off as an Old Oxonian as well as an Old Rugbeian, stating that he was educated at St. John's College, Oxford" Cullen (2014: 122).

4 Of course, much of queer theory has challenged the notion of camp's apolitical position since Sontag's "Notes on Camp," beginning with the works of Judith Butler and Judith Halberstam. This will be addressed in what is to come.

5 There are many sources on this, including: Denisoff (1998: 81–95); Thomas (1976: 117–30).

6 Citing Baudelaire and the *fin de siècle* aesthetics as Isherwood's early inspiration, Peter Thomas argues that *Mr Norris Changes Trains* (and the Berlin Stories generally) act as a "brilliant" chronicle of Weimar Berlin "because of *literary* and *not strictly political* loyalties" (118, emphasis added). He further suggests that politicizing *Norris* and *Goodbye Berlin* is a fundamental misunderstanding of both texts, and that if they are "read from the starting-point of their literary allegiances and not with a view of their political pedigree, they acquire a richer metaphorical texture and, finally a deeper political meaning" (118).

7 Tom Cullen (183). It is worth emphasizing that Cullen's compunction to adopt dramatic form for the rendition of this escapade suggests something of its inherently campy nature. It seems not even the biographer can describe Hamilton's antics without reference to the biographical figure as actor or artist within his own life.

8 Mary Adams Papers. SxMOA4/5/2. The Keep Archive, Sussex. Script from Answering You No. 1; 1941.

References

"Answering You" (1941), BBC Transcript. Mary Adams Papers. SxMOA4/5/2. The Keep Archive, Sussex. Script from Answering You No. 1.

Auden, W. H. (1977), *The English Auden: Poems, Essays, and Dramatic Writing: 1927–1939*, edited by Edward Mendelson, New York: Random House.

Bozorth, Richard R. (2001), *Auden's Games of Knowledge: Poetry and the Meanings of Homosexuality*, New York: Columbia University Press.

Carlston, Erin G. (2013), *Double Agents: Espionage, Literature, and Liminal Citizens*, New York: Columbia University Press.

Cullen, Tom (2014), *The Man Who Was Norris: The Life of Gerald Hamilton*, Sawtry: Dedalus Books.

Davenport-Hines, Richard (1995), *Auden*, New York: Pantheon Books.

Denisoff, Dennis (1998), "Camp, Aestheticism, and Cultural Inclusiveness in Isherwood's *Berlin Stories*," in Shannon Hengen (ed.), *Performing Gender and Comedy: Theories, Texts and Contexts*, 81–95, New York: Routledge.

Gay, Peter (1968), *Weimar Culture: The Outsider as Insider*, New York: Harper.

Hamilton, Gerald (1956), *Mr. Norris and I*, London: A. Wingate.

Harker, Jamie (2013), *Middlebrow Queer: Christopher Isherwood in America*, Minneapolis: University of Minnesota Press.

Hepburn, Allan (2005), *Intrigue: Espionage and Culture*, New Heaven: Yale University Press.

Isherwood, Christopher (1954), *The World in the Evening*, New York: Farrar.

Isherwood, Christopher (1976), *Christopher and His Kind: 1929–1939*, New York: Farrar.

Isherwood, Christopher ([1935/1939] 2018), *The Berlin Stories*, New York: New Directions.

Mosse, George L. (1985), *Nationalism and Sexuality; Respectability and Abnormal Sexuality in Modern Europe*, New York: Howard Fertig.

Page, Norman (1998), *Auden and Isherwood: The Berlin Years*, New York: Palgrave.

Sontag, Susan (1961), "Notes on 'Camp,'" in *Against Interpretation and Other Essays*, 275–93, New York: Picador.

Spears, Monroe (1963), *The Poetry of W.H. Auden: The Disenchanted Island*, New York: Oxford University Press.

Theweleit, Klaus (1987), *Male Fantasies: Volume 1*, translated by Barabara Ehrenreich, Minneapolis: University of Minnesota Press.

Thomas, Peter (1976), "'Camp' and Politics in Isherwood's Berlin Fiction," *Journal of Modern Literature*, 5 (1): 117–30.

2

Vanished Ladies

Helen MacInnes's *Above Suspicion* and Women in Spy Fiction

Kyle Smith

This chapter uses *Above Suspicion* ([1941] 2012) by Helen MacInnes as a starting point to consider representations of women in spy fiction. MacInnes's work creates complex female characters in espionage settings. *Above Suspicion* offers a number of constructions of the female spy that allow a discussion of the contrast between the involvement of women in intelligence work during the Second World War and the limited variety of figures offered up by the spy genre across the last century. MacInnes's novel also uses the figure of the tourist, a form of disguise often prevalent in the spy novel. The sociological theories of John Urry and Mimi Sheller on tourism and mobility allow reflections on the movements of the spy and tourist in MacInnes's text as well as the constraints and opportunities for women in intelligence work that also arise in contemporary spy fiction. MacInnes's texts offer comparisons with the increasing number of recent fictional texts by women on spying. The chapter focuses on novels by Natasha Walter (*A Quiet Life* [2016]), Manda Scott (*A Treachery of Spies* [2018]), and Lauren Wilkinson (*American Spy* [2019]). Texts such as these present a more complex and inclusive spy genre that was already suggested by the work of MacInnes.

Introduction

Svetlana Alexievich points to an important new and extensive visibility of women in the Second World War:

> During World War II the world was witness to a women's phenomenon. Women served in all branches of the military in many countries of the world: 225000 in the British Army, 450,000 to 500,000 in the American, 500,000 in the German . . .
>
> About a million women fought in the Soviet Army. They mastered all military specialities including the most "masculine" ones. A linguistic problem even emerged: no feminine gender had existed till then for the words "tank driver,"

"infantryman," "machine gunner" because women had never done that work. The feminine forms were born there, in the war. (2017: x)

This is from *The Unwomanly Face of War* where Alexievich, always the great sharer of forgotten stories by "ordinary people in extraordinary situations, focuses on the voices of Soviet Russian women who fought against the Nazis" (deGraffenried 2017: 144). This is a victory from which they seem to have been erased by Soviet and Russian authorities and from which Alexievich seeks to make them reappear (Yekelchyk 2019: 439–52). Alexievich's words are a good place to begin this chapter as I want to look at women being invisible and being made invisible, women in a military role that is ill-defined, badly defined, or undefined. And I want to consider how these challenges in definition exemplify women's disappearance in intelligence work while revealing strategies surrounding visibility.

At the core of this chapter is *Above Suspicion* ([1941] 2012), the first novel by the Scottish spy writer Helen MacInnes, which can help an analysis of representations of women in spy fiction. MacInnes's work (she wrote twenty-one spy novels) was often marked by strong and interesting female characters. This can be seen in the work written during the Second World War (*Above Suspicion, Assignment in Brittany* ([1942] 2013) and *The Unconquerable* ([1944] 1990) and those written across the Cold War (in texts like *The Venetian Affair* ([1963] 2013), *The Salzburg Connection* ([1968] 2013), and *Ride a Pale Horse* ([1984] 2014)). *Above Suspicion* allows a consideration of the space between representations of women in intelligence work during the Second World War and the limited variety of figures offered up by the spy genre across the last century. It also uses the trope of the tourist, a stock form of cover in the spy novel which sociological theories on tourism by Dean MacCannell (1976, 1992), John Urry (1990), and Mimi Sheller (2011: 1–12) will help to explicate. Sheller's and Urry's works on mobility (2006: 207–26) allow us to track the movements of the spy and tourist in MacInnes's text and see the limitations and possibilities for women in intelligence work that also emerge in contemporary spy texts. MacInnes's work offers comparisons with the increasing number of recent fictional texts by women on spying. I will refer to three specifically: Natasha Walter's *A Quiet Life* (2016), Manda Scott's *A Treachery of Spies* (2018), and Lauren Wilkinson's *American Spy* (2019).

The British spy novel was born at the beginning of the twentieth century and remains popular today. Across this period, it has reflected many of the fears and hopes of its audience and it has increasingly proved a form that works as a lens through which to focus on a variety of cultural and social issues (Carlston 2013; Hepburn 2005; Lassner 2016). It is a form that blends the adventure novel (but in a shrinking paranoid Empire) and the detective novel (but with an internationalized, and thus politicized, villain). Our notion of the spy genre is that it has traditionally not been feminine. Even in the twenty-first century Natasha Walter (*The Guardian* 2016) wrote of the spy genre still being "rigidly masculine." When we look at the most successful writers in the genre across the last century, we might notice changes in tone and content but whether we look at John Buchan, Ian Fleming, John le Carré, or Charles Cummings we see well-off, privately educated white men writing novels that revolve around, for the most part, well-off, privately educated white men. Walter, however, has acknowledged a growing variety of female centered spy texts in the last five years (Flood 2020). Also, there is a good deal of interesting research that reveals the variety of women (alongside MacInnes) writing spy novels and texts interested in the matters of spying (international politics, dissembling and its morality, surveillance) in the thirties, forties and fifties. For instance, there has been work focusing on Mary Allingham, Elizabeth Bowen, Ann Bridge, Katharine Burdikin, Agatha Christie, Pamela Frankau, and Storm Jameson.[1] These academic texts also reveal the fruitfulness of studying their texts closely and some of the reasons these, often successful, novels have not been considered in terms of academic study. In a sense what we have with these texts is another vanishing. Texts evade study because they are too "popular" or not popular enough, because they might be termed "middlebrow," because they are not "modernist" enough, because they do not fall easily into a single "genre."[2]

A nuanced picture of espionage fiction identifies a greater presence for women than we might imagine but it should not be overstated in fictional or historical terms. It is interesting to note that it only became even semi-legal for women to be employed as intelligence officers in the British military during the Second World War and, even then, the numbers remained small. Despite the limited numbers of women in the field and within the spy novel they do make some important appearances, though usually in limited roles and circumstances. This chapter will concentrate on women spies' invisibility and how recent texts make this sophisticated and nuanced.

Helen MacInnes took her detailed research into European politics and the diaries of her 1939 Bavarian honeymoon (with husband Charles Highet, academic and intelligence officer) and turned them into the spy novel *Above Suspicion* (MacDonald 1989: 285; Boyd 1983: 66–75). This novel gives us a woman spy writer who makes a woman spy front and center of the novel. MacInnes's representations of the woman spy are important and her text taps into the action and excitement of the form while offering more complex and ruthless elements of spycraft that the form can reflect—that mixture of the need to thrill and to appear authentic that Wesley Wark identifies in the genre (Wark 1991: 2). Also important are the connections between the spy and the tourist the form makes evident. Clive Bloom identified why the spy novel remains a pertinent genre when he termed it "*the* genre tied to international political and social tensions" (Bloom 1990: 1). The form's globalism, as well as revealing the engagement with contemporary politics, is often manifested through links between spying and tourism. From the earliest days of the genre, we can see in, for instance, Childers' *The Riddle of the Sands* (1903), holiday jaunts developing into adventures of international intrigue. Often, as with Maugham's *Ashenden* (1928), those who travel extensively become envoys for their country's covert operations. The jet-setting and the holiday playgrounds of the rich offer both fertile soil and the perfect backdrop for intrigue. This is clear in the "thrillers" on the Riviera (written at the turn of the twentieth century by the likes of William Le Queux and E. Phillips Oppenheim), in Ian Fleming's Bond novels of the 1950s, or the 2017 British American television mini-series *The Night Manager* (directed by Susanne Bier and based on the 1993 novel of the same name by John le Carré). Keith Holinshead emphasizes the importance of tourism as an integral concept more broadly when he suggests, "[t]ourism (and travel) matter in all kinds of protean identificatory, protean aspirational, and protean world-shaping ways. Few subjects are as axial in their human and societal reach [. . .] psychically, and politically" (Holinshead 2016: 309–16). Holinshead's parenthesis in this quotation leads to another important element: the protagonist who travels as a refugee, not a tourist. Although such figures differ starkly from the imperial spy drawn in the novels of writers like John Buchan, the reality is that the historical agents of the Second World War were much closer to the refugee and many modern spy texts reflect such a complex figure—a figure more likely to disappear, a figure more likely to be capable of disappearing. This is the figure who comes to the forefront of recent spy texts.

1. "The Lady Vanishes": Women Spying in Fiction

Women have seldom been central to the spy novel and often, in the past, the notion of a female spy was met with suspicion and skepticism. We might exemplify this with James Bond's initial reactions to Vesper Lynd—"What the hell do they want to send me a woman for?" he said bitterly. "Do they think this is a bloody picnic?" (Fleming 2003: 23). Yet, as recent research has made clear, more often than we might expect we see women as spies in the British spy novel. Perhaps it is because they are so good at being invisible when they appear outside of their assigned contexts that they make good spies. Here is the female figure at the center of Helen MacInnes's *Above Suspicion*, Frances Myles, about to kill an enemy who has been chasing her and her husband (Richard Myles) up the side of a hill: "He hadn't looked up to where she remained motionless behind the rock. If he had seen her, he ignored her; his eyes were fixed on Richard. He pulled out a revolver. [. . .] Frances raised the heavy stone which she had gathered in her two hands and threw it with all her strength" (MacInnes 2012: 221).

Perhaps it is this invisibility that makes women spies so good at what they do. Or perhaps it is what makes them vanish so often. Several times in MacInnes's novel, Frances will disappear for chapters at a time. She will rest exhausted in a car after the particular encounter mentioned above while her husband and his colleague rescue an important agent from under the noses of their enemies (MacInnes 2012: 229–47). Caught by the Nazis, she will disappear into the background as her husband and his male colleagues plan to rescue her (MacInnes 2012: 278–310). She then plays little part in that rescue, unable to even make out what is going on because she is blinded by a lamp shone in her eyes (MacInnes 2012: 320–1). Yet if Frances is not always central to the mechanics of the novel, the "thrill" of the adventure, she is its heart and mind entering into dialogue with characters and audience to consider the moral imperatives of the international politics at the core of the spy novel and considering the nature of spying as a woman. Lassner suggests, "MacInnes's women create social, emotional, and narrative havoc," and certainly Frances acts as a disruptive force (Lassner 2017: 230). And that, after all, is what a spy is.

MacInnes uses a variety of techniques that sit outside the notion of the objectivity of modernist texts to engage with the politics of her day, "by infusing her social and cultural settings with political propaganda" (Lassner 2017: 229). The opening chapters set up an idealized picture of Oxford and the novel begins with a casual stroll down Jowett Walk on a hazy June afternoon marked by a strong sense of community and tradition. These chapters are a preparation for the hectic movement to follow in most of the book, but the initial picture is also contrasted with mention of events that make clear that this is June 1939. So, for instance, we are told of the young college porter, newly a father, who joined the Territorial Army "in March, just after the seizure of Prague" (MacInnes 2012: 9). The Nazi invasion of Czechoslovakia is really the end of appeasement, a clear sign that Hitler has gone back on the promises of the Munich Agreement in September 1938 when the Nazis were given control of the Sudetenland. It is also at the end of March 1939 when Chamberlain stood up in the House of Commons and promised to defend Poland if it is attacked by the Nazis. This proved to be the spark for the Second World War in Europe. *Above Suspicion*, published while the Luftwaffe bombed Britain, takes the opportunity to reflect on the events and moral choices that led up to war with Germany only a few years previously.[3]

It is perhaps in her dialogue, though, that MacInnes most successfully questions important contemporary moral issues, such as appeasement, US neutrality, and the moral imperative to defeat Nazism. Again and again in MacInnes's text the female character is the one who engages in difficult conversations about politics. In Chapter 9 Frances talks to the American journalist Van Cortlandt about the end of appeasement ("we have come out of the ether") and confronts him about American "isolationism" (MacInnes 2012: 98). Her husband attempts to defuse this conversation as MacInnes gives Frances the dialogue the male characters fear to speak. In Chapter 2, a number of male characters choose to walk away from the Nazi Von Aschenhausen, but Frances stays to confront him and unsettle him. This allows MacInnes to engage with the moral issues behind going to war, as when Frances says, "I like to think of all people having their *Lebensraum*, whether they are Germans or Jews or Czechs or Poles" (MacInnes 2012: 27). Lassner suggests that MacInnes saw "defeating Nazi Germany was a primary war aim, but [. . .] sympathy and concern about the fate of Hitler's victims was also paramount, unlike the official Allied position" (Lassner 2017: 229).

Frances's role as spy is central to the novel and in this MacInnes's text also allows us to consider the expectations of women and their relationship to espionage. Frances is not only carrying out the role of spy, she also frequently considers what it is to be a woman spy. At the beginning of her holiday/mission, Frances moves through the French countryside by train taking in her fellow passengers: "[t]hat pinched little governess looked like a German agent. I've seen too much Hitchcock lately, she thought, at this rate I'll be worse than useless" (MacInnes 2012: 42). Frances is undoubtedly referring to *The Lady Vanishes* (1938), Alfred Hitchcock's adaptation of Ethel Lina White's *The Wheel Spins* ([1936] 1997: 160–4). This novel, though it seems to have a woman spy-hero, is actually a romance. Interestingly, the novel's spy plot is a facetious concoction of one of the male characters (it takes up only a couple of pages) that Hitchcock chooses to make central to his film. Eric Homberger suggests the character's comment shows the extent to which "spy-consciousness permeated popular mentality in the 1930s" (Homberger 1990: 81). At the center of Hitchcock's film is Miss Froy, the single-minded, eccentric governess (and undercover agent) on her way home after six years abroad. She is an older woman and thus easily dismissed from the minds of those who do not engage with her when she is kidnapped by her enemies. This is what makes her "vanishing" so plausible, whether characters ignore her disappearance because they genuinely do not remember seeing her or because they choose to see their own problems as more important than rediscovering her (Beckman 2003).

Frances Myles clearly signals the limited images of women within the world of surveillance and espionage through the "pinched little governess" (which suggests both Miss Froy and her enemies), but MacInnes gives us several outlines of the female operative in *Above Suspicion*. These female spies are confined (or revealed) by their invisibility, such as the ever watchful, interfering Nurnberg bookshop assistant Ottilie in Chapter Eight or the "conversational" Paris chambermaid in Chapter Five (MacInnes 2012: 54). Even Frances herself on holiday helps put her male partner (strangely out of place on his own) "above any suspicion" (MacInnes 2012: 12). He is also made safer by her presence, as they tell him, "You won't take risks if she is with you" (MacInnes 2012: 18). In these contexts, women serve the purpose of fulfilling expectations, a sort of necessary mood furniture without which the world seems odd and bare: they are below suspicion.

MacInnes also offers an operative slightly at odds with these invisible, sexless female spies. Near the beginning of *Above Suspicion*, Frances is told her friend at the Foreign Office, Peter Galt, had "got entangled with a spy" (MacInnes 2012: 10). Her reply is: "Well, I only hope she was beautiful" (MacInnes 2012: 10). Her response is meant to be humorous and disruptive (as much of her most interesting conversation is), and it ties into one strong stereotype of the female spy: the female agent as seducer. Our archetype for this is Mata Hari who Rosie White termed the "apogee of feminine espionage, but also the epitome of an Orientalised other" (White 2008: 1). John Buchan, the most successful of early spy novelists, encapsulates this popular image of a female enemy spy in *Greenmantle* [1916] with the figure of Hilda Von Einem. The novel's hero, Richard Hannay imagines her thus: "Sometimes I thought of her as a fat old German crone, sometimes as a harsh-featured women like a schoolmistress with thin lips and eyeglasses. But I had to fit the East into the picture, so I made her young and gave her a touch of the languid houri in a veil" (Buchan [1956] 1992: 245). Buchan's Von Einem captures the feared and shocking representations of moral and ethnic "impurity" of the female spy delineated already as we move across MacInnes's text. Buchan defines his villain in terms of the "strictures" of the Germanic and the "excesses" of the East. Then there are the sexual undertones—she is both fearfully ugly and mesmerizingly attractive. The old woman, the thin-lipped schoolmistress, and languid belly dancer represent images of what Buchan considers dysfunctional womanhood.

There is, however, a third way of looking at the female spy in MacInnes's novel. Rosie White offers a contrast to the figure of Mata Hari in the British concept of the spy: Edith Cavell. Cavell was a First World War British nurse in Brussels, who helped over 200 soldiers escape from German-occupied Belgium until she is captured by the Germans in 1915 and killed by firing squad:

> Edith Cavell has come to represent all that Mata Hari is not. Cavell's Englishness is to the fore in most accounts of her life; her identity as an English woman specifically cast in terms of appropriate femininity, "pure" whiteness and middle-class respectability. This representation of the good woman spy continued to

resonate during and after the Second World War in cinematic accounts of Cavell and the women of the SOE (Special Operations Executive). (White 2008: 1)

Cavell's role is as a spy who is not really a spy, just a good person, a saint even, as Singh (2015) says. As White suggested, this dichotomy is perpetuated after the First World War and during the Second World War and beyond. It helps sideline, romanticize, and whiten the real and fictionalized female spy and makes her, eventually, invisible. The Special Operatives Executive (SOE) employed several women as spies in the early forties and some of these were represented in films in the fifties and sixties. A good example is the film *Carve Her Name with Pride* (1958) where the blonde, privately educated, middle-class Virginia McKenna plays the dark-haired, half-French, half-cockney Violet Szabo (who was married to a French Hungarian). The film also emphasizes Szabo's nobility and sacrifice very differently from representations of how contemporary Second World War films depict spies (White 2007: 55–6). Films of this period that center on women war heroes tend not to dwell on the injuries and suffering at the hands of their Nazi jailors. It is silent, invisible, only hinted at, signaled by a wince rather than a description. We can see a very similar technique in *Above Suspicion*. Several times Frances is found putting makeup on scratches, bruises, and welts (MacInnes 2012: 238, 239, 339). She finishes the novel with her torture at the hands of Von Aschenhausen and his henchman remaining, for the most part, undescribed:

> They reached the stream, and they bathed their faces in the cool water. The bullet graze had bled a lot; it looked unsafe to disturb the bandage, so Richard hacked a piece off the shirt and bandaged on top of the bloodstained handkerchiefs. The clothes for her consisted of a nondescript belted grey coat, a grey beret, a shapeless dress and shoes and stockings. Richard had an ersatz tweed suit, a rough green felt hat, and a tie of indescribable hideousness. Frances dressed her hair and disguised the bruises on her cheek as well as she could with her one hand. It would be almost impossible to get the dress on without starting more bleeding. Richard helped her into her coat and even that was difficult enough. The shoes were too big, but fortunately they had straps. (MacInnes 2012: 339)

So *Above Suspicion* captures the limited representation of the female spy as it exists, for the most part, across the twentieth century: either invisible, sneaky, and sexless; invisible, sneaky, and sexualized or the saint suffering in silence. Yet, Frances is not a powerless domestic nor a figure merely shaped by men's desires: she thinks, acts, and speaks in ways that affect events, and engages with contemporary politics, and in that she "repudiate[s] the genre's restrictive roles for its women characters" (Lassner 2017: 234). However, the novel also highlights issues that reflect some of the challenges that did arise in the Second World War, as it is set on the cusp of war and published during the war. It reflects some real elements of spycraft and the concerns of actual spies in the period. It engages with the idea of women spying for their country and the concerns revolving around this for the existing order.

Recent spy novels echo many of the issues at the heart of MacInnes's novel, such as Natasha Walter's *A Quiet Life* (2016), the story of Linda Last, a diffident figure spying for the Soviets in 50s Britain and America, Manda Scott's *A Treachery of Spies* (2018), which starts as a present-day police procedural, but becomes a French Resistance story about the murder of a former *maquisard*, Sophie Destivelle, in Orleans and Laura Wilkinson's *American Spy* (2019), about a Black woman working for the FBI and the CIA to counteract revolution in Burkina Faso. In some ways Walter's *A Quiet Life* (2016) seems closest to MacInnes's book in its setting in the 1940s and 1950s and its untrained middle-class woman, even if its representation of women's roles in this period is marked by a more extensive feminist awareness. Walter's research into Melinda Maclean (the wife of the Cambridge spy, Donald Maclean) led to the fictionalization of Melinda as a spy. She has talked of how Melinda Maclean's contradictions attracted her:

> it was clear that she benefited from the stereotypes of the time about women and espionage. Though there had been many women working as spies during and after the world wars, they were often dismissed as the seductive courtesan (Mata Hari) or the martyred nurse (Edith Cavell), and neither of those stereotypes seemed relevant to Melinda. She kept up appearances with such aplomb. . . . nobody ever suspected that Melinda knew a thing. She was the good wife, reading her fashion magazines and looking after the children. It was only much later that it transpired she too had been a devoted communist. (Walter 2003)

Walter shows an invisible figure who uses this invisibility to her advantage. The "quiet life" of the title stands, in part, for the life, "a new start. A quiet life," Laura Last yearns for as her husband, spying for the Soviets, unravels (Walter 2016: 329). However, it also reflects the nature of the life Laura lives. She is a young, upper-middle-class woman of the period, who appears more an ornament than a fully functioning human being.[4] The Laura who sees "herself in the mirror, well dressed, quiet, unremarkable" is not a million miles from Frances in front of her mirror saying, "You'll do" (Walter 2016: 326, MacInnes 2012: 20). Last is a self-conscious watcher and recorder. She escapes to the Soviet Union because an additional feminine trait makes her appear so unimportant: "Her hands clasped over her huge belly: the epitome of femininity, alien, outside whatever masculine narrative, whether of espionage or alcoholism, the Foreign Office was constructing from Edward's disappearance. A pregnant woman is even more invisible than other women, Laura thought as she fell asleep, or rather, only her pregnancy is visible" (Walter 2016: 362).[5]

Wilkinson's *American Spy* (2019) begins with the excitement we might expect from a spy thriller—the reaching for a gun in a dark house where a noise has been heard. But this is punctured within the first sentence by the domestic. The figure who is creeping toward their bedroom having taken a Service automatic from their safe stands on a piece of Lego. There is a suggestion of children in these opening lines but quickly we move into the presence of an intruder and struggle which ends in the death of the intruder. The first word we hear from the children is "Maman" (Wilkinson 2019: 4). We do not fear for the spy, but the children, and the novel returns, again and again, to family concerns (the relationship with her mother, her sister, her father, even the murder of Fred Hampton takes place beside his pregnant partner). The novel ends with our spy's declaration that she hopes her children will be "agents of change" forcing us to think about the words "agent" and "agency" (Wilkinson 2019: 287).

2. "The Lady Vanishes": Women Spies in History

The nature of specific government agencies focused on intelligence plays an increasingly important role in spy fiction. Philip Knightley (2003: 35) argues that the British Secret Intelligence Service (SIS) was in part a reaction to the sensationalist spy narrative of William Le Queux. From the days when unnamed elements of the Establishment called upon gentleman amateurs to solve global problems (as in *Greenmantle* and *The Three Hostages* by John Buchan ([1956] 1992: 111, 700) we move through to a focus on the maneuvers between "espiocrats" in the branches of such agencies in the novels of le Carré (1993: 84). Wilkinson and Scott's novels focus on the present circumstances within the CIA. Martha Lakoff, the central culprit in the murders that initiate Manda Scott's novel, inhabits a very different world from the female spy we see in MacInnes's novel. It is not just that Martha Lakoff is far from the world of the amateur spy: she is not even a government agent. The police inspector Ines Picault suggests to Martin Gillard that Martha is CIA. He even suggests that it is "far darker than that. We're moving into a world where private enterprise calls the shots" (Scott 2018: 452). Similarly, *American Spy* (2019) considers contemporary issues around the privatization of counterintelligence where our central figure mistakenly believes she is working for the CIA in Burkina Faso but is in fact working for a much shadier enterprise to whom intelligence work has been farmed out. So, as in the past, the state agencies of intelligence are seldom shown entirely positively.

In *Above Suspicion*, the element of government intelligence Frances and her husband find themselves working for never takes on the clear role it has in these contemporary works, but it does capture some of the problems faced during the Second World War by real agents. In fact, the novel starts with the description of a breakdown in intelligence only too familiar during the Second World War:

> Until about five weeks ago we had the normal reports from him—accurate and regular. But since then, we have had no really informative messages. Two of them, in fact, were dangerously misleading. Fortunately, we had other sources of information about these facts which made us suspicious, and we didn't act on his advice. These suspicions were increased when two men, escaping from Germany by this route, disappeared completely. (2012: 14)

The situation that initiates the Myleses' adventure is prophetic of some of the most serious bungling within the complex world of British secret agents (specifically within SOE's F-section). The Gestapo took control of the French section of the SOE in the early forties and, despite a variety of clues (very like the one promptly acted on in MacInnes's novel), the Nazis collected agents, supplies, and information before signing off cheekily on June 6, 1944 (Helm 2005: 59). The failure to act on these warning signs led to the death of over 400 British agents. This included twelve women agents—the first British female agents sent into a foreign country in some sort of semi-officially sanctioned capacity.

As Alexievich suggested, the expansion of women's role in the military was an important one across all the major powers though the female spy was, in legal terms, an impossibility at the beginning of the Second World War: "The 1929 Geneva Convention and the 1907 Hague Convention on land warfare, the main instruments offering protection to prisoners of war, made no provision at all for protecting women, as women were not envisaged as combatants" (Helm 2005: 9). Also, the legal framework of the RAF, Navy, and Army in Britain barred women from combat. Nevertheless, female SOE agents were first authorized in April 1942. Peter Gubbins (Head of Military Operations in SOE) was confident in the abilities of women to succeed as agents and arranged for his recruits to be enlisted into the FANY (First Aid Nursing Yeomanry), a voluntary civilian corps (and thus outside the statutes of the military) (Helm 2005: 9–10). However, this quasi-legal status meant the women who died during the war were almost wiped from official records. Vera Atkins is a central figure in the story of female SOE agents. She oversaw the recruitment and deployment of British agents in occupied France. She had responsibility for the thirty-nine women SOE agents who were couriers and wireless operators for the various circuits established by SOE. After the war she traced 117 of the 118 missing F Section agents and she established the circumstances of the 14 deaths of women, twelve of whom had been murdered in concentration camps.[6] Atkins's tenacity persuaded the War Office that these twelve women, technically regarded as civilians, were recorded as killed in action (Helm 2005: 265). She worked to show their bravery, before and after capture, to help ensure they received official recognition by the British government (Helm 2005: 265). The intelligence scenario outlined at the beginning of *Above Suspicion* allows us to consider one of the most fearful elements for agents in the Second World War: the breakdown of communication and what that might mean. It becomes apparent that many of these agents did not only face death, but erasure. Only the work of Atkins and the historians who told her story and that of many of the female SOE agents helped prevent that erasure (Bailey 2009; Helm 2005; Pattinson 2007). The last forty years has been an exceptionally fruitful period in considering the roles of women in war situations more generally.[7] Much contemporary spy fiction by women entailed intense research, including all three of the novelists here, who use an extensive range of primary and secondary sources.[8] The best contemporary spy fiction reflects the most recent historical research.

3. "The Lady Vanishes": The Tourist and the Refugee

So, the breakdown in communications that initiates Frances and Richard Myles's adventures reflects events on mainland Europe concerning military intelligence and, though not common, women did serve in military intelligence on the front line in the 1940s. The Myleses are sent out as tourists to find whether a particularly important line of intelligence has been broken. There is an expectation that their findings will definitively decide whether this is a safe route of intelligence, or as Peter words it, "What we want to know is this -- before the harvests are gathered in, to put it bluntly—does the man still exist, or has he been sending us false messages to warn us that things aren't just right, or has he been liquidated" (MacInnes 2012: 14). MacInnes's choice to send out the couple as tourists in the summer before the Second World War allows interesting strategies in the narrative and enables important comment on an international situation in flux: it allows MacInnes to enact a "redefinition of propaganda as an instrument of [her] own political conviction" (Lassner 2017: 229). Frances and her husband move between two worlds: holiday and work (for their government). The spy novel genre has often utilized the figure of the tourist because it offers the agent such an excellent cloak of invisibility. Nothing clarifies this better than a close sociological reading of the tourist. It also allows us to track the transformation the tourist/spy undergoes as war grows closer, as the tourist allows a consideration of a more modern, bureaucratic traveler: the refugee. The worlds of the spy and the tourist in peacetime share many elements. Spy fiction developed when tourism became more accessible (Watson 1979: 55–6). The novel offers several contrasts between life before and during the war begins when the novel was published. Initially, MacInnes's novel looks back to a pre-war tourism where the Baedeker was the essential guidebook. This works as a central device throughout the novel: it serves as a badge of the tourist couple's authenticity; it offers banal meeting places for secret rendezvous; and it can be used for codes that can only be broken by someone conversant with this earliest of mass-produced travel manuals. Even when the heroes are uncovered as spies and are on the run the book continues to offer maps, route finders, and meeting places that will not arouse suspicion (MacInnes 2012: 30, 239, 262). The destinations and source of information, the planned and random movement, become identical for tourist and agent. In tourist terms the Baedeker works as, what Dean MacCannell the early sociologist of the tourist termed, a "marker" which he sees as essential to proving the authenticity of a sight (MacCannell 1976: 10). Without such a marker the tourist cannot identify a sight and thus cannot read the landscape in the manner he or she wants to. These markers denote safe meeting places to the spy and yet still appear innocent. In *Above Suspicion*, the Baedeker defines the spy's relationship with the landscape: the guide defines not only what the tourist sees, but also what the spy sees and provides a safe route through an unknown space.

The tourist and the spy are alike in *Above Suspicion* in other ways. First, and most obviously in this case, both report what they see. Initially, Frances wants to see the Germany and Austria she has known, and expects, as a tourist, as we read, "She opened a window and looked out on to the Konigstrasse. The houses had high steep roofs, some of them pitted with attic windows, while others turned the gable ends to the street. This was better, this was more like she had imagined" (2012: 73–4). The tourist's way of looking at her environment is at the center of John Urry's book *The Tourist Gaze* (1990), in which Urry compares it to the medical gaze at the center of Foucault's *Birth of the Clinic* (1973): "When we 'go away' we look at the environment with interest and curiosity. It speaks to us in ways we appreciate, or at least, we anticipate that it will do so. In other words, we gaze at what we encounter. And this gaze is as socially organised and systemised as is the gaze of the medic" (Urry 1990: 1). So, Frances's view of the Konigstrasse fulfills her touristic expectations, but, for the most part, Frances Myles's gaze denigrates what she sees: the Gothic architecture, the sausages, the coffee and the vindictiveness of the torture museum in Nurnberg (MacInnes, 2012: 78, 91, 111, 93). The "grandiose buildings," the uniforms and the "military tread" of Nazism bring nothing positive for Frances: "to all appearances the shops aren't any better, the restaurants aren't any better, the food is worse, so are the theatres and books" (MacInnes 2012: 82). As Jonathan Culler puts it in *The Framing of the Sign*, "the tourist is interested in everything as a sign of itself, an instance of a typical cultural practice" (Culler 1988: 155). Each of these "cultural practices" is a mark against German culture for political reasons and a prospective weak spot that a spy might turn to her advantage. So, Frances's words are also those of the spy (the collector and distributor of information). She is MacInnes's propagandist, writing in the heart of the war, aiming to undermine the authority of the enemy.

The spy and the tourist also share a love of home as MacInnes shows in *Above Suspicion's* opening in peacetime Oxford. The roses and poplars, Oxford colleges where one "sported the oak" for privacy, cricket, sherry, parties where academics talk of Gaudi, Picasso and Waugh and punts on the river, suggest an intelligent cosmopolitan world built solidly on tradition and convention (MacInnes 2012: 7, 9, 22, 34). Though imminent war hangs over the scene, it suggests a world worth saving and making much sacrifice to save. Frances takes this image of home into Germany. The tourist compares the new site with home. In times of peace the dissimilarities might make the tourist destination positive, but in times of war dissimilarities reveal the enemy's shortcomings. Even a positive encounter with a polite Austrian bellboy emphasizes this: "Frances suddenly realised that this was the first really friendly smile or voice they had met in two weeks. She thought of a London bus conductor or a policeman and felt a wave of homesickness strike her" (MacInnes 2012: 92). Britain here seems a specified, recognized, and organized society "at ease with itself." In contrast, Germany and Austria are viewed, as they are throughout the book, as dehumanized, grim totalitarianisms rife with bad manners which makes Frances yearn for the stability of her home, but also fear for that stability. The spy is driven by the same fears, and makes the same comparisons, as the tourist. One of the great invasion paranoias of the spy novel is that stable figures of the home landscape, like police officers and bus conductors, are the enemy in disguise.[9] Surely, if anything does separate the spy and the tourist, it is the fact that a spy is a better-than-average tourist, privy to more authentic experiences of the foreign culture in the line of duty. It is authenticity, according to MacCannell, that is the driving force behind tourists' actions (MacCannell 1976: 3). In Paris, the Myleses hear real French people singing songs and longing for there not to be another war (MacInnes 2012: 63). Moving into even more dangerous environments, Frances gets to walk about the streets wearing a dirndl, like an ordinary Austrian, and, perhaps even more exciting for the tourist, she is held captive in an actual Nazi fortress by real SS men (MacInnes 2012: 264, 310–30). As a spy she achieves a higher level of touristic experience by having encounters that are more authentic. As MacCannell puts it, "touristic shame is not based on being a tourist but on not being tourist enough, on a failure to see everything the way it ought to be seen" (MacCannell 1976: 10). What we seek as tourists is authenticity in a site or environment as if we had the eyes of a local. At points, we even want to stop being the tourist and become the local. This is really what happens in Helen MacInnes's *Assignment in Brittany* (1942), where our hero Hearne takes on the identity of a Breton farm owner (by chance, his physical double), while the original lies in an English hospital. The spy and the tourist both hark back to the adventurers, explorers and travelers of the nineteenth century adventure novel, or what Green terms, "the generic counterpart in literature to empire in politics" (Green 1979: xi). The confidence of the adventure form is replaced by paranoia in the spy genre in which the celebration of gaining an Empire is replaced with the fear of losing one. Add to that the fears of the early years of the Second World War: the skies over Britain threatened by the Luftwaffe, France defeated, the whole of Europe overwhelmed by the Nazis, British concerns in North Africa imperiled, the United States still neutral, the fear of being subsumed by the Empire building of the Nazis.[10] In peacetime the woman spy can hide as a tourist. What happens when political events or war define tourists not as being in disguise, but as targets?

Contemporary spy novels are not marked so much by the figure of the tourist (perhaps because of those imperial connotations), but they do show us travelers. Walter's shifts from Geneva to the United States and to England. Wilkinson's travels between the United States, Martinique, and Burkina Faso. Scott's moves from France to Scotland to England. Scott's book is marked by clear shifts between two time periods, but all three books are marked by fragmented shifts in time. This sense of movement, at least until the recent pandemic, seems an important element of the early twenty-first century. "All the world seems to be on the move," suggested John Urry and Mimi Sheller (2006: 207). They were talking about the new area of study they termed "Mobilities" and the contemporary importance of studying the nature of movement in the twenty-first-century world (how we move, how we stop, what processes affect our journeys, and how our identities affect these processes). Yet, this world on the move seemed to contain echoes of the circumstances in the Second World War, another era of unprecedented movement. The Second World War and the decades on either side of it were a period of exceptional upheaval caused by war, political unrest, and ideological hatred and fear—at its core those who were persecuted and deported to death camps, slave labor camps, and gulags and those who became unwanted refugees. The list of figures the article suggests are on the move contains many contemporary figures and yet many of them echo those forced to travel in the Second World War: asylum seekers, international students, terrorists, members of diasporas, holidaymakers, business people, sports stars, refugees, backpackers, commuters, the early retired, young mobile professionals, prostitutes, armed forces—these and many others fill the world's airports, buses, ships and trains (Sheller and Urry 2006: 207). Some of the areas of study within Mobilities ("Refugees and border politics—surveillance—raced and gendered spatialities") tie in with our study of a Second World War novel (Sheller 2011: 8). In many ways, an area of study that is interested in the "combined movements of people, objects and information in all of their complex relational dynamics" is almost a definition of the spy novel itself (Sheller 2011: 1; Sheller and Urry 2006: 209).

The tourist is a figure who moves through a fresh environment searching for authenticity. In times of war, authenticity becomes a particularly contested area. This tourist figure moves through a suddenly insecure environment searching for safety. This is what happens to Frances and Richard: their experiences allow MacInnes to offer a window on the dispossessed. It is interesting that two of the most important figures in defining the tourist sociologically (Dean MacCannell [1992] and John Urry[(1990]), move on to study more complex travelers (nomads, transnational workers, refugees). Urry (1990) especially offers us a way to look at the more complex travelers Frances and her husband point toward as we move toward the end of *Above Suspicion*.

MacInnes's novel, choosing to focus on events from 1938 and 1939 while written during the early period of the Second World War, floats between war on the verge of happening and war being experienced. Even at the beginning of the novel, Frances both recognizes the mobility of the well-off tourist and how war changes mobility: "Once you could walk over mountain paths and spend the evenings round a table in the village inn. There had been singing and dancing, lighthearted talk and friendly laughter. But now there were uniforms and regulations. Now you might only laugh at certain things. Now conversations with foreigners were apt to end in argument" (MacInnes 2012: 8).

Barriers go up—both physical and social. The tourists, as in the Myleses' case here, are relatively free due to their wealth, their education, and the confidence given to them by their stable social position. However, ironically, the changing "cultural practices" mean that tourists are also seen as spies. There is no getting "above" suspicion. The Myleses' "cover" is no longer so useful for the very reasons that make thirties Northern Europe a much less attractive tourist destination: its state-led distrust of the foreigner, its xenophobic patriotism. It is no longer an antidote to home or a reminder of it, except in the sense of reminding us of the superiority of "our" home, of "our" nation. The tourist's identity seems to offer a certain invisibility, and though the suspiciousness and surveillance of the state in the burgeoning dictatorship might make things less easy, the Myleses do manage to move about relatively freely for at least part of the novel. There are, however, spaces they cannot enter—as with this one in Nuremberg that MacInnes chooses to show us:

> From the quiet blackness of the little alley to the left of them came a bitter cry, the high, self strangling cry of fear or pain, or both. They looked at one another.
>
> "And just what was that," asked Richard quietly. He made as if to move into the alley. There was another cry. It made Frances feel sick. Van Cortlandt and Richard looked grimly at each other.
>
> "You stay here with your wife. I'll investigate." The American had taken a step along with Richard into the alley. "Halt!" The abrupt command came from behind them. The two men had increased their pace to a run, as they had seen the foreigners become curious.
>
> "Halt!" Van Cortlandt and Richard stopped they looked belligerently at the men. Frances came to the rescue.
>
> "Something's wrong—a murder or something—down there."
>
> The brown shirted men exchanged looks.
>
> "We advise you to take a walk," the older one said.
>
> "But something is wrong," the American protested.
>
> The trooper who was doing the talking said, "We advise you to take a walk. It is only a Jew's Alley." (MacInnes 2012: 113)

The tourist cannot see this but, as limited as they might be, they are not trapped in those alleys or in the concentration camps Mr. "Smith" (the man they rescue) helps Jews escape from (MacInnes 2012: 231). They glimpse a state-sanctioned violence but are moved on assiduously and they sense the danger in protesting too much. Lassner identifies the importance of this scene across several pages in *Espionage and Exile* (2016). She recognizes MacInnes as one of the few authors who "used their mass-market, popular fiction to dramatize the plight of European Jewry at a time when national governments and mainstream media were still ignoring it" (Lassner 2016: 70–118, 90–3).

Frances and her husband cannot maintain the dual role of tourist and spy as the war footing escalates and the opportunity to be above suspicion recedes. They survive because of the networks (Sheller and Urry 2006: 223–4) they have developed beyond the state—both the enemy's and their own. The connection with the spy network developed in Germany and Austria allows them access to new identity papers. There is the money of the American journalist, Van Cortlandt, and the Oxford student Thornley, Frau Schilt, and the disguise she offers. That nice bellboy in Innsbruck turns out to be a friend of their ex-housekeeper Anna—this couple offer maps out of Austria, and they offer secret rendezvous in shop changing rooms (MacInnes 2012: 92, 134, 269, 288). The fact that Von Aschenhausen went to university with Frances's husband (and that Richard learned good German at university) allows Richard to impersonate a senior Nazi on the phone. Frances can disappear and rest (when Thornley and Richard go off to rescue Mr. Smith, when Thornley and Van Cortlandt and her husband rescue her from her torturers). This suggests a certain level of passivity on Frances's part and yet she exists as part of a network of spies or at least a network of those who will resist the state (including a network of spies).

By the end of the novel the Myleses are no longer tourists, and we read,

> They were to travel on their German passports, complete with Italian entry stamps (Schulz had earned his money) towards Grenoble. If the station would accept their marks, they could catch an early morning train. If not, they would have to wait until the banks opened. Van Cortlandt and Thornley, cutting back on their tracks would drive through Lombardy until daylight made the car too dangerous. They would then get rid of it and make for the Swiss border if they hadn't reached it by that time. Van Cortlandt was confident that they would. They divided the marks they had and van Cortlandt emptied the smaller of the two suitcases to carry the dress and two extra shirts and socks for Richard. They could think of no other main points; the details would depend on quick wits and luck. They would meet in Paris, Van Cortlandt gave them the address of a hotel he knew. (2012: 340)

What a long way they have come from the novel's beginning amidst flowers, trees, and the river, and the sound of leather against willow, the cloisters of an Oxford college, drinks parties, and intellectual conversation.

Negotiating the border had changed for the Myleses: it was not the fluid, porous place it was in peacetime for the hill climber described at the beginning of this section. It now demands false papers, and it demands cash. It demands flexibility, quick thinking, imagination, and good fortune. The whiteness of their skin will help. Money will help. Frances, we feel, will disappear successfully and return home. For Frances still has a nation-state to return to, whose attributes we saw at the beginning of the book. The refugees fleeing Nazism were not so lucky, struggling to gain visas for other countries (including Britain) and struggling to deal with statelessness (as Arendt (2017: 353) suggests "what is unprecedented is not the loss of home but the impossibility of finding a new one"). The Myleses' network of social and cultural capital makes their escape so much more possible than it proves to be for many others. Other people from far afield in other people's ill-fitting clothes trying to find a way home.

We might think back to Frances's conversation with Von Aschenhausen in Chapter 2. It is by his clothes ("his Savile Row suit") that she identifies him as a Nazi rather than an "exile" (MacInnes 2012: 25). MacInnes sharpens the moral choice here—a German succeeding at this time can only be a Nazi. But she also emphasizes the necessity of war for the British (and by extension the Americans)—a war not just about protecting "our own" but defeating the morally indefensible, defeating an enemy who would remove citizenship, freedom, life from all those it deems "the bad" (MacInnes 2012: 26). The spies from SOE who disappeared into concentration camps were nearly all mixed nationality, on the cusps of different cultures rather than English. They were the children of parents who worked in Europe or were immigrants (or the children of immigrants) who had settled in Britain in an unsettled world.[11] They vanished. And many of them are only remembered in part because of Vera Atkins, a Romanian and a Jew who spent a large part of the war trying to have her application for British naturalization accepted (Helm 2005: 50–2, 132–3, 365–6).

Walter's hero vanishes at the end of her book too. In a sense, Walter wishes to reveal the woman behind the myth of the British spy, Maclean. Walter shows both the strengths and weaknesses of invisibility, of quietness—to show its possibilities and limitations. With Frances, in *Above Suspicion*, MacInnes (2012) does a strangely similar thing. Frances's invisibility is a strength—it means she can kill a man who does not even see her. She can disguise her bruises behind her makeup. Her very presence can stop her husband from doing anything too impulsive. Most importantly, however, she is not silent and she leads us into the most important discussions of the novel. Walter sees Frances as "a female spy with a sure intelligence, and who isn't sexually available" but suggests we shouldn't overstate "the originality or the feminism of MacInnes's vision" (*The Guardian* 2016). This is to miss what Lassner suggests, that "the novel's "international resistance," its antifascist critique and argument for British intervention belong to Frances's (Lassner 2017: 230).

Walter's Laura Last is also a contradiction of the expectations and stereotypes of the British female spy. She may start the book a tourist and end it in exile—but she gives up everything to be with her husband in the Soviet Union, Britain's archenemy. She is a figure of the Cold War, not the Second World War, but still, today, Laura Last has much to say to us about power and representation both as a woman and a spy. Similarly, Manda Scott's (2018) novel offers up a complex gendered identity, one marked by class and the traumas of war and power as they continue over time. Perhaps most interesting is Wilkinson's (2019) narrative. The novel offers a sophisticated picture of a broader world that is often just a picturesque backdrop in the spy novel. To consider Burkina Faso beyond French colonialism is to consider how Empire hangs over all the wars of the twentieth century, cold or hot. The book reflects on the details of Blacks murdered by the security services (such as Fred Hampton) to show how internal US security ties into race. The novel considers the nature of being a spy and its connectedness to the nature of being Black (reflecting on Black writers like Nella Larsen and Ralph Ellison and Black philosophers like Franz Fanon). The spy novel ceases to be the genre of powerful white men to become a way to think about gender, class, race, and Empire.

Conclusion

It may surprise us that a genre like the spy novel, so "rigidly masculine" for so long, could be used in these three modern texts to look at women's roles within society, yet this is something they share with MacInnes's text. *Above Suspicion* lays out the limited images of the female spy in cultural terms and reveals other possibilities seldom grasped for many decades after the text's publication. It reflects the form's fascination with travel and reflects the fears, change, and uncertainty the Second World War brought. It nods, unwittingly, to the British women spies who disappeared into the Nazi concentration camps. It engages in political discussion of the most pressing issues of its day, confronting questions of British appeasement, US neutrality, and Nazi treatment of the Jews. The growing range of contemporary novels about aspects of spying written by women reflects what a fruitful area of engagement espionage has become for historical and cultural representations of women working in the intelligence field.

I want to return to Alexievich (2017) to make one last point. Her text shows us a vast array of women at war—privates, majors, generals, cryptographers, tank commanders, pilots, foot soldiers, partisans, snipers, bakers, laundry workers, cooks, doctors, nurses, gunners, telephone operators telling us their experiences of war. These experiences reveal staggering bravery and stamina as well as dreadful destruction, both physical and mental. It also shows the vast complexity of life that is ignored when a huge percentage of the population is disappeared from a momentous event. The book declares the need to make one's presence felt. Like Elena Pavlovna Shalova, a KOMOSOL leader of an infantry battalion as it entered Berlin in 1945: "I wrote my name on the Reichstag . . . I wrote with charcoal, with what was at hand You were defeated by a Russian girl from Saratov" (Alexievich 2017: 315). How easy it is to wipe out charcoal, but this is a declaration of womanhood, of ordinariness, of nationalism, of community. And Alexievich's text reveals the complex and twisted situations that demand a heartrending invisibility. Pauline Kasperovich, a partisan during the war, tells the story of a mother whose partisan sons were captured by the Nazis after a shootout. She talks about how the boys' mother behaved as her sons were paraded through the village:

> The entire village stood there. Their father and mother stood there, nobody made a sound. What a heart the mother must have had not to cry out. Not to call. She

knew that if she began to weep, the whole village would be burned down. She wouldn't be killed alone. Everybody would be killed. For one German killed they used to burn an entire village. She knew . . . . There exist awards for everything, but no award, not even the highest Star of the Hero of the Soviet Union is enough for that mother . . . for her silence . . . (Alexievich 2017: 257)

The voices of forgotten people saved from vanishing. Not all voices and not always perfectly saved. But a more complex picture becomes possible, a more inclusive and nuanced picture. One that even has space for the bravery of invisibility and silence even as the text tries to reduce invisibility and silence. Alexievich's text is generated by oral history, but also through its creative arrangement. Historical research has done so much to create a more subtle picture of the past, as can fiction. It seems that the spy novel, often marked in the past by an imperial masculinity, is increasingly utilizing the fluidity of identity and globality of movement at its heart to offer more sophisticated and inclusive narratives.

Notes

1 Bold (2012: 31–53); Boyd (1983: 66–75); Ehland and Wächter (2016); Grundy Haigh (2016: 138–61); Hepburn (2005); Humble (2001); Lassner (2009: 113–30); Lassner (2016, 2017); Wheelwright (2019: 3–17).

2 Ehland and Wächter (2016); Grundy Haigh (2016: 138–61); Hepburn (2005); Humble (2001); Lassner (2009: 113–30); Bluemel and Lassner (2018).

3 Aster (2008: 443–80); Carter (2020); Hastings (2011); Holland (2010); Levine (2016); McDonough (2002); Mazower (1998); Overy and Wheatcroft (2009); Overy (2006); Rothwell (2002); Todman (2016).

4 "The women provided the colour between the black and white of the men's tuxedos, but that was all they seemed to be there for; these flashes—green, scarlet, blush and blue—between the black coats" (Walter 2016: 77).

5 We might also note this question of invisiblity in the sense that the killer of Manda Scott's Sophie Destivelle's proves to be "blonde, pregnant oh-so-helpful Martha" (Scott 2018: 452).

6 These were Andrée Borrel, Vera Leigh, Sonia Olschanezky and Diana Rowden who were executed at Natzweiler-Struthof on 6 July 1944; Yolande Beekman, Madeleine Damerment, Noor Inayat Khan and Eliane Plewman who were executed at Dachau on 13th September 1944; Denise Bloch, Lilian Rolfe and Violette Szabo who were executed at Ravensbrück on 5 February 1945, and Cecily Lefort executed in the gas chamber at the Uckermark Youth Camp adjacent to Ravensbrück in February 1945.

7 Anderson (1981); Cockburn (2007); Downs (2014); Enloe (2010, 2014); Elshtain (1995); Jensen (2008); Khan (2020); Roberts (2013); Rose (2004).

8 In Walter's (2016: 436–40) acknowledgements she refers to a variety of texts on the Cambridge Spies, the Blitz, the British Communist Party, McCarthyism. In Wilkinson's (2019: 290–3) acknowledgements she cites extensive research into the CIA, the Black Panthers and Burkina Faso. Manda Scott ((2018: 454–62) across an Afterword, a Bibliography and her Acknowledgements) refers to an impressive variety of texts on the SOE, French Resistance and the CIA.

9 Household ([1939] 1981: 81–2); Buchan (1993: 96); MacInnes (2012: 136).
10 Atkinson (2013); Hastings (2011); Holland (2016); Overy and Wheatcroft (2009); Todman (2016).
11 Here is some of the background of the twelve SOE operatives who died in concentration camps: Andrée Borrel (French); Vera Leigh (abandoned as a baby in Leeds she was adopted by an American and grew up around the outskirts of Paris); Sonia Olschanezky (her father a Russian Jew, her mother a German Jew); Diana Rowden (English, grew up in France); Yolande Beekman (half Swiss, born in Paris); Madeleine Damerment (French); Noor Inayat Khan (born in Moscow to an Indian Muslim father and an American mother); Eliane Plewman (born in Marseilles to an English father and a Spanish mother); Denise Bloch (French and Jewish); Cecily Lefort (English, she had lived in France with her French husband since the mid-twenties); Lilian Rolfe (English, grew up in Paris where her father worked); and Violette Szabo (born in Paris, father English, mother French, husband French Hungarian).

References

Alexievich, Svetlana (2017), *The Unwomanly Face of War*, London: Penguin.
Anderson, Karen (1981), *Wartime Women: Sex Roles, Family Relations, and the Status of Women in World War II*, Westport: Greenwood Press.
Arendt, H. (2017), *The Origins of Totalitarianism*, London: Penguin.
Aster, Sidney (2008), "Appeasement: Before and After Revisionism," *Diplomacy & Statecraft*, 19 (3): 443–80.
Atkinson, Rick (2013), *An Army at Dawn*, London: Little, Brown.
Bailey, Roderick (2009), *Forgotten Voices of the Secret War: An Inside History of Special Operations during the Second World War*, London: Ebury Press.
Beckman, Karen (2003), *Vanishing Women: Magic, Film, and Feminism*, Durham: Duke University.
Bloom, Clive (1990), "Introduction: The Spy Thriller: A Genre Under Cover?," in C. Bloom (ed.), *Spy Thrillers: From Buchan to le Carré*, 1, London: MacMillan.
Bluemel, Kristen and Phyllis Lassner (2018), "Feminist Inter/modernist Studies," *Feminist Modernist Studies*, 1 (1–2): 22–35.
Bold, Christine (2012), "Domestic Intelligence: Marriage and Espionage in Helen MacInnes's Fiction," *Paradoxa*, 24: 31–53.
Boyd, Mary (1983), "The Enduring Appeal of the Spy Thrillers of Helen MacInnes," *Clues*, 4: 66–75.
Buchan, John (1992), *The Complete Richard Hannay*, London: Penguin.
Buchan, John (1993), *The Power House*, Edinburgh: B&W.
Carlston, Erin (2013), *Double Agents: Espionage, Literature, and Liminal Citizens*, New York: Columbia University Press.
Carter, Benjamin Hett (2020), *The Nazi Menace: Hitler, Churchill, Roosevelt, Stalin, and the Road to War*, New York: Henry Holt.
Childers, Erskine, ed. (1903), *The Riddle of the Sands: A Record of Secret Service Recently Achieved*, London: Smith, Elder & Co.
Cockburn, Cynthia (2007), *From Where We Stand: War, Women's Activism and Feminist Analysis*, London: Zed Books.

Culler, Jonathan (1988), *Framing the Sign: Criticism and Its Institutions*, Oxford: Blackwell.
deGraffenried, Julie (2017), "Voices from Chernobyl: The Oral History of a Nuclear Disaster by Svetlana Alexievich, trans. K. Gessen," *The Oral History Review*, 44 (1): 144–6.
Downs, Laura Lee (2014), "War Work," in J. Winter (ed.), *The Cambridge History of The First World War, vol. III*, 72–95, Cambridge: Cambridge University Press.
Ehland, Christoph and Cornelia Wächter, eds (2016), *Middlebrow and Gender, 1890–1945*, Leiden: Brill.
Elshtain, Jean (1995), *Women and War: With a New Epilogue*, Chicago: University of Chicago Press.
Enloe, Cynthia (2010), *Nimo's War, Emma's War: Making Feminist Sense of the Iraq War*, Berkeley: University of California Press.
Enloe, Cynthia (2014), *Bananas, Beaches and Bases: Making Feminist Sense of International Politics*, Berkeley: University of California Press.
Fleming, Ian (2003), *Casino Royale, Live and Let Die, Moonraker*, London: Penguin.
Flood, Alison (2020), "'Nobody in Tesco Buys Spy Books by Women': How Female Authors Took on the Genre," *The Guardian*, 7 January. Available online: https://www.theguardian.com/books/2020/jan/07/spy-books-by-women-stella-rimington-manda-scott-charlotte-philby (accessed 19 July 2022).
Foucault, Michel (1973), *1926–1984. The Birth of the Clinic: An Archaeology of Medical Perception*, London: Tavistock.
Green, Martin (1979), *Dreams of Adventure, Deeds of Empire*, New York: Basic Books.
Grundy Haigh, Emma (2016), "The Adventures of the Lady Typist: Redefining the Heroic in Early Twentieth-Century Women's Spy Fiction," in C. Ehland and C. Wächter (eds), *Middlebrow and Gender, 1890–1945*, 138–61, Leiden: Brill.
Hastings, Max (2011), *All Hell let Loose: The World at War 1939–45*, London: Harper Press.
Helm, Sarah (2005), *A Life in Secrets: The Story of Vera Atkins and the Lost Agents of SOE*, London: Abacus.
Hepburn, Allan (2005), *Intrigue: Espionage and Culture*, New Haven and London: Yale University Press.
Holland, James (2010), *The Battle of Britain: Five Months That Changed History 1940*, London: Bantam Press.
Holland, James (2016), *The Rise of Germany, 1939–1941*, London: Corgi.
Hollinshead, Keith (2016), "A Portrait of John Urry—Harbinger of the Death of Distance," *Anatolia*, 27 (2): 309–16.
Homberger, Eric (1990), "English Spy Thrillers in the Age of Appeasement," *Intelligence and National Security*, 5 (4): 80–91.
Household, Geoffrey ([1939] 1981), *Rogue Male*, London: Penguin.
Humble, Nicola (2001), *The Feminine Middlebrow Novel, 1920s to 1950s: Class, Domesticity and Bohemianism*, Oxford: Oxford University Press.
Jensen, Kimberley (2008), *Mobilizing Minerva: American Women in the First World War*, Urbana and Springfield: University of Illinois Press.
Khan, Yasmin (2020), "Women and War in the British Empire," *War & Society*, 39 (3): 227–31.
Knightley, Philip (2003), *The Second Oldest Profession*, London: Pimlico.
The Lady Vanishes (1938), [Film] Dir. A. Hitchcock, USA: Metro-Goldwyn-Mayer.
Lassner, Phyllis (2009), "Under Suspicion: The Plotting of Britain in World War II Detective Spy Fiction," in K. Bluemel (ed.), *Intermodernism: Literary Culture in Mid-Twentieth-Century Britain*, 113–30, Edinburgh: Edinburgh University Press.

Lassner, Phyllis (2016), *Espionage and Exile: Fascism and Anti-Fascism in British Spy Fiction and Film*, Edinburgh: Edinburgh University Press.

Lassner, Phyllis (2017), "Double Trouble: Helen MacInnes's and Agatha Christie's Speculative Spy Thrillers," in C. Hanson and S. Watkins (eds), *The History of British Women's Writing, 1945–1975*, 227–41, London: Palgrave Macmillan.

Le Carré, John (1993), *The Night Manager*, London: Penguin.

Levine, Joshua (2016), *The Secret History of the Blitz*, London: Simon and Schuster.

MacCannell, Dean (1976), *The Tourist: A New Theory of the Leisure Class*, London: Macmillan.

MacCannell, Dean (1992), *Empty Meeting Grounds: The Tourist Papers*, London: Routledge.

MacDonald, Gina (1989), "Helen MacInnes," in B. Benstock and T. F. Staley (eds), *Dictionary of Literary Biography, vol. 87, British Mystery and Thriller Writers Since 1940*, 284–94, Detroit: Gale Research.

MacInnes, Helen ([1941] 2012), *Above Suspicion*, London: Titan Books.

MacInnes, Helen ([1942] 2013), *Assignment in Brittany*, London: Titan Books.

MacInnes, Helen ([1968] 2013), *The Salzburg Connection*, London: Titan Books.

MacInnes, Helen ([1944] 2013), *[The Unconquerable] While Still We Live*, London: Titan Books.

MacInnes, Helen ([1963] 2013), *The Venetian Affair*, London: Titan Books.

MacInnes, Helen ([1984] 2014), *Ride a Pale Horse*, London: Titan Books.

Maugham, William Somerset (1928), *Ashenden or the British Agent*, London: William Heinemann, Ltd.

McDonough, Frank (2002), *Hitler, Chamberlain and Appeasement*, Cambridge: Cambridge University Press.

Mazower, Mark (1998), *Dark Continent*, London: Vintage.

Overy, Richard (2006), *Why the Allies Won*, Pimlico: London.

Overy, Richard and Andrew Wheatcroft (2009), *The Road to War: The Origins of World War II*, London: Vintage.

Pattinson, Juliet (2007), *Behind Enemy Lines: Gender, Passing and the Special Operations Executive in the Second World War*, Manchester: Manchester University Press.

Roberts, Mary Louise (2013), *What Soldiers Do: Sex and the American GI in World War II France*, Chicago: University of Chicago Press.

Rose, Sonya (2004), *Which People's War?: National Identity and Citizenship in Wartime Britain 1939-1945*, Oxford: Oxford University Press.

Rothwell, Victor (2002), *The Origins of the Second World War in Europe*, Manchester: Manchester University Press.

Scott, Manda (2018), *A Treachery of Spies*, London: Penguin.

Sheller, Mimi (2011), "Mobility," *Sociopedia.isa*, 1–12. Available online: https://www.isaportal.org/resources/resource/mobility/ (accessed 19 July 2022).

Sheller, Mimi and John Urry (2006), "The New Mobilities Paradigm," *Environment and Planning*, 38: 207–26.

Singh, Anita (2015), "Revealed: New Evidence that Executed Wartime Nurse Edith Cavell's Network was Spying," *The Telegraph*, 12 September. Available online: http://www.telegraph.co.uk/news/bbc/11861398/Revealed-New-evidence-that-executed-wartime-nurse-Edith-Cavells-network-was-spying.html (accessed 19 July 2022).

Todman, Daniel (2016), *Britain's War: Into Battle, 1937–1941*, London: Penguin.

Urry, John (1990), *The Tourist Gaze*, London: Sage.

Walter, Natasha (2003), "Spies and Lovers," *The Guardian*, 10 May. Available online: https://www.theguardian.com/theguardian/2003/may/10/weekend7.weekend2 (accessed 19 July 2022).

Walter, Natasha (2016a), *A Quiet Life*, London: The Borough Press.

Walter, Natasha (2016b), "We've been Expecting You, Ms Bond: Why fiction needs more Female Spies," *The Guardian*, 11 June. Available online: https://www.theguardian.com/books/2016/jun/11/why-fiction-needs-more-female-spies (accessed 19 July 22).

Wark, Wesley, ed. (1991), *Spy Fiction, Spy Films and Real Intelligence*, London: Routledge.

Watson, Colin (1979), *Snobbery with Violence*, London: Eyre Metheun.

Wheelwright, Julie (2019), "Poisoned Honey: The Myth of Women in Espionage," *Queen's Quarterly*, 100 (2): 3–17.

White, Ethel Lina ([1936] 1997), *The Lady Vanishes*, London: Bloomsbury.

White, Rosie (2007), *Violent Femmes: Women as Spies in Popular Culture*, London: Routledge.

White, Rosie (2008), "Englishness and Espionage: Edith Cavell as the Good Spy," in C. Hart (ed.), *Heroines and Heroes: Symbolism, Embodiment, Narratives & Identity*, 1–13, Kingswinford: Midrash.

Wilkinson, Lauren (2019), *American Spy*, London: Dialogue Books.

Yekelchyk, Serhy (2019), "People's War, State's Memory?," *Canadian Slavonic Papers*, 61 (4): 439–52.

3

Helen MacInnes's *While Still We Live*

Gender, Secret Agents, and National Ethics

Michael T. Williamson

The purpose of this chapter is to consider how Helen MacInnes's early Cold War (1944–45) spy fiction is informed by earlier models of political and ethical engagement drawn from nineteenth-century women's historical fiction. How, I ask, does this literary historical inheritance shape gendered distinctions between "spies" and "secret agents" in ways that respond to questions about past, present, and future fates of Poland, a country which was partitioned in both the eighteenth and the twentieth centuries? In her first early Cold War novel, *While Still We Live* (1944), MacInnes urges readers to see the importance of Poland's postwar fate and to make it matter in ways that tie together British and Polish national identity. Writing before the Soviet liberation of Poland in 1945, while at the same time representing the occupation of Poland during the years of the Nazi-Soviet Treaty of Non-Aggression between 1939 and 1941, MacInnes creates a narrative that points both forward and backwards. This doubled narrative, which is both retrospective and anticipatory, is told through the perspective of Sheila Matthews, a Scottish woman stranded in Warsaw at the outbreak of the war. Sheila is recruited to serve as a secret agent by the Polish underground because she resembles a German spy, and in the guise of a German woman she witnesses how the Nazi occupation of Warsaw shifted rapidly from economic exploitation to mass murder. As MacInnes shifts her narrative of wartime domesticity from Warsaw to Polish partisan forest camps, she raises significant ethical questions for her American and British readers regarding the postwar fate of Poland.

These ethical concerns disrupt assumptions about the relationship between war writing and domesticity, especially assumptions that posit binary oppositions between the urgency of wartime ethics and the imagined self-absorbed inattentiveness of peacetime domesticity. In their introduction to *The Edinburgh Companion to Twentieth-Century British and American War Literature*, for example, Adam Piette and Mark Rawlinson argue that "war makes literature ethical" because "the spectacle and imagining of the death of others in state-sponsored conflict demands writing that pays due witness to that suffering [and] accompanies that suffering without recourse to the usual contractual conventions that govern polite engagement with a sophisticated and jaded readership" (Piette and Rawlinson 2016: 2). MacInnes, this chapter will argue, uses the already ethically engaged genre of the romantic historical novel, in which "the usual contractual conventions" to which Piette and Rawlinson so strongly object feature prominently, in order to transform "writing that pays due witness to suffering" into politically and ethically aware knowledge of geopolitical history.

This shift from the witnessing of suffering to the production of knowledge is explicitly gendered and explicitly national in the historical romance novel, particularly in the case of representations of Poland as a country that has been feminized by defeat and partition.[1] Since Poland can no longer be "known" through conventional modes of national identity performance, clandestine narratives of domesticity become important vehicles for knowledge about gendered national identity. The role of the woman secret agent in MacInnes's *While Still We Live* is neither to witness this suffering nor to restore Polish masculinity to a level of respectable agency. Rather, her goal is to establish a clear and compelling role for gendered partnership, in which ideological affiliations between people from different countries combine to shape a lasting resistance to Nazi tyranny and other forms of tyranny that might succeed it. Three main questions emerge from these representations. How does MacInnes's portrayal of a British woman secret agent in Poland serve as the background for narrating the Polish experience of aerial bombing and occupation in British terms? How do narratives of gendered resistance to both Nazism and Soviet Communism intersect with narratives about British identity in wartime Europe? Finally, how does MacInnes's translation of Polish wartime history into British terms seek to intervene in the anticipated fate of Poland after the war?

Although the title "Queen of Spies" rightfully belongs to Daphne Park, who served as a clandestine Senior Controller in MI6 during the Second World War, the role of "Queen of International Espionage Fiction" belongs to the Scottish author Helen MacInnes.[2] MacInnes's three main wartime novels, *Above Suspicion* (1941; MacInnes 2012), *Assignment in Britany* (1942; MacInnes 2013), and *While Still We Live* (1944, published in the United Kingdom as *The Unconquerable*), established her reputation as a writer of historical spy fiction that anticipated the entanglements of Cold War Europe. Her grasp of the political complexities of Nazi-occupied and Soviet-occupied Europe enabled her to document the work of espionage during the war, but she also posited relationships between espionage and postwar history that have been vexed by the reception, over decades, of women's war writing. In fact, postwar readers were convinced that MacInnes could only have gathered such accurate source materials, especially those related to Soviet agents in Poland, from contacts made by her husband, an agent for MI6, or from her own work as (they imagined) a spy herself. If, as Piette and Rawlinson put it in their introduction to *The Edinburgh Companion to Twentieth-Century British and American War Literature*, "war tends to alter the genres it inhabits" (Piette and Rawlinson 2016: 6), the assumption is that genre conventions must be overcome by experience.

Yet fantasies of "authentic" authorial experience in spy fiction are contingent on literary choices that have everything to do with genre and little to do with the author's direct lived experience. Those literary choices are themselves contingent on the genres available to writers in the literary marketplace, and women writers found significant opportunities for writing about war in the 1940s. It matters who inhabits the genre and who alters war through that inhabitation. Piette and Rawlinson, for instance, choose not to focus on women's war writing (only four out of the fifty-seven essays in their book give significant attention to women writers). Had their collection of essays been more informed by women writers' decisions relating to genre when writing about war, perhaps a different thesis might emerge: genre inhabits war, and its conventions alter the inheritances of war.

This chapter seeks to address the gendered oversights in Piette and Rawlinson's *Companion* by drawing attention to important contemporary sources for MacInnes's *While Still We Live* and by situating her novel in a longer and deeper tradition of women's war writing than the largely masculine-gendered approach favored by Piette and Rawlinson. The optimism of MacInnes's work may have been belied by postwar compromises, especially Roosevelt's concessions to Stalin regarding Eastern Europe, but these compromises do not cancel its ethical imperatives and do not erase the traditions of women's writing that give those imperatives their dynamic force.

Cold War spy fiction often laments lost opportunities and squandered lives, suggesting as Allan Hepburn puts it that "ethical action and justice cannot be disengaged from shoddiness and illegality" (Hepburn 2005: 169). MacInnes's Second World War novels, on the other hand, anticipate a Cold War in which relationships between British and European subjects are determined not by new morally relativist (or "shoddy") geopolitical alignments but by older, more historically informed affiliations through which moral action may be transmittable across a wide spectrum of differences. Those affiliations survive in the form of a two-hundred-year-old tradition of historical fiction by women, but they have been written out of both Cold War history and the literary history of the spy novel. By representing spying in gendered terms derived from the genre of the historical romance, MacInnes urges readers to imagine national identity as a process of discovery in which multiple affiliations and multiple identities, often in exilic form, become the basis for imagining long-term ethical resistance to tyranny.

For Sheila Mathews, the Scottish protagonist of MacInnes's most politically complex wartime novel, *While Still We Live*, this process of discovery involves stretching and breaking boundaries around national "character." The novel is set in Poland between 1939 and 1940, and as MacInnes works to develop deep fictive kinship ties between Poles and British citizens, she uses the figure of the spy as the vehicle through which clandestine forms of previously submerged identity can be articulated. In fact, spying becomes an inherited feature of national character. Sheila's father, Charles, was executed in Poland for spying in 1916. The details surrounding his death are shrouded in mystery, but it later becomes clear that he was a "secret agent" who was connected in an obscure way with the Russian intelligence operative, by 1939 part of the Soviet NKVD, who also "runs" Sheila as an agent. Sheila's ethical-intellectual journey as she works to lay claim to her father's clandestine moral inheritance—especially his ability to "fight in [his] own way [. . .] with [his] brains, secretly, courageously" (MacInnes 2017: 76) for a losing cause in the name of justice—mirrors the reader's own journey across both national and gendered boundaries. That journey is explicitly gendered in the novel. An orphan who has spent most of her life alone, in her diary, Sheila muses, "I felt if I learned about Poland, I might learn something of my father" (78), and her naïve curiosity is gradually replaced by a strong sense of the nobility of Polish suffering and the kinship that comes from shared trauma. "It was pleasant," Sheila quips, tongue in cheek, "to share things, even air raids, with people" (MacInnes 2017: 132). As this rather perverse moment of self-awareness indicates, Sheila's identification with Polish suffering is markedly different from that of her male counterparts in the first half of the novel.

This difference becomes acute during the Blitz of Warsaw during the first weeks of September 1939. A group of Americans and British subjects are caught in Warsaw and confined to a single apartment together. Whereas Sheila is incapacitated by fever and grief, her foil, the socialist-leaning American newspaper reporter Mr. Stevens projects his own frame of reference onto events. The contrast is striking. Sheila merely murmurs, "I've been lying here thinking about London" (140), a line of thinking that might not have meant much to British readers in 1939, during the Blitz of Warsaw, but which would have resonated much more powerfully as a shared experience of bombardment by the time the novel was published in 1944. Stevens, on the other hand, engages in imaginative speculation as he maps the lived reality of the siege of Warsaw (and for British readers, the experience of the Blitz), onto a native New Yorker apocalyptic fantasy of catastrophe:

> "New York . . . ," Stevens was saying, "All the bridges under heavy air attack. Brooklyn and Queens levelled to the ground. Last ditch stands by soldiers in all the outlying boroughs. Manhattan itself under heavy artillery fire. Airplanes swarming over. The Empire State Building gone, and all the blocks around it. The stations just a heap of twisted girders. Radio City a ragged shell, with burst water-mains pouring down Fifth Avenue. The museums in flames. The Metropolitan and Times Square a shambles. The Medical Center in ruins. All its equipment gone. Blood running down the trolleycar lines on Broadway. The dock area one line of blazing warehouses. No power, little food, less water. Gaping windows, crushed walls, buildings smashed to pieces." (MacInnes 2017: 140)

What is for Stevens a speculative fantasy that will remain so throughout the war is for Sheila an anticipation of actual catastrophe. The differences between the British and US civilian experience of the Second World War could not be cast more sharply. Sheila's slow journey toward kinship with an "other" is the antithesis of Stevens' immediately realized imaginative exercise in apocalyptic narcissism. Whereas Sheila painstakingly confronts Polish suffering, Stevens simply replaces Poles with New Yorkers. This difference in imaginative sympathy is the difference between reporting events from Stevens' perspective, shielded by the diplomatic safety of the press corps, and understanding events from the genre-based perspective of the woman spy whose "mission," as Phyllis Lassner argues, "is an odyssey into the political consciousness of the integrity of a nation that lies beyond the cultural and historical consciousness of the Western liberal democracies" (Lassner 2016: 93). Learned affinities, not apocalyptic fears, guide Sheila as she embraces Polish suffering and resilience.

Lassner points out that MacInnes was not alone in her efforts to use popular fiction to establish connections between Polish and British people, especially through narratives that highlight "the translation of women's social and economic security into political consciousness," a process that "criticizes privileged isolationism" (Lassner

2016: 82). This translation takes an interesting form as it shapes current events into both a retrospective moral reckoning and a projected future moral history, since the "fate of the fragmented nation [Poland] lies in Sheila's developing political agency, metonymically designated as Britain's moral consciousness" (Lassner 2016: 93). MacInnes's "political fantasy of exile as moral rescue" (Lassner 2016: 93) positions Sheila as a secret agent whose "intelligence" (information passed on from Poland to Britain) reinforces Britain's decision to stand against Nazism when the USA and USSR would not. More importantly, given the date of the novel's publication, this intelligence serves to bolster the position of the Polish government in exile and to pressure the USA into supporting a free democratic Poland against Soviet interests. As the contrast between Sheila's and Stevens' responses to the siege of Warsaw suggests, the psychic nature of the novel's political fantasy is essential to its moral force. Because MacInnes also works within the conventions of the historical romance, however, the emotional trajectory of the novel matters as much as its political and ethical trajectories. The narrative is, after all, not only an exercise in translation of the term "spy" into the more morally and politically viable "secret agent." It is also an important translation of the historical romance novel into another popular literary form, one that resists the imposition of ideologies of resistance and gendered self-abnegation onto domestic spaces and identities.

That MacInnes should work on multiple overlapping frontiers—historical and emotional, national and international, domestic and militarily operational, clandestine and overtly sentimental—in 1944 is not surprising, given recent scholarly discussions of spy fiction and the gendering of national hybridity. As Ann Rea observes, spy fiction begins in the early 1900s with narratives that feature unstable frontiers, uncertain boundaries of identity, and shifting loyalties, such as Rudyard Kipling's *Kim* (1905). In these narratives, "the spy's hybrid identity creates an affinity for pluralism" that "undermines any sense of impermeable frontiers" (Rea 2019: 76). Often unwittingly, the spy's movement toward pluralism contributes to fluid geopolitical situations that, more often than not, serve imperial rather than local interests. By the end of 1944, with the liberation of most of Poland by the Soviet Red Army, those imperial interests shifted dramatically from Nazi to Soviet claims on Poland. The Polish government in exile thus functioned as a displaced vestige of a former nation whose anticipated postwar boundaries were a moral as well as political matter. Yet while the Polish government in exile is often the focus of Polish/British spy fiction, as is the case with Alan Furst's *The Spies of Warsaw*, MacInnes is more interested in the spy's role at the intersection between wartime domesticity, including the experience of homelessness, and public rituals, especially shopping. Reactions to this domesticity create dramas of "shifting loyalties" for women that, along similar but importantly different lines from the male writers whose work shapes Rea's argument, engage the woman spy in the work of "becoming a frontier." In particular, MacInnes's focus on the degree to which Nazi economic power affected all aspects of public Polish life during the early phases of the occupation from 1939-1940, including the circulation of goods, is an important part of this affinity for a gendered pluralism that links women's experiences of domesticity to wartime spying. The shift from political to economic subjugation prefigures a more murderous shift toward enslavement and the mass murder of nearly

3 million Polish Jews and 1.8–1.9 million non-Jewish Poles. Conveying that shift, for MacInnes, becomes a matter of representing the growing abnormality of the everyday under Nazi occupation.

Sheila thus becomes a vehicle for shaping wartime moral consciousness into a redemptive narrative of sympathy and responsibility for a nation that had been crushed yet not wholly vanquished in 1944, as the Warsaw ghetto uprising, the Warsaw uprising, and continued partisan activity demonstrated to the world. In a particularly interesting scene, Sheila is taken by a Nazi officer to a Polish clothing shop during the initial days of the occupation. Sheila is impersonating a Polish German spy, and the Nazi officer thinks that she should look more like someone "worthy" of working as a spy for the Nazis:

> She had seen what it was like to be defeated by the Germans; now, she was seeing the other side of the picture [. . . .] She had never seen so many little groups of people all so intent for their own little purposes, and yet all coming under, one large theme: loot. Breughel, she decided, could have filled one of his enormous canvasses with them. He would have enjoyed their petty preoccupations and painted them into one sweeping satire. Here in this corner, would be two airmen measuring stockings. Here the soldier with the nightdress in front of him. Here the three Gestapo men stretching girdles to see if the rubber was good (they ought to know a lot about rubber with their experience in clubs). Here the two officers each with an armful of perfume bottles and bath salts. Here the lacquered blond with her hand held under the lace and ninon bed jacket. And behind the hundred little groups would be the ragged outline of a murdered city, a pyramid of bones, and a mad woman wandering. (MacInnes 2017: 327–8)

Unlike Stevens' fantasy of New York under siege, Sheila's depiction of occupied Warsaw as an adaptation of Breugel's *Massacre of the Innocents* is brutally real, largely because it is based on the transformation of otherwise normal, peacetime events, such as shopping, into a masquerade of greed and brutality. Sheila's experience as a witness to war profiteering, about which British readers felt considerable resentment in their own country by 1944, shifts from satire to documentary witnessing in a flash. As is the case during the siege of Warsaw, MacInnes carefully directs the reader's attention away from the relative safety of projected fantasy (in this case, satire rather than apocalyptic fantasy) toward the brutal realities of occupation. The vignette serves as a commentary on W.H. Auden's description of Breughel's *The Fall of Icarus* in his 1938 poem, "Musée des Beaux Arts." Auden's poem highlights the strange complicity of the "everyday" (which is sometimes viewed in salvific terms), when he points to "some untidy spot / Where the dogs go on with their doggy life and the torturer's horse / Scratches its innocent behind on a tree" (Auden 1976: 179). MacInnes's deft extension of this line of thinking pulls the reader into a world in which an indifference to suffering, so delicately managed in Auden's meditation, becomes a horror that permeates all domestic rituals. How, MacInnes asks, can one go on with life indifferent to Polish suffering, when Germans shop cheerfully as Poles are murdered by the millions? The collapse of time between the 1939 Nazi/Soviet occupation of Poland and the mass killings (including the Holocaust by bullet) of 1941–43 sets a moral standard for behavior in which the shying away of pacifists, apologists, and postwar appeasers becomes impossible.

MacInnes's later descriptions of Polish refugees who are machine-gunned by German planes offer further literary documentation of German atrocities, and as the net closes on Sheila and the Polish partisans in the forest, she listens with horror to accounts of Nazi anti-partisan reprisals:

> The men of Korytow will all be shot. The old women will be dumped out on the frozen plains northeast of Warsaw and left to wander. The middle aged are sent as serfs to Germany or are given the dirtiest duties about the barracks. The younger women and girls will be sent to the soldiers' brothels. The children will be sent to the Nazi camps. They will be taught to be slaves. (MacInnes 2017: 466)

Representing the resistance to this fate (which might have been the fate of all Europeans, including the Soviets and the British, had the Nazis won) is a main part of the political work of MacInnes's novel. Yet Polish subjects are not subjugated victims in the novel. Instead, they inhabit the realm of the resistant, the defiant, the "Unconquerable," however subjugated they may be. This transformation is essential to MacInnes's imagination of an independent postwar Poland. Indeed, whereas in the first half of the novel Sheila functions as a figurative frontier of knowledge, the second half of the novel points to a postwar world in which the future of a liberated Poland is marked by intimations of dependence, with Poland at the mercy of the Soviet Union or dependent on Allied advocacy, rather than by a restoration of interwar independence.

The anxieties related to this anticipated dependence are conveyed not through political narrative but through the conventions of the historical romance novel. Most interestingly, this form enables MacInnes to re-gender geopolitical alliances in ways that stress the ethical unfolding of the magnanimity in defeat as an alternative to revolutionary resistance. In doing so, she translates the suffering, brooding presence of Polish masculinity, long a feature of British women's romance fiction, into terms that challenge the absolutist claims on women's affections that characterize the political romance novel of the 1940s and 1950s.[3]

That Poland should be the subject of politically inflected early Cold War romance narratives is not surprising, since as Lassner points out "With a thousand-year history of invasion and occupation by such adjacent imperial powers as Germany and Russia, the attempts of Poland to recover its sovereignty lent themselves to mythic narratives of undaunted heroism" (Lassner 2016: 93).[4] Heroism is not, however, the dominant characteristic of the type of British women's war writing about Poland that MacInnes inherits from nineteenth-century women writers such as Jane Porter and Elizabeth Barrett Browning.[5] Rather, the genre is populated by valiant, doomed, morally redeemable fallen men whose suffering engages the affections of British women. MacInnes's detailed representations of life in Nazi-occupied Poland, which so closely resemble dispatches from secret agents in the field, are undoubtedly the product of secret intelligence. They are also a consequence of the literary genre in which MacInnes works: the conventions of literary forms—romance fiction inflected by spy fiction and cast as wartime propaganda—produce historical and moral knowledge. The historical romance thus produces the kind of "intelligence" one would expect from a spy. Under the cover of writing retrospective documentary wartime fiction about the invasion of Poland in 1939, MacInnes writes anticipatory speculative national propaganda designed to garner support for Poland's postwar independence.

In doing so, she follows a trend established during the 1930s and 1940s in anti-Nazi propaganda fiction by women. Lassner characterizes the work of this propaganda as follows:

> Neither heroes nor anti-heroes, neither femmes fatales nor matinee idols, their men and women spies occupy a challenging narrative space that questions and revises distinctions between exile and espionage as action, state of being, and gendered identity [. . . .] as they activate their missions, they also critique and revise official and conventional political convictions. In the process, women spies exile themselves from the domestic sphere and their private roles. The result is a revisionist double agency. (Lassner 2016: 70)

As illustrated above, in *While Still We Live,* the "challenging narrative space" that Lassner observes becomes significantly complicated by parallels between the British experience of the Blitz and the novel's retrospective narration of "the Nazi sack of Warsaw." Whereas MacInnes's earlier novels consider the effects of war on the tourist economy and on the experience of rural domesticity in Western or Central European countries annexed or occupied by the Nazis (Austria and France, in particular), *While Still We Live* reveals for a British, American, and colonial British audience the far more violent extent of the Nazi invasion and occupation of Poland. MacInnes details the mass murder of entire villages, the machine gunning of columns of refugees, and the prolonged bombing of a Warsaw utterly unable to defend itself. MacInnes began the novel during this period and continued to write during the Blitz, the partition of Poland into Nazi and Soviet-occupied zones, the murder and enslavement of Poles, and the commencement of what is now known as the 1941–42 "Holocaust by bullet." Her outrage at the fate of Poland is clear, and it is matched by her outrage at the relative indifference of the United States, represented by Stevens, to this fate. News regarding the mass murder of Jews in Eastern Europe was published steadily and prominently, beginning in 1940, and Stevens' casual moral and ethical indifference is particularly enraging to Sheila, who knows the fate of Poland's Jews without having access to the resources Stevens has as a journalist.[6]

MacInnes is not alone in her anger and in the urgency with which she argues the Polish cause. Poland has been represented in novels by British women since the early nineteenth century as a site for representing Britain's melancholy, subjugated, romantic, and morally regenerative European double. In spy fiction, this doubling creates fictive boundaries, as the spy becomes a "frontier" created by a long history of fictional affiliations between Britain and Poland. The partition of Poland in the 1790s becomes, as Thomas McLean observes in *The Other East and Nineteenth Century British Literature: Imagining Poland and the Russian Empire*, "a remarkable nexus of Romanticism and sensibility: the moment when the sublime military hero falls, and accepts his fall with humanity and concern for others" (McLean 2012: 70). These fictional affiliations are underscored by strong cultural affiliations. Poland was both a site for Scottish emigration (by 1640 over 30,000 Scots had emigrated to Poland, to be followed by another wave after the Congress of Vienna), a vector for nationalist independence (Bonnie Prince Charlie was half Polish), and a hybrid reference point for Scots-Irish settlers in the Appalachian region of the USA, signposted by the towns of Warsaw, Kentucky and Warsaw, North Carolina (McLean 2012: 72). After the Second World War, marriages between Poles and Protestant Scottish women "led to friction," perhaps because of religious differences but also perhaps because, "Polish men prided themselves on their attractiveness to British women" (Webster 2013: 619). Poland is also historically an imaginary geographical space in which "exotic, non-normative representations of gender," (Webster 2013: 615–16) especially feminized and traumatized men, contributed to non-normative notions of national identity.[7] This is not merely a matter of the genre conventions of fiction, as there is considerable evidence that, as Wendy Webster puts it, many British women married Poles in order to "flout the rules of sexual patriotism, continuing the shift to increasingly multinational and multi-ethnic families and communities in Britain" (Webster 2013: 621).[8] As the aftermath of British fictional engagements with Poland in the early nineteenth century "encouraged later readers to welcome exiles who arrived in Britain after the failed Polish uprisings in 1831, 1846, and 1848," (McLean 2012: 85) so too did writers like MacInnes "do their bit" to encourage a widening of British identity and women's political engagement.

In fact, the first decades of the nineteenth century marked an important redefinition of women's historical romance fiction, as "historical process" (Lokke 2004: 19). The specificity of women's historical fiction shifted the genre away from speculative utopianism and toward practical engagements with current historical events. As Kari Lokke argues, historical fiction by women shifted from "embodying the infinitely receding horizon of the unapproachable ideal" and instead "became a rich field of social endeavor and political praxis" (Lokke 2004: 19–20).[9] Twentieth-century spy fiction by women represents an essential continuation of this shift toward "historical process." The larger purpose of spying is, after all, to gather and disseminate information about places or peoples that might otherwise be neglected in favor of more dominant modes of historicizing or more standardized modes of drawing ideological distinctions. That this knowledge is shaped by the ideological interpretation of the spy—and that it often emerges as propaganda—does not necessarily make it a less valuable contribution to the broadening of international horizons. Despite propaganda's limitations (the chief of which is its tendency to erase cultural difference in favor of archetypal sameness), MacInnes enables the British reader to wonder, as the ethicist Paul Ricouer asks, "If another were not counting on me, would I be capable of keeping my word, of maintaining myself?" (Ricoeur 1995: 341). Instead of providing a distorting mirror-land onto which British people project their anxieties, she offers an extension of British selfhood into an ethically imagined future of postwar Europe.

The extension of British women's selfhood into Poland emerges most strikingly in Jane Porter's *Thaddeus of Warsaw*, first published in 1803 and republished throughout the nineteenth century in a staggering eighty-four editions. As companion texts published almost 150 years apart, the novels offer important interventions into the tradition of women's war writing. Like MacInnes, who was praised for the accuracy of her descriptions of partisan warfare, readers were not certain "whether to treat [*Thaddeus of Warsaw*] as fact or fiction" (McLean 2012: 66). Porter's novel was deliberately marketed as a romance spy novel, and it features the first appearance of the figure of the alienated, shattered, yet defiant Polish male exilic protagonist, a prototype for the Byronic Hero of the Greek independence movement. Porter's protagonist, Thaddeus Sobieski, travels to England as an unwilling cultural secret agent, under no one's influence but his own, intent on securing British popular support for a Poland torn asunder by partition in the 1790s. As a series of English women attempt to seduce him, Thaddeus requires that they recognize a nascent Polish democracy as an alternative to other revolutionary forces, especially French republicanism, as a precondition for the bestowal of his shattered affections upon them. The romance novel thus creates what one critic describes as "a biblical typology in which the protagonists of the historically set [novel] act as moral forbears [who offer up] an embodied future for current, political movements" (Kasmer 2012: 93). These movements included Scottish responses to the Clearances, Italian and Greek independence movements, and Polish independence movements. Porter's reasons for writing about Poland are forthright. She writes in her preface, "Wishing to pourtray a character which Prosperity could not intoxicate, nor Adversity depress, I chose Magnanimity as the subject of my story" (Porter 1845: viii) because "Poland seemed the country best calculated to promote my intention. Her struggles for independence, and her misfortunes, afforded me situations exactly fitted to my plan" (ix–x—quoted in McLean 2012: 70). Thaddeus's revivifying generosity changes British society and widens British understanding of Europe beyond France, Spain, and Germany.[10]

Representing Polish masculinity as magnanimous is essential to MacInnes's interventions into the Polish/British historical romance narrative. As the daughter of a secret agent and as a representative of Britain's international moral standing, Sheila's reflections on the lives of Polish partisans in the forest are necessarily politicized. Polish partisans represent the future of Poland:

> Life was primitive and simple; work was hard, the sense of danger was constant. But perhaps because there was no time to sit and brood, perhaps because each man had learned savagely and cruelly why they were fighting, for what end they were fighting, there was a unity of a broad and deep kind [. . . .] It was the best kind of unity, for each of those men was still an individualist. You could see that in their reactions and unexplained prides. (MacInnes 2017: 481)

At the heart of the partisan group, Sheila finds Adam Wisniewski, a tall "dark young man in uniform" whose brown eyes affect Sheila immediately, freezing "the smile on her lips into self-consciousness" (MacInnes 2017: 22), when she first meets him at the novel's outset and whom the jealous, socialist-leaning Stevens had described earlier as a "proto-fascist" because of his interest in women and horses (MacInnes 2017: 484). As the political plot of the novel shifts to historical romance, Sheila muses,

> If Wisniewski had lived up to the label Steve had pinned on him, he would now be sitting in Warsaw or Cracow, collaborating with the Nazis. There he would have

had women and horses and a comfortable house; there he would have seen the people who opposed him either killed or imprisoned. If this man were a fascist by inclination, he would have welcomed the chance to "cleanse" his country of the people he disagreed with. He wouldn't be working with them. living with them, all political differences buried under a common battlefield. Fascists never buried politics. They kept them sharpened, like a dagger to plunge in your back [. . . .] Not one Pole had accepted the chance to gain the whole New Order and lose his own soul by working with the enemy. The reward for their refusal was always torture and death for themselves, imprisonment and persecution for their families [yet] nothing the Nazis could do would convince or persuade the Poles to become Nazis, or the allies of Nazis. (MacInnes 2017: 484–5)

As Adam becomes a symbol for Poland, Sheila's defense grows stronger and points to a recognition of Poland as a country that is morally superior to other countries that were either actively complicit, such as France, or that like the United States made "America First" excuses to keep out of the war:

All the so called "enlightened" would have had Poland quite taped and labelled. Poland was "feudal" Poland was "undemocratic," Poland was "fascist." And now the Poles are giving a demonstration to the world of what honour and freedom really mean [. . . .] Their honour is real, not just national vanity. And the more they refuse to cooperate, the more they suffer. Korytow, and the hundred other Korytows, would still be standing today if the Poles would only cooperate. How many countries, even the most democratic ones, would pay this price for their honour? (MacInnes 2017: 485)

MacInnes's readers might at this point be reminded of her earlier spy novel, *Assignment in Brittany*, set in the chaotic aftermath of the Dunkirk evacuation yet published after the breakup of the Nazi/Soviet alliance and the Nazi invasion of the Soviet Union.

Assignment in Brittany offers a distinctly harsh view of international identity: it is preoccupied with the spectre of invasion, not only the invasion of France and the Soviet Union but also the possible invasion of the United Kingdom, and much of the novel contrasts the feeble and conflicted resistance of the French, the vacillations of the Bretons as they negotiate between independence from France and resistance to Nazi occupation, and the imagined ferocious resistance of the British to any form of occupation. In particular, the resistance to occupation on the part of the British secret agent Hearne serves as an allegorical field of reference for speculation about British behavior. While the French sleep easily in their beds at night, the British would be "maniacal" under occupation, Hearne speculates, and in doing so he draws strands of imaginative sympathy to the doomed Polish resistance to Nazi invasion in 1939.

Like Hearne, whose spying is complicated by the unstable national and cultural frontiers between French and Breton identity, Sheila's cultural and political affiliations are mediated by two types of partition: political and emotional. She describes her political allegiances according to the conventionally partitioned discourse of interwar period, telling her "handler," Mr. Olzcak, "My conservative friends say I am a radical. My communist friends say I am a reactionary. So obviously I must be a liberal" (MacInnes 2017: 79), but her emotional connection with Adam is what activates her political consciousness. Unlike Hearne, she is a woman spy in an historical *romance* novel, a form in which romantic engagement, self-discovery, and moral agency (or Porter's "magnanimity") are inseparable. As Kari Lokke points out, the nineteenth-century tradition of women's writing in which "disappointment with Romantic passionate love becomes a catalyst for the cultivation of heightened political, spiritual, and historical awareness" initiates a wave of narrative innovation that includes Madame de Stael's *Corrine, or Italy*, Mary Shelley's *Valperga*, Bettine von Arnim's *Die Gunderode*, George Sands' *Consuela*, and Isak Dinesen's *The Dreamers* (Lokke 2004: 7). MacInnes's *While Still We Live* represents an early Cold War iteration of this shift in awareness, as Sheila discovers an identity that is affiliated with a nation, not an ideology.

Indeed, because of the ideologically overdetermined discourse of partisan resistance during the Second World War, especially resistance mediated by the Soviet Union, discoveries of identity come at a price in spy fiction, particularly for women, and particularly when "identity" is determined by "heroic" conceptions of national and ideological action. Domesticity is often regarded in spy fiction as an impediment to moral action. Intimate domesticity is an even greater liability for women war writers, particularly when it is scrutinized within the context of ideologically staged dramas.[11] Allen Hepburn's observation that the male spy often "wants to eradicate intimacy in order to work efficiently" (Hepburn 2005: 170) is particularly helpful in highlighting the differences between spy and romance traditions. In the romance tradition in which MacInnes works, intimacy is not to be eradicated or avoided. In fact, it is precisely the mode of experience by which knowledge is produced.

MacInnes's possible source for her description of partisan activity in *While Still We Live* offers a glimpse of this combination of intimacy and knowledge. During 1941, when MacInnes was working in New York City on the research for *While Sill We Live*, the world-famous photojournalist Margaret Bourke-White was in the USSR working on her book *Shooting the Russian War*, published in early 1942. Both MacInnes and Bourke-White were actively engaged in writing anti-Nazi propaganda designed to push the United States into declaring war on the Germans. *Shooting the Russian War* also serves as one of the earliest descriptions of partisan activity in Nazi-occupied Europe.[12] In fact, Bourke-White's accounts of the mixture of demoralization, stupidity, fanaticism, and blank indifference expressed by Nazi prisoners, especially in the face of unexpectedly strong resistance from both the Red Army and partisans behind the lines, demonstrated that the Nazis could be stopped by tanks, trucks, and armored vehicles sent to the USSR through the Lend-Lease program with the United States.[13]

That the Nazi defeat was temporary and soon reversed was less relevant than the significance of Soviet resistance.[14] Bourke-White is keen to present this resistance in sharp contrast to that of nations that have capitulated:

> In the Soviet Union when territory is captured one does not see the swarms of refugees which have clogged the roads of other invaded countries [especially France]. The government has previously instructed civilians to stay and become partisans. They have been given directions in the art of sniping and in guerilla

warfare, and if their village is captured they know just what they are expected to do. Guerillas cannot win a war, but they can do a great deal to make the enemy uncomfortable. (Bourke-White 1942: 259)[15]

Sixty-three detachments, totaling 4,855 "irregular combatants" made up of both men and women, including a woman whom Burke-White came to know as "Tanya" who served as a nurse by day and as an artillery position spotter behind the German lines by night, operated behind the German rear.[16]

MacInnes transposes Bourke-White's description of partisan activity in Ukraine further west, to Poland, and her descriptions of partisan warfare offered important ethical lines of distinction as the lines of Eastern European partition that began the Cold War started to be drawn. This ethical dimension to women's war writing has been largely obscured by expectations derived from ideas about domesticity and politics that diminish the significance of affection and romance as vectors for historical engagement.

Women who are involved in revolutionary underground or partisan warfare, for example, face expectations that follow a consistent narrative pattern defined by the conventions of literary genre as much as by ideology. This pattern ranges across national and ideological boundaries in surprising ways. Despite the significant differences between European and Asian contexts during the 1940s, for example, novels written in China during the 1940 and 1950s convey similar assumptions about women's roles at the intersection between spy fiction and historical romance to those of British writers.[17] As Haiyan Lee points out, the literary formula "revolution plus romance" necessitates a sublimation of identity and the evacuation of private, domestic experience. According to the formula, "a bourgeois romantic, at the end of a tortuous *affaire de coeur*, overcomes his or her 'privation' by plunging into revolutionary torrents" (Lee 2010: 643).[18] In these narratives, the "exteriority of the other [. . .] obliterates the ethical (feminine) self" (Lee 2010: 643) by subsuming the private and domestic experience of the world into ideological frameworks that expose the foolishness of individuated sentimental attachment in the face of group identity. Lee writes

> Underground activism is premised on a schizoid conception of the self in which the ideologically committed mind [. . .] is detached from and remains haughtily indifferent to the experiential body. One pretends to relish the promised pleasures of life under occupation while cherishing secret allegiance to a higher purpose of righteous principles. However mired the body is in senseless enjoyment, the mind remains incorruptible. The debasement of the body is really a baptism of the senses through which the true revolutionary heart is tempered. (Lee 2010: 644)[19]

Although we might not expect the conventions of the nineteenth-century Bildungsromane to mitigate against the politically salvific elements of Chinese fiction, the line between writing anti-Communist propaganda in China and MacInnes's wartime depiction of spying in Poland is not as thick as it might first seem to be.

In *While Still We Live*, Sheila faces ethical choices that are strikingly similar to those addressed by the Chinese writer Eileen Chang in her espionage fiction published during the 1940s. Instead of using espionage fiction to consolidate ideological positions, Chang provides spaces for ethical openness and possibility, as Haiyan Lee notes when she argues that

> on the one hand, [Chang] deflates the sanctimony of revolutionary politics by laying bare its ruthless instrumental, patriarchal, and totalizing logics; on the other hand, she depicts the bourgeois social not as mere bad faith, or the realm of "weightless irrelevance," but as an inescapable modern condition that requires both a stoic appreciation of the ordinary and a guarded openness for contingent transcendence. The realm of bourgeois vacillation is, paradoxically, also the basis of ethical hope. (Lee 2010: 653)[20]

Like Chang's protagonist Jiazhi in "Lust, Caution," who was modeled on the real-life spy Zheng Pingu, Sheila's "bourgeoise vacillation" involves choosing between romantic partnership and becoming a member of a partisan revolutionary cadre.

In fact, having barely survived a physical and psychic fracturing of identity during the Blitz on Warsaw and the Nazi occupation in September of 1939, Sheila's role as a double agent turns every decision she makes into a moment of possible "bourgeoise vacillation" as she manages to negotiate an identity split between her internal British sympathies for the Poles and the façade she must maintain as the double for a Nazi spy, whom she uncannily resembles. As she is coached into her role as spy, Sheila is told by her handler, Mr. Olszak, "You have been caught up in a chain of events, which will make it dangerous for us to have you here unless we trust you fully. I know you aren't against us. But that isn't enough" (MacInnes 2017: 84). When she later joins a group of Polish partisans, Olszak comments on her relative privilege as a British citizen in Poland: "Hardship and danger destroy fewer people than indulgence [. . . .] Each generation suffers so that its children will be strong, for children whose fathers have escaped hardship come to think that life is too easy. Soon they believe that easiness is life. There is no greater danger to a country when its citizens assume that danger no longer exists" (MacInnes 2017: 116–17).

Much of the first half of the novel is devoted to confirming this stifling view, which is both ideologically based in resistance rhetoric and formally based in the structure of the political romance. Needless to say, British and American readers in 1944 would find the gap between Sheila's British experience of the war and their imagination of the Polish experience of the war considerably narrowed. Although MacInnes's strategy of doubled Polish/British identity is clear throughout the novel, however, the parallels between the London Blitz and the Warsaw Blitz, and between British resolve and the Polish resistance can only go so far. The conventions of the genre of the historical romance novel demand that Sheila be torn between the promise of domestic happiness and the duties of a resistance fighter. More to the point, the realities of history make an affiliation between the British experience of the war and the Polish experience of the war utterly incompatible.

After she is captured during a roadblock raid on a Nazi officer's car, Sheila slowly sheds her invented cover as a Nazi spy and becomes integrated into the world of Polish partisans and into the moral and ideological conflicts that shaped Eastern Europe during early stages of the Cold War. In the forest, Olszak chastises her for her romantic attachments, telling her that "we have no families, no loyalties except one alone—our country [. . .] however heartsick and despairing you may be, you will take comfort from the fact that we are all part of each other" (MacInnes 2017: 236). Although this appeal draws on nationalist sympathies, Olszak reports to the Soviet-run Polish Communist Party, not to the Polish government in exile in London. In the forest, with Polish partisans, Sheila moves defiantly away from this idealization of collective identity, and she quotes her secret agent uncle, whose "contempt for revolution" she inherits (MacInnes 2017: 578).

What began as an attempt to raise British consciousness about the fate of Poles during the war thus becomes a novel about the redemption of British international identity in a world of rigid ideologically defined geopolitical boundaries. Sheila is in Poland to find out more about her father, who was shot in Warsaw by the Germans in 1916, a few months before her birth. Her father, it turns out, had been a secret agent working for the Russians in German-occupied Warsaw. His job, like Sheila's job a generation later, was to convey information about the occupying German forces to Soviet-controlled resistance groups.

Olszak, who "ran" Sheila's father as an agent, fully expects Sheila to follow in her father's stead and to inherit the cause of international socialism for which he gave his life. His recruitment effort depends on a mixture of blackmail and persuasion, and a moralized distinction between "the spy" and "the secret agent" makes up the root of his argument. When Sheila asks if her father was a spy, he replies:

> A spy, to me, is someone who finds out information for a certain amount of money. The money smothers this conscience if he is a traitor. If he is a patriot, the money softens the lack of public recognition. But there is another word which I prefer to give to men who care neither for money nor for any recognition. Their lives are often ruined; they may meet an unpleasant death; but they fight in their own way—with their brains, secretly, courageously—because all that matters to them is what they are fighting for. I think it is only fair to give them full credit for that. Shall we say that your father was a secret agent? (MacInnes 2017: 76)

The lure of this definition of a "secret agent" as one who fights with a courageous mind for an ideological system, as opposed to the sordid "spy" who operates for material gain, suggests an ethical and moral frontier, a creative moral conscience that justifies a schizoid conception of the self. Conscience is the superior moral alternative to modern "consciousness." Whereas "consciousness" and "intelligence" can be bought and sold, a moral conscience activates a presence of mind, a sense of purpose, something to fight for.

According to the legal definition of a "wartime spy" according to *Article 29 of the Annex to the Convention (IV) Respecting the Laws and Customs of War on Land* (1907), "a person can only be considered a spy when, acting clandestinely and under false pretenses, he [*sic*] obtains or endeavors to obtain information in the zone of operation of a belligerent, with the intention of communicating it to the hostile party."[21] Judging by Olzcak's redefinition of spying, it appears that between 1907 and 1944, the "false pretenses" of spying, especially the deceptions of impersonation, became subsumed within "false consciousness," as ethical behavior became a matter for internalization and the "schizoid conception of the self" in the "ideologically committed mind" promised a core true self surrounded by an imposter's external veneer. When gendered male, this schizoid conception of selfhood mirrors the vexed relationship between field agent and spy master.[22]

With its roots in an earlier century, one that genders the historical romance differently from the disenchantments of twentieth-century political romance, MacInnes's *While Still We Live* resists a rhetoric of "true selves" eroded by the acts of dissembling required of spies. Instead of following Mr. Olszak's political romance script, Sheila and Adam travel across Poland to Olszak's mother's house in the mountains as they work to smuggle Sheila back to England, where she can report on Polish partisan activities and gather support for Poland from British and American politicians. MacInnes approaches this new role for Sheila as a secret intelligence-gatherer and documentarian, far closer to Bourke-White's role as a reporter than to the role of the self-abnegating revolutionary whose misogynistic function Chang exposes, with deft assurance and a strange humor. Madame Olzcak, Mr. Olzcak's mother, translates his ideologically based definition of spying into a domestically based extension of the virtuous home as a synecdoche for the virtuous nation. Whereas Mr. Olzcak urged Sheila to adopt the burden of her father's sacrifice and sense of ideological purpose, Madame Olzcak offers her an opportunity to embrace the role of a British wife of a Polish cavalry officer whose intelligence regarding Polish resistance must be shared internationally, not used in an anticipated Cold War of emotionally starved ideological attrition and negation. Instead of functioning as a tortured secret agent sacrificed for a cause, as Mr. Olzcak would have her do, Sheila is given permission to marry Adam by Madame Olzcak, whose position is both operationally and morally higher than her son's. In a scene of romantic love and consummation uncommon in most male spy fiction, MacInnes switches briefly to Adam's perspective as he watches a pensive Sheila absorb the new inheritance offered by Madame Olzcak:

> Sheila had risen from the chair, and having made that effort seemed incapable of more. She didn't speak. There was a strange brooding look on her face. For a moment, he was jealous, and then cursed himself for a selfish fool. Jealous of the ghost of a dead father . . . jealous of the moments when her thoughts were not his. He lowered the lamp, saw its flame flicker and die. By the light of the fire, he watched her hands slowly fumble at the waistband of her skirt. Then she looked at him, and now she was thinking only of him. Even before she spoke, he came over to her. "Adam." (MacInnes 2017: 646–7)

The sexual consummation of Sheila's marriage cannot mask the horrors of the fate of Poland between 1939 and 1944, but it can activate a different form of geopolitical intelligence and inheritance than that posited by the political romance or by the geopolitical machinations of superpowers.

Against the legacy of weariness and doubt that marks later Cold War spy fiction, MacInnes thus translates depoliticized male melancholy into feminine passion.[23] This model follows a narrative arc established in the nineteenth-century historical romance. As such, it offers us a different form of inheritance for spy fiction, one that works against patrilineal descent by offering a matrilineal line of "semi-resistance and semi-retreat" that is neither stranded in history, as Chambers would have it, nor incapacitated by the ideological bifurcations that underscore the "ruthless instrumental, patriarchal, and totalizing logics" that Lee argues are part of the "sanctimony of revolutionary politics" in fact and fiction (Lee 2010: 653).

MacInnes's novels explicitly question the subjects of the "serious" thriller, which Michael Denning itemizes as "the uncertainty of the authority for the protagonist's actions, the lack of a clear-cut 'good,' and the ensuing issues of innocence and experience, identity and point of view" (Denning 1987: 63). With certainty and a conviction that national identity is both porous and transmittable, MacInnes's orchestration of the confluence of conventions from romance and historical novels can be particularly interesting to postwar readers who value transnational affiliations over national identities, especially identities that they might regard as jingoistic or invented to serve national interests. An assertion of British national identity becomes, as MacInnes's spies impersonate Central Europeans, a more complicated moral principle of identification and empathy. The emergence of middlebrow studies, especially of middlebrow literature by women, has thankfully made it unfashionable to speak with disdain about romance plots, the emergence of moral agency, or the complicity of national identity in the ruination of revolutionary utopian collectivity. We are all the better for this turn, and for having with us MacInnes's retrospective and future-oriented documentary historical romance fiction. Depictions of the fate of Poles under Nazi and Soviet occupation are rare in British fiction, and it was not until the recent publication of Timothy Snyder's *Bloodlands* in 2010 and his more recent *Black Earth: The Holocaust as History and Warning* (2016) that the fate of Poles became common knowledge in the United States. Perhaps, then, it is not "the million useless things" of quotidian life that we need to remember now. Perhaps, rather, it is the force of an ethical propaganda by women writers, forged out of a fusion of romance novel conventions and the secret intelligence provided by the middlebrow romantic spy novel, which should move us and call us back into historical memory.

Notes

1 See Kasmer (2012: 91–110).

2 See Hayes (2016: 10–22). Park was named Senior Controller to the senior ranks in the British Intelligence system in no small part because of her work with the Operation Jedburgh paratroopers.

3 For discussions of these political romances, see Huang (2005) and Wang (2004). Many of these romances, especially those written in or about China, denigrated narratives of domesticity in order to bolster expressions of ideological commitment, especially commitments to communism. Anticommunist narratives tended to focus on the destruction of a woman's right to choose (especially sexual partner, pregnancy, and occupation) in collectivist societies.

4 Phyllis Lassner argues brilliantly that MacInnes deftly points to the mass murder of Jews at a time when such news, although easily available to readers of major newspapers and magazines in the United States, was not readily absorbed. See also Wested (2017: 51–2 and 83–8) for a discussion of Poland and the Cold War.

5 See McLean (2012), for a discussion of the relationship between Polish national failure and feminine domestic British restoration.

6 See Norich (2007: 127–30) for a list of articles related to the Holocaust published between 1940 and 1942.

7 If Lord Byron's *Mazeppa* represents the male Polish hero at his lowest point, George Eliot's Will Ladislaw, is the most cheerfully refined version of the type of the Polish Briton, and as the agent of change in the novel it is he who successfully carries forward a program of reform in *Middlemarch*. For a discussion of Ladislaw and the male romantic hero, see Wilt (2014: 53–86).

8 Webster (2013: 621).

9 By way of contrast, Diana Wallace argues in *The Woman's Historical Novel: British Women Writers, 1900–2000*, (2005) that "women's historical novels suggest a subterranean current of resistance to the suppression which was entailed in women's wartime and post-war lives" (88). See also Lokke (2004: 22). In Lokke's view, the shift is more interior than "subterranean," and she argues that "the oppositional nature of women modernists' meditations on female creativity lies in their exploration of a free-floating, multivalent creative and spiritual self, already prefigured in the novels of women writers of Romanticism. For modernist women writers, however, this self is dissolved into labyrinthine genealogical and mythic cycles rather than historical effort" (22). MacInnes's historical fiction offers a middlebrow alternative to this modernist self-dissolution.

10 Kasmer (2012: 93) argues that Porter's novels "advance a conservative, Tory political agenda that advocates [for] monarchism and a naturalized social hierarchy for the moral good of the British nation. In embracing a conservatism associated with a preference for romance and chivalry, ideals promoted by Edmund Burke in *Reflections of the Revolution in France* (1790), Porter affords the genre of romance with a historical and political currency" (93).

11 See Hepburn (2005). Hepburn argues that in John le Carré's *The Spy Who Came in from the Cold*, "Leamas wants to eradicate intimacy in order to work efficiently" (170). See also Rea (2019: 69–75).

12 Bourke-White (1942). This important book faded into obscurity as the United States entered the war, and its quick journey to oblivion suggests the dangers of obscurity that women writers face when they explore international affiliations and fictive forms of kinship.

13 Bourke-White's account of the aftermath of the battle for the Yel'nya bridgehead in early September 1941 survives as one of the few descriptions of the only Soviet victory in 1941 (it was short-lived, as the Nazis retook the bridgehead a few weeks later). See Bellamy (2007: 246–7).

14 Bourke-White's account of the battle can be cross referenced with the Soviet reporter Grossman (2007: 39–41). Neither journalist was interested in producing propaganda.

15 Bourke-White (1942: 259).

16 See Bellamy (2007: 239–88). Although it has been portrayed as both naïve Soviet propaganda and as coercive American propaganda, Bourke-White's photo essay simply reflects the situation as she found it. Partisan activity did "delay and divert the Germans' drive forward," the Nazis "neither understood nor considered partisan activity a threat" in the region (Bellamy 2007: 239), 80 detachments totaling 2,409

fighters were trained to operate behind enemy lines, and 434 detachments totaling 12,561 fighters were "stay-behind parties which would be activated when the Germans rolled past them" (Bellamy 2007: 268). These are not imagined numbers, and in representing their activity Bourke-White also conveyed the temporary demoralization of German troops, who thought their war would have been over in a matter of weeks. For an excellent discussion of women writing about war, see Mackrell (2021).

17 See Lassner (2016).

18 Lee (2010: 640–56). See also Lee (2007).

19 Lee (2010: 644).

20 Lee (2010: 653).

21 https://avalon.law.yale.edu/20th_century/hague04.asp#art29.

22 The disdain and distrust that Peter Guillam and George Smiley express toward the field agent Rickie Tarr in *Tinker, Tailor, Soldier, Spy* highlights an important tension between the economic and selfish sexual potency of the male secret field agent and the institutionally embedded constraints faced by intelligence organizations, or those who organize and preside over the process of spying. As a secret agent, Rickie spies, impersonates, and encourages all sorts of "false pretenses" and false intimacies for money, whereas the spymasters Guillam and Smiley organize and coordinate these efforts and frame the information they receive for their national and institutional employers. The ideological and nationalist elements of the organization thus scorn their personal, economic and sexual residues. Yet Percy Alleline, the head of the Intelligence Services, expresses his disdain for "young Guillam" in much the same way, since Peter is, after all, the recruiter and manager of field secret agents. Taints, it turns out, can be inherited, and le Carré has made a career of undermining the ideological, national and institutional dimensions of intelligence gathering, casting the entire network as just short of, and sometimes over the line of, perverse and impotent. It is no surprise that his latest novel, *A Legacy of Spies*, is narrated by Peter Guillam and tells the story of his experiences as a compromised, sexually potent and ideologically impotent, secret agent. The constant high wire act of dissembling, impersonating, masking, veiling, switching between public and private selves, both of which are infiltrated by inauthenticity, and (perhaps the worst) acting always on the behalf of others drives us away from affiliations of any kind and renders suspect any kind of identification, especially the passport and its role as a document of inherited national identity. The erosion of identity is perhaps the legacy of the twentieth-century male spy narrative.

23 See Chambers (1993: 59). Chambers' description of the melancholic anger expressed by late nineteenth-century French writers is surprisingly akin to male melancholia in Cold War spy fiction. Chambers argues that between the "extremes of resistance and retreat, the decentered self of the melancholic subject—that vaporized, faltering, lacking subject of a new textuality—occupies a precarious middle ground of semi-resistance and semi-retreat, a ground neither of resistance nor of retreat, which is that of the oppositional or 'depoliticized'" (59).

References

Auden, Wystan Hugh (1976), *Collected Poems*, ed. E. Mendelson, New York: Vintage.

Bellamy, Chris (2007), *Absolute War: Soviet Russia in the Second World War*, New York: Vintage.

Bourke-White, Margaret (1942), *Shooting the Russian War*, New York: Simon and Schuster.

Chambers, Ross (1993), *The Writing of Melancholy: Modes of Opposition in Early French Modernism*, Chicago: University of Chicago Press.

Denning, Michael (1987), *Cover Stories: Narrative and Ideology in the British Spy Thriller*, New York: Routledge.

Grossman, Vasily (2007), *A Writer at War: A Soviet Journalist with the Red Army, 1941–45*, trans. R. Chandler, New York: Vintage.

Hayes, Paddy (2016), *Queen of Spies: The Autobiography of Daphne Park*, London: Gerald Duckworth and Co, Ltd.

Hepburn, Allan (2005), *Intrigue: Espionage and Culture*, New Haven: Yale University Press.

Huang, Nicole (2005), *Women, War, Domesticity: Shanghai Literature and Popular Culture of the 1940s*, Leiden: Brill.

Kasmer, Lisa (2012), *Novel Histories: British Women Writing History, 1760–1830*, Lanham: Farleigh Dickinson University Press.

Lassner, Phyllis (2016), *Exile and Espionage: Fascism and Anti-Fascism in British Spy Fiction and Film*, Edinburgh: Edinburgh University Press.

Lee, Haiyan (2007), *Revolution of the Heart: A Genealogy of Love in China, 1900–1950*, Stanford: Stanford University Press.

Lee, Haiyan (2010), "Enemy under My Skin: Eileen Chang's *Lust, Caution* and the Politics of Transcendence," *PMLA*, 125 (3): 640–56.

Lokke, Kari (2004), *Tracing Women's Romanticism: Gender, History, Transcendence*, New York: Routledge.

MacInnes, Helen (2012), *Above Suspicion*, New York: Titan.

MacInnes, Helen (2013), *Assignment in Brittany*, New York: Titan. Originally published New York: Harcourt, Brace, and World, Inc., 1942.

MacInnes, Helen (2017), *While Still We Live*, New York: Titan. Originally published as *The Unvanquished* by Little, Brown, 1944.

Mackrell, Judith (2021), *Going with the Boys: Six Extraordinary Women Writing From the Front Line*, New York: Picador.

McLean, Thomas (2012), *The Other East and Nineteenth Century British Literature: Imagining Poland and the Russian Empire*, New York: Palgrave Macmillan.

Norich, Anita (2007), *Discovering Exile: Yiddish and Jewish American Culture during the Holocaust*, Stanford: Stanford University Press.

Piette, Adam and Matthew Rawlinson, eds (2016), *The Edinburgh Companion to Twentieth-Century British and American War Literature*, Edinburgh: Edinburgh University Press.

Porter, J. (1845), *Thaddeus of Warsaw*, New York: The American News Company. Originally published 1803.

Rea, Ann (2019), "'Subtle Covenants': Dispossession, Frontiers, and the Internationalist Education of Fiction's Spies," *Pennsylvania English*, 40 (1): 54–78.

Ricoeur, Paul (1995), *Oneself as (An)Other*, Chicago: University of Chicago Press.

Snyder, Timothy (2010), *Bloodlands: Europe between Hitler and Stalin*, New York: Basic Books.

Snyder, Timothy (2016), *Black Earth: The Holocaust as History and Warning*, New York: Tim Duggan Books.

Wallace, Diane (2005), *The Woman's Historical Novel: British Women Writers, 1900–2000*, New York: Palgrave.

Wang, David Der-wei (2004), *The Monster That Is History: History, Violence, and Fictional Writing in Twentieth-Century China*, Berkeley: University of California Press.

Webster, Wendy (2013), "'Fit to Fight, Fit to Mix': Sexual Patriotism in Second World War Britain," *Women's History Review*, 22 (4): 607–24.

Wested, Odd Arne (2017), *The Cold War*, New York: Basic Books.

Wilt, Judith (2014), *Women Writers and the Hero of Romance*, New York: Palgrave.

4

"Some Other Man Who Would Have to be Set Aside"

Burgess, Maclean, and the Adversarial Spy in Ian Fleming's *From Russia with Love*

Oliver Buckton

This chapter will argue that the conflict between James Bond and Donovan Grant, his Soviet/SMERSH counterpart in *From Russia with Love*, exemplifies the "adversarial spy" noted by critic Emma Grundy Haigh. The disruption of Bond's supremacy as a spy-hero—of whom his author, Ian Fleming, was growing weary—is linked to the departure from the conventional narrative formula of the Bond novels. The threat the "adversarial spy" poses toward the hero, Bond, is coded as a challenge to his masculinity and sexuality, initiated by the displacement of Bond by Grant at the novel's opening. Fleming's use of this "adversarial spy" device in this, the fifth Bond novel, is linked to the spy scandals of the 1950s, involving "Cambridge Spies" Burgess, Philby, and Maclean. The sexual transgressions of Burgess, in particular, led to an association of espionage and treason with homosexuality, a constellation that surfaces in *From Russia with Love* with the "Committee of Inquiry" into Burgess and Maclean, to which Bond is initially assigned, and in the sexual aberrations of SMERSH villains, Grant and Rosa Klebb. The chapter explores how other powerfully masculine figures—including Bond's ally, Darko Kerim of the Turkish Secret Service—pose a threat to Bond's role and dominance as spy-hero.

Ian Fleming's fifth James Bond novel, *From Russia with Love*, published in 1957, departs intriguingly from the narrative structure that Fleming had established in his previous four Bond novels: *Casino Royale, Live and Let Die, Moonraker*, and *Diamonds Are Forever*. Each of the first four novels begins *in medias res* with James Bond about to be launched on, or preparing for, a mission. Bond is then called into the office of his boss, M, and assigned a mission that pits Bond against a major villain (typically an agent of SMERSH, the Soviet spy agency) who threatens the security and/or economy of Britain and its allies. *From Russia with Love* (FRWL), however, begins with a striking description of a male body: "The naked man who lay splayed out on his face beside the swimming pool might have been dead. He might have been drowned and fished out of the pool and laid out on the grass to dry while the police or next-of-kin were summoned" (Fleming 1957: 1).

Despite the obvious difference from the established formula of the Bond novels, the reader will probably register this man's resemblance to James Bond.[1] Like Bond, he is physically powerful—we learn he "was immensely strong and the bulging muscles at the base of the neck hardly yielded"—and his possessions, the "little pile of objects" containing "typical badges of the rich man's club," are similar to Bond's preference for expensive gadgets (Fleming 1957: 4, 1). Fleming's familiar notation of superior brand names—his watch is "a Girard-Perregaux model designed for people who like gadgets"—is reminiscent of Bond's pleasure in such objects.[2] However, the reference to "the ridge of fine blond hairs above the coccyx" alerts the knowing reader (who has read previous Bond novels) that this man cannot be 007 who, we learn in Fleming's debut novel *Casino Royale*, has dark hair (Fleming 1957: 1–2). Hence, the identity of this man emerges as an enigma at the novel's opening. Yet, even after this realization of our mistake, the deferral of Bond's appearance in the novel will have significant implications for the narrative that follows, affecting the status of Bond as protagonist and as a symbol of British postwar masculinity.[3]

Whether or not the reader is lured into mistaking this man for Bond (suggesting 007's interchangeability), there remains an intriguing resemblance between the as-yet anonymous "man" and our familiar hero. For example, the description of this man's "small cruel lips" (Fleming 1957: 3) recalls the "cruel mouth" of Bond first described in *Casino Royale* and also noted in the SMERSH photograph of Bond, which features "a wide and finely drawn but cruel mouth" (Fleming 1957: 50).[4] Fleming soon reveals the man's identity—"His real name was Donovan Grant, or 'Red' Grant. . . . He was the Chief Executioner of SMERSH, the murder apparat of the M.G.B.," meaning that Grant is the Soviet counterpart of Bond, a professional killer and the prize asset of his own secret Service (as Bond, with his "licence to kill" and 00-status, is a uniquely valuable agent of SIS) (Fleming 1957: 8). Crucially, Grant is a British defector to the Soviet Union: the offspring of a hasty union between a German and an Northern Irish woman, he served in the British army but switched sides to the Soviet Secret Service, because it offered him more opportunities for killing. Unlike Bond, Grant boasts of his appetite for murder, "I am an expert at killing people. I do it very well. I like it" (Fleming 1957: 18). He proves his credentials to the MGB Colonel by killing a German spy, Dr. Baumgarten. This role of a British defector to the Soviet Union as Bond's antagonist links the novel to the scandal of the Cambridge spies that still haunted British intelligence in the later 1950s and remains a key historical context for *FRWL*.

When James Bond eventually appears in Part II of the novel, he is reluctantly serving on a SIS "Committee of Inquiry dealing with the delicate intricacies of the Burgess and Maclean case" (Fleming 1957: 102). Identifying the spy scandal of Burgess and Maclean, the "Missing diplomats" who defected to the Soviet Union in 1951, Fleming presents Bond as the virile British spy-hero needed to counteract the damaging effects of the notorious episode. These "delicate intricacies" include the sexuality of the double agents, which was part of the scandalous context of the case. Bond is faced with the prejudice of the Committee Chief, Captain Troop, RN, who asserts, "I thought we were all agreed that homosexuals were about the worst security risk there is. I can't see the

Americans handing over many atom secrets to a lot of pansies soaked in scent" (Fleming 1957: 103). Troop's comments touch on two key anxieties of the SIS in the aftermath of the Burgess-Maclean scandal. First, given Burgess's flamboyant homosexuality, there was a fear that SIS had been infiltrated by homosexuals secretly working for the Communists; and second, that the scandal would damage the privileged British access to American nuclear secrets.[5]

The associations between communism and homosexuality, especially in the paranoid world of Cold War espionage, have been touched on by Burgess's biographer, Andrew Lownie: "The Soviet intelligence service had discovered that the penalties for homosexuality meant that homosexuals had to live part of their lives in secret and formed a tight and loyal network, which if penetrated, could be very fruitful. It was felt that Burgess's knowledge of, and contacts within, the homosexual world could prove very useful" (Lownie 2015: 53). Further, the idea that the homosexual agent might be inclined to turn against his own organization and spy for the enemy, is suggested by George Steiner: "the homoerotic ethos may have persuaded men, such as Blunt and Burgess, that the official society around them . . . was in essence hostile and hypocritical. It was, consequently, ripe for just overthrow and espionage was one of the necessary means to this end" (cited Lownie 2015: 73).

James Bond's purpose as a fictional spy-hero, therefore, is partly to lay to rest the anxieties that the SIS had become penetrated by "soft" agents and was vulnerable to homosexual blackmail. As Christine Berberich argues, "James Bond, the ultimate British spy, is the response to those double-crossing agents Burgess and Maclean, and ultimately represents Britain as a whole" (Berberich 2012: 23). Yet Bond's heterosexual performance is not reliable, as Allan Hepburn reminds us: "He [Bond] has sex with whichever women throws herself in his libidinal path—except women who show interest in him [. . .] Random seduction does not make Bond sexy, only opportunistic. Indeed, he treats sex mechanistically" (Hepburn 2005: 189). Interestingly, promiscuity is one thing Bond has in common with Guy Burgess, described by one of his lovers as "the most promiscuous person who ever lived. He slept with anything that was going and he used to say anyone will do" (Lownie 2015: 81). If Burgess's homosexual promiscuity made him untrustworthy in the eyes of his superiors, Bond's heterosexual promiscuity will actually be exploited by M for the Cold War against the Soviet Union.

In *FRWL*, Bond's phallic, heterosexual masculinity is defined and affirmed in his conflict with the SMERSH colonel Rosa Klebb. Klebb is depicted as a sadistic and cruel lesbian, who desires Tatiana Romanova sexually. Thus Bond's—and M's—geopolitical contest with the Soviet Union (SMERSH) is worked out through his rivalry with Klebb for control and possession of Romanova. As Funnell and Dodds express it, "Klebb is depicted as a predatory lesbian suitor who challenges Bond for the affections of the Bond Girl" (84). The film version of *FRWL*, they point out, "remains faithful to Fleming's unflattering descriptions of [Klebb] as a character" (Funnell and Dodds 2017: 284). Critically, Klebb "attempts to deny Bond and his phallic masculinity which according to [Jeremy] Black is emblematic of the maleness of the British secret Service (and public anxieties at the time of homosexual double agents who fled to the Soviet Union in the 1950s such as Guy Burgess)" (84–5). In similar vein, Ian Kinane notes that Klebb also shares the common trait of Bond villains, of being physically grotesque: "often the villains' moral decrepitude is signalled in their physical disability or repulsiveness" and he cites "Rosa Klebb's toad-like visage" as a prime example (Kinane 2021: 186n6).

However, Donovan Grant, meanwhile, is a reminder that, even by the mid-1950s, British heterosexual masculinity is still under threat from Soviet spy machine. From SMERSH's perspective, Bond's "weakness for women" proves that he is "therefore not homosexual" (Fleming 1957: 61).[6] However, their own man Grant is not only a defector from the British army, but he is defined as asexual. From the female masseuse's point of view in the opening chapter, what disturbs her about Grant is "the sexuality of the man. The indifference of these splendid, insolently bulging muscles" (Fleming 1957: 6). We learn that none of his killings of girls is sexually motivated: "That side of things, which he had heard talked about, was quite incomprehensible to him" (Fleming 1957: 14). In place of the promiscuous homosexuality of Burgess and ambiguity of Maclean, Grant is the sociopath, driven by bloodlust not ideology, for whom "only the wonderful act of killing . . . made him 'feel better'" (Fleming 1957: 14). While this removes Grant as a threat to Bond for sexual possession of the Bond Girl, his asexuality arguably makes him more lethal as an assassin. Hence, the flipside of Bond's special status as Britain's top agent, is that his weaknesses and mistakes—linked to his heterosexual promiscuity—not only reflect on 007 himself but also undermine Britain's national prestige generally.

Ironically, Bond himself may be the embodiment of this perceived "softness" of SIS. When Bond first appears in the novel, indeed, he is suffering from the effects of the "soft life," specifically the boredom and inertia he experiences when not on a mission: "Just as, in at least one religion, *accidie* is the first of the cardinal sins, so boredom, and particularly the incredible circumstance of waking up bored, was the only vice Bond utterly condemned" (Fleming 1957: 97). Of course, there are other "vices," such as homosexuality, that were more worrying to the critics of SIS, but the fear Bond has of growing "soft" has the effect of compromising his virility. Again, in this respect, Bond resembles Grant who is first seen indulging in the "soft life" at the Soviet holiday dacha "on the south-eastern coast of the Crimea" (Fleming 1957: 11). But where Grant is able to snap out of his lassitude instantly, Bond struggles to do so.

Bond's opportunity to escape from such "accidie" comes in the form of an urgent call from M, whose close relationship with 007 is the most enduring male relationship throughout the series of novels. As James Chapman notes, M is "a symbolic father-figure who endows Bond with power and authority (his 'licence to kill')" (Chapman 2007: 27). Bond's function is that of a guided missile that M will launch against their country's enemies, the ringing of Bond's red telephone being "the signal that had fired him, like a loaded projectile, across the world towards some distant target of M's choosing" (Fleming 1957: 106). Yet unknown to Bond, Grant—an even more formidable weapon—has also been "launched" against him by the enemy Soviet spy agency, SMERSH.

Grant's function in *FRWL* is a prime example of what Emma Grundy Haigh has characterized as the "adversarial spy," in relation to whom the spy-hero's identity must be defined. As Haigh argues,

> The real source of the adversarial spy's power is not the threat he poses to Britain or British society. It is instead the threat he poses to the spy-hero or, more precisely, the

relation he has to the spy-hero. The adversarial spy is more than just the spy-hero's opposite in the enemy camp; he is also Other to the spy-hero's own divided subjectivity. As such, the adversarial spy is both that which the spy-hero seeks to define himself against, and that which the spy-hero desires to become. (Haigh 2012: 17)

FRWL, more so than other Bond novels, reflects this duality of the spy-hero and the adversarial spy. Like other Bond villains—but also like Bond himself—Grant is of mixed ethnicity (German Irish, while Bond is Scottish Swiss) and he has turned against England—in whose military he served—and chosen to work for the Russians, because of "their brutality, their carelessness of human life, and their guile" (Fleming 1957: 15). Having risen to the top of his profession and gained the respect of SMERSH through his ruthless killing, Grant now suffers from boredom and futility similar to Bond's: "What could he aim for now? Further promotion? More money? More gold nicknacks? More important targets? Better techniques?" (Fleming 1957: 26). From Grant's perspective, we discover his chief desire is for a worthy adversary against whom he might prove his superiority: "was there perhaps some other man whom he had never heard of, in some other country, *who would have to be set aside* before absolute supremacy was his?" (Fleming 1957: 26, emphasis added). Grant's role as adversarial spy is confirmed when he is sent by SMERSH to execute the *konspiratsia* or "death warrant" against James Bond, thereby aiming a further catastrophic blow against Western intelligence during the Cold War.

Throughout their contest, Bond's masculinity is superseded by Grant's adversarial superiority in key areas of their struggle. He is not only more physically powerful than Bond but also more ruthless as a killer. Indeed, Grant has been introduced by Ian Fleming primarily for this very purpose—to eliminate the spy-hero that had become a burden, a reminder of Fleming's "bondage" to his own character.[7] Grant's special significance is that he is matched against Bond in a "duel" that dramatizes the wider antagonism between East and West in the Cold War: a global duel, Fleming implies, that the West is in danger of losing.

By setting up a deadly duel between East and West—represented by Russia (Grant, Klebb), and Britain (Bond, M) respectively—the structure of *FRWL* is itself "double." Notably, Part I is set in Russia, while Part II is set in Britain and in Istanbul and on the Orient Express—illustrating that the two "sides" of the Cold War are mirror images of each other, like two opposing players in a chess match with spies and agents as pawns. Istanbul thus becomes a liminal space, a location on the border between East and West where the "game" of espionage is played out. *FRWL* was, as critics have noted, the novel in which Fleming tried to live up to his promise, to take seriously his friend Raymond Chandler's suggestion that his writing should "try for a little higher grade" (Fergus Fleming 2015: 229). While Ian Fleming resisted this suggestion, *FRWL* demonstrates his ambition to transcend the formulaic spy story and attempt a more complex structure. By "doubling" Bond with several other male characters, Fleming signaled his self-reflexive awareness that the masculine supremacy of his spy-hero was at once a response to, and under threat from, the spy scandal of Burgess and Maclean. Like Grant, Burgess and Maclean represent the adversaries within who turned against their native country in order to serve Russia.

To provide a broader context for the role of the "adversarial spy" in Cold War spy fiction, I will briefly turn to the work of Fleming's contemporary spy novelist, Helen MacInnes. Like Fleming, MacInnes also invoked the scandal of Burgess and Maclean in the context of an adversarial spy relationship. In *North from Rome*—published in 1958, the year after *FRWL*—MacInnes delves into a network of Communist agents in Italy and links them to the Cambridge spies. The struggle between her protagonist— an American writer named William Lammiter—and his communist adversary, Luigi Pirotta, is played out under the influence of another British double agent, Evans, with whom Pirotta holds secret conspiratorial meetings. Described by British agent Brewster as "a friend of [Donald] Maclean's," Pirotta is "the professional Communist," whose goal is "To spread his empire around the world" (MacInnes 2012: 113). To this end, like SMERSH, "he will plot dissension, destruction, and hate. . . . To the professional Communist, people are always expendable" (MacInnes 2012: 113).

MacInnes represents Pirotta's adversarial relationship with the novel's protagonist, Lammiter, as a sexual rivalry between agents of the East and West. Lammiter's adversarial relationship with Pirotta is confirmed when his American fiancée, Eleanor Halley, travels to Rome and becomes romantically involved with the aristocratic Pirotta. By the time Lammiter arrives in Rome, she has decided to marry Pirotta and end her relationship with the American. Eleanor's jettisoning of Lammiter in favor of Pirotta is an emasculating rejection that plunges Lammiter into identity crisis. He assures Eleanor that "I don't hate him because he calls himself a count" (MacInnes 2012: 15)—rather, he hates Pirotta because he desires the same woman, and has a greater power to attract and "possess" her. The ideological struggle of East vs West is played out through the sexual rivalry between the adversarial spies. As Christine Bold writes, the sexual relationship in the novel is used to shore up the "Anglo-American union" as "the heroine affiances herself to the wrong man, thereby discovering both political conspiracy and male violence against women." In [*North from Rome*] the man's Italian ethnicity is the sign of his untrustworthiness. The resolution of the adversarial spy plot can only be achieved when "[Eleanor] return[s] to the first, white American love" (Bold 2012: 45).

There is an intriguing parallel between the roles of Eleanor Halley in *North of Rome* and Tatiana Romanova in *FRWL*. While one is from the United States and the other is from Russia, both are sexually attractive women who mediate between the adversarial spies. As Funnell and Dodds point out, FRWL "emphasizes Romanova's heterosexuality and desirability through her sexual encounters with Bond and past history of male lovers. She is set up as a female lure and successfully initiates a sexual relationship with Bond" (Funnell and Dodds 2017: 83).

Though Grant does not desire Romanova, Rosa Klebb, Grant's boss, apparently does, and tells her "your body belongs to the state" and then appears suggestively before her "wearing a semi-transparent nightgown" (Fleming 1957: 84, 85). Romanova "belongs" to SMERSH, and has been selected as a "beautiful lure" to draw Bond into the "killing bottle" where Grant will eliminate him. Exploiting Bond's "weakness for women," SMERSH selects their most desirable member of State Security, "a very beautiful girl indeed" who pledges her loyalty to the state embodied by Rosa Klebb, confirming "I would obey" any orders, including orders to seduce "an English spy" (Fleming 1957:

70, 80, 83). Tatiana is strongly contrasted in the novel (as in the film) with Klebb, her superior officer. As Funnell and Dodds note, in contrast to Klebb's physical ugliness, "Romanova is presented with a more traditionally and aesthetically feminine image, which positions her as an object of desire for Bond" (Funnel and Dodds 2017: 81).

Fleming's novel comments on the paradox of the two agents, Bond and Romanova, "thrown together from enemy camps a whole world apart, each involved in his own plot against the country of the other, antagonists by profession, yet turned, and by the orders of their governments, into lovers" (Fleming 1957: 195). Eventually, Tatiana will choose Bond over Klebb and SMERSH. From her initial role as Bond's "adversary," she will be transformed into the battleground between the Soviet Union and Britain. As in *North from Rome*, the Cold War adversarial spy relationship is fought over the body and mind of a beautiful woman, and takes place on a journey traveling from East to West.[8] Just as Lammiter defeats the Communist plot by winning back Eleanor from Pirotta, Bond's success in seducing Tatiana is tantamount to success in defeating her masters.

However, this Cold War triumph over the Soviets was somewhat of a chimerical fantasy for Britain in the 1950s. As James Chapman observes, Fleming's fictional bolstering of the British Secret Service was "an ironic view given the extent of Soviet penetration of the British intelligence services at the time" (Chapman 2007: 33). Indeed, Chapman points out that *FRWL* "seems like nothing less than a highly programmed attempt to restore the reputation of Britain's intelligence community at a time when it had been severely compromised" (Chapman 2007: 33). The revelation that Cambridge-educated, highly placed, and esteemed officials in the Foreign Office and Secret Intelligence Service, Burgess and Maclean, had been Soviet double agents shook the confidence of the public in its government and its intelligence services. Suspicion then fell on Kim Philby, who was ironically head of the counter-espionage division of SIS responsible for thwarting the espionage by the Soviet Union. Philby was publicly accused of being the "third man," but was exonerated by Foreign Secretary Harold Macmillan in Parliament, in November 1955, due to lack of concrete proof of his treason.

Paradoxically the message of *FRWL* is the exact opposite of "bolstering": rather, the plot exposes the weaknesses and folly of the British Secret Service, and even highlights the vulnerability and incompetence of Bond. Ultimately, Bond is merely a disposable pawn in SMERSH's chess game, the ultimate purpose of which is "to destroy the myth and thus strike at the very motive force of this organization" (Fleming 1957: 43–44). The image of Cold War antagonism as a deadly chess game is dramatized in the chess duel between SMERSH's chief of planning, Kronsteen, and his adversary, Makharov. The "two faces of the double clock"—also referred to as "the enemy clock"—that times the players' moves, foreshadows the inevitable approach of adversarial conflict between Grant and Bond (Fleming 1957: 55). Moreover, the reference to "the two faces of the chess clock show[ing] different times" registers the conflict across divergent time zones between the Cold War antagonists (Fleming 1957: 55). While the two players are compatriots, any misapprehension that this is a friendly match is soon dismissed by Kronsteen's "slanting black eyes [which] looked down with deadly calm on his winning board" (Fleming 1957: 55–56). Kronsteen's ruthless, predatory method typical of SMERSH, and revealed in metaphorical terms: "first he stripped off the skin, then he picked out the bones, then he ate the fish" (Fleming 1957: 56).[9] Anticipating that his opponent "would be writhing in agony like an eel pierced with a spear," Kronsteen's duel to the death reflects the high stakes of the Cold War and the hostility even between members of the same "side" (Fleming 1957: 57).

Both sides of the Cold War are prone to rust with inactivity. Just as Grant was shown suffering from surfeit and lassitude—he is "sick of [roses] and longed to get to Moscow to be and away from their sweet stench"—so Bond is depicted in a similar state of malaise: "The blubbery arms of the soft life had Bond round the neck and they were slowly strangling him" (Fleming 1957: 11, 97). The impression that Bond has gone "soft" reinforces the impression that the British Secret Service has been emasculated by the spy scandals. The source of Bond's malaise, like Grant's, is that he currently lacks a dangerous mission—"peace had reigned for nearly a year. And peace was killing him" (Fleming 1957: 97).

M's role as Bond's boss is to reinvigorate 007 by his "gift" of a mission involving seduction of a beautiful Russian agent. Bond, of course, is the playboy bachelor who, in Fleming's previous novel, *Diamonds Are Forever*, had warned his American lover Tiffany Case that he was ineligible for marriage: "Matter of fact I'm almost married already. To a man. Name begins with M. I'd have to divorce him before I tried marrying a woman. And I'm not sure I'd want that" (Fleming 1956: 199). With this affirmation of Bond's emotional commitment to M above any woman, along with M's disapproval of Bond's "womanizing" and his evident relief that Bond did not marry Tiffany, we recognize the homoeroticism that informs their relationship (Fleming 1957: 106–7). Bond and M are confirmed as the male couple—thus possibly vulnerable to homosexual blackmail—and the language of love is again invoked when Bond "looked across into the tranquil, lined sailor's face that he loved, honoured, and obeyed" (Fleming 1957: 106). SMERSH confirms that M "does not drink very much. He is too old for women"—but not, apparently, for men (Fleming 1957: 44). However, any suggestion that Bond's disinclination for marriage to a woman stems from homosexual leanings is disavowed by his heterosexual promiscuity. Bond's "love" for M is displaced by his willingness "to pimp for England" (Fleming 1957: 117). Even Bond's acceptance of the improbable story that Tatiana Romanova, the Soviet cipher clerk, is in love with him, reflects obedience to M's will: "Bond was sold. At once he accepted all M's faith in the girl's story, however crazy it might be" (Fleming 1957: 112). Bond's only concern from now on will be "the dowry she was bringing with her"—the Soviet Spektor machine (Fleming 1957: 118).

Living in a clubland world of male homosocial bonds, this male spy couple are dangerously blind to the larger picture—falling easily into the Soviet trap that we have already seen laid by General G and his cohorts. With the references to Burgess and Maclean—the highly placed traitors within the British Foreign Office—Fleming shows the archaic "Old Boy" structures of British intelligence failing to match the ruthless chess-playing genius of the Soviet spy machine. In his desperation to obtain a Spektor cipher machine, M will recruit the assistance of a key ally, Darko Kerim, in Istanbul. Yet even this non-adversarial spy casts some doubt on Bond's masculine superiority.

The character of Darko Kerim, head of Station T in Istanbul, is another more effective double of Bond.[10] Initially, Kerim is an extension of M's official quasi-paternal authority—possessing power in his own domain, located on the crucial border of East and West. Notably, Bond's first impression of Kerim is of intimidating physical force and vitality: "Bond was six feet tall but this man was at least two inches taller and gave the impression of being twice as broad and twice as thick as Bond. Bond looked up into two wide apart, smiling blue eyes in a large smooth brown face with a broken nose" (Fleming 1957: 127).[11] Unlike M and Bond, Kerim is deeply suspicious of the honey trap that uses Tatiana Romanova as bait for Bond, demonstrating the Turk's superior instincts: "He tapped the side of his nose as if he was patting a dog. 'But this is a good friend of mine and I trust him . . . if the stakes were not so big, I would say to you "Go home my friend. Go home. There is something here to get away from."'" (Fleming 1957: 132). This combination of instinctual cunning and physical force prompts Bond to reflect on Kerim's attractiveness: "What a man for Head of Station T! . . . He was the rare type of man that Bond loved, and Bond already felt prepared to add Kerim to the half dozen of those real friends whom Bond, who had no 'acquaintances,' would be ready to take to his heart" (Fleming 1957: 137–8).

As Ian Kinane has argued, Kerim belongs to a category of ethically dubious characters for whom Bond, like Fleming, "harbours great affection" (Kinane 2021: 182n59)—a category that also includes Enrico Colmbo in "Risico" and Marc-Ange Draco in *On Her Majesty's Secret Service*. Interestingly, Kinane points out that "each of these men are portrayed as dependable, larger-than-life characters who adopt a pseudo-paternal role towards Bond" (182n59). Eco had argued that these hybrid characters shared qualities of the villains, yet ended up becoming Bond's cherished allies. The "paternal" role sheds new light on both Kerim's authority over Bond and Bond's love for this surrogate father-figure.

Yet despite being "loved" by Bond, Kerim becomes a threat to Bond's supremacy as protagonist. Not only is he physically larger and more imposing than 007, but Kerim also embodies a domination that makes Bond a subservient figure: "A hint of authority behind the loud friendly voice reminded Bond that this was the Head of Station T, and that Bond was in another man's territory and juridically under his command" (Fleming 1957: 126). Bond concedes to Kerim, "I'm under your orders here. You tell me what to do and I'll do it" (Fleming 1957: 130), a direct echo of CIA agent Felix Leiter's acknowledgment of Bond's dominant role in *Casino Royale*: "I'm under your orders and I'm to give you any help you ask for" (Fleming 1953: 45).

Moreover, the rugged vitality of Kerim is a reminder not only of the "soft life" from which Bond is suffering but also of the decline of Britain's imperial potency more generally. The scandal of Burgess and Maclean's defections, and the humiliation of the Suez affair of 1956, have left Britain's international prestige in tatters. Kerim's advocacy of the ruthless treatment of their enemies elicits a surprising admission from Bond: "I quite agree about the Russians. They simply don't understand the carrot. Only the stick has any effect. Basically they're masochists. . . . They love the knout . . . . As for England, the trouble today is that carrots for all are the fashion" (Fleming 1957: 179–80). For Bond, the "soft life" in England is not just an individual disease but a collective, national crisis of confidence.[12] The decline of Britain's imperial power, a form of national emasculation, is certainly one of the postwar changes Bond laments: "At home and abroad. We don't show teeth any more—only gums" (Fleming 1957: 180). In this way Kerim anticipates another more virile ally of Bond's, Tiger Tanaka in *You Only Live Twice* (the last Bond novel published during Fleming's life). When Bond goes to Japan to ask Tanaka for access to a vital intelligence source called MAGIC 44, Tanaka casts doubt on the worthiness of Britain to receive it: "You have not only lost a great Empire, you have seemed almost anxious to throw it away with both hands. . . . when you apparently sought to arrest this slide into impotence at Suez, you succeeded only in stage-managing one of the most pitiful bungles in the history of the world" (Fleming 1964: 80). Like Kerim, Tiger forces Bond to confront the unpleasant reality that he, and Britain, have gone soft.

Kerim's role as a more potent masculine counterpart of Bond is highlighted in the scene in which he cold-bloodedly assassinates a deadly rival: the Bulgarian SMERSH agent, Krilencu. Kerim apologizes for this killing in advance, implying that Bond is not strong enough to stomach such ruthless violence: "Well, don't blame me if you don't like this. . . . It's going to be a straight killing in cold blood. *In my country* you let sleeping dogs lie, but when they wake up and bite you shoot them. You don't offer them a duel" (Fleming 1957: 174, emphasis added). Bond and Kerim watch the huge poster of Marilyn Monroe, from which another man—the target—appears: "out of the mouth of the huge shadowed poster, between the great violet lips, half-open in ecstasy, the dark shape of a man emerged and hung down like a worm from the mouth of a corpse" (Fleming 1957: 178). It is as though the beautiful woman is aroused, "the great violet lips" suggesting a vagina from which the man is born only to die. In this surreal birth scene, Krilencu is metaphorically born into death, becoming a victim of the beautiful femme fatale and her "ecstasy." For all Bond's celebrated expertise in combat, and his "licence to kill," his function in this scene is reduced to the marginal role of observer (Fleming 1957: 176). After the kill, Bond feels "a moment of resentment against the life that made him witness these things," reinforcing his role as a passive spectator to the violence, rather than a participant (Fleming 1957: 179). Bond's passivity is explained by a longstanding distaste for ruthless assassination: "Bond had never killed in cold blood, and he hadn't liked watching, and helping, someone else do it" (Fleming 1957: 179). The contrast between Kerim's ruthless methods and Bond's squeamishness, is self-evident: "In a way it had been a long duel, in which the man had fired twice to Kerim's once. But Kerim was the cleverer, cooler man, and the luckier and that had been that" (Fleming 1957: 179).

Kerim also supplants Bond in his traditional stronghold of gadgetry, having a sniper's rifle concealed in his walking stick: "Barrel from the new 88 Winchester . . . . Put together for me by a man in Ankara"—and also possessing a state-of-the-art Sniperscope (Fleming 1957: 177).[13] While Bond was equipped by Q-branch with a "smart-looking little bag . . . with fifty rounds of .25 ammunition . . . between the leather and lining of the spine" together with "a flat throwing knife, built by Wilkinsons, the sword makers" these weapons prove useless (Fleming 1957: 115). Bond's lack of high-tech weaponry warns the reader he is ill-prepared for his own deadly duel with his SMERSH counterpart Donovan Grant, a man who has no such scruples about killing in cold blood and possesses the latest gadgets of his trade. Although Bond does not yet *know* that he is engaged in this long duel with Grant, the reader already anticipates the confrontation and suspects that the "cleverer, cooler man" will triumph. Evidently, Fleming has more interest in creating these new masculine characters than in the fate of the spy-hero whom he dismissed, in a letter to William Plomer as a "cardboard booby" (Pearson 1966: 406).

Bond's face-to-face meeting with Grant eventually takes place on the Orient Express during Bond's journey from Istanbul to Paris with the Spektor decoding machine, accompanied by Tatiana Romanova. On his train journey, Bond is reading Eric Ambler's *The Mask of Dimitrios*, acknowledging Ambler's pioneering role as the spy novelist who foregrounds the political complexities of the Balkans in his fiction. Yet the allusion to this novel by Ambler—himself a friend of Fleming's—is hardly auspicious for Bond as a spy-hero, as Ambler's protagonist, Charles Latimer, is displaced from the center of the narrative by an adversarial spy, the villain Dimitrios Makroupolus.[14]

Although he had never met Grant before, "Bond's eyes were drawn to him, as if it was someone he knew, as the man approached up the platform" (Fleming 1957: 227).[15] The uncanny attraction, and the mysterious sense of kinship between two men who are inscrutably linked in the narrative despite being strangers, is key to the adversarial spy relationship. While observing Grant's intimidating physique, it is evident Bond feels none of the admiration or affection for another man's physical vigor that he expresses for Kerim: "He looks like an athlete, thought Bond. He has the wide shoulders and the healthy, good-looking bronzed face of a professional tennis player going home after a round of foreign tournaments" (Fleming 1957: 227). Bond simply observes Grant's physical strength without any emotion, as though sizing up an antagonist. Moreover, as the description proceeds, it conveys the sinister character of Grant beneath the "golden" surface, which reinforces the reader's knowledge of his deadly profession:

The man came nearer. Now he was looking straight at Bond. With recognition? Bond searched his mind. Did he know this man? No. He would have remembered those eyes that stared out so coldly under the pale lashes. They were opaque, almost dead. The eyes of a drowned man. But they had some message for him. What was it? Recognition? Warning? Or just the defensive reaction to Bond's own stare? (Fleming 1957: 227)

The fact that Grant is now carrying the same Q-branch model of briefcase as Bond heightens the impression of their doubling. The M.G.B. has yet again penetrated SIS, with Grant's successful impersonation of a SIS agent. This scene also initiates the penetration by Grant of Bond's space, a significant move in their duel. In her discussion of the significance of "masculine space" in dueling, Jennifer Low argues, "the frequency with which fencing manuals conflate the body and the defensive ward suggests that the penetration of the ward was interpreted as penetration of the body. In fencing, a combatant gains a psychological advantage from invading his opponent's space" (Low 2003: 44). Hence, when the two men meet on the Orient Express, Nash (Grant) invades Bond's space, sharing Bond's compartment, which, significantly, is Number 7 (Bond's code number), suggesting that Grant is usurping Bond's identity (Fleming 1957: 201). Funnell and Dodds point out, moreover, that the spaces in which Grant threatens to dominate Bond, are themselves gendered: "although Grant does not compete with Bond for the affections of the Bond girl, he does challenge Bond's masculinity (in the cabin and dining room) and dominance in a space that is often feminized. Thus, Bond's defeat of Grant on the train takes on patriarchal significance and can be linked to his seduction of Romanova and mission recovery, after being forced to leave the Orient Express prematurely" (Funnell and Dodds 2017: 175). Nash (Grant) then further intrudes on Bond's space by taking his weapon, a symbol of his potency as a spy, as we learn "Bond hated someone else touching his gun. He felt naked without it" (Fleming 1957: 239).[16]

Unlike Kerim, Grant's adversarial relation with Bond is clearly malevolent. In fact, there are numerous warning signs that Nash/Grant is dangerous and hostile. These warnings begin with the unsettling—the "Windsor knot" of his tie which for Bond "was often the mark of a cad" (Fleming 1957: 230). But they soon proceed to the deeply sinister, as "the pale eyes swiveled to meet his. There was a quick red glare in them. It was as if the safety door of a furnace had swung open. The blaze died" (Fleming 1957: 231). Bond's conclusion is disturbing—"There's madness there all right, thought Bond, startled by the sight of it. Shell-shock perhaps, or schizophrenia" (Fleming 1957: 231). Grant can be read here as a projection of Bond's own fragmented self, the uncanny "recognition" of his counterpart being symptomatic of Grant's embodiment of the dark side of Bond's lethal profession. The reason Bond is "startled" by Nash, and almost fatally blind to his role as an enemy, is that to recognize this Bond would first have to acknowledge him as a dark double of Bond himself, an adversary equipped with the same deadly skills and marked by a similarly troubled history and possessed by "madness."

Tatiana's role as mediator between adversarial spies is reinforced as she tells Bond she "does 'not trust' his [Grant's] eyes" (Fleming 1957: 235). Tatiana warns Bond that in Russian Grant's assumed name of "Nash means 'ours.' In our Services, a man is *nash* when he is one of 'our' men" (Fleming 1957: 235). Failing to take Tatiana's warning, Bond dismisses this ominous interpretation as a coincidence: "Nash is quite a common English name. He's perfectly harmless" (Fleming 1957: 236). Bond also ignores that Nash is also a homophone of "gnash," a word evoking violent rage. As elsewhere, Bond's failure to take a woman's insights seriously have dire consequences. Tatiana's suspicions reveal more than just that Nash is a Soviet agent ("ours")—it also points to the affinity between Bond and Nash, between SMERSH and the SIS: Grant/Nash is "one of our men" not only because he is impersonating a British agent, but because the methods and motives of the two "sides" are so similar. This doubling of spy-assassins is visualized by Fleming in a striking mirror image as Bond is standing facing the train window, when "Nash's face slid up alongside his in the dark glass. Nash came very close so that his elbow touched Bond's" (Fleming 1957: 237).[17]

It is fitting that the culmination of Bond's duel with Grant takes place on the Orient Express, traveling from East to West, crossing the symbolic "iron curtain" of the Cold War. Having failed to heed either the sinister message issued by Grant's eyes with their "red glare," or Tatiana's warning about the Russian meaning of his name, Bond is trapped and held captive by his enemy. We already know that Grant's preferred method of killing is by strangling or cutting throats (from Chapter 2). Kerim has warned

Bond, "you must keep your sword sharp" (Fleming 1957: 156), perhaps alluding to the Wilkinson knives in his briefcase. But without the protection of either Kerim or M, Bond is powerless against the assassin, to whom he has foolishly handed over his own gun. Grant's function here is to remind Bond of his fictional identity, based on earlier novelistic agents: "No Bulldog Drummond stuff'll get you out of this one" (Fleming 1957: 244). Grant offers a rude awakening that Bond is outdated and ill-equipped for modern conflict.

By contrast, Grant is equipped with a lethal gun concealed inside a book. The volume containing the weapon, Tolstoy's *War and Peace*, suggests the superior literary pedigree of Russian agents (Tolstoy's magnum opus trumping Ambler's spy thriller). It is hard to miss the implication that Grant, in seeking to eliminate Bond, is acting on behalf of Fleming as well as of SMERSH: as he gloats to Bond, "You see, old man, you're not so good as you think. You're just a stuffed dummy and I've been given the job of letting the sawdust out of you" (Fleming 1957: 243). Fleming, having grown tired of Bond, has "given the job" to Grant—a more powerful adversary of Bond who had usurped him from the novel's opening—to "put him aside." Yet, even as Bond looks death in the face, he is given a miraculous reprieve by his merciful creator. Fittingly it is one of Bond's (and Fleming's) most dangerous habits—his compulsive smoking—that comes to his rescue.[18] Lacking the "explosive toys" of Grant, Bond is forced to resort to more primitive methods, as the shield of his cigarette case "slipped . . . between the pages of his book" fortuitously blocks Nash's bullet (Fleming 1957: 250). Ambler's *Mask of Dimitrios* helps to save Bond's life, even though its protagonist is anything but heroic.

Having survived, Bond realizes that he has been a pawn in SMERSH's conspiracy, berating himself that "conceit and curiosity and four days of love had sucked him along on the easy stream down which it had been planned that he should drift" (Fleming 1957: 251). Bennett and Woollacott argue that "Bond frustrates the villain's conspiracy by an unexpected piece of phallic improvisation. Red Grant—opposed to Bond as the body that doesn't respond to women versus the body that must—makes his mistake in relying unduly on the power of the gun, apparently unaware of the fact that, in this particular novel, knives and swords are constructed as the true centre of phallic authority" (Bennett and Woollacott 1987: 140). Rather, though, it is phallic authority itself that the novel calls into question, as the most potent weapon of all will be yielded by a woman, whose weapons supplant guns as the tools of violence. Bond's subsequent actions seem to support this idea, as he extracts "the flat-bladed throwing-knives, two edged and sharp as razors" (Fleming 1957: 254). Indeed, in Fleming's description the razor-sharp knife he had previously "mocked" becomes an extension of Bond's own body, able to penetrate where Grant's apparently more potent weapon had failed: "the fist with the long steel finger, and all Bond's arm and shoulder behind it, lunged upwards . . . .He held the knife in, forcing it further" (Fleming 1957: 255). The sexual tenor of this description is heightened by the "ghastly wailing cry" from Grant that follows penetration and the "convulsive twist" his body makes. Even Grant's dying response suggests a sexual assault, as "slowly, agonizingly, the two huge hands *groped* for him" (Fleming 1957: 255, emphasis added).

Bond ultimately triumphs because, unlike in the assassination scene with Kerim where he is a passive spectator, he is able to appropriate Grant's superior killing weapon for himself: "Suddenly Bond's scrabbling fingers felt something hard. The book! How did one work the thing?" (Fleming 1957: 256). The noise made by the gun is a surprisingly anti-climactic "Click!" but "Bond felt the recoil," and the "hands on his legs . . . going limp" followed by the "terrible gargling noise" confirms Grant's final demise (Fleming 1957: 256).

Grant's asexuality is reiterated throughout the novel, for example in the fact that as a young man who murdered women, he never showed any sexual interest in his victims. When gloating to Bond that Tatiana has been used to lure him in a honey trap, Grant again reminds us he is "Not interested in that sort of thing myself" (Fleming 1957: 246). Grant's lack of sex drive, rather than its excess, is used to demonize him and contrast him to Bond's heterosexual promiscuity. It also establishes a pattern of sexual "abnormality" in the agents of SMERSH itself. Grant's fatal mistake in his duel with Bond is arguably misreading the conventions of the literary genre in which he appears. Grant's previously cited dismissal of the popular spy genre is his undoing, for it is precisely "Bulldog Drummond stuff"—the miraculous interception of his bullet by Bond's book-cigarette case armor, and the gadgets Bond uses—that saves Bond's life and gives him the advantage. At the same time, this scene confirms Fleming's view of the fictional spy as a simplistic, fallible hero.

Having spared Bond in the duel with Grant on the Orient Express, Fleming does not offer a second reprieve in the luxurious Paris hotel room where Bond goes to meet Rosa Klebb. Suggestive of an erotic rendezvous, this Parisian hotel bedroom is where Bond encounters the "more masculine image" of Klebb, one "that confirms her authoritative and unattractive position in the narrative" (Funnell and Dodds 2017: 83). Here Klebb's concealed shoe blade, her poisoned "sting" of the scorpion, sends Bond "crash[ing] headlong to the wine-red floor" gasping for breath Fleming 1957: 268). With this echo of the Homeric "wine dark sea" Fleming perhaps reaches for an epic conclusion to the career of his famous hero. Less grandiosely, Fleming had finally found an enemy agent capable of ridding him of the "stuffed dummy." It is ironic, given Bond's disregard for the advice and insight of women, that his apparent assassin is a female agent. The phallic power of 007 has been decisively defeated by a stiletto.

Fleming came to view his own relationship with James Bond as an adversarial one—a kind of duel in which only one of them could survive. The positive critical reception of *FRWL* may have prompted Fleming to reconsider his abrupt aborting of Bond's career for—despite the fact that Bond made more mistakes than in any of the previous adventures—the novel was a critical success. The effect of a positive reception was propitious, but it pales by comparison with the approval of another American hero—US president John F. Kennedy—who included *FRWL* in the list of his ten favorite books of all time, published in *Life* Magazine: as Chapman remarks, "Fleming's (and Bond's) stock had never been higher than at this moment" (Chapman 2007: 44). Many saw parallels between the famous fictional superspy and the glamorous young American president. As Ian Kinane notes, "The fact was not lost on many that, with his charm, vitality and good looks, Kennedy 'certainly imitated [Bond] to a degree no President has even remotely approached before' . . . . The playboy Bond found life in the playboy president" (Kinane 2021: 22). This endorsement from the most powerful and popular leader in the Western world—a symbol of America's twentieth-century supremacy—led to *FRWL* being chosen as the basis for the second Bond film produced by Albert "Cubby" Broccoli and Harold Salzman. Ironically, the novel in which Fleming tried in vain to eliminate his spy-hero with the assistance of a Soviet adversary, proved to be the work that—more than any other—catapulted Bond into perpetual international stardom. Today, the global reach of James Bond in popular culture reminds us of the outcome of this duel between creator and character. The fictional Bond remains alive, well into the twentieth century, thriving long after the death of the man who gave birth to him.

Notes

1 Interestingly, Umberto Eco examines this opening as an example of Fleming's literary technique of the "aimless glance" (Eco 1984: 166) rather than as a major departure from his conventional narrative structure.

2 As Christine Berberich observes, "Fleming celebrates consumerism in general and brands in particular" (Berberich 2012: 17) and this man's luxurious tastes seem consistent with Bond's.

3 As Fergus Fleming observes, "Unconventionally, Fleming started the book with a long description of Grant—who ranks as one of his most carefully imagined villains—and even less conventionally he ended it by killing his hero" (Fleming 2015: 111).

4 This resemblance is reiterated with the narrator's comment about Grant, "there was something cruel about the thin-lipped rather pursed mouth" (Fleming 1957: 6).

5 As Peter Hennessy argues, Britain was worried in the 1950s about being left behind in the nuclear arms race, citing Labor's Foreign Secretary Ernest Bevin: "We've got to have this thing [the atom bomb] over here, whatever it costs. We've got to have the bloody Union Jack on top of it" (51). Hennessy also notes that the Burgess-Maclean scandal meant that "what today would be called the sexual preferences of those within the reach of PVing [positive vetting] were added to the scope of inquiry on the grounds that certain activities could, if concealed or illegal, leave an official liable to blackmail by a hostile intelligence service" (Hennessy 2010: 103).

6 Claire Hines has written at length of the close relationship between James Bond, Ian Fleming, and *Playboy* Magazine, specifically noting the voyeuristic pleasure of the magazine's readers and their identification with Fleming's spy-hero (Hines 2018: passim]. As Anna Aslanyan notes, "although there is no evidence that Bond's tastes were influenced by *Playboy*, his sexual conquests generated a lot of content for the mag[azine]" (Aslanyan 2018: 30).

7 Fleming's growing discontent with his literary work was revealed in letters to Chandler, in which Fleming admitted, "probably the fault about my books is that I don't take them seriously enough . . . . If one has a grain of intelligence it is difficult to go on being serious about a character like James Bond . . . my books are straight pillow fantasies of the bang-bang, kiss-kiss variety" (Fleming 2015: 228).

8 As Funnell and Dodds note, "The conversion fantasy of Tatiana Romanova in *FRWL* takes place on a train traveling westward and the film uses an onscreen map to depict her journey from NATO-supporting Turkey through the former Yugoslavia . . . to her eventual arrival in NATO-supporting Italy and the city of Venice" (Funnell and Dodds 2017: 103).

9 In Terence Young's film version of *FRWL*, Kronsteen's opponent is a Canadian chess player, which emphasizes the Cold War opposition of East vs West while avoiding a direct confrontation of the Soviet Union and the USA. As Funnell and Dodds point out, the film "opens with a chess match between a Canadian player (Adams) and Kronsteen, an Eastern European grandmaster who produces a stunning victory over his Western opponent" (Funnell and Dodds 2017: 80–1).

10 Eco argues that Kerim represents "a variant that is discernible only in a few other novels," that of a "strongly drawn being who has many of the moral qualities of the Villain, but . . . fights on the side of Bond" (Eco 1984: 150).

11 Even Bond's signature brand of "Morland cigarettes" of Grosvenor Street London is eclipsed by Kerim's exotic blend: "It was the most wonderful cigarette he had ever tasted—the mildest and sweetest of Turkish tobacco in a slim long oval tube with an elegant gold crescent" (Fleming 1957: 120, 128).

12 As Christine Berberich argues, despite "Fleming's celebration of conspicuous consumption through the repeated 'branding' which can be found in his novels and which reflects the shift from austerity to affluence in the 1950s," he is "strangely ambiguous . . . in favour of some social changes yet fundamentally opposed to (many) others" (Berberich 2012: 14).

13 In Terence Young's film version of *From Russia with Love*, the rifle—rather than being acquired by Kerim—is part of the equipment issued to Bond by Q at the beginning of the film. Even though Bond never pulls the trigger—Kerim insists on doing so—his possession of the rifle nonetheless establishes him rather than the Turk as the possessor and master of technology.

14 There is an intriguing echo of Charles Latimer's name in that of William Lammiter, the protagonist of *North from Rome*. Apparently MacInnes also was influenced by Ambler's writer-turned-spy.

15 Ironically it is at the very moment that Bond "felt happy" with Tatiana, that he sets eyes on his deadly double, Grant, whose appearance is romantically described: "A shaft of sun lit up the head of one man who seemed typical of this happy, playtime world. The light flashed briefly on golden hair under a cap, and on a young golden moustache" (Fleming 1957: 226, 227).

16 This line would later be appropriated for the dialog of a female spy, Severine (Bérénice Marlohe), in the twenty-third EON Bond film, *Skyfall* (2012).

17 This visual doubling of Bond and Grant is developed at greater length in Terence Young's film version of *From Russia With Love* (1963), which substantially enhances Grant's role in the plot. Rather than disappearing into the background—as he does for much of the novel—the film's Grant (Robert Shaw) shadows Bond throughout the film.

18 Bond's consumption of seventy cigarettes a day, revealed in *Casino Royale*, mirrors Fleming's own rate of smoking, by most accounts.

References

Aslanyan, Anna (2018), "Rev. of the Playboy and James Bond," *Times Literary Supplement* (Issue 6203), September 7.

Bennett, Tony and Janet Woollacott (1987), *Bond and Beyond: The Political Career of a Popular Hero*, New York: Methuen.

Berberich, Christine (2012), "Putting England Back on Top? Ian Fleming, James Bond, and the Question of England," *The Yearbook of English Studies*, 42, Literature of the 1950s and 1960s: 13–29.

Bold, Christine (2012), "Domestic Intelligence: Marriage and Espionage in Helen MacInnes's Fiction," in Robert Lance Snyder (ed.), *Espionage Fiction: The Seduction of Clandestinity*, 31–53, Vashon Island: Paradoxa.

Chapman, James (2007), *Licence to Thrill: A Cultural History of the James Bond Films*, Revised edition, London: I.B.Tauris.

Eco, Umberto (1984), "Narrative Structures in Fleming," in *The Role of the Reader: Explorations in the Semiotics of Texts*, 144–72, Bloomington: Indiana University Press.

Fleming, Fergus, ed. (2015), *The Man with the Golden Typewriter: Ian Fleming's James Bond Letters*, London: Bloomsbury.

Fleming, Ian (1953), *Casino Royale*, Las Vegas: Thomas and Mercer.

Fleming, Ian (1956), *Diamonds Are Forever*, Las Vegas: Thomas and Mercer.

Fleming, Ian (1957), *From Russia with Love*, Las Vegas: Thomas and Mercer.

Fleming, Ian (1964), *You Only Live Twice*, Las Vegas: Thomas and Mercer.

Fleming, Ian (1965), *The Man With the Golden Gun*, Las Vegas: Thomas and Mercer.

From Russia with Love, Dir. Terence Young. Eon, 1963.

Funnell, Lisa and Klaus Dodds (2017), *Geographies, Genders, and Geopolitics of James Bond*, London: Palgrave MacMillan.

Haigh, Emma Grundy (2012), "In Light of the Other: The Hero and the Adversarial Spy," in Robert Lance Snyder (ed.), *Espionage Fiction: The Seduction of Clandestinity*, 11–29, ParVashon Island: Paradoxa.

Hennessy, Peter (2010), *The Secret State: Preparing for the Worst 1945–2010*, London: Penguin.

Hepburn, Allan (2005), *Intrigue: Espionage and Culture*, New Haven: Yale University Press.

Hines, Claire (2018), *The Playboy and James Bond: 007, Ian Fleming, and Playboy Magazine*, Manchester: Manchester University Press.

Kinane, Ian (2021), *Ian Fleming and the Politics of Ambivalence*, London: Bloomsbury.

Low, Jennifer (2003), *Manhood and the Duel: Masculinity in Early Modern Drama and Culture*, New York: Palgrave.

Lownie, Andrew (2015), *Stalin's Englishman: The Lives of Guy Burgess*, London: Hodder & Stoughton.

MacInnes, Helen (2012), *North From Rome*, London: Titan.

Pearson, John (2013), *The Life of Ian Fleming, 1966*, London: Bloomsbury.

5

Bond, Colonialism, and the "Other"

Christine Berberich

This chapter will assess and problematize the figure of James Bond as a representative of a normative white Britishness that repeatedly marginalizes ethnic-minority characters. Taking in the social-political context of the Cold War and British decolonization, it argues that Bond is repeatedly upheld as the victorious representative of a powerful Britain in a way that ignores the *Realpolitik* of the day. Ethnic-minority males are repeatedly "othered" in the novels by serving as mere foils to Bond's allegedly superior masculinity. The chapter will also assess the even more marginalized representation of ethnic-minority women that are, more often than not, merely reduced to their sexualized physicality. The chapter thus argues that Fleming's novels display a racially motivated misogyny that appears to be driven by the attempt to reassert a not only outmoded but racist colonial discourse no longer in keeping with its times.

* * *

The Opening Ceremony for the 2012 Olympic Games in London started with two icons of Britishness: Her Majesty the Queen and James Bond, 007, the agent with a license to kill. The worldwide audience loved this surprising interaction between the Queen and Bond actor Daniel Craig which included a helicopter flight over London that took in all of the capital's iconic sights—Big Ben and the Houses of Parliament, the London Eye, Tower Bridge—and that culminated in a spectacular pretend jump, naturally with Union Jack parachutes, into the Olympic stadium.[1] This opening segment of a stunning Opening Ceremony was wildly popular with the viewing public for its seemingly joyful celebration of British icons, and because it showed the Queen from an unexpectedly mischievous side. From the vantage point of the cultural commentator, however, it was not unproblematic: the music accompanying the helicopter flight was the culturally laden "Dambuster March"; when they flew over Parliament Square, the large Churchill sculpture came to life and smilingly waved. Contemporary Britishness, supposedly being celebrated to set up a worldwide sporting event, was conflated with the at best nostalgic, at worst mythical commemoration of the Second World War. And, of course, the lines between "fact" and "fiction" were further blurred through the choice of the film's two protagonists: a *real* person and a *fictional* character. Since his first appearance in 1953, the fictional secret agent 007, James Bond has, for people all over the world, become synonymous with Britishness. As the leading Bond scholar James Chapman points out, "Bond is so indelibly associated in the popular imagination with a particular image of Britishness" (130). Celebrated and lauded as the quintessential Gentleman, Bond has, seemingly, upheld British, but in particular *English* values since the 1950s. His inclusion in the Opening Ceremony alongside the Queen—a real person and head of state representing British values and institutions more than anyone else—*might* consequently have been just a bit of fun. But it becomes problematic if the history of the cultural construct that is James Bond is considered: his creation in the 1950s to promote an unquestioning British superiority at a time when Britain, while becoming a more affluent and fairer, less hierarchical society, saw a decline in its global status as its Empire dissolved. Bond rose to fame throughout the late 1950s and the 1960s during the Cold War, when the British secret agent was often, though not always, seen to be victorious over the "devious" powers of, in particular, the Soviet Union and other "foreign" agents. Read in this context, then, the inclusion of Bond in the Olympic Opening might seem incongruous with a 21st-century sporting celebration.

Britain emerged from the Second World War victorious, but badly shaken. For the former world power, victory had come at a high price. The country was economically weakened, victory only having been secured with the help of the Allied nations. By 1945 it was clear that Britain would no longer be a predominant world power, that this was a role carved up by the United States and the Soviet Union. Much of postwar Britain lay in ruins; rationing was in effect until the early 1950s. The population was war-tired and starved of entertainment and hope, and this mood was slow to change.[2] By the time Ian Fleming published the first James Bond novel *Casino Royale* in 1953, things had started to look up. As I have shown elsewhere, the early 1950s were important years for Britain gradually emerging from war-time austerity: the Festival of Britain of 1951 was to mark the centenary of the Great Exhibition of 1851 but, simultaneously, to show Britain's recovery; the coronation of Queen Elizabeth II in 1953 seemed to ring in an new Elizabethan era.[3] All this, however, happened simultaneously with the rapid progress of decolonization that well and truly marked Britain's demise not only as an imperial but also as a world power: Indian Independence in 1947 rang in a veritable surge of independence of former British colonies. Israel (formerly Mandate Palestine), Myanmar, and Sri Lanka gained independence in 1948 and most African and Caribbean Colonies became independent throughout the late 1950s and early 1960s. This demise of Britain as a world power was sealed during the Suez Crisis of 1956 when American intervention forced Britain into a humiliating withdrawal from the conflict. It was against this backdrop that Ian Fleming created James Bond, the ultimate spy who repeatedly saves not only Britain but the world from the brink of destruction. In his seminal work *The Politics of James Bond* of 2001, Jeremy Black writes, "[Bond] was, and is, an image of toughness, sharpness, cleverness and male sexuality, a national and class stereotype, that Fleming sought to identify anew with the British after . . . the Second World War" (Black 2001: vii). As Black makes clear, Fleming consciously created Bond to assert a strong image of Britishness—tough, sharp, clever, masculine—to bolster the country's declining self-belief and morale. In a world where the word "Britain" did not seem to hold much currency anymore, Bond emerged as an upholder of traditional British values and morals that are, again and again, victorious in a battle between "right" and "wrong." As Fleming biographer Ben MacIntyre states, "Bond is . . . a political fixer, the embodiment of the hope that Britain still plays a vital part out there" (MacIntyre 2008: 197). As such, the novels "fix" world affairs, rig events and provide an alternative, although frequently nuanced history.

Completely disregarding the *Realpolitik* of his age, where power came to solely lie with the Americans and the Soviets, Fleming celebrates a reactionary, nostalgic notion of national identity that repeatedly sees the British winning the day and so pretending to have more power and influence than they really had. In *From Russia with Love*, for instance, the head of the Russian secret organization SMERSH singles out the British Secret Service as the only serious contender in the world: "Every country has good spies and it is not always the biggest countries that have the most or the best. . . . England is another matter . . . I think we all have respect for her Intelligence Service" (Fleming 2002b: 35-6). While Bond's lack of discipline weakens him in this novel, and indeed the novel ends with Rosa Klebb almost killing him, Bond still represents Britain. As its seemingly sole defender and, by extension, the Western world, he is repeatedly drawn into world affairs and conspiracy, combating megalomaniac individuals or enemy states. Reflecting the Cold War context of their conception, the enemies in Bond's earlier adventures are almost exclusively agents of SMERSH, the "official murder organization of the Soviet government . . . a contraction of 'Smiert Spionam,' which means 'Death to Spies,'" thus emphasizing the Cold War division of West versus East (Fleming 2002a: 25).

The agents who fight for SMERSH are not always Soviets but, more often than not, have other ethnic origins—in the early novels usually harking back to the Second World War, in later novels taking on evil geniuses from former British colonies. As such, and as Cynthia Baron has outlined, "007's exploits remain steeped in the discourse of 'Orientalism' . . . in order to justify Western imperialism" (Baron 2003: 135). This Orientalism repeatedly celebrates Britishness as strong, masculine, powerful and assertive, and in a very definite opposition to the exoticized "others" who are shown as different, effeminate, indecisive, and, ultimately, weak. This chapter will read the figure of Bond, the celebrated representative of "Britishness," against the backdrop of decolonization and the Cold War. It will argue that there is a problematic juxtaposition at the heart of the Bond franchise: the permanent and binary recurrence between good (Bond/Britain and the West, generally represented by the United States) versus evil (the racial, ethnic, ideological "Other"). Bond, the Alpha Male and representative of an already obsolete British colonial rule, is presented at the pinnacle of a hierarchy that sees "foreigners," especially those of a different ethnic background, considerably further down the power line. They act as mere foils for Bond to display his innate British superiority. Fleming marginalizes both male and female ethnic and racial "others" in order to unquestioningly uphold Western, but in particular British values. Finally, the chapter further argues that, while male "Others" serve as suitable opponents for Bond, there simply to be crushed, ethnic or racially different *women* are further marginalized and visible only in their physicality in the novels. Fleming thus displays a problematic, racially motivated misogyny—not only toward women but also toward his effeminate, male antagonists—that suggests a British urge to reassert an outmoded colonial discourse of "superiority" and "inferiority" out of place in the second half of the twentieth century.

* * *

It is a rare thing indeed for Bond to fight an enemy from within his own lines, from his own country.[4] Black talks about Fleming's, "disinclination to look for evil among the British" (Black 2001: 19). In the early Bond novels, his enemies, generally in cahoots with the Soviets, have a clear connection to battle lines drawn up during the Second World War. In *Casino Royale* (1953), Bond's archenemy Le Chiffre is described via stereotypical racial characteristics: "ears small, with large lobes, indicating some Jewish blood," as "probably a mixture of Mediterranean with Prussian or Polish strains," a man of "large sexual appetite" and "flagellant" (17); Sir Hugo Drax, from the 1955 novel *Moonraker*, is of German origin and a prominent former Nazi; Emilio Largo in *Thunderball* (1961) is Italian, and so, presumably, a former Fascist; Dr. No is half-German, half-Chinese; Auric Goldfinger is a Latvian with a war past; Ernst Stavro Blofeld, who appears in various guises in the novels *Thunderball* (1961), *On Her Majesty's Secret Service* (1963), and *You Only Live Twice* (1964), is of Polish and Greek origin, and seemingly a shape shifter who does not shy away from radically changing his own appearance in order to pass undetected on his way to world dominance. These men are the creative evil geniuses who pull the strings in the background: deviants because of their origin or their sexual orientation, their former opposition to Britain during the war, having learned their evil trade more often than not in Nazi training camps. While their background clearly sets them apart from the *British* spy who represents the desirable norm, Bond often finds himself impressed by them. He notes, for instance, Dr. No's "professionalism," pondering that he "was obviously a man who took immense pains"—and, as such, a worthy opponent (Fleming 1988: 317). Their background, with clear links to former enemy Germany, keeps the war-time opposition and discourse alive. Winning over these Germans or Nazi-trained criminals, Bond can, again and again, relive the glory of VE Day without having to acknowledge the help provided by the Allies to achieve victory in 1945. Bond fights these "other" opponents by himself, the lone Englishman—once more into the breach, dear Bond!—taking on the killers of the world.

What makes the Bond novels problematic for a 21st-century readership is their continuous juxtaposition of Britishness against other countries and, in particular, other races. Gilberto Triviños, for instance, has written that it is, nowadays, impossible to say that Fleming's work is merely entertaining.[5] The Bond novels, with their celebration of innate British superiority, are inherently political—despite Fleming's own repeated insistence that he himself was "a totally non-political animal," not "involved" or "engaged," and without a "message for suffering humanity."[6] This is particularly apparent when Fleming describes characters with different ethnic and racial backgrounds. Not considered "worthy" enough to be the real opponents in most cases, they function as mere minions, albeit dangerous ones, only there to show Bond's perceived superiority over them. In *Dr. No*, for instance, there are the Chigroes, mixed-race "Chinese Negroes" who form the backbone of Dr. No's Empire (Fleming 1988: 212). The novel starts with a particularly unsavory description of three of them, three blind "Chigro" beggars, "bulky men, but bowed" that are seen to "shuffle along" (Fleming 1988: 212). The language Fleming applies here has distinct Orientalist undertones: the men are "bowed" rather than walking upright; they "shuffle" rather than move with firm steps, suggesting something underhand and sly. Contrasted with the affluent setting of

Richmond Road in Jamaica, "they made an unpleasant impression"—simply judged on their appearance which is different from that of the wealthy *white* inhabitants of that street (Fleming 1988: 213). They are directly—and unfavorably—contrasted to the four white men gathered for a game of cards: the "Brigadier in command of the Caribbean Defence Force, . . . Kingston's leading criminal lawyer, . . . the Mathematics Professor from Kingston University, . . . [and to] Commander John Strangeways, RN (Ret.), Regional Control Officer for the Caribbean . . . the local representative of the British Secret Service" (Fleming 1988: 212). After this introduction—the affluent and influential white men representing British colonial power versus the ragged and unfavorable "Chigroes"—it is unsurprising to the reader that the three blind beggars turn out to be assassins who kill Strangeways and his assistant Mary Trueblood. It is in particular, this latter juxtaposition, the "big Negro with yellowish skin and slanting eyes" who shoots the defenseless woman, the golden-haired "Trueblood," that sets up the racial divide in this novel (Fleming 1988: 218). When Bond himself is captured by Dr. No's henchmen, they all turn out to be "Chigroes" too, large men with "brutal, squinting" faces, characterized by "sweat smell," trained killing machines without individual or independent thoughts or morals (Fleming 1988: 314). Throughout the novel, the "Chigroes" are described with ugly or animalistic characteristics: "brown and yellow eyes," "purple blubbery lips parted in a sneer," as "apes" who "look dumb enough," with "brownish teeth worn to uneven points by years of chewing sugar-cane" (Fleming 1988: 317, 319, 362). This theme of depicting other races in animalistic terms is continued in other Bond novels. In *Goldfinger*, for instance, the Korean Oddjob is repeatedly referred to as "that Korean ape," with a particular focus on his Asiatic facial features that set him apart from the Caucasian Bond: "a square flat yellow face," "slanting eyes in the flat yellow mask" (Fleming 1988: 562, 593, 599, 473, 507). Another former war enemy, the Japanese in *You Only Live Twice* (1964), are repeatedly described as "sly," "inscrutable," "sadistic" or "wily," with "brown face[s]" and "slit eyes" (Fleming 1964: 5, 6, 30, 243). And there is also the shady Cuban Major Gonzales in the short story "For Your Eyes Only," who ruthlessly has old Colonel Havelock and his innocent wife massacred. His two Cuban henchmen are described, again, as having "animal eyes" and "brown monkey-hands" (Fleming 1964: 49, 53). This proliferation of animal descriptions for non-white characters gives the Bond novels a clear racist undertone. For Baron, Bond is thus "an imperial hero, who provided a way for Britishness to continue to be defined in opposition to the 'dark' people of the world," and Vivian Halloran has referred to the "white Anglo-Saxon superiority over 'mongrelized' races" in Fleming's novels (Fleming 1988; Halloran 2005: 159).

This juxtaposition of "Britishness" versus "Otherness," of, quite literally, "white" against "Black," is particularly prominent in Fleming's second Bond novel *Live and Let Die*, first published in 1954. The cover for the 1956 Perma book edition of *Live and Let Die* already—and not at all subtly—illustrates this juxtaposition between white and Black: a near-naked Bond and a shackled and skimpily clad Solitaire (in a suitably virginally white swimsuit) form an illuminated circle in the middle of the image, surrounded, on the margins, by threatening Black characters. Due to this position, the viewer's gaze is automatically drawn toward her prominent chest. Over this scene of sexualized violence presides Mr. Big, fully clothed, leering, located at the side of the image, sitting at a desk counting gold coins.[7] Although Bond here again has to fight against an agent of SMERSH, this time he has to confront "Mr. Big," his first and, to date, only opponent of African origin in the novels. Whereas later novels mainly depict other-race henchmen and assistants and marginalize them through the use of animal imagery as has been outlined above, *Live and Let Die* offers, from the very beginning, a discourse about "otherness," about the situation of African Americans in the United States and about their general "difference" from everybody, but in particular from the "hero" James Bond. Mr. Big is introduced by M as "probably the most powerful negro criminal in the world," the "head of the Black Widow Voodoo cult and believed by that cult to be the Baron Samedi himself" (Fleming 1963c: 17). As Black has shown, the depiction of Mr. Big, "allows M and Bond to offer their views on the ethnicity of crime, views that reflected ignorance [and] the inherited racialist prejudices of London clubland" (Black 2001: 11). With this brief introduction, Mr. Big is simultaneously elevated—"the most powerful criminal"—and again belittled (Fleming 1963c: 17). As the head of a powerful Voodoo cult, he is immediately exoticized, marginalized, shown to be part of some exotic mumbo jumbo that rational men, such as Bond himself, would never believe in. Bond's immediate disbelief about Mr. Big's power is symptomatic: "I don't think I've ever heard of a great negro criminal before. . . . Chinamen, of course, the men behind the opium trade. There've been some big-time Japs, mostly in pearls and drugs. Plenty of negroes mixed up in diamonds and gold in Africa, but always in a small way. They don't seem to take to big business" (Fleming 1963c: 18). Bond's speech highlights his innate belief in the superiority of other races over Africans that are, in his opinion, not even capable of turning out great criminals. But Mr. Big's special abilities are quickly explained as being due to his mixed-race heritage—"he's not pure negro. . . . Good dose of French blood. Trained in Moscow, too" (Fleming 1963c: 18). What a great criminal needs, evidently, is some "white" blood and white mentorship, even if it comes from an ideologically dubious background, such as the Soviet Union. Mr. Big's mixed-race background is also, again, symptomatic of the division of the world into Britain's allies (mainly the United States) and enemies, both old and new: France is, historically and traditionally, and despite her status as "Ally" during the First and Second World Wars, an opponent for Britain; the Soviet Union is the ultimate postwar enemy. Tellingly, Mr. Big's name is an acronym for "Buonaparte Ignace Gallia," a play on Napoleon Buonaparte, the French Emperor and historical archenemy of the British (Fleming 1963c: 20). Bond's hypocrisy and bias become particularly clear when comparing Mr. Big's "dubious" mixed-race heritage with the far more positive one of Quarrel, the Cayman Islander who assists him in *Live and Let Die* and makes a reappearance, only to tragically die, in *Dr. No*: Quarrel's "blackness" is more acceptable for Bond as he is descendant "from a Cromwellian soldier or a pirate of Morgan's time" and has been trained by the British (Fleming 1988: 238). His blackness is described as a soothing, calming, and usually gleaming "brown," set apart distinctly from Mr. Big's "grey-black skin" (Fleming 1988: 241, 239). As Gerald Early has shown, Quarrel, largely thanks to being Bond's friend, is depicted as "a white man's idealized version of a black companion—strong, loyal, brave, and not too black looking" (Early 1999: 191). For Vivian Halloran, this distinction between the mixed-race Mr. Big (bad) versus the similarly mixed-race Quarrel (good) is symptomatic of Fleming's fascination with miscegenation, in particular his belief that mixed-race characters combine their different national identities but do not blend them (Halloran 2005: 161). This accounts for Mr. Big's negative depiction, as he combines the doubly dubious Caribbean and French backgrounds, whereas Quarrel is acceptable due to the British part of his genetic makeup.

Throughout *Live and Let Die*, negative depictions of racially other characters abound. Harlem in New York, which Bond visits with his CIA counterpart Felix Leiter, is shown to be a place that is entirely outside of "normative" perceptions of the United States, a place inhabited by "minds that still recoiled at a white chicken's feather or crossed sticks in the road—right in the middle of the shining capital city of the Western world" (Fleming 1963c: 51). It is the "capital of the negro world," and, as such, a place that is "other," that is suspicious and that is, ultimately, highly dangerous (Fleming 1963c: 42). Even the shops are depicted as different from those in other New York boroughs, full of "lucky charms and various occultisms" and, simply due to their difference, deeply *unheimlich* to Bond (Fleming 1963c: 50). Chapter headings such as "Nigger Heaven" might still have been in usage in 1954 but certainly jar uncomfortably with 21st-century postcolonial sensibilities (Fleming 1963c: 44). Bond and Leiter ridicule the language spoken by the locals, described as "straight Harlem—Deep South with a lot of New York thrown in" (Fleming 1963c: 47). Though dressed up for the occasion, the Harlem residents are described with clearly racist overtones: "the air was thick with smoke and the sweet, feral smell of two hundred negro bodies. The noise was terrific—an undertone of the jabber of negroes enjoying themselves without restraint . . ." (Fleming 1963c: 55). Their "feral" smell is again linked to animals; their language a mere "jabber," something clearly deemed to be uncivilized. The scene is set for an otherworldly experience for Bond, suitably rung in by "Voodoo drummers from Haiti" and the naked dancer G-G (Fleming 1963c: 57). It is from this backdrop of exoticized music and dance that Bond is abducted and introduced to the world of Mr. Big and his violent henchmen. His first encounter with Mr. Big is again depicted in suitably animalistic and horrifyingly racist terms—Mr. Big is described as having "animal eyes, not human" that "seemed to blaze," with a wide nose not "particularly negroid. The nostrils did not gape at you," with a "monstrous head that had an overall awe-inspiring, even terrifying" effect (Fleming 1963c: 64–5). He is surrounded with Voodoo paraphernalia. His personal guards are referred to as "clumsy black apes" (Fleming 1963c: 62). Fleming here once again plays with racial stereotypes in order to mark out the enemy as "Other," and this theme is continued once Bond has tracked Mr. Big down to Jamaica where the criminal has held the entire island in check with his voodoo rituals that play on local fears and superstitions. Jamaica thus serves, as Baron has said in a different context, "as a 'natural' site for colonial adventure" (Baron 2003: 140)—a place steeped in seemingly primeval beliefs and myths that is waiting for the rational representative of the colonial master race to restore law and order and to inevitably emerge victorious. Mr. Big falls foul of the trap he set for Bond, being eaten by the very sharks that he had earmarked to kill Bond, and the colonial order, the problematically assumed supremacy of the white man, is re-established. Triviños refers to the pervasive myth of the Bond novels that reinforces beliefs in the superiority of white over Black, of British masculinity over other races.[8] As such, he sees Fleming, as a Western writer, trapped in a Manichean representation of West versus East, capitalism versus communism, white versus other colors, that should not even have been acceptable in the 1950s and that perpetuates a mythical worldview and a deeply problematic take on history. For Triviños, this represents a process of *dehistoricizing*: real-life political events of the 1950s and 1960s are blatantly ignored and even falsified in order to present an alternative history where the white man still rules supreme (Triviños 1985–6: 118). And it is this that, according to the Black Power activist Eldridge Cleaver, accounted—and potentially, and very worryingly, still does— for their popularity. In *Soul on Ice* (1968) he claimed that "The 'paper tiger' hero, James Bond, offering the whites a triumphant image of themselves, is saying what many whites want desperately to hear reaffirmed: 'I am still the White Man, Lord of the land, licensed to kill, and the World is still an empire at my feet'" (Cleaver 1968: 104).

This unquestioning celebration of male superiority is continued in Fleming's depiction of women throughout the Bond novels. In fact, the Bond novels and, by extension, the films, have become (in)famous for their problematic representation of women.[9] Robert Arp and Kevin S. Decker explain that "Bond's treatment of women is a glaring case of objectification" (Arp and Decker 2006: 203). They outline that the Bond novels apply the "Male Gaze" to show women as "other"; "that is, inferior physically, mentally and socially—and perhaps even as inherently wicked" (Arp and Decker 2012: 203). Many of the now-famous Bond "girls"—in itself a problematic and belittling title for the novels' women—are shown to be "damaged:" a broken nose in the case of Honeychile Ryder, who is also a former rape victim, in *Dr. No*; Gala Brand in *Moonraker* has a mole on her right breast; Tiffany Chase in *Diamonds Are Forever* is also a former victim of a gang rape; Domino Vitali in *Thunderball* has a limp; Kissy Suzuki in *You Only Live Twice* is a beauty but has work-roughened hands with broken fingernails; and *Goldfinger's* Pussy Galore, famously, starts out as a lesbian, clearly an unthinkable concept for Fleming, before Bond "rescues" and converts her. As such, the women are already shown as "inferior" to Bond's unquestioned masculinity that does not show any weaknesses.[10] Their main role is, again, to bolster Bond's male ego and confirm his strength. Despite the fact that it is often the "girls" who provide valuable clues or help to Bond, it is, ultimately, he who is always shown to rescue them, and to reap the (sexual) reward for that at the end of the novels; the women always, and inevitably, end up sexualized, subjugated to and, quite literally, underneath the Alpha Male that is Bond. As Tony Bennett has shown, "the figure of Bond functioned as an ideological shorthand for the appropriate image of masculinity . . . In a period that experienced a considerable cultural redefinition—a flux and fluidity—of gender identities, the figure of Bond furnished a point of anchorage" (Bennett 2017: 8). At a time that saw, in real social and political terms, women's emancipation and increasing sexual liberation from the yoke of patriarchy, Bond again relegates women to subjugated roles, to objectified playthings, assuring his male readers that all is still well and as it should be in the world of gender inequality.

As Black has shown, "women were accorded only a secondary place in the novels" and their role is even further marginalized if they are of different racial background (Black 2001: viii). There is a small number of ethnically diverse walk-on parts for women; examples include the Black dancer G-G in *Live and Let Die*; the Black-Chinese photographer Annabel Chung in *Dr. No*; Miss Taro, the beguiling Chinese SPECTRE agent in *Dr. No*. In the novels, however, there is a marked absence of ethnic-minority women who are romantically or sexually involved with Bond. The one notable exception is Kissy Suzuki in *You Only Live Twice*, who, however, has become "Westernized" through having lived and worked in the United States for some time. Unlike the film franchise that has moved with the times by developing some more prominent parts for racially "other" or mixed-race actresses—one can think here of Trina Parks's representation of "Thumper," one of Willard Whyte's two female guards in *Diamonds are Forever* of 1971; Gloria Hendry in *Live and Let Die* (1973) with whom James Bond (played by Roger Moore) shares a kiss; Grace Jones's memorable depiction of Mayday in *A View to a Kill* of 1985; Halle Berry's character Jinx in *Die Another Day* of 2002; or, most recently, Naomi Harris's reincarnation of Miss Moneypenny starting with *Skyfall* of 2012—women of, in particular, African background play a very marginalized role in the Bond novels. Most often they appear all but briefly and in attitudes of servitude. There is, for instance, Agatha, "a huge blue-black Negress" who works for Colonel Havelock, or, also in *For Your Eyes Only*, "Fayprince, a pretty young quadroon . . . training as second housemaid" (Fleming 1963b: 46). The usage of the term "quadroon" here is in itself noteworthy—it denotes a person of mixed-race heritage, generally one-quarter Black, and is a term deeply steeped in the language of slavery and so, obviously, language that should have been defunct even in the 1950s. If Black female characters *do* appear in a seemingly professional capacity, they are generally belittled. In *Live and Let Die*, for instance, Bond is startled to see a "negress at the wheel, a fine-looking negress in a black chauffeur's uniform" and ponders how unlikely it is to see "a negress driving a car . . . A negress acting as chauffeur is even more extraordinary" (Fleming 1963c: 6). Yet, although her role is so noteworthy, she does not appear in the novel again. She is merely a foil for Bond to voice his racially motivated and misogynist thoughts—a *professional* woman! a *woman* driver! a *Black* woman driver!—a mere object that passes through his line of vision but neither leaves a lasting impression nor deserves a more extended role.

For Bond, the objectification of women starts, in the first instance, with a gaze, with his knowing and appraising look. Bond is quick to sexualize the ethnically diverse women he encounters—just as he does with all the women in the novels—but also does not shy away from subjecting them to violence, more often than not committed on his behalf by somebody else. In *Dr. No*, the "Chigro" photographer Annabel Chung is manhandled by Quarrel on Bond's behest; he patronizes her and uses violence to gain information from her. Finally, she becomes a sexualized object because of the size of her "Mount of Venus, the soft lozenge of flesh in the palm below her thumb" that suggests that "her'll be good in bed," as Quarrel knowingly informs Bond (Fleming 1988: 247). Similarly, in *Live and Let Die*, Bond watches the voodoo dancer G-G during his night out in Harlem. Although he finds her attractive—with a "small, hard, bronze, beautiful" body—he once again immediately compares her to an animal. Appearing, at first, akin to an exotic bird—"the cloak of black feathers came away from the front of her body and spread out into a five-foot black fan. She swirled it slowly behind her until it stood up like a peacock's tail"—her face reveals the features of a wilder animal: "her lips were bared slightly from her teeth. Her nostrils began to flare. Her eyes glinted hotly . . . It was a sexy, pug-like face—*chienne* was the only word Bond could think of" (Fleming 1963c: 57–8). Just as Bond has no qualms comparing her male counterparts to "apes," he does not stop at comparing a beautiful woman to a dog.

It is remarkable that, despite his alleged sexual prowess and his role as sexual predator, the literary Bond is never shown to actually sleep with a Black woman. That act, again, would not fit into Fleming's highly segregated world where "white" was on one side, "Black" on another and the dividing line was not to be crossed. In *Quantum of Solace* of 1960, for instance, Bond is assured by the Governor of Nassau that "it would never have occurred to this young man to have relations with a coloured girl" (Fleming 2008: 112). This comment is preceded by Bond's own and rather crude assertions that "the only trouble with beautiful Negresses is that they don't know anything about birth control" (Fleming 2008: 112). Women of color are here reduced to objects again, out only to ensnare white men and to reproduce. The quote also hints at a potential loss of control for the otherwise dominant white. As Christine Bold has asserted, "It is no secret that Fleming's fiction ritually works to objectify and infantilize its 'girls,' as these sexually mature women are routinely named; moreover, because women are often exoticised in terms of their racial and ethnic heritage, the novels mount a politics of colonisation across a broad front" (Bold 2003: 172). The Bond novels thus seem to want to include an "exotic" element through the presentation of racially other women, yet at the same time want to exert total control over them and deny them any individual agency.

The racially "other" characters in the Bond novels thus have a very clear-cut role to play: they are meant to be seen as inferior, there to be subjugated and ruled by the whites in general, but the British in particular. The question that needs to be asked is why Fleming still felt this representation to be necessary in the 1950s, at a time when Britain needed immigration from her former colonies in order to fill vital work positions and keep industries going. Starting with the Empire Windrush in 1948, immigrants from the former colonies started arriving in Britain, officially invited to come to work, assured of a warm welcome that, in reality, was not even lukewarm. Politically, there were also lots of changes, with many of those former colonies increasingly being governed by native rulers: in 1963, for instance, Jomo Kenyatta became the first Black prime minister of Kenya, just a year before the country declared itself a Republic. The answer—unsatisfying and racist, yet revealing—can be found in a comment from M early on in *Live and Let Die*: "the negro races are just beginning to throw up geniuses in all the professions—scientists, doctors, writers. . . . After all, there are 250,000,000 of them in the world. Nearly a third of the white population" (Fleming 1963c: 18). At a time when, rightly and correctly, the end of colonialism rang in the beginning of a period of emancipation for former subjugated subjects, offering them opportunities to start careers, to fill positions previously only held by the ruling white men, it was the whites who had the primeval fears, not the Blacks with their voodoo; the whites who were scared of being outnumbered, of being overtaken, of being marginalized by a surge of Black activity. The Bond novels thus actively contribute to perpetuating a worldview that was rapidly becoming obsolete in real terms: the supremacy of white over Black, of male over female. As Cannadine says, the "Bond novels . . . are quite extraordinarily patriotic, fervently embodying the same beliefs in the greatness and innate moral superiority of England"—yet, simultaneously, they succeed only in creating an "international fantasy world" that has no bearing on reality (Cannadine 1979: 47, 55). They are relics, outmoded and overtaken already by real-life events in their own time. At the same time, however, they seem to appease the anxieties of those who were worried about changing power balances at the time.

The Bond films, by contrast, have tried to mask the original texts' racism a bit; there are more racially diverse characters to be found in leading roles there. Even Felix Leiter, Bond's friend and ally in the CIA, was played by African American actors, Bernie Casey in *Never Say Never Again* of 1983 and, more recently, Jeffrey Wright in *Casino Royale* (2006), *Quantum of Solace* (2008), and *No Time to Die* (2021). It is now more common to see ethnically diverse actresses—the aforementioned Halle Berry or Naomi Harris, for instance—in leading roles in the Bond films. Yet even the successful Bond film franchise is still under the shadow of the fiction that preceded it and that, as Ashley Fetters put it in no uncertain terms, has a "history of subtly nasty racist bullshit:" discussion of having Bond played by a Black actor (Denzel Washington was mentioned, but in particular Idris Elba) was short-lived (Fetters 2015). And although Elba is still pushed by some as a particularly interesting choice for a new Bond, the actors who are now touted to replace Daniel Craig as the next Bond—Tom Hiddleston, James Norton, Tom Hardy—are clearly, and resolutely, white.[11] At the time of revising this chapter, Lashana Lynch, a *Black* British *female* actor, has appeared in *No Time to Die* as the new 007 after Bond's seeming retirement. Her role, which caused so much gossip, consternation (for some), and celebration (for many others), eventually turned out to be not a leading role in the film. Given the rather peculiar ending of *No Time to Die* (no spoiler), the rumor mill is now busy debating whether or not her role will be reprised in the next Bond outing on the silver screen.

It is, consequently, in light of the clear racism depicted in the Bond texts, the marginalization and exoticization of racially "other" characters, the continued subjugation and belittling of women, especially those of color, as well as even the contemporary film franchise's reluctance to make a clear anti-racism statement by appointing a "Black" actor to play Bond, that the inclusion of the fictional character James Bond was so problematic in the Opening Ceremony of the 2012 Olympics. It might have been an amusing scene. But, coupled with the war iconography used in it, it was a throwback to the 1950s. As Triviños makes clear, "las novelas de Bond no divierten. Pervierten"—the Bond novels do not entertain, they "pervert": they pervert reality, they pervert history (Triviños 1985–6: 107). Fleming's racially motivated and misogynist worldview was already out of keeping with the time when he first created Bond in 1953. His novels should thus only be read with the clear understanding that they are dinosaurs, obsolete representatives of a bygone time that has no relation to what Britain in the twenty-first century should be celebrating.

Notes

1   https://www.youtube.com/watch?v=xW5abat5NEU.
2   See Ferrebe's *Literature of the 1950s* for more details on life in postwar Britain.

3 See my "Putting England Back on Top? Ian Fleming, James Bond, and the Question of England" (2012: 13–29).

4 "Red" Grant, however, in *From Russia with Love*, is a defector from Britain, albeit Northern Irish on one side and German on the other.

5 Triviños (1985–6: 107). The original reads "Hoy non es possible admitir . . . según la cual los libros de Fleming no quieren instruir sino sólo entretener, divertir."

6 Quoted in Cannadine (1979: 48); Fleming (1963a: 14).

7 Find the image at http://salmongutter.blogspot.co.uk/2015/05/paperback-875-live-and-let-die-ian.html.

8 See Triviños (1985–6: 111): "James Bond . . . sobre todo realiza las oscuras aspiraciones del lector que cree en la superioridad del blanco sobre el negro, en la perversidad del comunismo, en la inferioridad de los latinos, rusos, búlgaros o polacos, en la malignidad de los orientales, en la monstruosidad homosexual o en la maldad de los judíos."

9 See here, in particular, Germanà's recent *Bond Girls* (2019).

10 This depiction of women is limited mainly to the novels. The films, certainly the more recent ones, approach women in a slightly more positive way. In the Daniel Craig version of *Casino Royal*, for instance, Bond shows himself sympathetic to the past history of Vesper, a former victim of rape.

11 See https://www.independent.co.uk/arts-entertainment/films/news/next-james-bond-8-list-daniel-craig-idris-elba-tom-hiddleston-aiden-turner-jamie-bell-a7219891.html.

References

Arp, Robert and Kevin S. Decker (2006), "'That Fatal Kiss': Bond, Ethics, and the Objectification of Women," in Jacob M. Held and James B. South (eds), *James Bond and Philosophy: Questions are Forever*, 201–13, Chicago: Open Court.

Baron, Cynthia (2003), "Dr No: Bonding Britishness to Racial Sovereignty," in Christoph Lindner (ed.), *The James Bond Phenomenon: A Critical Reader*, 135–50, Manchester: Manchester University Press.

Bennett, Tony (2017), "The Bond Phenomenon: Theorising a Popular Hero—A Retrospective," *The International Journal of James Bond Studies*, 1 (1): 1–34.

Berberich, Christine (2012), "Putting England Back on Top? Ian Fleming, James Bond, and the Question of England," *Yearbook of English Studies*, 42: 13–29.

Black, Jeremy (2001), *The Politics of James Bond: From Fleming's Novels to the Big Screen*, London: Praeger.

Bold, Christine (2003), "'Under the Very Skirts of Britannia': Re-Reading Women in the James Bond Novels," in Christoph Lindner (ed.), *The James Bond Phenomenon: A Critical Reader*, 169–83, Manchester: Manchester University Press.

Cannadine, David (1979), "James Bond & the Decline of England," *Encounter*, 53: 46–53.

Cleaver, Eldridge (1968), *Soul on Ice*, New York: Delta Books, 1992.

Early, Gerald (1999), "Jungle Fever: Ian Fleming's James Bond Novels, the Cold War, and Jamaica," *New Letters*, 66 (1): 139–63.

Ferrebe, Alice (2012), *Literature of the 1950s: Good, Brave Causes*, Edinburgh: Edinburgh University Press.

Fetters, Ashley (31 October 2015), "A Brief, Depressing History for a Black James Bond," *GQ Magazine*, np. Accessible at https://www.gq.com/story/brief-history-black-james-bond (accessed 5 March 2018).

Fleming, Ian (May 1963a), "How to Write a Thriller," *Books and Bookmen*, 14.

Fleming, Ian (1963b), *For Your Eyes Only*, London: Signet.

Fleming, Ian (1963c), *Live and Let Die*, London: Pan Books Ltd.

Fleming, Ian (1964), *You Only Live Twice*, London: Jonathan Cape.

Fleming, Ian (1988), *Dr. No*, London: Coronet.

Fleming, Ian (2002a), *Casino Royale*, London: Penguin Books.

Fleming, Ian (2002b), *From Russia with Love, Dr No & Goldfinger*, London: Penguin Books.

Fleming, Ian (2008), *Quantum of Solace*, London: Penguin.

Germanà, Monica (2019), *Bond Girls: Body, Fashion and Gender*, London: Bloomsbury Academic.

Halloran, Vivian (2005), "Tropical Bond," in Edward P. Comentale, Stephen Watt and Skip Willman (eds.), *Ian Fleming & James Bond: The Cultural Politics of 007*, 158–77, Bloomington: Indiana University Press.

MacIntyre, Ben (2008), *For Your Eyes Only: Ian Fleming and James Bond*, London: Bloomsbury.

Triviños, Gilberto (1985–6), "Heroes (y) Monstruos en la narrativa de Fleming," *Acta Literaria*, 10–11: 103–31.

6

"Learn, Babies, Learn"

Race, Representation, and John Birch Society Activists Julia Brown and Lola Belle Holmes

Veronica A. Wilson

In 1962, Julia Clarice Brown, a middle-aged Black woman and former communist, publicly revealed nine years of service as an FBI informant in the Communist Party of the United States (CPUSA). For three days she testified before the House Committee on Un-American Activities (HUAC), describing her experiences as an "undercover agent" in Cleveland.[1] Brown identified more than 100 persons as CPUSA members or sympathizers. HUAC subpoenaed eighteen accused individuals to answer her charges. All pled the Fifth Amendment, refusing to discuss alleged party memberships, radical activism or beliefs, or personal knowledge of Brown. Despite this, HUAC praised Brown's patriotism, emphasizing her contribution to the struggle against communism. Soon Brown told various versions of her story to the media and before paid audiences, becoming a "professional anticommunist" until the early 1970s (HUAC 1962).

In 1963 African American labor activist Lola Belle Holmes "surfaced" as a six-year FBI informant in Chicago-area communist and civil rights circles. She testified before the Subversive Activities Control Board (SACB) that she had joined several organizations affiliated with the CPUSA, reporting to Bureau handlers about those groups' members, activities, and ideological agendas. Like Brown, Holmes reported that these "fronts" were controlled by the CPUSA and ultimately the Soviet Union. She alleged that Reds in the United States had not retreated from revolutionary objectives despite public statements to the contrary. Her testimony was used to convict former Illinois CPUSA leader Claude Lightfoot of failing to register with the US Department of Justice as a foreign agent—a violation of the McCarran Internal Security Act passed by Congress in 1950.

A sewing machine operator at a novelty company, Holmes had attended numerous Chicago-area CPUSA events and training workshops. She described Lightfoot and other African American leftists as sham civil rights activists whose true loyalties lay with Moscow. Having been "outed" as an FBI informant, Holmes could no longer continue in that capacity, and she soon became a witness for HUAC as well as on the lecture circuit as a supposed expert on communism as an internal security threat.[2]

FBI and HUAC contacts helped Brown and Holmes build lucrative anticommunist careers. In 1963 both became speakers for the right-wing John Birch Society (JBS); soon the JBS published Brown's memoir of years in the CPUSA and FBI (Brown 1966). By 1964 both women opposed the entire civil rights movement, particularly the Reverend Dr. Martin Luther King, Jr. Holmes's and Brown's passionate anticommunism outweighed concerns that African Americans suffered second-class citizenship. Their crusade seemingly "trumped" their racial identities at a time when identity politics became increasingly central to US politics and society.

This chapter analyzes how Brown's and Holmes's opposition to the civil rights movement grew even as mainstream public opinion moved in the opposite direction. It examines the considerable influence these women's narratives had within right-wing circles, despite being virtually unknown in US history today. Finally, this chapter concludes with questions for further analysis of how Brown's and Holmes's representations of themselves, the Black freedom struggle, the Reverend Dr. Martin Luther King Jr., and the CPUSA impacted American politics and the civil rights movement.

When Brown and Holmes first appeared before HUAC and the SACB, they were virtually unknown to the American public. Within Midwestern CPUSA and civil rights circles, however, they had played active roles for several years. Brown began left-liberal activism in 1947, after moving to a racially integrated, middle-class area of Cleveland with her husband J. Curlee Brown. White neighbors befriended the Browns and discussed racial problems. Julia claimed she had rarely experienced discrimination but was appalled at stories of police brutality, housing discrimination, lynchings, and other injustices. Holmes by contrast lived in a predominantly Black area of Chicago and was attracted to Progressive Party–supported civil rights and labor organizations. Both women grew suspicious when friends seemed interested in grooming them for communism, and Holmes worried that her Progressive Party background hurt her job prospects in a growing Cold War climate (FBI Holmes File Memo 1956: 1–2).[3]

Brown welcomed her neighbors and their friends' racial egalitarianism. Later she explained: "So here, I thought, is a group of white people on my side. . . . Absolutely no difference. No segregation. It was just as if they didn't know the difference between Negro and white." Soon Brown joined the Civil Rights Congress (CRC), an organization of liberals and communists who provided attorneys to fight civil rights violations against African Americans and government prosecution of leftist radicals. Around Christmastime she joined the CPUSA (HUAC 1962: 993–1003; "I Was a Spy for the FBI" 1961: 96.). For her part, Holmes remained concerned about civil rights and progressive causes but joined the CPUSA only at the FBI's request in 1957.[4]

Initially, Brown felt restricted by her limited education. Needing to work for a living, she left school after the tenth grade and moved from Atlanta to a series of northern cities. After marrying Curlee, she helped build his truck hauling business and to purchase and manage rental properties. Through hard effort, the Browns achieved middle-class status by 1947. Julia's commitment was not to a working-class revolution, but to improving conditions for African Americans (HUAC 1962: 1003.). She believed the CRC would work to prevent lynchings and police brutality, yet it concentrated on defending CPUSA leaders arrested for conspiracy to overthrow the US government[5]

(HUAC 1962: 1004–5). Claiming to have witnessed neither police brutality nor other racist violence throughout her years in Atlanta, Chicago, Philadelphia, Detroit, and Cleveland, Brown decided the CRC overdramatized such problems to manipulate African Americans and foment civil strife.[6] Meanwhile, Holmes reached similar conclusions in her association with Chicago-area communists, who seemed more concerned with CPUSA and Moscow's priorities than the needs of working-class people of color.

Brown's final straw was the discrimination she allegedly experienced in the Cleveland CPUSA. She lived in southeastern Cleveland but had to join a party section on the opposite side of the city, because that group was integrated while the southeastern group remained lily-white. Her duties consisted of secretarial and chauffeur work in addition to the chores rank and file members routinely performed, such as distributing pamphlets and selling subscriptions to the *Daily Worker* (HUAC 1962: 1001–3). By late 1948, Brown believed the CPUSA did not genuinely support civil rights reform, and that it was "teaching us to hate our employer" and "trying to destroy everything that I stood for" (HUAC 1962: 1008–10). She removed her house sign supporting Progressive Party presidential candidate Henry Wallace, posting a placard for Harry Truman instead. In 1950 she went to the FBI. Brown explained her sense of letdown after meeting an agent who seemed unfazed by her revelations:

> The Communists had made a fool of me by playing on my desire to be a good citizen. Finally, discerning the evil intent that lurked behind such phony facades . . . , I had naively assumed that I was alerting the nation to a secret peril. . . . Except for a very understanding husband, I had no one to console me, no one with whom I could talk. . . . [F]riends and acquaintances in my neighborhood had long ago ostracized me because of my association with people they knew or suspected were Communists. (Brown 1966: 34–5)

As a communist, "[s]o subtle had been my enslavement," she claimed in racially charged terms, "I had not realized how completely I had been mastered" (Brown 1966: 35–6). She reveled in her restored freedom: church activities, new friendships, ball games, and caring for their rental properties.[7] In 1951 the FBI asked her to rejoin the CPUSA as an undercover informant. Within weeks she joined the CRC-affiliated Sojourners for Truth and Justice—a Black women's organization combating racial discrimination. Sojourners urged officials to offer redress for lynchings, segregation, police brutality, and poverty—and for CPUSA concerns, such as the government's revocation of singer Paul Robeson's passport. Brown believed some Sojourners "were really trying to fight for civil rights," while the communists in the group refused to support a reformist organization, effective or not. Once they began losing control over the organization to moderate members who wanted to focus on racial issues alone, they dissolved it[8] (HUAC 1962: 1030–9).

Finally, Brown was appalled by CPUSA efforts to "infiltrate" the National Association for the Advancement of Colored People (NAACP), whose leadership had purged most suspected party members or sympathizers from its ranks. Even the staunchly racist FBI Director J. Edgar Hoover routinely assured the public that the NAACP was not "communist infiltrated or controlled" despite Red attempts to join the association. Hoover's staff constantly investigated the NAACP, stating that the NAACP worked for "full racial integration and equality *within* the present form of government"[9] (FBI, "Communist Party and the Negro" 1956).

Brown moved to Los Angeles in 1960, ceasing her undercover work for the Bureau. The CPUSA had tightened internal security due to the Smith Act trials, and, as Brown's presence confirmed, justifiably feared FBI spies in their midst. Brown had fallen under suspicion when comrades had caught her taking notes during Ohio party conventions. When she moved to Los Angeles, she began preparing her memoir and her appearance before HUAC[10] (HUAC 1962: 1094–5, 1103).

Once Brown's HUAC testimony was complete, she soon became a fixture on the anticommunist lecture circuit. By 1963 the JBS added her to its stable of right-wing spokespersons traveling the country to lecture educational, civic, and patriotic organizations about the alleged communist threat. Unlike "mainstream" anticommunists, Birchers insisted that the *internal* Red conspiracy posed a graver danger to US interests than Soviet expansion abroad, maintaining that most US leaders and institutions were already co-opted by communism. This paranoid view was the JBS "party line" at its 1958 founding by businessman Joseph Welch and remains its official stance to this day.[11] By 1965 the JBS had approximately 80,000 members, several hundred local chapters, 400 bookstores, its own publishing house, and dozens of speakers in its American Opinion Speakers Bureau.[12]

Before becoming a JBS speaker, Brown told an interviewer for *Ebony* magazine that the CPUSA "prostitute[ed] the legitimate grievances of Negroes to further its own end." African Americans must understand that the CPUSA was dedicated to violent revolution, not civil rights reform. Yet the party was "weaker today among Negroes than it was 10 years ago," she maintained. "Over the entire United States, I feel sure there are no more than a few real dyed-in-the-wool Negro Communists . . ." ("Spy for the FBI" 1961: 94–5).

In her early anticommunist career, Brown reiterated her faith in Black Americans, especially the NAACP, in which she believed communists had "little or no" influence. Her optimism lay in her conviction that "the extent of Communist penetration among Negroes is sometimes exaggerated by well-meaning but uninformed persons." She disagreed with former President Harry Truman, who allegedly stated that the sit-in movement was communist-inspired: "Truman was wrong. The communists would have never inspired a movement based on passive resistance. They don't believe in that. They don't do anything that's decent. But after it started, they tried to jump on the bandwagon" ("Spy for the FBI" 1961: 95). Communists had briefly infiltrated the NAACP Chicago chapter, she said, but executive secretary Roy Wilkins "moved in and cleaned up" the organization. She concluded, "I'm 100 percent with the NAACP and I think they are doing a wonderful job" ("Spy for the FBI" 1961: 95). After she joined the NAACP, someone recognized her as a communist and spread the word. "They didn't say anything to me," she explained, "but you could feel the air getting cold. . . . Oh, they are smart guys down in Cleveland, those NAACP guys" ("Spy for the FBI" 1961: 102).

In 1962 Brown told *Sepia* magazine: "The Communist Party is definitely exploiting the Negro—the ones they can get into the party. Anywhere they can find a dupe, they will find him. I was one . . . ." When CPUSA leaders went underground after the Smith Act trials, Brown opined, "[M]ost of those who have gotten out of the party are people of my race. Most . . . are religious people—very religious. Religion and communism are just like gasoline and fire. They don't mix"[13] ("Communist for FBI" 1962: 12.)

Yet she revealed new bitterness. "Mrs. Brown," Sepia's interviewer stated, "suffered considerable persecution from Negroes because of her role as a Communist spy for the FBI. . . . 'So many people seem to be angry with me because I have exposed my people along with others,' Mrs. Brown says" ("Communist for FBI" 1962: 12). My research has uncovered no early commentary critical of Brown, but she may have started getting the phone threats and hate mail she later claimed to receive as a JBS speaker. Perhaps loved ones disapproved of her secret life with the Bureau or supported communist civil rights efforts. At any rate, a new self-righteous tone appeared in her rhetoric.

More ominously, Brown criticized African Americans she believed shared communist goals, stating: "The aims of the Communist Party and those of the Black Muslim movement are apparently similar in many respects. The Communists have ordered party members to encourage and aid Negroes to establish separate states within the United States" ("Communist for FBI" 1962: 12). Here Brown equated Black nationalism (which encouraged Black self-sufficiency) to the former CPUSA goal (abandoned in the 1950s) of establishing an African American socialist nation in the South. With the 1920s "Black belt nation" theory meant to attract people from Marcus Garvey's "back to Africa" movement, the CPUSA presaged some 1960s Black nationalist rhetoric, including ideas promoted by Malcolm X.[14] As for Brown, this was a foreshadowing of tactics to come.

In 1963 Brown was hired by the JBS speakers' bureau. Making at least $100 per speech, she delivered dozens of speeches every year from 1963 to 1970 (with an estimated fifteen speeches per month in 1968-69), and sporadically between 1971 and 1979. Brown forged a lucrative career, making more money than she could have in almost any other job she might have obtained as an African American woman with a tenth-grade education.[15] FBI handlers groused that she was "financially ambitious"—a quality, they implied, unbecoming in a Black woman.[16] Her memoir *I Testify* sold several thousand copies upon release in 1967 and several thousand more at Brown's JBS appearances.[17]

Yet *I Testify* is hardly an accurate text, or a consistent representation of Brown's earlier attitudes. Reflecting the preferences of her publisher, the Birch Society's Western Islands press, Brown's largely ghostwritten memoir echoes the JBS "line" on civil rights as a communist plot to destroy the United States. A text that marks Brown's (d)evolution from a pro-civil rights activist to her later incarnation as a JBS fixture and supporter of Alabaman segregationist governor George Wallace, *I Testify* praises the NAACP, but exaggerates communist "infiltration" of the civil rights movement, painting a far grimmer picture than Brown had done even a few years previously in her magazine interviews (Brown 1966: 48–59, 106–56).[18]

Moreover, *I Testify* promotes African American self-help (rather than direct-action protest) as the best remedy for discrimination. In the tradition of Booker T. Washington, Brown advises that bigotry "can best be fought with . . . a dignified determination to defeat discrimination by better example." Civil disobedience or "bad behavior" might "be cited as a justification for continued discrimination. I want my people to be accepted, not just tolerated" (Brown 1966: 59). In keeping with JBS priorities, *I Testify* sees communism as the ultimate threat, and bigotry a lesser concern to be defeated gradually. Insisting she had never witnessed police brutality, Brown described:

> incidents where every effort was made by misguided Negroes to provoke law enforcement officers into some action which might be propagandized as police brutality. You may be certain that [they] were doing this under instructions from some directing force.... In general, the people of my race have a profound respect for authority. They will not deliberately challenge that authority unless incited to it by diabolically clever brainwashing. (Brown 1966: 160–1)

The implications are chilling: police brutality is a myth, and rabble-rousers lure police into reprisals that radicals exploit to undermine government legitimacy. Published mere months after the Watts riot, *I Testify* argues that urban uprisings have nothing to do with unemployment, substandard housing, poverty, or police brutality, nor with viable grievances against public officials. Instead "diabolical" radicals use naïve African Americans to foment racial strife and destroy social harmony.[19]

Throughout their careers, Brown and Holmes played on anxieties of white Americans traumatized by the Cold War, urban riots, campus demonstrations, the growing welfare state, and the civil rights movement. Their speeches were popular because they told whites what many wanted to hear: outside agitators were responsible for the upheavals; most Black Americans were incapable of violence; and if the Red menace were defeated, direct-action demonstrations and white backlash would end. Such rhetoric fit into a long-time Southern tradition of blaming "outside agitators"— Northerners, civil rights activists, communists—for Black dissatisfaction. Frequently addressing the *Brown v. Board of Education* decision and 1964 Civil Rights Act, Brown and Holmes supported white suspicions that such policies were un-American. By the mid-1960s, most Americans polled believed that communists had infiltrated civil rights groups and caused the riots. Brown, Holmes, and other militant Cold Warriors exploited and encouraged such conspiratorial thinking.

By 1964, the Reverend Dr. Martin Luther King and his disciples became Brown's and Holmes's primary target. Like most JBS speakers (and FBI officials), they insisted that King was part of the communist conspiracy to spark racial tensions leading to a violent socialist revolution. Such claims gained credence as violent white backlash met King's efforts across the South. In hundreds of speeches (with titles such as "To Tell All My People," "I Too Have a Dream," and "Learn, Babies, Learn") Brown and Holmes expanded on this theme while King's influence grew in the movement and society.[20]

Warning audiences of the dangers King posed as a Red dupe whose appearances triggered racial clashes that contradicted his allegedly hypocritical non-violent philosophy, Brown labeled King the "most violent non-violent man in America," and "the biggest enemy of my people." Brown accused President Lyndon Johnson, who signed the Civil Rights Act and Voting Rights Act into law and created programs to assist poverty-stricken Americans, of doing "more for Communism than any other president."[21]

Not to be outdone, Holmes insisted that as the former "darling of the Communist Party," she knew the Reds "do not want improvement in the lot of the Negro people. . . . They want oppression and depression of the Negro people to continue" because communists needed something to "thrive upon."[22] In reference to civil rights protests, urban riots, and the emergent Black Power movement she charged: "the Negro is growing mad, and it is caused by the civil rights movement. Their leaders are driving them to their own destruction. It is directed by the Kremlin," from which "all the rioting, looting, killing, and marches come." In the same speech she charged that Moscow had infiltrated American labor unions, the US Justice Department was turning the nation "over to the Kremlin," and that she possessed "documented evidence" of Dr. King's connections to the CPUSA. Rather confusingly she opined:

> We as a race have done more to retard our progress than any white man ever did. . . . We have been lazy and complacent and given over to the theory that white is right. I want to work compassionately for civil rights for all, not just Negroes. All we have to do is prove our worth and take advantage of our opportunities.[23]

Both women constantly reiterated this theme of African American self-empowerment. The best solution was for Blacks to build their own businesses and promote free enterprise. Brown insisted that she hated discrimination, but the civil rights movement was too politically and morally compromised to bring about positive change. A "genuinely anti-Communist civil rights movement" (which she never precisely defined, just as Holmes did not more clearly explain herself above) would gain her full support. But the current movement opposed "patriotic Negroes."[24] Communists had convinced Black people that "a Negro section of a city is necessarily a ghetto," making "Negroes see their dwelling places as inferior . . . thus paralyzing Negro initiative."[25] After the Watts riot Brown insisted, "There are no real slums in Los Angeles, little or no discrimination. . . . Those who refused to work were getting welfare," so Watts had "little or no poverty. What did these people want that any law-abiding citizen could not have?"[26]

While most of Holmes's speeches were delivered in the Midwest and West, JBS chapters arranged Brown's engagements to coincide with King's visits to Southern cities, claiming that King canceled appearances rather than deal with the suspicions Brown aroused in the community. I have found several such boasts in multiple newspapers and suspect that King's cancellations were coincidental. Brown prided herself, however, on dissuading African Americans from participating in demonstrations. When King failed to show or to muster a sizeable grassroots response in various communities, Brown and the JBS interpreted it as their anticommunist victory.[27]

No matter their impact on King's plans, however, these speakers reinforced racism and the white violent backlash, just as JBS opposition to 1964 Civil Rights Act and 1965 Voting Rights Act did.[28] Yet Holmes and Brown refused to publicly recognize this fact. Instead, they insulted, shouted at, and ignored audience members who tried to call such issues to their attention. Relying on information gleaned from FBI and

JBS sources (some were Klan allies), Brown and Holmes repeated charges that King attended a "Communist training school" in 1957 and had Red advisors.[29] It is difficult to gauge how much these JBS speakers harmed the civil rights cause. It is fair to say that such conspiratorial narratives and paranoid representations of a genuinely grassroots movement not only echoed, but helped shape and sustain, the white backlash of the 1960s and 1970s. This resulted in the rise of the New Right and its opposition to affirmative action; the public repudiation of busing to desegregate northern schools; and lawmakers' rejection of antipoverty programs and additional civil rights legislation. This was, of course, part of the JBS agenda, particularly for the farthest right-wing and white supremacist JBS chapters in the South and far West.

Brown was politically active into the 1970s and 1980s, attempting to prevent the creation of a national holiday commemorating King's birthday and life's work. After King's assassination, Brown portrayed him as communist-led and -inspired, arguing that radicals must have killed him when he did not "do things their way" (which begged the question of how "duped" King could have been in the first place). Alleged assassin James Earl Ray must have been part of a Red conspiracy to eliminate the civil rights leader they once manipulated for their diabolical ends. Baseless suppositions such as "King was getting soft," and "the Communists had used him all they wanted to," pepper her later speeches.[30]

For her part, Holmes made equally dubious and shocking assertions. She repeatedly accused the Kremlin of arranging John F. Kennedy's assassination, as well as King's.[31] In 1967 Holmes apparently visited civil liberties lawyer and Warren Commission critic Vincent Salandria, insisting that the CIA had not plotted Kennedy's assassination, as Salandria believed—but that J. Edgar Hoover and Lyndon Johnson had done so. Holmes's allegations, delivered under alias as a supposed New Orleans nurse named Rita Rollins, never became part of her 1960s public record, but both her private and public conspiracy-peddling may provide hints as to Holmes's paranoid state of mind in the late 1960s.[32] "Violence in the streets," she repeatedly insisted, "is inspired by organized Communism—*not* by white racism." By 1968 she claimed that Black churches were dominated by communist clergy, War on Poverty funds were used to organize urban riots, and America's future hinged on electing segregationist George Wallace to the presidency. Holmes had voted for him in 1968, she told shocked and gladdened audience members, and would do so again in 1972.[33]

Such musings inspired grassroots conclusions about King's activism, his death, and the riots following his assassination. "King was probably murdered by a Communist," wrote a woman to the Billings, Montana *Gazette*: "[H]is death will add more to the atmosphere of hatred and violence, than he could have done alive." Everywhere King went, he inspired "sex orgies in the streets, riots, arson, looting, killing and contempt for civil authorities." Why was it "up to . . . people like Brown and Holmes [to] bring the facts to light?"[34] In 1969 Brown claimed that communists had assassinated Robert Kennedy too, and for similar reasons.[35]

Lest we write off Brown and Holmes as political outliers with little impact, we should note that they addressed packed (and mostly white) venues. Dozens of letters to newspaper editors cite Holmes and especially Brown as authorities on the alleged CPUSA-King conspiracy and civil rights and Black Power movements, and more than three hundred newspaper stories presented their speeches in neutral or favorable terms. Contemporaries admired Holmes's mix of traditional "masculine" and "feminine" qualities, describing her as years younger than her actual age, and praising her fashion sense, trim figure, and rapid-fire ability to counter hecklers with well-chosen words or loud counteraccusations. They were impressed that the "light-skinned" Julia Brown looked like "the cultured wife of a successful businessman . . . or a prominent clubwoman," yet was a courageous FBI informant.[36] Some people who disbelieved portions of these women's messages began to question their own opinions. Others simply were persuaded by their spirited deliveries, melodramatic narratives of danger and derring-do, and snappy rejoinders to leftist or liberal hecklers in the crowd. Admirers believed that Holmes and Brown still lived in constant danger from Red retaliation. Brown risked "her life every day just by speaking wherever she [was] invited," opined a Michigan woman.[37]

Holmes lived until 2005 but disappeared from the public scene in 1971. In the late 1960s she grew more shrill, rambling, and argumentative, interrupting and insulting audience members. Several school boards and university administrations, concerned Holmes might spark student protests and local racial unrest, canceled planned appearances on their campuses.[38] In 1967 Manhattan, Kansas officials denied permission for Holmes to use the city auditorium; unable to find an alternate venue, she delivered her speech from a flatbed truck in a local pasture.[39]

Excusing her lack of invitations from African Americans, Holmes always claimed activists had "banned" her from Black groups. In a rare 1968 Southern gig, she spoke at a Black-owned restaurant in Jeffersonville, Indiana, where she praised Wallace and criticized civil rights workers. Within hours of her departure a crowd of 150 locals firebombed the cafe and attempted the same at two other businesses. Firefighters confronted brick-throwing protestors who vandalized their trucks. Officials imposed a curfew the following night and the restaurant suffered at least $1000 in damage—more than $8000 in today's currency.[40] At one of Holmes's final appearances, she chaired a panel at the 1969 JBS Independence Day celebration in Boston, but her three African American speakers failed to show. The best she could do was "hold court" on her own, delivering a campaign speech for Wallace on the hotel mezzanine. Taking audience questions, she opined that communists had frightened her panelists from appearing, and flatly stated that she would not want her daughter to marry a white man.[41] After such embarrassments, and with dwindling JBS members and finances to arrange her appearances and draw sympathetic crowds, it is little wonder Holmes soon retired.[42]

Years after Holmes vanished from the lecture circuit and Brown retired from regular public speaking, Brown made some of her last public appearances, testifying before Congress in 1978 and 1979 in opposition to the proposed Martin Luther King commemorative holiday. Sponsored by conservative South Carolina Senator Strom Thurmond (a long-time ally of the JBS) and Georgia Congressman (and JBS member) Larry McDonald, Brown urged Congress not to honor King, whom Hoover had once called "the most notorious liar in the country," concluding, "If this measure is passed . . . , we may as well take down the stars and stripes . . . and replace it with a red flag."[43]

Brown's and Holmes's careers leave us perhaps with more questions than answers. Other than reading about letters to the editor, packed houses for their speeches, and praise from right-wing Americans, how are we to measure their influence? It is impossible to know how many people "converted" to their message, or how many were already predisposed to believe. Right-wing author Alan Stang stated that the mainstream media has virtually ignored African American anti-civil rights stories. Holmes and Brown are not the sorts of activists whom women's historians admire or most African Americans wish to acknowledge. They are rarely mentioned, much less taken seriously, in the civil rights histories I have consulted, yet may have tangibly impacted the movement. Certainly, they negatively influenced people named before HUAC and SACB and in their years in the FBI, but even sympathetic histories of American communism say little or nothing about such Black informants—either the damage they caused the party or their harm to progressive causes generally.

Throughout their many public performances and their increasingly inaccurate and paranoid representations of the Black freedom struggle, Brown's and Holmes's pride in their accomplishments was clear. Thus, it would be fallacious, reductive, and in fact racist to write them off as self-hating Black women or victims of false racial consciousness. Instead of simply ignoring or lambasting them, historians must grapple with ways to fairly explain right-wing African Americans and to make accurate sense of strong-willed, independent Black women who rejected liberal or leftist political positions normatively associated with feminism and civil rights. Growing exploration of the ethics of representation reminds us that we must grant fair treatment to the motives of all marginalized historical actors and rhetors—even, or perhaps especially, those with whom we passionately disagree.

Feminist scholars Jacqueline Jones Royster and Gesa E. Kirsch challenge us to "ask new and different questions and to find new and better ways to listen to the multidimensional voices that are speaking from within and across" the lines dividing us from our subjects of study (Royster and Kirsch 2012: 4). Royster and Kirsch explain that historians must utilize their "critical imaginations" to responsibly contextualize arguments about our subjects and their intended purposes, as well as their actions and effects (Royster and Kirsch 2012: 72). Piecing together fragmented and frequently biased sources such as FBI files, HUAC and SACB testimony, magazine interviews, and digitized newspaper archives to critically analyze Brown's and Holmes's choices and impacts is automatically a risky business, in the absence of personal writings left behind by these women and made available to researchers. In addition, I have the advantage of hindsight. Holmes and Brown helped create an atmosphere that empowered white supremacists and thus perhaps inspired King's assassination, but they could not have predicted the violent tragedies of the late 1960s when they embarked on their JBS careers earlier in that fraught decade. No historical actors can fully understand their own positionalities in relation to contemporary events, any more than Brown and Holmes could have predicted or averted King's murder in April 1968, Robert Kennedy's slaying mere weeks later, or George Wallace's near-assassination in 1972.

Theorist Judith Butler reminds us that all public rhetors face the challenge of misrepresentation by others; as soon as Brown and Holmes uttered a single word in the public sphere, their words and body language were interpreted by others independently of Brown's and Holmes's wishes. In Butler's terms, Brown's and Holmes's public appearances (and Brown's largely ghostwritten memoir) were "performatives" with "signifiabilities" or significance that could not "be controlled by the one who utters or writes, since such productions are not owned by the one who utters them" (Butler 1992: 241). Thus, such performatives "continue to signify in spite of their authors, and sometimes against their authors' most precious intentions" (Butler 1992: 241). In short, Brown and Holmes had every reason to be frustrated when civil disturbances worsened throughout the 1960s, despite—or perhaps sometimes partially because of—their earnest rhetorical efforts.

Furthermore, Elizabeth Lowry's analyses of indigenous women's rhetoric challenges us to take seriously and not avert our eyes from the justifiable anger of marginalized women (Lowry 2021). Certainly, Brown and Holmes possessed numerous valid reasons for their dramatic cumulative anger: racism, urban upheaval, marital strife, economic struggles, exceedingly limited career alternatives, and genuinely appalled conviction that the postwar society in which they belatedly had managed to achieve somewhat comfortable economic circumstances was falling apart at the seams. While their FBI informant positions provided one lucrative, anonymous, and relatively secure outlet for their expressions of anticommunist anxiety and hostility, that "safe" outlet ended for both women when they testified before HUAC and the SACB in the early 1960s. After that, they became targets of communist hatred and sometimes liberal scorn.

Both women seem to have experienced genuine anguish when Black people condemned them or refuted their increasingly conspiratorial rhetoric. On the other hand, the JBS tours provided generous pay far from domestic work or the assembly line; considerable yet biased public acclaim; and opportunities for Brown and Holmes to give "the Reds" and civil rights activists as good as they got—for a few years, at least, until the gigs became too dangerously divisive and began to vanish. Seeing their careers slowly dry up and encountering increasingly militant young people at nearly every speaking tour in the late 1960s, it is little wonder that both women became hostile and paranoid. Significantly, despite ritualistic JBS and other right-wing commentators' insistence (from the 1960s through the early twenty-first century) that Holmes and Brown were American heroes deserving respect, homage, and commemoration, no one has created archives for their papers or even a depository for newspaper coverage about them. For all their admiration of Black conservative anticommunists, JBS officers and journalists refuse to discuss past and present organizational details with most "outsiders," including JBS interactions with Brown and Holmes. Atop their many reasons for righteous anger, these women lived long enough to become virtually forgotten by their own supposed allies.

Only years of painstaking research in Bureau and digitalized newspaper archives have enabled me to compile this much information on these women, about whom the civil rights, Black history, and women's history literatures are almost completely silent. With ethical and empathetic scholarly imperatives in mind, my analyses of Brown, Holmes, and their Black conservative Cold War allies continue. As Gesa E. Kirsch reminds us, scholars must engage "historical women's lives respectfully and meaningfully," not only in terms of *our* present-day concerns, but according to *their* values and sensibilities as well (Royster and Kirsch 2012: 7). Such projects, no matter how emotionally frustrating or limited by fragmentary evidence, are critically important to more fully understand the complex interconnected workings of race, gender, and politics in the American past and present.

Notes

1   FBI officials, especially Director J. Edgar Hoover, emphasized that informants were not "agents," but employees of the FBI. They did not share the professional status of licensed and trained FBI investigators, who earned the title of "Special Agent." The media, however, tended to use more exciting nomenclature when discussing undercover operatives, so it is hardly surprising that some informants appropriated such titles as well.

2   Attorney General Robert Kennedy insisted that Lightfoot register with the SACB as a member of the CPUSA, and thus an agent of the Soviet Union. The CPUSA challenged the McCarran Act, eventually winning a 1965 US Supreme Court victory in *Albertson v. Subversive Activities Control Board*, which ruled that individual registrations were equivalent to self-incrimination under the Fifth Amendment. In 1968 Congress decided that organizations such as the CPUSA no longer needed to register with the Justice Department. The SACB ceased operations by 1973 and essentially was dissolved by Congress in 1993. In these hearings, Brown revealed that over six years of FBI work, she had progressed from earning $10 a week to making $200 a week in 1963 (plus reimbursed expenses). Two hundred dollars in 1963 is equivalent to over $1800 in 2021 currency. See https://www.usinflationcalc ulator.com/. For newspaper story examples see: "Woman Says She Was FBI Agent in Communist Party," Galesburg (Illinois) *Register-Mail*, 25 January 1963, 3; and "Surprise Witness," Decatur (Illinois) *Daily Review*, January 26, 1963, 1.

3   A 1952 state representative candidate for the Illinois Progressive Party and outspoken supporter of Progressive presidential candidate Henry Wallace in 1948, Holmes worried in the 1950s that these activities had invited employers' suspicions that she was a communist, although she had signed a mandatory workplace anticommunist affidavit. A longtime member of the International Ladies' Garment Workers Union (ILGWU) Local 212 in Chicago as well as a left-liberal, Holmes had supported civil rights efforts and labor unions for years, but now these affiliations might harm her job prospects—part of why she turned to the FBI for assistance with convincing her employer of her anticommunist bona fides. Soon she became a paid informant to fight CPUSA influence in progressive, civil rights, and labor circles. See FBI Holmes File Memorandum (1956: 1–6).

4   Holmes's biographical information is difficult to find. Unlike Brown, she gave no national magazine interviews and wrote no published memoir. We must interpret her life based on the frustratingly partial and frequently biased data found in HUAC transcripts, FBI files, JBS sources, and newspaper coverage of her public appearances. I have made several attempts to contact Holmes's descendants in the Chicago area and through ancestry websites, to no avail.

5   The Justice Department hoped to destroy the party through intimidation and bankruptcy. CPUSA allies protested the arrests and trials from 1949 until the 1950s, when the Supreme Court effectively overturned the Smith Act (Horne 1988).

6   Brown's middle-class status and integrated neighborhood may have sheltered her from police violence, particularly in urban ghettos. Or she may have overemphasized her

arguments to gain the favor of HUAC's conservative members. Holmes, by contrast, lived in the South Side of Chicago, more exposed to urban racial problems in that location.

7 The Browns' 123rd Street residence in Cleveland was a triplex. They rented apartments on the second and third floors. Rental incomes and profits from Curlee's truck-hauling business enabled them "to live comfortably and to bank an appreciable sum each month" (Brown 1966: 36).

8 Also see McDuffie (2011).

9 Also see Powers (1987); Leonard (2005): 16–23; and Brown (1966): 87–9, 100–3, 124–7.

10 The FBI had so infiltrated the CPUSA that by the late 1950s, perhaps one-third of the party was secretly in the Bureau's employ. In identifying alleged Communists, Brown accused another Black informant. With FBI permission, Melvin Hardin admitted he had been an informant for eight years, and his wife for four. See "A Communist for the FBI 'Exposes' Another One," *New York Times*, June 7, 1962, 15.

11 By 1965, "responsible" conservatives condemned JBS ties to anti-Semitic and white supremacist organizations. The JBS publicly denied such bigotry, but some members joined groups such as the Ku Klux Klan and Christian Identity movement. See Diamond (1995); Epstein and Forster (1967); and Powers (1995).

12 Cited in the most recent comprehensive work on the JBS, Mulloy (2014). It is important to recognize that, due to the JBS's secrecy and notorious reluctance to share data about their member numbers or identity to outsiders, membership figures are only estimates based on investigators and academics' painstaking calculations. The Society tended to overinflate its numbers in its newsletters and speeches.

13 "Communist for the FBI," *Sepia*, September 1962, 12.

14 Ibid., 11. Bureau officials commiserated that Brown should only discuss activities about which she had firsthand knowledge, opining that Brown "is not qualified to assert herself as a spokesman for what is happening in the CP across the country." See Julia C. Brown HQ file 100-382107-70.

15 For fees see "Negro Speakers at Birch Group 'Seminar' Assail Rights Drive as Red Plot," *New York Times*, March 21, 1966, 23.

16 Agents worried she might "capitalize on her experience in the Communist Party to her financial advantage, and for the prestige she may believe such publicity will afford her." See Julia Brown Los Angeles FBI File, #A-12, SAC (Special Agent in Charge) Cleveland to SAC Los Angeles.

17 JBS supporters often purchased multiple copies for school and public libraries, to counter "Communist" views on civil rights.

18 Brown lamented that ghostwriter Carleton Young expressed views of the "lunatic right," yet her speeches included long excerpts from *I Testify*. Brown never repudiated the book and thanked Young in her acknowledgements. See FBI Los Angeles File, serial #A-129, SAC Los Angeles to J. Edgar Hoover, August 8, 1963; and Los Angeles File, serial #A-119, SAC Los Angeles to J. Edgar Hoover, March 28, 1963.

19 For analysis of the Watts riot that takes into account the socioeconomic factors Brown ignored, see Horne 1997.

20 Holmes or the JBS speakers' bureau here satirized "Burn, Baby, Burn," a slogan attributed to Black radical H. Rap Brown in the late 1960s, denoting his hope for urban riots as instruments of revolutionary social change.

21 "Communist Movement Told," *Lima* (Ohio) *News*, April 26, 1964, 42; "Former Counterspy Says Nation Infiltrated with Reds," *Nashua* (N.H.) *Telegraph*, May 28, 1964, 1; and "King a Pawn, Says Negro," *Kingsport* (Tenn.) *Times*, September 14, 1965, 1.

22 "Ten Ejected by HUAC in Chicago," Madison, Wisc. *Capital Times*, May 26, 1965, 4.

23 "Negro Hits Own Race," *Delaware County* (Pa.) *Daily Times*, August 26, 1966, 14.

24 "Infiltration Tactics Told by Ex-Communist," *Lebanon* (Pa.) *Daily News*, March 10, 1967, 1, 21.

25 "Negro in Birch Talk Hits Rights 'Dupes,'" Long Beach, Ca., *Press-Telegram*, September 25, 1964, B-2.

26 Brown (1966: 280–1).

27 Brown spoke in Petersburg, VA. in advance of King's appearance. A JBS spokesman said, "We do frankly hope that [Brown's] appearance will lead to King's trip here being cancelled." Petersburg *Progress-Index*, March 21, 1968, 15. JBS activist Alan Stang sometimes accompanied Brown to help "explain the scheme before [King's] terrorists arrived to foment animosity." In Sandersville, GA, Brown and Stang told audiences "which organizations and people [King] worked with and fronted for . . . , what his purpose was. We explained that he was trying to divide the races and foment violence . . . ." Stang, "Martin Luther King, Jr.: Communist Fraud," http://www.etherzone.com /2004/stang011604.shtml.

28 "Calls For Large Attendance, Boycott Asked for Julia Brown's Free Speech," *Danville* (Va.) *Register*, March 24, 1968, 13. Brown's appearances sparked opposition. Officers of Danville's Blanks Club urged "citizens of good will to refrain from attending" her speech. The Club was "composed of some of the city's most influential and successful Negro business and professional leaders" —evidence of Brown's limited appeal to "respectable" African Americans.

29 The Highlander Folk School in Monteagle, TN trained activists for pacifist and civil rights work. King visited the school in 1957 and was photographed near a CPUSA member. The photographer, Klansman Edwin Friend, tailed King for the Georgia Commission on Education, which wanted "evidence" of a Red conspiracy with which to discredit civil rights activism. The Commission's report can be found here: http:// mdah.state.ms.us/arlib/contents/er/sovcom/result.php?image=/data/sov_commission/ images/png/cd06/041961.png&otherstuff. This infamous photo graced many southern billboards: https://www.loc.gov/pictures/item/98503183/.

30 "TACT Speaker Claims Civil Riots Red-Led," *Tucson Daily Citizen*, August 3, 1968, 19.

31 "What Will the Communists Do Nov. 8?" Appleton, Wisconsin *Post-Crescent*, September 25, 1969, 4. In this appearance Holmes insisted Communists had a destructive plan for 8 November 1969, but she refused to clarify. When Oshkosh State University Young Republicans questioned her, she dismissed it as "smart talk." The 1964 Civil Rights Act, she said, had been written by Communists during her tenure in the party.

32 Kelin (2007: 345–8, 369). Attorney Vincent J. Salandria (1926–1990) continued to claim CIA involvement in the Kennedy assassination, insisting (with little basis, according to most political historians) that the president was murdered by "the national security state" for trying to end the Cold War. For more, see Salandria (2004).

33 "Woman Blames Communists for Street Violence," *La Crosse* (Wisc.) *Tribune*, January 30, 1969, 3; "Woman Speaks for Wallace, Saying Negroes Communists," *Los Angeles Sentinel*, March 27, 1969, A–1; "Speaker Alleges OEO Funds Are Financing Racial Strife in U.S.," Kalispell, Wisconsin *Daily Inter-Lake*, February 25, 1969, 1.

34 "'Facts' On King," *Billings Gazette*, April 12, 1968, 4.

35 "Charleston Loaded with Reds, Former FBI Informant Feels," Charleston, West Virginia *Gazette-Mail*, February 16, 1969, 5.

36 "Undercover Agent Tells Experiences," Waterloo, Iowa *Daily Courier*, February 7, 1971, 39.

37 "Great Black Americans Listed," Benton Harbor, Michigan *News-Palladium*, January 21, 1972, 2.

38 "Board Rejects TACT Speaker at La Crescent," *Winona* (Minn.) *Daily News*, March 20, 1968, 9.

39 "Civil Rights Platform a Truck Bed," *Kansas City Times*, July 26, 1967, 38. Manhattan is home to Kansas State University. Worried about campus turmoil, the city commission also canceled a JBS showing of *Anarchy, U.S.A.*—a film about University of California at Berkeley students protesting San Francisco HUAC hearings in 1960.

40 "Pro-Wallace Talk Triggers Violence," *Florence* (S.C.) *Morning News*, July 14, 1968, 2. For 1968's versus current monetary values, see https://www.usinflationcalculator.com/ (accessed February 10, 2022).

41 "Is the John Birch Society Losing Its Grip?" *Anniston* (Ala.) *Star*, August 10, 1969, 5. The author attributes drastically reduced convention attendance (approximately 1,000, compared to 2,000–3,000 in previous years) to the JBS virtual takeover by the 1972 George Wallace presidential campaign.

42 Jeffersonville lies across the Ohio River from Louisville, Kentucky. The Louisville race riots of May 1968 had spilled over into the same predominantly Black Jeffersonville neighborhood—making it a predictably risky endeavor to host Holmes in the first place. The restaurant, Tex's Barbeque House, was able to rebuild. As for the shrinkage of the Birch Society, Mulloy estimates that at its heyday in the mid-1960s, the JBS had 60,000–70,000 members. Its growing notoriety drove some conservatives away throughout the 1960s, and in the 1970s new right-wing grassroots organizations lured potential members away into projects to reinstate school prayer, overturn the 1973 *Roe v. Wade* Supreme Court decision to legalize abortion rights, abolish sex education in public schools, and oppose ratification of the Equal Rights Amendment. It did not help that JBS founder Robert Welch embraced conspiracy theories of ancient Illuminati who ran the world and controlled global Communism for their own inscrutable and malign purposes. See Mulloy (2014: 183–9).

43 "Famous Black Birchers: Red, White, and Blue American," and "An Anti-Communist Negro Makes This Appeal: Please Don't Help Glorify Martin Luther King," The John Birch Society website, http://www.jbs.org (accessed January 5, 2006).

References

Brown, Julia (1966), *I Testify: My Years as an F.B.I. Undercover Agent*, Boston: Western Islands.

Butler, Judith (1992), *Bodies That Matter: On the Discursive Limits of "Sex,"* New York: Routledge.

"Communist for FBI," (September 1962), *Sepia*, 11–12.

Diamond, Sara (1995), *Roads to Dominion: Right-Wing Movements and Political Power in the United States*, New York: Guilford Press.

Epstein, Benjamin R. and Arnold Forster (1967), *The Radical Right: Report on the John Birch Society and Its Allies*, New York: Random House.

Federal Bureau of Investigation (1956a), "The Communist Party and the Negro." Cited at independent scholar Ernie Lazar's "John Birch Society's Endless Enemies" website, http://birchers.blogspot.com.

Federal Bureau of Investigation (1956b), "Lola Belle Holmes File Office Memorandum: Chicago Special Agent in Charge to Director J. Edgar Hoover," 7 February.

Horne, Gerald (1988), *Communist Front?: The Civil Rights Congress, 1946–1956*, Rutherford: Fairleigh Dickinson University Press.

Horne, Gerald (1997), *Fire This Time: The Watts Uprising and the 1960s*, Boston: Da Capo Press.

House Committee on Un-American Activities (1962), "Hearings before the Committee on Un-American Activities: Communist Activities in the Cleveland, Ohio, Area," *87th Congress, 2nd Session, 4–6 June 1962*. Washington: U.S. Government Printing Office.

"I Was a Spy for the FBI" (March 1961), *Ebony*, 16: 94–8, 100, 102–3.

Kelin, John (2007), *Praise from a Future Generation: The Assassination of John F. Kennedy and the First Generation Critics of the Warren Report*, San Antonio: Wings Press.

Leonard, Kevin A. (2005), "'I Am Sure You Can Read between the Lines': Cold War Anti-Communism and the NAACP in Los Angeles," *Journal of the West*, 44 (2): 16–23.

Lowry, Elizabeth (2021), "Invitational Anger," in Amy E. Dayton and Jennie L. Vaughn (eds), *Ethics and Representation in Feminist Rhetorical Research*, 57–69, Pittsburgh: University of Pittsburgh Press.

McDuffie, Erik S. (2011), *Sojourning for Freedom: Black Women, American Communism, and the Making of Black Left Feminism*, Durham: Duke University Press.

Mulloy, D. J. (2014), *The World of the John Birch Society: Conspiracy, Conservatism, and the Cold War*, Nashville: Vanderbilt University Press.

Powers, Richard Gid (1987), *Secrecy and Power: The Life of J. Edgar Hoover*, New York: Free Press.

Powers, Richard Gid (1995), *Not Without Honor: The Story of American Anticommunism*, New York: Free Press.

Royster, Jacqueline Jones and Gesa E. Kirsch (2012), *Feminist Rhetorical Practices: New Horizons for Rhetoric, Composition, and Literary Studies*, Carbondale: Southern Illinois University Press.

Salandria, Vincent J. (2004), *False Mystery: Essays on the Assassination of JFK*, Louisville: Square Deal Press.

7

"A New Class of Domesticity"

Home, Abroad, Foreignness, and Masculinity in Len Deighton's *The Ipcress File* and John le Carré's *The Spy Who Came in from the Cold*

Ann Rea

Two spy novels published in the early 1960s, Len Deighton's *The Ipcress File* and John le Carré's *The Spy Who Came in from the Cold* (Deighton 1962; le Carré 1963), surprisingly perhaps, depict domesticity as a central preoccupation, something readers might expect narratives of espionage to exclude. In these texts, a complex sense of domesticity also signifies the spy's sense of his nation, as his home country. Both texts depict tensions between domesticity and its opposites, variously what is "abroad," and therefore foreign, or simply the public sphere, as opposed to the home. "Domesticity" here can connote both being "at home," with the comforts of home, among the intimacy of others in emotional warmth, on one's home soil, or Britain, as opposed to being out in the field, as a spy. The terms "foreign" and "abroad" are therefore associated with "the cold" in le Carré's novel, but in Len Deighton's novel there are more positive "foreign" influences at work on the home. The as-yet-unnamed Harry Palmer's[1] domestic life reveals and helps to prompt a cultural change, especially in British masculine behavior, in the early 1960s, as Britain emerges from postwar austerity. Deighton depicts Harry's taste for continental influences in gastronomy and cooking,[2] showing his cosmopolitan, sophisticated masculinity that amounts to a youthful modernization of British manhood. These mostly Mediterranean influences allow him, in turn, to defiantly, even impudently, assert a modern, middle-class, *chic* challenge to the traditional, upper-class, public school English Establishment of the Service. The film adaptation of the novel by Harry Saltzman popularizes these aspects of Palmer still further by associating him with Swinging London and fashionable style in his short raincoat[3] and trendy glasses. In contrast with Harry's swinging, modern dress and exotic, Mediterranean food, Leamas in le Carré's text inhabits enduring vestiges of austerity Britain, and a powerlessness that we might locate in Britain's Cold War politics, and in the influence on postwar British culture of French existentialism.[4] These both contribute to Leamas's domestic impoverishment, and professional and civic disempowerment, couched as a universal national experience. Against this, Leamas counters a desire for domesticity and romantic love that compounds with his disempowerment in the Service.[5] He exhibits a version of masculinity driven by duty, to both his country and to the woman in his life, which produces a stalwart inability to express emotion in turn linked to his belief that spies should exist without emotional warmth because of the security risks it poses. So le Carré's novel opposes ideas about being at home and abroad in a complex way, since Leamas craves the domestic life he is excluded from, and potentially as an Irishman, craves full inclusion in the Service and the Britain that also exclude him.[6] Meanwhile, Deighton's protagonist introduces foreign epicurean elements into his domestic life, thereby refreshing Britain's masculine domestication, perhaps partly in response to the perception that, after the exposures of Burgess, Maclean and Philby, the Service and even Britain itself, have been emasculated.

For many writers and readers, though, espionage fiction allows an imaginative engagement with a variety of positions in the nation, even, perhaps, treason. Erin Carlston urges that the fictional spy offers "the trope of treason, [. . . as] a way of registering a genuine and profound sense of alienation, skepticism or even outrage," and that with Britain's growing bureacratization in the mid-1960s, fictions of espionage can offer an imaginative resistance to approved relationships to organizations (Carlston 2013: 6). Both Alec Leamas and Harry Palmer encounter difficult truths about the Service and the country they have pledged to serve, including a confrontation with their own powerlessness within that structure. Leamas must face betrayal by the Circus which countenances Mundt's—the former Nazi's—double agency and its willingness to manipulate Leamas himself and Liz, and even to expend her to protect Mundt. The "thrills" in *The Ipcress File* show Palmer observing Britain's involvement in the plot in Lebanon, in which he throws a sticky bomb, killing the man who had sat beside him on the plane. He impassively witnesses the American test of a nuclear bomb, powerless in relation to the Establishment figures around him, some of whom, like Dalby, will prove to be traitors. Both agents stand as ordinary men with access to special, insider knowledge about the complexities and perfidies among the British themselves and their allies, and so serve as bridges to these worlds for readers. As Rosie White comments, "Where Buchan and Fleming describe fantasies of individual agency, Deighton and le Carré indicate a lack of agency, describing anti-heroic little men locked within bureaucratic machines" (White 2007: 33). The fictions describe the agents' place within Britain, therefore, as much as in the wider world, and so consist of domestic narratives about the home country, and the kind of place these men, and readers, can occupy within it, as well as within domesticity.

Fictions of Espionage and Domesticity

A truism of literary criticism about spy fiction, especially imperial adventure spy novels by, for example, John Buchan, is that the male protagonist becomes a spy to avoid the stifling emasculation of domesticity. Richard Hannay, newly returned from the Empire, feels listless and enervated in London, fretting with boredom until the case draws him in.[7] Espionage, like the Empire, offers stimulating adventure, promising to test the man's mettle and prevent the introspection that might lead to melancholy or depression. Home appears inhospitable to the colonial man,[8] this fiction implies, as if he belongs on foreign soil, albeit British imperial soil, which will liberate his version of masculinity. The imperial spy novel, the source of later spy fiction, was not domestic fiction, although we can certainly argue that like later spy fiction it is middlebrow:[9] spy fiction generally repudiates domestic life, at least until the 1960s, before which its spy protagonists barely eat, sleep and bathe, never mind observing epicureanism and taste in domestic interiors. The plethora of domestic details in the early pages of *The Spy Who Came in from the Cold* and *The Ipcress File*, in descriptions of the surroundings of senior members of the Service, who remain at home while the spy is "out in the cold," evoke the domestic life in England that spies usually relinquish. Le Carré's portrayal of the bureaucratized, middle-class masculinity that appears universal in postwar Britain,[10] and that may explain the enormous popularity of this fiction, also places enormous constraints on Leamas, but Harry Palmer uses an iteration of domesticity to assert an impudent, aspirational, middle-class, if perhaps ultimately merely gestural, masculinity with internationalist sympathies. Deigton might suggest that, powerless in the nation overall, and certainly powerless in the larger world, Palmer can at least exert power over his domestic life and his presentation as masculine.

The Ipcress File and *The Spy Who Came in from the Cold* disrupt the simple binary between home and abroad, and between feminine and masculine spheres, in protagonists who crave domesticity or embrace aspects of it. Leamas craves affection and domestic comfort—to "come in from the cold"—and Harry Palmer embraces continental sophistication in food and domestic interiors, making them acceptably masculine and heterosexual because they denote sexually attractive modern distinction. In Harry Saltzman's film adaptation of *The Ipcress File* in particular, Harry's Swinging London style offers clear visual meaning and appeal. In the novel, his sophisticated taste in food denotes his awareness of London's Mediterranean immigrants whose delicatessens and restaurants elevate English food to continental gastronomy. When he is in the field, his knowledge of foreign places and food provides readers an element of exotic vicarious tourism.[11] This sophistication in turn asserts a challenge, at once meritocratic, middle-class, urban, and youthful, to the stuffy "Establishment" pedigrees of his superiors in the Service. His aspirational continental sophistication counters more traditional, English, class-bound ideas of elegance.[12] Palmer's democratized glamour allows a kind of display often anathemized for English men and offers a middlebrow guide to readers wishing to emulate it.[13] Compellingly, this embrace of the foreign and continental taste and style occurs at a historical moment that critic Jed Esty[14] characterizes as an inward turn in British culture, and a "shrinking" of Britain's sense of its place in the world, produced by the loss of the Empire.[15]

Jed Esty, in arguing that Britain's culture turned inward in this period toward a "national particularism," overlooks middlebrow fictions of espionage that examined Britain's place in the world, its reduced diplomatic power after the Second World War and especially after Suez, and the resulting sense of emasculation (9). This fiction depicts Britain in a postwar, Cold War world order defined, largely, by the Iron Curtain which created new constructions of foreignness and domesticity. Michael Denning marks a sharp contrast to Esty's formulation of British culture as inward-looking, when he asserts,

> The [. . .] major appeal of the spy thriller is its map of the world. [T]he thriller takes the globe as its setting; [. . . and] its map shows not simply the "exotic," but an entire world system, an international order of nations. This map was drawn with the hand of Empire [. . . and] remains one of the few genres, popular or literary, that are able to tell an international plot. If these plots often provide mystified and mendacious maps to the international order, it is perhaps less the fault of the genre than of the culture and society which can only imagine the relations between nations and peoples through the conspiracies of secret agents and spies. For a genre is finally a cover story for a culture, and in this lies the success and failure of the spy thriller, its utopia and its ideology. (Denning 1987: 152)

These cover stories can engage in the exploration of existential dilemmas facing the spy as the citizen of a world order in which identity and citizenship can appear contingent, and where workers can confront powerlessness in the growing bureaucracies. And espionage narratives depict responses to Britain's shrinking political role in the world, various constructions of masculinity and men's place in the institutions of the modern world, as well as the possibilities for masculine relationships to the domestic space, and by extension to the country, from which they were excluded in the imperialist adventure novel.

The Spy Who Came in from the Cold and *The Ipcress File* portray domesticity for their spies quite differently. In le Carré's novel, domestic life represents what the spy must protect, and increasingly the safety and emotional warmth that Leamas craves but must repudiate to avenge his agents' deaths. Many, many uses of the word "cold" in the novel's opening chapters signify the various meanings of the spy's exclusion from domesticity. During a break in his initial interrogation in Holland, Leamas walks near the sea and sees a woman feeding bread to the seagulls. We read,

> He knew what it was then that Liz had given him; the thing that he would have to go back and find if ever he got home to England: it was the caring about little things—the faith in ordinary life; the simplicity that made you break up a bit of bread into a paper bag, walk down to the beach and throw it to the gulls. It was this respect for triviality which he had never been allowed to possess; whether it was bread for the seagulls or love, whatever it was he would go back and find it; he would make Liz find it for him. A week, two weeks perhaps, and he would be home. Control had said he could keep whatever they paid—and that would be enough. With fifteen thousand pounds, a gratuity and a pension from the Circus, a man—as Control would say—can afford to come in from the cold. (le Carré 1963: 85)

Even so, in the novel's opening scenes, we see that Leamas despairs of "agents the world over" who make themselves vulnerable because of an attachment to a woman (le Carré 1963: 5–6). His agent Karl Riemeck, who dies in the opening scene at the Berlin Wall, left behind his lover Elvira who told Leamas, "He trusts me. He told me everything" (le Carré 1963: 4). Leamas thinks "That damned woman [. . .] and that fool Karl who'd lied about her. Lied by omission, as they all do, agents the world over" (le Carré 1963: 5–6). In turn, as Alice Ferrebe comments, when Leamas falls in love with Liz, "their intimacy is indicative of professional and personal failure," and "Leamas's act of love makes him vulnerable to feminine weakness and a failure of control" (Ferrebe 2005: 85). Leamas's identity as a spy must exclude intimacy, love, trust, safety and "faith in ordinary life" (le Carré 1963: 85). Not only is this damaging to the spy's psyche, but it becomes unsustainable, hence the security breaches caused by what Graham Greene called "the human factor."

Leamas will later learn that Mundt, as a double agent, caused the deaths of Riemeck and his other agents, with the collusion of the Circus. The domestic phenomenon that leads to their deaths is finally not intimacy with a woman, but the perfidy of the British Service, the officials *at home*, running a former Nazi double agent and treating Liz and Fiedler as expendable in the pursuit of a "greater" cause. The novel's ending leaves us struggling to understand the title since Leamas chooses to die on the eastern side of the Berlin Wall even though George Smiley appears to strive to confirm that Liz is dead, and then waits for Leamas to escape to the west: his death leaves Leamas on the wrong side of the Iron Curtain, and therefore permanently "out in the cold," as we think at first. But consideration that Leamas has chosen death with Liz upon learning of his betrayal by the British Service, Control and Smiley suggests a different interpretation of the title, in which Leamas succumbs to the appeal of domestic life, emotional intimacy, loyalty to Liz and the end of his work as a spy. For Leamas, coming in from the cold indicates his desire for "triviality," "the faith in ordinary life" and includes domestic safety, emotional commitment, and warmth (le Carré 1963: 85). But earlier in the narrative we read a startling depiction of the psychological and existential threat to the spy in his assumption of "cover," or the role that he performs, in Leamas's case as pretending to defect to the east:

A man who lives apart, not to others but alone, is exposed to obvious psychological dangers. In itself, the practice of deception is not particularly exacting; it is a matter of experience, of professional expertise, it is a facility most of us can acquire. But while a confidence trickster, a play-actor or a gambler can return from his performance to the ranks of his admirers, the secret agent enjoys no such relief. For him, deception is first a matter of self-defence. He must protect himself not only from without but from within, and against the most natural of impulses; though he earn a fortune, his role may forbid him the purchase of a razor, though he be erudite, it can befall him to mumble nothing but banalities; though he be an affectionate husband and father, he must under all circumstances withhold himself from those in whom he should naturally confide.

Aware of the overwhelming temptations which assail a man permanently isolated in his deceit, Leamas resorted to the course which armed him best; even when he was alone, he compelled himself to live with the personality he had assumed. [. . .] Leamas, without relinquishing the power of invention, identified himself with what he had invented. The qualities he exhibited to Fiedler, the restless uncertainty, the protective arrogance concealing shame, were not approximations but extensions of qualities he actually possessed; hence also the slight dragging of the feet, the aspect of personal neglect, the indifference to food, and an increasing reliance on alcohol and tobacco. When alone, he remained faithful to these habits. He would even exaggerate them a little, mumbling to himself about the iniquities of his Service.

Only very rarely, as now, going to bed that evening, did he allow himself the dangerous luxury of admitting the great lie he lived. (le Carré 1963: 120–1)

In these brief dangerous moments, Leamas admits the hope that Fiedler is walking into the trap that Leamas believes he and Control are laying, and he wonders whether Fiedler is the "special interest" they seek to identify. We read, "In matters of that kind he was wholly uninquisitive: he knew that no conceivable good could come of his deductions. Nevertheless, he hoped to God it was true. It was possible, just possible in that case, that he would get home" (le Carré 1963: 121). This explicit reference to "home" as the end goal of the operation and the locus of Leamas's hopes, adds poignancy to the portrayal of Leamas's practice of cover, his implicit trust in the Service, and his acquiescence to his own inferior and unenlightened place in that system.

For Alice Ferrebe, the portrayal of Leamas's reaction to his betrayal by the Service entails consideration of his gender and she draws our attention to the description of Leamas on the eastern side of the Wall when she quotes, "he stood glaring round him like a blinded bull in the arena" (le Carré 1963: 24). She observes, "The metaphor employed here is instructive. The bull incorporates strength and virility even amidst its confusion, of course, but the arena in which it demonstrates these qualities is built and controlled by a greater power" (Ferrebe 2005: 85). Going further, Ferrebe notes,

> The narrative does emphasise the purely subjective nature of one mortal's viewpoint—the reader is unaware for a portion of the novel that Leamas is merely faking treachery so as to achieve the goal of his mission. However, the incomplete nature of this subjectivity is revealed to be characteristic of a position lower down the intelligence hierarchy, for, as Peters confirms with Leamas: "it's part of our work only to know pieces of the whole set-up." (Ferrebe 2005: 97)

Ferrebe helps us to see that, with our limited information as readers, until just over halfway through the novel, even about whether the protagonist is defector and traitor or the one betrayed, we are in a position that metafictionally mimics the limits of the spy's knowledge and power. As Ferrebe, again, explains, "The radical possibilities of admitting the instability of subjectivity are countered by the conviction of an absolute, male-controlled morality" (Ferrebe 2005: 85). Leamas passively submits to the Circus's operation, as a result of which their collusion with Mundt and betrayal of Leamas come as a complete surprise. As Ferrebe says, "Leamas's universe is wholly logocentric and ultimately whole: somewhere, someone knows the truth. That truth, too, is perceived to have a strongly nationalistic stamp—the guarantee of English rational behavior, the imperial moral high ground. [. . .] Leamas's allegedly existential activity is ultimately directed at maintaining a colonial, logocentric, patriarchal status-quo" (Ferrebe 2005:

85–6). Instead, Leamas must confront that the Service occupies a low moral ground, in its collusion with Mundt.

Because he occupies a lowly place in the system, his knowledge is circumscribed, as Ferrebe observes, "for, as Peters confirms with Leamas: 'it's part of our work only to know pieces of the whole set-up'" (Ferrebe 2005: 97). The lowly agent unquestioningly accepts his passive role in this "colonial, logocentric, patriarchal status-quo" until he realizes the extent of its exploitation of him, Liz and Feidler (Ferrebe 2005: 97). What Ferrebe does not consider is whether, if Leamas's "cover" identity as Irish is really true, his place on this hierarchy is further diminished. This English, patriarchal and logocentric system requires the powerlessness of the comparatively menial, and perhaps not even British, man within it. Leamas becomes like the citizens whom espionage claims to protect, and so he sees the family car crushed between the twin juggernauts of Communism and capitalism as he dies.

The Spy Who Came in from the Cold's early pages show Leamas disparagingly noting the domestic details that Control fusses with on the home front while the spy endures the exigencies of being "out in the cold." After the opening scene at Checkpoint Charlie when Leamas watched Reimeck being brutally gunned down, the narration places Leamas in Control's office in London for the interview that effectively exploits Leamas's reaction to Reimeck's death and sets him up to believe that he will pursue Mundt. Even though he is suffering from "metal fatigue" and needs time at home, Alec Leamas agrees to avenge his agents by "taking care of Mundt" (le Carré 1963: 15). Tod Hoffman describes le Carré's account of how he came to imagine Leamas:

> He [le Carré] was in the bar at London airport when a "very rough-edged, kind of Trevor Howard figure" sat down beside him and ordered a large Scotch. He paid with several coins of sundry currencies. He drank up and left. Le Carré goes on, "I thought I picked up a very slight Irish accent. And that was really all, but there was a deadness in the face, and he looked, as we would have said in the spy world in those days, as if he'd had the hell posted out of him. It was the embodiment, suddenly, of somebody that I'd been looking for. It was he, and I never spoke to him but he was my guy, Alec Leamas, and I knew he was going to die at the Berlin Wall." (Hoffman 2001: 75)

Chronically out in the cold, like the man le Carré observed in the London airport bar, Leamas can have no domestic respite to fulfill his psychic, emotional needs even though Control manipulates him by suggesting that he can admit the need for respite. Control articulates the text's first indication of a spy's need to come in from the cold when he bewilders Leamas by saying, "We have to live without sympathy, don't we? That's impossible of course. We act it to one another, all this hardness; but we aren't like that really, I mean . . . one can't be out in the cold all the time; one has to come in from the cold . . . do you see what I mean?" (le Carré 1963: 14). Control's sense of "the cold" already depicts it as an emotional state, even while he also probes and even exploits Leamas's need to remain in the field to avenge his agents' deaths.

This scene in Control's office shows odd domestic details that contribute to Leamas's sense of Control as femininized by his desk job in London, safe from risk. Leamas notes the "shabby brown" cardigan which he supposes was knitted by Control's wife (le Carré 1963: 12). Control fidgets with the electric fire in his office commenting, "It's so dry, that's the trouble. [. . .] Beat the cold and you parch the atmosphere. Just as dangerous" (le Carré 1963: 12). Le Carré's use of the dramatic "dangerous" here is masterful. Leamas has just seen his last agent murdered, with many others preceding him. Dry air hardly seems a danger. The banality of Control's domestic fussing, with his "horror of drafts" and the difficulty of getting coffee made by the "new girls" conflates his cosseted, even emasculated position on the domestic front distant from foreign postings and agents "out in the cold." This adds irony to Control's remarks that Reimeck was probably "blown" by Elvira, his lover, and the danger of romantic relationships, for agents in the field at least, which Leamas resolves to prevent in the future though he will ultimately succumb himself. And, of course, Control clumsily attempts to explore Leamas's feelings about what Control euphemizes as "heavy weight of expenditure" among his agents, but he only succeeds in increasing Leamas's combination of defensiveness and scorn for Control. We see Leamas's reaction to Control's, "one has to come in from the cold . . . d'you see what I mean?" when we read, "Leamas saw. He saw the long road outside Rotterdam, the long straight road beside the dunes, and the stream of refugees moving along it; saw the little aeroplane miles away, the procession stop and look towards it; and the plane coming in, nearly over the dunes; saw the chaos, the meaningless hell, as the bombs hit the road" (le Carré 1963: 14). At the moments of greatest horror, in this scene and in the novel's final scene on the eastern side of the Berlin Wall, Leamas "sees" traumatic images of the slaughter of ordinary people. Twice he imagines the family in the little Fiat which he had narrowly missed on the autobahn and later, as he meets his death at the Wall he sees a family car crushed between the two juggernauts that metaphorically represent Cold War powers. "Ordinary people" are repeatedly invoked as the symbol of the purpose behind espionage. Control moralizes, "We do disagreeable things so that ordinary people here and elsewhere can sleep safely in their beds at night," and we can note that "ordinary people" are always associated with their domestic lives, and here not just at home, but in bed (le Carré 1963: 14). Effectively, domestic life is what the Service claims to protect. To Control Leamas replies, "I can't talk like this" and agrees to stay "out in the cold a little longer" thinking, "Anything to avoid talking" (le Carré 1963: 14). He agrees to avenge his agents by "taking care of Mundt" even though he is "burnt out" and needs time at home, which Control appears to see, but Leamas also sees that to admit he needs to come out of the cold would require an admission of his worst memories.

Spies like Leamas seek to protect the ordinary family in the car on the *autobahn*, seeing them as the symbol of domestic life, but when he sees it again "smashed between great lorries" at the moment of his death at the end of the novel, it serves as the nightmare realization that domesticity and "ordinary life" will never be his and that the British Service does not really protect ordinary people from the opposition between the Soviet Union and the United States. And Control's moral equivocation masks the truth that the Service will collaborate with Mundt, the former Nazi, against Jewish Feidler, Liz, and their own man Leamas. Effectively Leamas's commitment to protecting "ordinary people" leaves him permanently out in the cold and dying in east Berlin.[16] In spite of himself though, Leamas comes to know Liz even though this relationship may have been instigated as part of the Circus's plot to fend off challenges to Mundt from within the *Abteilung*, by which they sought to protect their double agent. Again, the "human factor,"[17] people's tendency to form loyalties based on affection, often irrationally, can function as a subversive force that undermines obedience to authority. Ironically, of course, Control is deeply immersed in, and also compromised by domesticity, even as he makes permanent Leamas's exclusion from it.

The Spy Who Came in from the Cold and *The Ipcress File* as Bachelor Fiction

Bachelors in fiction offer a distinct challenge to conventional domesticity, as we see in both Alec Leamas and Harry Palmer. Nicola Humble argues in her account of the phenomenon of the popular bachelor narrative in the 1880s until the 1920s that "Bachelor texts become less prevalent after the Second World War" (Macdonald 2011: 91).[18] While their popularity may dwindle,[19] nevertheless, I believe, Len Deighton continues and refreshes the tradition in ways that reveal the attitudes of the time in which he wrote. Humble acknowledges that in "adventure stories—John Buchan's Richard Hannay novels, or 'Sapper's' tales of Bulldog Drummond—the guiding initial assumption is that the business of adventure is a job for a single man" (Humble 2011: 90).[20] While this certainly applies to *The Spy Who Came in from the Cold*, the grimness of Leamas's bachelorhood owes much to le Carré's portrayal of him in an *austerity* Britain.[21] Instead of cooking gastronomic delights, Leamas appears to skip meals in favor of liquid lunches, at least as part of his cover. Liz cooks him dinner at her flat when they begin to know one another and takes him food when he is ill with 'flu, but that she does so marks him as vulnerable. His flat is "bitterly cold" at the top of a "dingy staircase" and has "threadbare curtains" (le Carré 1963: 32, 35). He only has one pillow and no cushion, so she folds his coat to support his head. And the scene in the grocer's shop which, as part of the creation of his cover leads to Leamas's arrest, maintains a delicate balance between displaying the depth of Leamas's decline and portraying the grocer as a figure of resentment, in an austerity Britain in which the grocer would be the point of contact between, most often, the housewife and the policies of the Ministry of Food, as rationing even increased in the 1950s, arousing intense public animosity. Grocer-proprietors of small corner shops, like Ford, who refuses to extend credit to Leamas, might stand as widely reviled figures in postwar England. At the same time, in another version of the distinction between the use of the term "domestic" to denote "British" nationality, Leamas accepts the label as "foreign" in appearing to be potentially Irish when he assumes his cover. Leamas's appearance of disintegration relies on stereotypes of the Irish as disloyal, and not wholly part of the English domestic front. And Leamas exploits these perceptions in staging his disintegration, perhaps even encouraging speculation that he is Irish, as a means of creating doubt about his commitment to the Secret Service before he appears to defect, something which will both be validated and serve as justification, in his exploitation and betrayal by them.

Although Deighton's novel was published one year before le Carré's, *The Spy Who Came in from the Cold* depicts an earlier period of postwar austerity than Deighton's Swinging London emerging into the relative affluence of the 1960s, especially in terms of food. Leamas's meager bachelor life diverges sharply from appealing portrayals in bachelor novels of a liberating alternative to married domesticity for the consumption of a masculine middlebrow audience of, presumably, mostly married men for whom fantasies of bachelor life would carry immense reading pleasure. Leamas's bachelorhood offers few attractions, and he yearns for a domestic life with Liz, instead of living an appealing alternative to marriage as characters in bachelor novels tended to do. *The Ipcress File*, however, presents domestic life and the mundane domestic details of bureaucratic white-collar work as *potentially* feminizing, even though Harry Palmer impudently liberates himself from these constraints in his highly competent masculine domesticity and sophistication by cooking gourmet food. By grounding his version of domestic bachelor masculinity in the higher standards of continental cosmopolitanism, however, Deighton makes the novel less *threateningly* domestic for his masculine readers, and simultaneously offers Harry higher aspirations beyond his Burnley, Lancashire working-class background. In the newly meritocratic England in which a bright scholarship boy can rise, the Establishment still seeks to exclude those without a public school or regimental tie, but Harry's Oxford education, knowledge of art, music and fine, gourmet food allow him to assert himself impertinently against Ross, Dalby, and other Establishment men in the Ministry who are effeminized and even marked as homosexual, by their taste in furnishings, their gardening and fussy bureaucratic office life. Indeed, the novel gains humor from Harry's defiance of their assertions of superiority. Even his choice of clothes in Chapter 13 tells us that he, "picked a suitable dark grey striped wool and nylon, with a white shirt, and handkerchief, plain brown tie, and brown shoes to add a touch of rebellion" (Deighton 1962: 90). His recurring questions about his expenses, and the games he plays with Dalby to convince him to increase his expense allowance, remind us that he depends on his salary. Dalby accuses Harry of insubordination too but unchastened, Harry retorts at one point, "Forgive me if my lack of ignorance is an embarrassment to you" (Deighton 1962: 46). Impertinence is an accusation that can be leveled at a middle-class man who refuses to accept his designation as inferior to an upper-class man and offers a marked contrast to Leamas's passive acceptance of the role Control offers.

Thinking of *The Ipcress File* in the context of the late-nineteenth and early twentieth-century tradition of the bachelor novel, a middlebrow form,[22] allows us to explore the ways in which it also departs from that tradition, extends and challenges Humble's narrative about bachelor fiction, and reveals changing thinking about masculinity in the 1960s. Quintessentially middlebrow in his aspirational use of sophistication to improve his social status, Harry Palmer appealed to a wide audience in the middlebrow narrative tradition, with his promise of instruction to the aspiring reader in bachelor, continental sophistication. Harry also offers instruction in the modern urban alternative to pre-war social rigidity of bureaucratic life, even as he reveals the domestic characteristics of that work in all their utter banality: the tussles over expense reports, the tea money and the Nescafé that refuses to dissolve. And the film uses visual style and glamour to take this instruction further. Casting Michael

Caine with his working-class London accent changes Harry's characterization to make him more metropolitan, less middle-class, and to associate him more directly with Canadian director Harry Saltzman's sense of the aesthetics of London.[23] Palmer's brand of British domestic masculinity with continental, as opposed to English domestic culinary knowledge is simultaneously emphatically heterosexual, and even promises heterosexual erotic success. Harry notes that, as in le Carré's novel, the Minister who stays at home on the domestic front is feminized and even queered: on the very first page his flat is described as being, "furnished like Oliver Messel did it for Oscar Wilde," with its Sheraton and Heppelwhite chairs.

In the aftermath of Burgess, Maclean and Philby's defections, anxiety surrounding gay men in the Service contributes to the emphatic reassertion of heteronormative masculinity in Deighton's portrayal of Palmer. His defiance of the Establishment class tacitly includes suspicion about their sexual orientation, as much as for their outdated privilege. As Erin Carlston observes, "US politicians and the American press increasingly promulgated the view of Great Britain as a nation of effete, left-leaning and unreliable pederasts, in marked contrast to the deference they had generally shown the British before World War II," and the British dependence on what the United States saw as "the chummy reluctance of one Harrovian or Etonian to doubt the integrity of any other Old Boy" that led to Britain's failure to name and punish Philby (Carlston 2013: 209, 210). Britons increasingly shared this view of the British Service and the government under Eden as effeminate, after Suez. Fiction by Fleming and Deighton offers various reassurances of masculinity to assuage these homophobic anxieties.

The turn-of-the-century bachelor novel excluded sexual activity, even indicating a requirement for celibacy, in some cases.[24] By 1963, however, sexual mores no longer preclude sexual activity for the bachelor.[25] This works in conjunction with the fact that the narratives scrutinize, and their popularity relies on, what Humble refers to as "the *shape* of the bachelor's domestic life. [. . .] *How* a bachelor lives, and particularly the degree of comfort in which he does so," which surely accounts for the appeal of these novels to a wide readership, perhaps one predominantly of married men. Because, of course, these narratives foreground the portrayal of the bachelor as "an attractively escapist figure to a male readership," although in the 1960s the bachelor inhabits this space alone, even in Leamas's case, in an increasing awareness of his own loneliness (Humble 2011: 92). As Humble argues, "The ideal of independent masculine domestic space is an enduring fantasy at the centre of all bachelor narratives," and in the case of Deighton's fiction, might include women visitors, lured there by at least the temptation of good cooking (Deighton 1962: 103). By the 1960s for the bachelor spy, sexual adventure is a part of his adventure story, even if Leamas and other le Carré protagonists often either crave the emotional solace of domesticity and the "triviality" of coming in from the emotional and domestic cold of austerity.

Len Deighton's novels about Harry Palmer deviate from Humble's tradition in important ways. Firstly, and most obviously, Palmer has no bachelor "chum" to share his eccentric domestic establishment. While he clearly lives as he wants in bachelor independence, he lives well by many of the markers of conventional uxorious domesticity and in particular, he cooks and eats well; nevertheless, Harry has no flatmate to offer a superior alternative friendship to marital intimacy. Unlike Holmes

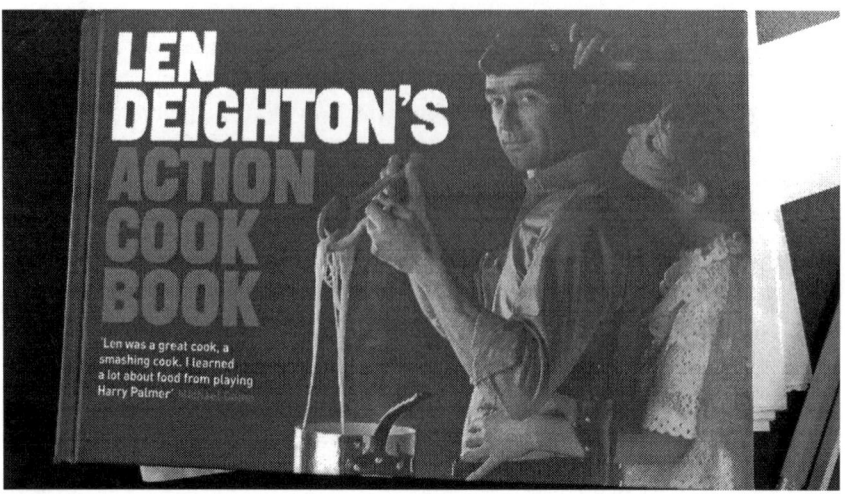

Figure 6 Cover illustration of *Len Deighton's Action Cook Book*. Reprinted by permission of HarperCollins Publishers Ltd. © (1965) Len Deighton.

and Watson, Bertie Wooster and Jeeves, his single state avoids the "closely woven strands of anxiety and pleasure" contained in the implications that these fictional pairs are at the very least queer in not conforming to heteronormative married domesticity, with its restraints and repressions. Humble's characterization of bachelors between 1880 and 1960 depends on the implied vague homoerotic bond between the bachelor companions. Unlike them, Harry Palmer is not celibate: instead, his sophisticated bachelor domesticity appeals not only to male readers but makes him attractive to women, with his cooking offering part of this attraction.

Len Deighton and Mediterranean Culinary Influences

Len Deighton published his cook book, the quintessential middlebrow genre, in 1965, entitled, unambiguously, *Len Deighton's Action Cook Book: Len Deighton's Guide to Cooking and Eating* (1965), which compiled his weekly "Cook Strips" from the *Observer* newspaper. Begun for his own purposes, when Deighton wanted to avoid getting food stains on his collection of classic cook books, he explains in the Introduction,

> I was an art student and it was inevitable that the notes included little diagrams and drawings. During a dinner party, Ray Hawkey, a graphics specialist who was at the time radically changing newspaper design, came into the kitchen and spotted the fluttering collection of recipe notes. He suggested they could be published if they were more carefully drawn and my scribbled lettering replaced by that of a lettering expert. [. . .] To build up a credible supply of cook strips I retrieved old notes from where they had been stuffed behind the flour bin on the top shelf. For this reason

the early recipes were mostly the ones that I liked best and had cooked regularly. And that is why *Action Cook Book* remains so personal. (Deighton 2009: 7–8)

Deighton's mother taught him to cook, although he also learned by working in restaurant kitchens and picking up tips from immigrants from, for example, Hungary, and also by learning about food from his travels in Portugal, where a fisherman taught him how to cook squid. But the subtitle, *Len Deighton's Guide to Eating* recalls our attention to the enjoyment of the products of his kitchen, as well as to their production, and serves as an aspirational guide to cosmopolitan food. It also replaces the impetus behind cookery books written for women, that they would cook food for *other* people to eat. His Introduction recalls that the recipes he learned from his mother, "[r]*is de veau*, tripe, brains, tongue and the rich fragrant stew that only oxtail produces were all dishes that my mother had shown me how to cook, for during the war these were available in addition to the meat ration" (Deighton 2009: 10). The publication moment of not only *Len Deighton's Action Cook Book* but also the early spy novels that feature Harry Palmer, coincides with Britain's slow emergence from austerity's continuing wartime cooking and rationing, under the influence of Elizabeth David and her efforts to improve English cooking and food tastes. In her history of cook books and their influence on the culture surrounding food and on "the attitudes and aspirations of the class to whom it is addressed" (Humble 2005: 144) Nicola Humble accounts for Elizabeth David's postwar influence:

> In 1950—bang!—Elizabeth David burst onto the culinary scene like a firework, like the rising sun, like the clear note of the church bell on a Greek island. With the publication of her work *Mediterranean Food,* she liberated the postwar British from their hell of shortages and spam, ushering aubergines, olive oil and avocados into the shops and single-handedly revolutionizing our food habits and tastes . . . Or that's how the story goes. (Humble 2005: 125)

The reality instead was that, with the continued shortage of these exotic ingredients, David's book had relatively small influence on its publication in 1950, except for those who read it as "a sort of fantasy literature," for a sense of the sunshine and delicious food it described. The cheaper paperback Penguin edition in 1955 not only sold more copies but, as Humble observes,

> By that date rationing was over and most of the ingredients David discussed (chick peas, olive oil, pine nuts, tahini, salami, mozzarella and so on) were available to those prepared to hunt for them. The most excessive claims made for Elizabeth David are those that accord her responsibility for the import and distribution of exotic foodstuffs, but the food shops around Soho were already supplying such delicacies to the Italian cafés and restaurants that had begun to spring up in the area immediately after the war (run by immigrants now released from wartime farm labour). (Humble 2005: 126)

Readers of *The Ipcress File* will remember Harry's stop at such a delicatessen in Soho to buy salami and the garlic butter which melts in his pocket during the adventures that follow. Humble notes then that Elizabeth David, "reached a wider (though still pretty exclusively middle-class) public at the very moment when food controls had at last been lifted, offering them a vision of vibrant new flavours, exotic destinations, and food as an integral part of a cultured, informed and well-lived life" (Humble 2005: 127). Even so, "it was the generation of the mid-1960s who cooked her cassoulets, splashed about olive oil and treasured their unwashed omelette pans—not that of 15 years earlier" (Humble 2005: 135). And Len Deighton's cookbook and his Harry Palmer novels offer the same exotic food and destinations.

And Deighton's *Action Cook Book* has a chapter called "Bachelor Foods (The Quick Cook)," which still emphasizes quality: "no one is ever in such a hurry that they should eat some of the pre-packaged foods I see on sale in my grocer's, let alone feed them to friends" (*Action Cook Book* 65). And the book provides basic instruction for the bachelor who needs to learn from scratch: the "Read This First" section begins, "I have assumed little or no knowledge on the part of my reader" (Deighton 2009: 11). The book explains how to shop for ingredients and maintain a functioning pantry, which wines to serve with the foods, how to insist that the butcher perform some basic preparatory tasks, and suggests that if he grumbles, find another butcher. Delightfully unpretentious, Deighton argues,

> even the serious student of good food (only some of whom are cooks) will learn enough to justify reading it. Throughout this ACTION COOK BOOK I have given the classic recipes for the dishes without substitutes or short cuts except where I have stated otherwise. All I have cut out is the smoke-screen of mystique and witch-doctory; professional cooks have no time for that and neither, I suggest, have you. (Deighton 2009: 12)

The book's marketing invokes the "sex appeal" of bachelor cooking of a sophisticated, continental type and encourages us to conflate Deighton's culinary skill with Harry Palmer's. Oddly, perhaps, a blurb by Michael Caine on the front cover says, "Len was a great cook, a smashing cook. I learned a lot about food from playing Harry Palmer" (Deighton 2009: cover). A further publisher's blurb on the inside cover of the 2009 edition notes, "*The Action Cook Book* was once an instructional book for the bachelor male—a guide to sophisticated cooking for the would-be Harry Palmer" (Deighton 2009). It alerts us too to the fact that "If you look carefully at Harry Palmer's kitchen in the classic film *The Ipcress File*, you will notice a newspaper pinned on the wall. This is one of Len Deighton's classic 'cook strips'" (Deighton 2009). This odd conflation of Deighton with Harry Palmer, and vice versa, co-opts Harry's appeal to male readers as a marketing strategy for Deighton's cook book, and also Deighton's cooking skill as a testament to Harry's prowess in the kitchen, that other kind of "action!"

By the early 1960s, the spy novel has moved away from the imperial adventure novel's sense of the home as threatening to a man, and in le Carré and Deighton, the spy instead craves the home or embraces it instead of expressing his masculinity in a colonial setting that serves as an extension of Britain. Leamas yearns to come in from the cold, even in its austerity Britain iteration, and he holds an uncritical trust for the Service that ultimately betrays him, perhaps because he is Irish, although his identity is unstable. Leamas also seems to crave full inclusion in the Service that he relies on to provide the means to gain revenge on Mundt, though he is ultimately disillusioned. Even though it was published a year earlier, *The Ipcress File* shows Palmer embracing facets of a post-austerity domestic life, notably food, not only to consume it but also to actively produce it. This embrace includes continental and other "foreign" cultural elements. In this curiosity about and sympathy for what lies outside Britain, Palmer not only belies Jed Esty's claims about Britain's postwar inward turn but also establishes a challenge to the existing protocols of how a spy should behave, which in turn depend on older, male, public school authority figures who seek to remind him of his inferior social place. When Dalby asks him, "Think you can handle a tricky little special assignment?" Palmer replies, "If it doesn't demand a classical education I might be able to grope around it" (Deighton 1962: 10).

Impudently reminding his "superiors" not only of their assumptions about his place and his defiance of their opinion of him, Harry asserts a meritocratic, middle-class emphatically heterosexual authority imbued with youthful, continental sophistication against the Establishment seen, by the British public, as effete, ineffective, treacherous and homosexual. By considering the novels as middlebrow, we not only can understand how these texts can assert a revision and reassertion of masculinity for a postwar, Cold War Britain struggling with the emasculating implications of the loss of global relevance that a Cold War middle-class readership appears willing to associate with the Establishment. In addition, Palmer pushes back against, and in his cover Leamas appears to also push back against, the limitations and humiliations of the increasing bureaucratization of the working man's life. While Leamas is shown to be exploited, betrayed, and ultimately expended by his employers, Palmer, at least in the early novels,[26] asserts a defiance that serves as a form of authority. Leamas becomes like the "ordinary people here and elsewhere" whom the Service claims to protect, in his final scene at the Berlin Wall, but ends up caught between juggernaut superpowers in a metaphor for Britain itself in its new powerlessness (le Carré 1963: 14). Harry Palmer, meanwhile, instead asserts a new impertinent, middle-class, masculine authority, firmly heteronormative and perhaps ultimately homophobic, that can only witness America's influence over Britain's foreign policy without exerting influence. Ordinary readers of the middlebrow novel of espionage might see their own international powerlessness in both protagonists or might seek to assuage their anxieties by emulating Palmer's domestic and sexual power, even as they follow Deighton's instructions for continental culinary sophistication.

Notes

1   Harry Palmer appears in *The Ipcress File* (1962), *Horse Under Water* (1963), *Funeral in Berlin* (1964), *Billion Dollar Brain* (1966), *An Expensive Place to Die* (1967), *Spy Story* (1974), and *Twinkle, Twinkle, Little Spy* (1976), although in *The Ipcress File* Deighton does not name his protagonist.

2   Christine Berberich's "Putting England Back on Top? Ian Fleming, James Bond, and the Question of England" notes that the Ian Fleming James Bond novels also exhibit

what she calls, the "preoccupation with food and drink [. . .] that is symptomatic of the time," in its celebration of French cuisine (Berberich 2012: 17). Berberich explains this by noting Fleming's "own passion for it and his wish to impress his readers with his knowledge of the local delicacies of various corners of the globe" (Berberich 2012: 18). She also posits that Fleming may, "wish to instruct his readers [in true middlebrow, aspirational advice-manual style!] in how to act and what to order when abroad," although she also notes Fleming's "revelling in the fact that food, so long on the restricted list, was gradually becoming easier to obtain" (Berberich 2012: 18).

3 Toby Manning argues that the "white raincoat [Richard] Burton sported as Leamas recalled [Harold] Wilson's characteristic 'classless' Gannex raincoat [. . .] whilst channelling Burton's previous anti-establishment role in John Osborne's *Look Back in Anger*" (Manning 2018: 63–4). Manning argues that this "modernized, social democratic Britain of Harold Wilson's Labour, all high-rise estates, technology, the Beatles, classlessness, collectivity and Gannex raincoats" works in opposition to Oxford, in le Carré's fiction, which stands in turn for the "establishment veneration of tradition over modernity" (Manning 2018: 96). For Manning, then, the raincoat Burton wears as the screen Leamas attributes classlessness to Leamas. The short, beltless raincoat that Michael Caine wears as Palmer in the film of *The Ipcress File* carries different connotations, marking him as young, attractive and a trendy participant in Swinging London.

4 For a discussion of the influence of French existentialism on postwar British culture, see Alice Ferebbe (2005 and 2018).

5 As Allan Hepburn observes, the male spy often "wants to eradicate intimacy in order to work efficiently" (Hepburn 2005: 170).

6 For further discussion of the Irish spy and his vexed relationship to Britain, see my own, Rea (2019).

7 In the first pages of *The Thirty-Nine Steps* Hannay remarks,

> I had been three months in the old country, and was fed up with it. [. . .] The weather made me liverish, the talk of the ordinary Englishman made me sick, I couldn't get enough exercise, and the amusements of London seemed as flat as soda-water that has been standing in the sun. [. . .] Here I was, thirty-seven years old, sound in mind and limb, with enough money to have a good time, yawning my head off all day. I had just about settled to clear out and get back to the veld, for I was the best bored man in the United Kingdom. (Buchan 1994: 1)

8 Rosie White asserts that *The Spy Who Came in from the Cold* "contradicts the heroic exploits of Orczy's, Buchan's and Fleming's spy heroes" (White 2007: 31).

9 Middlebrow domestic fiction, beginning in the 1920s and 30s, allowed women and men to explore and evaluate new ideas about domestic life, sexuality and marriage, and was of course largely dismissed by critics. It has received some critical attention recently, although not until 1987, and spy fiction has not been considered as middlebrow. For a thorough summary of the problematic history of the term "middlebrow," see Nicola Humble's *The Feminine Middlebrow Novel, 1920s to 1950s: Class, Domesticity, and Bohemianism*. Critical efforts to reappraise this important fiction include, among others, Kate Macdonald's introduction to *The Masculine Middlebrow, 1880–1950: What Mr. Miniver Read*, Ann Ardis's *Modernism and Cultural Conflict, 1880–1922*, and Mary Grover's *The Ordeal of Warwick Deeping: Middlebrow Authorship and Cultural Embarrassment* (2009).

10 Rosie White quotes Leroy L. Panek who, as she says, "astutely states that 'le Carré uses the spy organization to examine not necessarily spies, but the way in which men serve institutions and institutions serve men'" (White 2007: 31).

11 This goes beyond the Mediterranean when, for example, in *The Ipcress File* Palmer offers evocative descriptions of the landscape of Lebanon and detailed, knowledgeable and appreciative descriptions of the food.

12 Faye Hammill notes the perceived need to push back against middle-class assertions of style when she considers Genevieve Antoine Dariaux's aristocratic style, *A Guide to Elegance: A Complete Guide for Every Woman Who Wants to be Well and Properly Dressed on All Occasions,* published in 1964. Dariaux conservatively reasserted upper-class markers of style, and yet, as the title suggests, offered to make this knowledge available to "Every Woman," even as she reinvokes upper-class superiority in matters of elegance (Hammill 2010: 196–204).

13 As both Nicola Humble (2001) and Faye Hammill (2010) elucidate, middlebrow fiction can both display sophistication, and offer a guide to attaining it. Middlebrow culture often offers guides to emulating chic to the aspiring reader who hopes to improve their status.

14 Esty (2004) argues that "English intellectuals translated the end of empire into a resurgent concept of national culture" (2). Esty argues that this amounts to a "postwar reclamation of England's cultural integrity and authenticity" in the wake of modernism (3). This concept entails a belief that Britain's cultural power declined with its global-political authority, so that postwar literature became "minor." This amounted to "shifting the terms of debate from British decline to English revival," accompanied by a "lost universalism and restored particularity" (6). Before this, colonial discourses "shaped and haunted" the sense of Englishness existing during the Empire, Esty argues, and concomitantly, "the end of empire might be taken to augur a basic repair or reintegration of English culture itself" and might lead to a "restored knowability of the home culture" (7). This amounted, he claims, to a "new apprehension of a complete national life—an insular romance of wholeness, or at least of layered social knowability" (Esty 2004: 8) Esty explains,

> Most of the writers taken to represent English literature of the midcentry, Greene, Waugh, Orwell, Auden, Larkin—remain committed to a literature of existential male antiheroism in a world of corrupt politics and culture. This constellation of writers became representative figures in part because their canonical-humanist conception of literary value, combined with their historical sense of pervasive national decline, seems to have accorded with the dominant assumptions of midcentury English criticism embodied in the figure of F.R. Leavis. By contrast to the aging modernists, their career trajectories tend to move further away from, not closer to, the ambiguous embrace of national identity or book politics. (Esty 2004: 9)

15 See Carole K. Fink (2014) for an explanation of Britain's position after the Suez crisis. This crisis, in part the result of the decolonization of Egypt and anti-colonial feeling, placed Britain amidst tension between the USSR and the US, in efforts to secure access to oil reserves in the Middle East, as well as shipping routes. President Eisenhower refused to support British Prime Minister, Anthony Eden's pact with Israel to seize the canal and topple Egypt's President Nasser, thus undermining Britain's power in the region and on the international stage. Eden was forced to resign amidst humiliation that suggested emasculation and the loss of not only the Empire but also Britain's global primacy to America and Russia. See also Tony Judt, *Postwar* (2005).

16 Rosie White describes the British Service in Deighton's and le Carré's novels as, "a bureaucracy in decline, liable to inter-agency rivalries, betrayal, infiltration by enemy operatives and the human emotions of greed and ambition" (White 2007: 30).

17 This phrase originates in Graham Greene's novel, *The Human Factor,* 2008, whose protagonist, spy Maurice Castle, owes his loyalty to the Soviet Union that rescued his Black South African wife's family, instead of to the British Service, his employers. The concept of human allegiances at odds with national or political loyalties is a common trope in fiction of espionage.

18 Humble charts the emergence and huge popularity of what she labels, "Fantasies of Men without Women," but posits that the bachelor narrative comes to an end with Cliff Richard's song "Bachelor Boy" in 1963. At the same time, though, she notes that, "In adventure stories—John Buchan's Richard Hannay novels, or 'Sapper's' tales of Bulldog Drummond—the guiding initial assumption (as with their literary heir James Bond) is that the business of adventure is a job for a single man" (Humble 2011: 90).

19 Humble (2011) pinpoints the death of bachelor fictions in 1963, with the release of Cliff Richard's song, "Bachelor Boy," ironically the same year as the publication of *The Spy Who Came in from the Cold* (Humble 2011: 91–2).

20 Rosie White argues that "concurrent with Richard Hannay's development as a professional spy is the development of Hannay as a domesticated Englishman rather than a restless colonial. If the Hannay novels take the protagonist on a journey from amateur to professional, they also map his development from lonely bachelor to contented husband" (White 2007: 22). Fiction of espionage, then, has engaged with the matter of the spy's domesticity even since its early days.

21 For an in-depth exploration of life in postwar Britain and the economic condition of austerity, see Kynaston (2008).

22 In her discussion of the phenomenon of the bachelor novels of the late-nineteenth and early twentieth century, Nicola Humble notes that they "cover the 'middlebrow' publishing spectrum, including memoirs, cookbooks, cartoons, and essay collections as well as novels, and their existence in such numbers suggests that the very word 'bachelor' must have been confidently expected to offer an immediate appeal to readers" (Humble 2011: 91).

23 See McMahon (2012).

24 See Humble's discussion of Israel Zangwill's *The Bachelors' Club* and *The Celibates' Club,* 2011 (Humble 2011: 97–8).

25 See Nicola Humble's 2011 essay, "From Holmes to the Drones" that examines turn-of-the-century bachelor fiction, in which she asserts, "Moving into the early twentieth century, it may well be that a gradual relaxing of social mores made sex outside marriage more possible for middle-class men and therefore marriage itself somewhat less attractive—though this is very difficult to quantify" (Humble 2011: 92).

26 Robert Snyder argues that in the later fiction, Palmer becomes compromised by the "political necessity" he confronts (177).

References

Ardis, Ann (2008), *Modernism and Cultural Conflict*, Cambridge: Cambridge University Press.

Berberich, Christine (2012), "Putting England Back on Top? Ian Fleming, James Bond, and the Question of England," *Yearbook of English Studies*, 42: 13–29.

Buchan, John (1994), *The Thirty-Nine Steps*, Mineola: Dover Publications.

Carlston, Erin G. (2013), *Double Agents: Espionage, Literature, and Liminal Citizens*, New York: Columbia University Press.

Deighton, Len (1962), *The Ipcress File*, London: Triad Grafton.

Deighton, Len (2009), *Action Cook Book: Len Deighton's Guide to Eating*, London: Harper Perennial.

Denning, Michael (1987), *Cover Stories: Narrative and Ideology in the British Spy Thriller*, London: Routledge, Kegan Paul.

Esty, Jed (2004), *A Shrinking Island: Modernism and National Culture in England*, Princeton: Princeton University Press.

Ferrebe, Alice (2005), *Masculinity in Male-Authored Fiction 1950–200: Keeping it Up*, London: Palgrave Macmillan.

Ferrebe, Alice (2018), *The 1950s: A Decade of Modern British Fiction*, London: Bloomsbury Academic.

Fink, Carole K. (2014), *Cold War: An International History*, Boulder: Westview Press.

Greene, Graham (2008), *The Human Factor*, Middlesex: Penguin Classics.

Grover, Mary (2009), *The Ordeal of Warwick Deeping: Middlebrow Authorship and Cultural Embarrassment*, Madison: Fairleigh Dickinson University Press.

Hammill, Faye (2010), *Sophistication: A Literary and Cultural History*, Liverpool: Liverpool University Press.

Hepburn, Allan (2005), *Intrigue: Espionage and Culture*, New Haven: Yale University Press.

Hoffman, Tod (2001), *Le Carré's Landscape*, Montreal: McGill-Queen's University Press.

Humble, Nicola (2001), *The Feminine Middlebrow Novel, 1920s to 1950s: Class, Domesticity and Bohemianism*, Oxford: Oxford University Press.

Humble, Nicola (2005), *Culinary Pleasures: Cookbooks and the Transformation of British Food*, London: Faber and Faber.

Humble, Nicola (2011), "From Holmes to the Drones," in Kate Macdonald (ed.), *The Masculine Middlebrow: What Mr. Miniver Read. 1880–1950*, 90, Basingstoke: Palgrave Macmillan.

Judt, Tony (2005), *Postwar: A History of Europe Since 1945*, New York: Penguin Books.

Kynaston, David (2008), *Austerity Britain*, London: Bloomsbury.

Le Carré, John (1963), *The Spy Who Came in from the Cold*, New York: Pocket Books.

Macdonald, Kate (2011), *The Masculine Middlebrow: What Mr. Miniver Read. 1880–1950*, Basingstoke: Palgrave Macmillan.

Manning, Toby (2018), *John le Carré and the Cold War*, London: Bloomsbury Academic.

McMahon, Gary (2012), "Harry Palmer, Michael Caine and *The Ipcress File*," *Film International*, 10 (2): 56.

Rea, Ann (2019), "'Subtle Covenants': Dispossession, Frontiers, and the Internationalist Education of Fiction's Spies," *Pennsylvania English*, 40, no. 1 (Winter): 54.

Snyder, Robert Lance (2018), "'Arabesques of the Final Pattern': Len Deighton's Hard-Boiled Espionage Fiction," *Papers on Language and Literature*, 54 (2): 155–213.

White, Rosie (2007), *Violent Femmes: Women as Spies in Popular Culture*, Abingdon: Routledge.

8

A Queer Thing

The Older Woman Spy

Rosie White

The older woman spy contradicts many popular stereotypes. In contrast to most fictional representations of the spy, she is not young, active, or male. In short, she is not James Bond. Yet there are a number of older women spies in fiction, film, and television series who take their narratives in unexpected directions. The ones I examine here are all white, Anglo-American, and ostensibly bourgeois; deviation from standard typologies of espionage narratives is thus limited. As spy fictions necessarily recount the workings of power, this limitation is not too surprising. In fact, as in fiction, the history of "the second oldest profession" offers itself as a map of white power (Knightley 2003).[1] Even the most notorious female spy, Mata Hari, was a white Dutch woman. Margareta Zelle MacLeod was married to a colonial army captain and subsequently made a necessary living as a "Hindu" dancer in Paris following their divorce, thus establishing the fictional trope of seductive female spy through many iterations of the "Mata Hari" figure in fiction and film (Wheelwright 1992). Julie Wheelwright's account of Margareta's career demonstrates the extent to which espionage in the West is embedded in discourses of class, colonialism, and illicit sexuality, all of which conspired to ensure that Mata Hari was sentenced to death in 1917. Subject to the fantasies of her interrogators, as Eva Horn observes, Mata Hari inadvertently confirmed the "mass hysteria" of the day, where a woman had only to slightly diverge from ideals of the properly feminine to be accused of espionage: "Spies are suspected everywhere. People amass in groups, manhandle the unfortunate victims, and deliver them to the police [. . .] hundreds dragged a girl to a policeman because somebody had accused her of being a man in disguise" (Erich Mühsam 1914, cited in Horn 2013: 170). Margareta Zelle MacLeod was not properly bourgeois or sexually respectable, and the image she had mined for a career onstage as an "Eastern" dancer meant that she was not white enough to survive her trial. The older women spies discussed here are notably distinct from the "Mata Hari" stereotype which continues to haunt women in espionage, as their age seems to remove them from the need to be sexually available to a male protagonist. Whereas Mata Hari conforms to the fantasy of women spies as *femmes fatales* these older women are more akin to what Eva Horn calls "the invisible functionary, the secretary and silent organizer" (2013: 171). Elsbeth Schragmuller was one of most successful "functionary" spies for Germany in the First World War; so much so that the French mythologized her as "a mixture of cocaine addict and gun-toting dominatrix" (Horn 2013: 194). In a 1936 essay Schragmuller proposed that women had a particular aptitude for espionage:

> Structurally the intelligence service presupposes certain psychological components that can be neither learned nor acquired in the pursuit of a given profession. . . . Women possess these psychological skills to the same degree as men. It may well be that women, given their more strongly developed emotional constitution, are better equipped in this respect than men, which explains the role they play in the intelligence service. (cited in Horn 2013: 194–5)

This chapter addresses the older woman as a queer figure, who disturbs masculine mythologies around espionage and at the same time challenges dominant discourses about ageing femininity. The older woman spy evokes a different account of espionage, "queering" its necessary skills and demonstrating that Bond's athletic combat is not necessarily the most efficient way of working. In doing so these figures engage with historical and current debates about women in public life, particularly working in professional roles. Although in the UK campaigns around the Gender Pay Gap may have shed light on financial inequities, it does not denote a general improvement. The Fawcett Society's *Sex and Power 2020* report noted fields which were "slipping back and stagnating," such as the number of women in senior civil service roles, which had decreased from 31 percent in 2018 to 21 percent in 2020. No women of color were employed in such roles. The statistics for public appointments were equally poor:

> The Public Appointments Commissioner is responsible for monitoring appointments to numerous arms-length bodies, such as the UK Statistics Authority, the Environment Agency and the Care Quality Commission. These bodies are key players in the way our country is run, yet the latest data from 2018–19 shows that the percentage of chair appointments made to women was just 31%, falling from 44% in 2017–18. (Kaur 2020: 9)

Those negative statistics are echoed in the fictions I discuss in this chapter, where older women are ignored, marginalized, and invisible. That invisibility is what enables them to work as such effective spies. Their perspectives from outside the boardroom, beyond the norm and the "visibility" of powerful men, offer an implicit critique of the workings of power. Bodies such as the civil service, the UK Environment Agency, and the CQC are implicated in these narratives as organizations that fail to value their female employees, overlooking their skills to the detriment of their own systems.

Older women who work in espionage can travel below the radar of enemy secret services, as evidenced by the story of a real spy, Melita Norwood, a Soviet agent who was exposed—but not prosecuted—in 1999, after forty years undercover in the British nuclear industries. Norwood was pre-empted by a fictional character. Dorothy Gilman's popular novels featuring Mrs. Emily Pollifax, a retired widow from New Brunswick, New Jersey, present espionage as a logical late-life career choice for any resourceful woman. Connie Sachs in John le Carré's Smiley novels has a marginal but pivotal role, while Beryl Reid's performance in the BBC adaptations offers a powerful vision of an ageing female agent. Academic work on gender and ageing has noted how the process of growing old can be understood in relation to queer theory, unraveling stable notions of selfhood and challenging discourses which present identity as immutable (Sandberg 2008). With reference to these and other examples, this chapter examines the older female spy in conjunction with work on queer identities, proposing that such figures disturb the ontological certainties of Fleming's famous agent and gesture toward a more productive understanding of ageing femininities.

There is a growing body of academic material on gender and ageing across the humanities and social sciences. In an overview of literary portrayals of ageing for the Cambridge *Introduction to Gerontology* Diana Wallace notes that feminist writing has been quick to engage with ageing, not least because women are more subject to cultural scrutiny: "because they live longer and are subject to particularly brutal expectations about youth, beauty and sexuality" (Wallace 2011: 400). Much of the work on women and ageing begins with reference to Susan Sontag's essay on "The Double Standard of Ageing," first published in 1972, which has become a foundational text for debate about ageing and gender. In this piece Sontag marks out the ways in which the English-speaking world has constructed ageing women as subject to the double jeopardy of cultural prejudices regarding both gender and old age. Ageing, like all forms of identity, is culturally specific. We are "aged by culture" (Gullette 2004; see also Woodward 1999, 2006). For white middle-class women in Western Europe and America during the late twentieth century, Sontag proposes that ageing is "a moveable doom" experienced decade by decade after forty (1972: 33). Older women in Western culture, she argues, unlike older men, are not afforded respect but rather become subjects of cultural abjection: figures of ridicule and disgust. In a study of jokes about older women Ruth Shade lists pejorative accounts of older women as trivial, invisible, forgetful, mean-spirited, intimidating, toxic, embarrassing, over-talkative, unattractive, sexually frustrated, undesirable, and both sexually predatory and sexually moribund (Shade 2010: 74–8). If postfeminist Western media privileges the "girl" as a sexually attractive and productive figure, the older woman is frequently her abject Other (Wearing 2007). Older women are often represented in popular media as unsexual, asexual, or (if sexually active) as ridiculous or disgusting. They tend to be depicted as sexually and professionally redundant and thus unproductive in every sense.

As Sontag argues, the double standard of ageing—that ageing is culturally different for men and women[2]—is about the double jeopardy of gender and age for the older woman. Femininity alone has its own range of negative stereotypes:

> Women are not expected to be truthful, or punctual, or expert in handling and repairing machines, or frugal, or physically brave. They are expected to be second-class adults, whose natural state is that of a grateful dependence on men. And so they often are, since that is what they are brought up to be. So far as women heed the stereotypes of "feminine" behaviour, they *cannot* behave as fully responsible, independent adults. (Sontag 1972: 38)

Aspects of Sontag's analysis continue to resonate with representations of the older woman in the twenty-first century. Adding age to femininity offers additional forms of depreciation: "The double standard about ageing sets women up as property, as objects whose value depreciates rapidly with the march of the calendar" (Sontag 1972: 38). In a postfeminist context such depreciation is allegedly held at bay by representations of women who are shown to be holding back the years by 'successfully' ageing, but only in specific and acceptable ways. Sarah Falcus and Katsura Sako note that in contemporary popular film and television it is "difficult to imagine ageing "successfully" without recourse to youthing [*sic*] and capitalist consumption" (Falcus and Sako 2014: 205). Women who do not actively fight the signs of ageing are often consigned to social and cultural invisibility. Such cultural stereotypes, of course, provide a fantastic cover story for any spy.

The double jeopardy of the older woman makes her the perfect secret agent. As Sontag notes, expectations of women's abilities in general—and older women's abilities in particular—are so low as to offer them a position below the radar of public life. Stereotypical forms of labor done by women, as cleaners, carers, or low-status administrators, offer them access to locations where information can be acquired. Horn's "invisible functionary" from the First World War is the model here: "As clerks and secretaries these [women] may have disappeared into the great apparatus, but in fact they regulated access, communication and secrecy" (Horn 2013: 171, 191). The story of Melita Norwood is an example of how femininity can be employed as a cover and also a form of protection. Femininity combined with other derogated forms of identity in the West, such as being working-class, over fifty, or not Caucasian, can make women invisible. It can also offer a form of agency, depicted in film and television representations of women spies and assassins, such as *La Femme Nikita* (Luc Besson, 1990). More recently in *Killing Eve* (BBC 2018–2021) Villanelle employs stereotypical roles (waitress, dominatrix, nurse, seductress) in her work as an assassin; another assassin is called the Ghost, because she is an Asian woman who gains access to her targets as a cleaner.

The older women's *invisibility* is thus a professional advantage should she choose to pursue a career in espionage. Older female spies have the potential to escape scrutiny and punishment by virtue of the very prejudices which Sontag outlines. At the end of her essay Sontag argues that women need to escape those stereotypes of ageing femininity; "Women should allow their faces to show the lives they have lived. Women should tell the truth" (Sontag 1972: 38). The figure of the older female spy—when she appears in the press, in fiction and in popular film and television—embodies a kind of truth by *contradicting* the notion of older women as culturally, physically and professionally redundant. She is a person of interest in this regard. Melita Norwood is one of the most notorious British examples of a successful older woman spy; a Soviet agent whose cover was "blown" in 1999 when she was eighty-seven. The then-home secretary, Jack Straw, was told that it was "inadvisable" to prosecute her (Cunningham 2005). As with any information in the public sphere regarding spies, there may be more to this story than the press reports but, at the very least, Norwood's ability to evade prosecution indicates the confusion produced by a spy who is not only female but also elderly. The consternation expressed by her friends and family following her exposure was reported in her obituary six years later: "The neighbours were gobsmacked; her daughter expressed amazement;

and Norwood, with typical British phlegm, said: 'I never considered myself a spy, but it's for others to judge.' Then she politely closed her front door to the media, and Bexleyheath went about its daily business, respecting the privacy of former Agent Hola behind her privet hedge" (Cunningham 2005). Many of the press images from the 1999 story about her career in Soviet espionage depict Norwood in her garden, surrounded by roses. She is represented as very old, very English, and very ladylike—an unthreatening, lovely old lady, in suburban retirement. These images, together with the gently humorous comment about the "privet hedge," call to mind Agatha Christie's Miss Marple, or Ealing comedies such as *The Ladykillers* (Alexander Mackendrick, 1955), where an elderly widow, Mrs. Wilberforce (Katie Johnson) inadvertently foils a gang of crooks who raid a security van full of cash. The elderly spy is depicted as a comic anomaly: a harmless eccentric. Yet Norwood had a forty-year career as one of the Soviet Union's most successful agents in the West, easily rivaling the Cambridge spies. As a lowly clerk and secretary at Non-Ferrous Metals, a British company involved in nuclear weapons development, she gained access to government documents which she passed to the KGB in the 1930s. Norwood was open throughout her career regarding her membership of the British Communist Party and had been known to British intelligence since the 1960s. When the press arrived on her doorstep in 1999 Norwood was unrepentant, telling them: "I would do it again" (*The Telegraph* 2005).

Melita Norwood's career in espionage, like her ability to weather the press storm around her subsequent exposure, was predicated on her age and gender:

> When further evidence came to light [regarding Norwood's activities] following [Vasili] Mitrokhin's defection [to the West in 1992], junior MI5 staff decided not to pursue an investigation because it "might have led to criticism for harassing an old lady," and eventually the law officers too decided not to prosecute. The decision led to an investigation by the Commons Intelligence and Security Committee, which concluded that MI5 had made a series of "serious failures." (*The Telegraph* 2005)

Her friends in Bexleyheath were aware of Norwood's political leanings because for many years she had given them copies of the communist newspaper *The Morning Star,* yet her obituaries tend to depict her as eccentric. This is very different from press accounts of Kim Philby or Anthony Blunt who are unequivocally seen as traitors. Norwood's story is marked by the amazement of her neighbors and of the journalists themselves. Who would have thought that a "little old lady" would do such a thing? Yet the "little old lady" proves an impenetrable cover story, inspiring a biography and at least one novel based on Melita Norwood's career as a spy (Burke 2008; Rooney 2013).

The Melita Norwood case in 1999 had been anticipated by a fictional depiction of an ageing female spy. Dorothy Gilman published fourteen novels featuring Mrs. Emily Pollifax, of New Brunswick, New Jersey; the first in 1966 and the last in 2000 (White 2012). In the first novel, Mrs. Pollifax is a sixty-year-old widow from the suburbs who finds her family and her various hobbies insufficiently rewarding. Following a visit to her doctor, who prescribes antidepressants, Mrs. Pollifax volunteers to work for the CIA, pursuing a childhood ambition to become a spy. She becomes a "walk-in" at Langley, arguing that her age and gender *qualify* her to be a spy:

"I've come to volunteer. I'm quite alone, you see, with no encumbrances or responsibilities. It's true that my only qualifications are those of character, but when you reach my age character is what you have the most of. I've raised two children and run a home. I drive a car and know first aid, I never shrink from the sight of blood and I'm very good in emergencies."

Mr. Mason looked oddly stricken. He said in a dazed voice, "But really, you know, spying these days is not bloody at all, Mrs.—Mrs.—"

"Pollifax," she reminded him. "I'm terribly relieved to hear that, Mr. Mason. But still I hoped that you might find use for someone—someone expendable, you know—if only to preserve the lives of your younger, better-trained people. I don't mean to sound melodramatic, but I am quite prepared to offer you my life or I would not have come." (Gilman 1966: 8–9)

Emily Pollifax demonstrates the resourcefulness of her age and experience throughout the series. The idea of the older woman spy as a disposable resource, however, indicates a more serious aspect to these comic fictions. While much of the appeal of the Mrs. Pollifax novels is the comic anomaly of a "little old lady" and the spy drama, their storylines also address darker aspects of the genre. Mrs. Pollifax is tortured and imprisoned during her assignments. She suffers but she also makes unlikely allies, deploying aspects of her age and gender to her advantage. In the exchange above from the first novel in the series Gilman addresses the "disposable" aspect of the elderly head-on. If, as Sontag argues, older women are objects of depreciating value, then Mrs. Pollifax takes that stereotype and turns it on its head. Disposability becomes Mrs. Pollifax's advantage, her Unique Selling Point both within the narrative as a CIA agent and in the novels as commercial fictions, offering comedy, adventure, romance, and a subtly political debate about gender and ageing.

The press accounts of Melita Norwood, like the adventures of Dorothy Gilman's Mrs. Pollifax, thus *queer* popular representations of the spy. They challenge the fantasy of the Bond hero in several ways, most notably by reversing the notion of age as a disadvantage. For Norwood and Pollifax being a "little old lady" is both a cover and a means of access to particular situations, a way of forming unexpected alliances. Because older women are regarded as cultural waste, they are potentially freer to explore different social and geographical territories, deploying the "double standard of ageing" to their advantage. Such figures offer an ironic commentary on the phallacies of Fleming's hero, indicating the fantasies James Bond plays upon, such as immortal youth, unbounded ability, imperial heritage, and patriarchal supremacy (Bennett and Woollacott 1987; White 2012). Older women spies deliver a view of and from the margins; culturally marginalized by their age and their gender, they are often represented as eccentric, unstable, and *queer*.

I am mobilizing the term "queer" in this context as a verb and calling upon a history of critical work in queer theory. To queer something indicates a questioning of the secure division between masculine and feminine, gay and straight, young and old. Queering unsettles categories and reframes debates. From early work in the field, such as Michael Warner's *Fear of a Queer Planet* (1993), queering has been employed to question the security of white, bourgeois, heterosexual identities by interrogating the lapses, elisions, and gaps in their construction. This radical potential is paradoxically indebted to a history of homophobia in Western culture. In his examination of queer (rather than gay or lesbian) as a category, Warner asserts: "The insistence on 'queer'—a term initially generated in the context of terror—has the effect of pointing out a wide field of normalization, rather than simply intolerance, as the site of violence" (Warner 1993: xxvi). Queering, in this context, is thus positioned as a means of changing the epistemological standpoint of a debate about identities rather than establishing putative "equality" with a supposed "norm." Where being called "queer" has historically been used as a means of controlling, attacking, and denigrating subordinated individuals and groups regarding their gender and sexuality, deploying a queer strategy has the potential to turn the spotlight on those in power and force them to acknowledge their privilege. The older woman spy in fiction, film, and television can be a queer agent in this regard.[3]

Recent work on gender and ageing has begun to argue that ageing is itself a queer process, as time unpicks the security of the self as a person in the world. To become old, to retire, to begin to deal with the physical and emotional shifts that attend ageing is to confront the mutability of identity, but also to potentially remake it (Sandberg, 2008). This is not a comfortable process, and the association of age and ageing with death and infirmity may explain the discomfort which often shadows representations of older people. It is this very discomfort—the uncanny sense that we recognize our own futures in depictions of ageing—that makes the older woman in espionage narratives such a compellingly queer figure. She troubles the ontological stability of the "truth" within such stories. She disrupts certainties, undermines the stability of identity, potentially makes the reader a little uncomfortable.

One notable example of that discomfort is the character of Connie Sachs in John le Carré's Karla novels. Le Carré's famous trilogy, beginning with *Tinker, Tailor, Soldier, Spy* in 1974, is *about* ageing and growing old. George Smiley is a retired agent called back into the Service in order to find a mole at his (unidentified) agency, whose headquarters are known as the Circus. When Oliver Lacon commissions Smiley he asks: "You'll take the job, clean the stables? Go backwards, go forwards, do whatever is necessary? It's your generation after all. Your legacy" (le Carré 1974: 86). In this passage Smiley is called upon to resolve a problem. Much like the detective protagonist in crime fiction he is required to bring order to a disordered world. Yet he is asked to do so because he represents that older generation of spies that have fostered the problem in the first place; it is his "legacy." George Smiley is an ageing agent in the first novel, who continues to age as the series proceeds. Yet while Smiley is a central figure in the novels, we are offered little account of his ageing body.

Instead, much of the shame and abjection of ageing is displaced onto another retired employee of the Circus, Connie Sachs. Smiley goes to visit Connie at her home in Oxford during *Tinker, Tailor, Soldier, Spy* and our first sight of her is written in a notably visceral manner:

> The door opened part way, held on a chain; a body swelled into the opening. While Smiley in the same instant gave his whole effort to seeing who else was inside the house, two shrewd eyes, wet like a baby's, appraised him, noted his briefcase and his spattered shoes, flickering upward to peer past his shoulder down the drive,

then once more looked him over. Finally the white face broke into a charming smile, and Miss Connie Sachs, formerly queen of research at the Circus, registered her spontaneous joy. [. . .]

She was a big woman, bigger than Smiley by a head. A tangle of white hair framed her sprawling face. She wore a brown jacket like a blazer and trousers with elastic at the waist and she had a low belly like an old man's. A coke fire smouldered in the grate. Cats lay before it and a mangy grey spaniel, too fat to move, lounged on the divan. On a trolley were the tins she ate from and the bottles she drank from. (le Carré 1974: 112)

Connie is depicted here as an example of dysfunctional ageing. Most notably she is not appropriately heterofeminine. Connie is too tall, her body and clothing disturbingly masculine. Physically and sexually ambivalent, her size and appearance in this passage from the first novel connote the lesbian identity that emerges more explicitly in the third novel of the trilogy, *Smiley's People* (1979). The description rankles with disgust at Connie's age and abject physicality. The "low belly like an old man's" presents her as outside "proper" femininity. She is not well-groomed or sculpted by exercise. Her diet of booze and processed foods from tins is unrestrained, just as her domestic surroundings are squalid and unkempt. Connie is emphatically *not* domesticated. Unconcerned with traditional feminine skills such as home-making, her flat is barely functional, with a drinks trolley repurposed as the repository of detritus from her meals. Connie's leaking, unconfined body is beyond age; she has the moist eyes of a child but the sharp observational skills of an experienced agent. The reference to the fat, mangy dog and several cats relates this older woman to the non-human world of beasts.

Much of this description corresponds to the misogyny embedded in what Sontag described as the double standard of ageing: "The revulsion against ageing in women is the cutting edge of a whole set of oppressive structures (often masked as gallantries) that keep women in their place" (Sontag 1972: 38). Above all, Connie does not know her place. This encounter is marked by an incongruously girlish flirtatiousness, as Connie greets Smiley as her "oldest, oldest lover" and talks about how she "loved all her gorgeous boys" (le Carré 1974: 112, 127). Geraint D'Arcy argues that "le Carré allows Sachs to possess a different kind of capital for which she also has no market: her sexuality, a capital which her arthritic body and advanced age renders mostly untradeable" (D'Arcy 2014: 284). Yet this is not a straight deal of any kind. Connie appears fully aware of her age and this sexualized language may be understood as a form of camp banter. She understands her lack of sexual capital and the impact of her ambiguously ageing appearance, but she does not *care*. Instead, the flirtatious language makes fun of Smiley, who is not just her "oldest lover" but her "oldest, *oldest* lover" (my emphasis). Connie and Smiley are colleagues who know each other far too well to misunderstand the joke. They are a dying breed. Compared to most of Smiley's peers in these novels Connie is exceptional because of her age and gender. She is one of the few women in the profession from that generation. Connie is clearly marked in this passage as inappropriate in her behavior and in her appearance. She is not respectable, not behaving in a manner which is "proper" to her gender or her age. She drinks, swears, and is rude about the senior officers in the Circus during the ensuing conversation with Smiley. She is too sharp for her own good and she has endured.

Connie Sachs's memory is central to this first novel in le Carré's Karla trilogy. As the former "queen of research at the Circus," she is a human archive, the memory of that intelligence community. Connie may be understood as a synecdoche for the thousands of women who have worked in the British Secret Services since their inception, not as agents but as researchers, administrators, archivists, and typists. Tammy Procter proposes those women's work as essential to the Establishment and maintenance of British intelligence: "As clerks, supervisors, report writers, translators, printers, searchers, messengers and historians, women made it possible for a tiny spy-tracking office created in 1909 to become a massive information clearinghouse by the end of the war" (Proctor 2003: 53). Connie is also emblematic of what often happens to such women in any large organization. They are kept in the margins in low-paid roles and disposed of when necessary. When she is no longer useful Connie is sacked, told by "That personnel cow" that she has lost her "sense of proportion" (le Carré 1974: 114). Yet Connie's memory and, by implication, her "sense of proportion," is startlingly accurate. At Smiley's prompting Connie launches into a lengthy account of an episode in the history of the Circus, beginning "Once upon a time there was a defector called Stanley, way back in sixty-three . . ." (le Carré 1974: 115). Her narrative covers twelve pages, peppered with names and dates which she has committed to her archival memory. She tells Smiley how she spotted a double agent, Aleks Polyakov, the Soviet handler for a mole inside the Circus, only to be told "to put him out of your silly woman's mind," and subsequently sacked (le Carré 1974: 126). Connie's marginal role within the Service gives her a clearer view of what is happening. She has a privileged place in le Carré's trilogy, queering the authority and power of the Circus's senior staff, setting the Secret Service on a kilter and putting their mission in question. She is key to Smiley's discovery of the mole, thus offering her a significant position as a beacon of truth within the narrative.

Connie Sachs has long been thought to have been based on MI5's real "queen of research," Milicent Bagot. Bagot was one of the few women to rise from the ranks of the "Registry Queens," MI5's central records office staffed entirely by women, to become an assistant director (Sisman 2015a): "Bagot was also one of the first to raise doubts about Kim Philby. Younger officers were wary of her as a stickler for meticulous office procedure; moreover she was a difficult colleague, whose robust opinions were expressed with passionate conviction. But her memory for facts was so extraordinary as to have passed into office folklore" (Sisman 2015b: 191). Bagot was the first to warn MI5 that Philby had been a member of the Communist Party, a fact he later denied, and that denial was key to exposing him as a Soviet agent (Evans 2006). In le Carré's authorized biography, he denies that Bagot was the model for Connie, instead naming Diana Mumford, "a member of the English ladies' bridge team who had worked at Bletchley Park" (Sisman 2015b: 191). Whether we should be convinced by this latter assertion is open to question, as le Carré himself acknowledges: "I'm a liar," he explains. "Born to lying, bred to it, trained to it by an industry that lies for a living, practised in it as a novelist" (Sisman 2015b: xiv). When Bagot died in 2006, *The Times* headlined the report of her death as "le Carré's 'Connie'": "Milicent Bagot, a spinster devoted to her secret work, knew more about the spread of communism than anyone else in MI5, which was why she was thought to be the model for Connie Sachs, the eccentric Soviet expert in *Smiley's People* and *Tinker, Tailor, Soldier, Spy*" (Evans 2006). Even these brief descriptions of Bagot's life indicate a certain uneasiness about a woman in the Intelligence Services. She is a "*spinster* devoted to her secret work," an "*eccentric* Soviet expert" (my emphases), terms which denote that she was not neatly positioned within a heterosexual matrix; that she somehow did not *fit* despite her expertise and efficiency. The older, senior woman in intelligence, as in any public body, is a queered figure.

Fabio Cleto notes the etymological alignment of queerness and eccentricity— "Strange, odd, peculiar, eccentric, in appearance or character"—and its relation to camp: "The estranging, alienating effect of eccentricity, anticonventionality, or perversion of doxastic prescription links *queer* with its 'troubling inauthenticity'— witness the occurrences of *queer money*, 'counterfeit money', at least since 1740 (cf. OED Supplement 1982: 972)" (1999: 12–13). In le Carré's novels, Connie Sachs embodies all these categories. Her gender and sexuality are disturbingly unbounded and this is translated into her appearances on screen, particularly in the BBC adaptations of *Tinker, Tailor, Soldier, Spy* (1979) and *Smiley's People* (1982), where Connie is played by Beryl Reid. The casting of Reid is noteworthy. As a cabaret performer, comedian, and character actor, Reid's career had already encompassed several roles which problematized heterofemininity. Like Milicent Bagot, many obituaries following Beryl Reid's death in 1996 described her as "eccentric."

Beryl Reid identified as heterosexual but a number of her film and television roles implicitly and explicitly referenced queer sexualities, such as the butch maths mistress in *The Belles of St Trinians* (Frank Launder, 1954). Her performance as June Buckridge in *The Killing of Sister George* (Robert Aldrich, 1968), a grim rendering of an intergenerational lesbian relationship, was ground-breaking in its explicit representation of queer desires. Reid's primary work was in character comedy, a tradition in which performers create a character distinct from their own public persona that becomes a self-contained "act":

> It is a formula which permits considerable flexibility . . . it can allow the performer to show off a skill or to involve us closely in the fate of a character we come to care about. In fact it can walk on the edge of drama while ensuring that we do not lose sight of the comedian-as-author. This framework makes it possible for a performer to wield unusual power. It emphasizes woman as controller; she does not "play herself" but creates a multiplicity of selves before the audience—selves which more conventional theatre practices might deny her. (Gray 1994: 162)

This tradition lends itself to a queer dynamic that cuts through or exposes social norms and Beryl Reid's work took full advantage of this. In her character comedy work Reid troubled binary understandings of gender and sexuality, deploying costume, regional accents, and physical theater to undercut the naturalization of straight, white, middle-class identity (White 2014). That heritage of queered comedy performance is brought to bear on Reid's role as Connie Sachs in *Tinker, Tailor, Soldier, Spy* (BBC 1979).

Reid plays Sachs as full of anger and sentiment. Unlike George Smiley (Alec Guinness), who remains impassive and largely unreadable throughout this series and the BBC's adaptation of *Smiley's People*, Connie is a leaky parcel of nostalgia, despair, and rage. The television series transposes phrases from le Carré's work into Reid and Guinness's script. While Reid is slighter and smaller than le Carré's description of Connie Sachs, the costume, makeup, and setting all closely follow the novel. As in the novel, Sachs is the sharp and winsome human archive of the circus, narrating how she spotted Polyakov and watched him for eight years before being sacked. This scene was filmed over two days on location in a house in Oxford, then reshot following technical problems with the footage. The director, John Irvin, suggested that Reid emphasize Sachs's bitterness and Reid was nominated for a BAFTA for her performance (Reid 1984: 230–2). Smiley is shown arriving in Oxford and walking through a snowy university quad before heading out to the suburbs where Sachs lives in a grubby bedsit. Day turns to night during his journey. Even in daylight the landscape is drained of color, almost monotone, while Sachs's room is furnished in dull shades of grey and brown. The sequence draws upon *film noir*, employing shadows which stretch across the protagonists' faces, the camera moving closer in as their conversation proceeds. Joseph Oldham notes how *Tinker, Tailor, Soldier, Spy* was part of a burgeoning tradition of quality British television drama and the first of such series to be entirely shot on film (2013: 732). The literal and metaphorical darkness of *noir* cinema is called upon in this sequence, as is that genre's predilection for claustrophobia, the camera showing little of the setting but zooming in on Connie's face. If Reid plays Sachs as weepy and emotional, she also demonstrates Sachs's archival memory and sharp wit. The visual aesthetic implies that there is more going on beneath the surface. Toward the end of the sequence Reid launches into a final speech about Sachs's "lovely boys" as the camera focuses unmercifully on her pale and aged face: "Hey ho, halcyon days [. . .] Poor loves, trained to empire, trained to rule the waves. Englishmen could be proud then. They could, George. All gone, taken away. Bye-bye world. If it's bad George don't come back—promise? I want to remember you just as you were. My lovely, lovely boys—promise?" As the speech begins, Sachs is drunk and tearful; by the end, George has already closed the door behind him and she is alone. The extreme close-up reveals every wrinkle; after she has spoken Reid turns her head away and bites her lip, as if regretting what she has said. Although this scene is full of pathos and regret, Sachs appears fragile but unbowed. Reid seems older than Guinness in this sequence (she was in fact five years his junior), and the close-ups emphasize this. Reid worked on her performance to replicate Connie's arthritic hands and clumsy movements (Reid 1984: 230). If Smiley is retired, Connie in this sequence is *aged*, with all the infirmities that presage an early death. Her tears, her anger, and her dislike of "the real world" position Connie as abject in her queered, ageing femininity.

All of this could connote a stereotype; the monstrous old woman, subject to the "double standard of ageing." Yet in le Carré's fictions and the BBC adaptations, Connie is not demonized, derogated, or ignored. Certainly, the novels and adaptations depict her as sentimental, nostalgic, enraged, and even pathetic. Her abjection may be understood as representing a more critical view of the British intelligence agencies. In the BBC's adaptation of *Smiley's People* (1982) Smiley once more seeks out Connie

Sachs for her memory, but this time the exchange has a different tone. Sachs is dying, only able to move with a walking frame and even more crippled by arthritis. She has moved out of Oxford and lives in the Oxfordshire countryside with a younger woman, echoing Reid's earlier role in *The Killing of Sister George*. The adaptation once again closely follows le Carré's novel; indeed, le Carré rewrote the script for *Smiley's People* after the original version was deemed unsatisfactory (Oldham 2013: 733). Connie and her partner, Hilary—also a former Circus employee—run a kennels and animal refuge: "Merrilee Boarding. All pets welcome. Eggs!" Their eccentric rural idyll is interrupted by Smiley's visit. Once again, he arrives at dusk and, as they talk, the night draws in. This time Connie has a more comfortable home and a partner who cares for her. In the novel their home is chaotic:

> For an office, they had the roll-top desk laden with bills and flea powder; for a bedroom the brass double bedstead with its heap of stuffed toy animals lying like dead soldiers between the pillows; for a drawing-room Connie's rocking-chair and a crumbling wicker sofa; for a kitchen a gas ring fired from a cylinder; and for decoration the unclearable litter of old age. (le Carré 1979: 218)

The set of the television adaptation is equally chaotic but also comfortable; there is a roaring fire with an oil painting above it and while the house is messy it is clearly a refuge not just for the animals but also for Connie and Hilary. Reid plays Connie Sachs in *Smiley's People* as a stronger figure. She is less tearful and more adversarial. Connie is less nostalgic in this second series, urging Guinness's Smiley to let the past go. Smiley harangues Sachs to get the information he needs, telling her to "Wake up and be useful!" The television series, like the novel, demonstrates how Smiley is driven by his obsession with finding his Soviet adversary, Karla, to the extent that he is willing to sacrifice his ethics. This makes it all the more significant that, as an emblematic figure for older women in professional and public life, Connie expresses her distress and is vindicated. Connie Sachs is an outsider, but her point of view is privileged. She is the oracle who tells Smiley the truth, or at least supplies him with information that leads him to the truth. Reading these narratives through Connie Sachs gives spy fiction a fascinating spin.

Le Carré's novels and the BBC adaptations offer very different accounts of ageing through Smiley and Connie. Smiley is a prime example of "successful ageing," a term attributed to the work of Jon Rowe and Robert Kahn (1987). Rowe and Kahn define "successful ageing" as avoiding illness, remaining physically fit and socially engaged (1987; see also Sandberg 2008: 120–1). The idea of "successful ageing" has been critiqued for its alignment with neoliberal discourses of the self-sufficient social subject; it is applicable primarily to a white, middle-class consumer. Successful ageing in these terms means *not ageing* as far as is humanly possible, remaining "youthful," able-bodied, not being a burden on the state. "Successful ageing" is what many Western governments are now investing in, as are some private multinationals, as a means of keeping us functioning as consumers well into later life (Sandberg 2008: 122–7). Smiley exemplifies "successful ageing" because he appears largely untouched by age. He is active, able-bodied, and a dedicated public servant. Connie is evidently less "successful." In the BBC's 1982 adaptation of *Smiley's People*, as in the novel, she is clear about her decline: "It's death, that's what I'm suffering from." More than this, Connie is *defiantly* unsuccessful at ageing. She refuses to carefully maintain her body and her home. She voices the truth about ageing: that it is not always pleasant or easy and that death is the only endgame. In embracing disreputable old age, Connie exposes the limited scope of "successful ageing" and its relation to a history of Western capital (Shildrick 2015). For women, "successful ageing" means assuming the role of a little old lady and effectively disappearing, not taking up too much space and time, being quiet, dressing "appropriately." Connie refuses this. She holds the knowledge that Smiley needs and speaks from a position outside the Circus. Connie Sachs represents an eccentric, queered alternative to "successful ageing" in her Oxfordshire "dacha" where "all pets [are] welcome without discrimination" (le Carré 1979: 216). Connie's failure to age "successfully" indicates a different perspective on femininity and ageing.

In *The Queer Art of Failure* Judith Halberstam proposes: "We can . . . recognize failure as a way of refusing to acquiesce to dominant logics of power and discipline and as a form of critique" (2011: 88). Halberstam's "queer art of failure" posits an alternate regime of resistance and survival on the margins, which seems an uncannily accurate account of Connie Sachs's role in the le Carré novels. More than a single instance of an eccentric character who offers a queered worldview, however, Connie's failing old age represents a radically critical reading of spy fictions. Connie correctly names the executive of the Circus as inhuman and inefficient. If intelligence agencies represent the state bodies they serve this offers a trenchant commentary on the workings of power. Like her factual and fictional peers, Melita Norwood and Emily Pollifax, Connie Sachs represents a different kind of secret agent. The older woman spy in this regard may be understood as a critical catalyst in the espionage narrative, questioning the corporate ethics of intelligence and exposing the intersectional absences in neoliberal discourses of "successful ageing."

Reading espionage fictions from the perspective of these older female characters, whether they are protagonists or marginal figures, demonstrates the limitations of hegemonic white masculinities which Western espionage narratives have predominantly offered. Such fantasies are at the center of Fleming's Bond novels and their cinematic adaptations. Like Bond himself, those film franchises promote excessive consumerism through dreams of omnipotence. Viewing such narratives from the standpoint of women like Mrs. Pollifax and Connie Sachs raises larger questions about the ethics of such phallocentric fantasies in the twenty-first century. As we emerge—hopefully—from the ravages of a global pandemic and begin—hopefully—to take responsibility for the damage we are doing to our planet, these fantasies are unsustainable. The emotional intelligence, vulnerability, and ethics of care that inform the older women spies discussed in this chapter could offer a more productive and sustainable future.

Postscript

During the process of writing and revising this chapter a British intelligence agent and former Director General of MI5, has been lurking in the background. Stella

Rimington was the first woman to command a major Intelligence Service in the UK. Her professional background in archives and libraries links her to the "invisible functionary, the secretary and the silent organizer"—women like Milicent Bagot and to the fictional Connie Sachs—but she has been far more successful than that model (Horn 2013: 171). I would not categorize Rimington as a "queered" figure, other than in terms of her exceptional status as a woman in such a senior position. Unlike Connie, and perhaps Milicent Bagot, Stella Rimington was fully incorporated into the British Secret Service; one of her roles was to identify "subversion" within government organizations such as the British Civil Service. Rimington, then a senior MI5 officer, was part of a 1980s inter-departmental group addressing Subversion in Public Life, drawing up a secret blacklist of civil servants, including teachers, under Margaret Thatcher's government. People who were identified as "subversives," such as those involved in the Trotskyist group Militant Tendency, were denied promotion, or covertly moved to roles where they could cause the least disruption (Cobain 2018). Stella Rimington's time as Director General in the early 1990s shifted the image of MI5 as she "instituted a policy of greater public openness," including releasing some files to the National Archives at Kew (https://www.mi5.gov.uk/dame -stella-rimington). This may be understood as a strategic move by MI5 to represent itself as democratic, modern, and egalitarian. Rimington's autobiography, chimes with this ethos, significantly titled *Open Secret* (2001). It is a carefully edited version of her life. Stella Rimington has had a remarkable career, moving up from the ranks through MI5 in an era when women's work in any profession was far from easy. My question would be what "service" means in this context. Like the civil service, Britain's Secret Services are represented as serving the national good, yet both bodies necessarily serve the government in power. Documents made available at Kew in 2014 raise difficult questions about MI5's role in the miners' strikes of the 1980s (Travis 2014). Serving a government which facilitated neoliberal economic and social policies demonstrates the extent to which such bodies enabled a regime whose effects continue to resonate in British social and political life.

In a waspish review of Rimington's autobiography David Rose notes the omission of details about the Melita Norwood case, where questions were asked about MI5's failure to recognize the Soviet spy: "When Rimington gave her evidence, in camera, to an inquiry into the affair by the Parliamentary Intelligence Oversight Committee, she said she could not remember what she had been told about Norwood, and could not explain her service's inaction. In fact, she was briefed extensively, six years before the story surfaced" (Rose 2001).

As a result of her evidence Rimington's successor took the blame for that failure. Rose also argues that Rimington's claim to have changed the culture within MI5 was not entirely accurate:

> Rimington claims, more or less singlehandedly, to have transformed a bastion of brutal sexism into one of political correctness. It is an account bitterly disputed by some of her female colleagues, who say they remember a woman principally devoted to personal advancement, who did little to foster other women's careers. While nearly half of MI5's staff are women, there are still very few in senior

grades, and their numbers reflect average proportions in Whitehall as a whole. (Rose 2001)

If we take these accounts of Rimington at face value, she represents the opposite of older women discussed in this chapter. Rather than the productive "failure" of Connie Sachs, which is "a way of refusing to acquiesce to dominant logics of power," Stella Rimington represents "success" (Halberstam 2011: 88). In her "service" she enables neoliberal capitalism, without critique or contradiction. Rimington's successful intelligence career, and subsequent success as an author, raises questions about what such "success" entails, and at what cost?

Professional success in neoliberal times is predicated on subjects "constituted as self-managing, autonomous and enterprising" individuals (Gill and Scharff 2011: 5). These are the fantasies that underpin James Bond; an *Übermensch* dedicated to a notionally benevolent and moral state. The reality is far less noble; neoliberal feminism as espoused by "successful" women in senior roles, such as Sheryl Sandberg, advocates "an individualistic, entrepreneurial ideology that is complicit with rather than critical of capitalism" (Gill 2016: 617). William Boyd's *Restless* (2006) offers a more critical account of "success" in the Secret Services, recounting the story of Eva Delectorskaya, an ageing female spy who has lived a life undercover after being betrayed by a double agent during the Second World War. Boyd places Eva's narrative alongside that of her daughter, Ruth, as they track down the intelligence officer who betrayed her, now a pillar of the British Establishment. Ruth is engaged in left politics and encounters the murky workings of intelligence agents infiltrating radical movements in the 1970s. This story is critical of the state and its machinations, encouraging the reader to consider the cost of international politics, particularly for women. It demonstrates the love and trust between Ruth and her mother, despite the years of lies that ensured Eva's safety. Ruth worries about her mother, observing her constant watchfulness, waiting for the enemy to come for her: "you don't need to have been a spy, I thought, to feel like this" (Boyd 2006: 324–5). Ruth and Eva's narratives interrogate the role of government agencies; how they can inadvertently destroy some people, often women, while rewarding others, mostly men, who play the game. And here we are, living through a global pandemic, war in Europe, and an economic crisis. Perhaps it is time to think differently about what we see as a "successful" individual, or intelligence agency, or governing body.

Notes

1 The espionage work of women of color has only recently been acknowledged, as in the case of Noor Inayat Khan, who worked under the codename "Madeleine" for the SOE in occupied France during the Second World War (Dalton 2012).

2 Sontag does not address other forms of difference, such as race, class, and sexuality, in this essay.

3 It is worth noting that while Erin G Carlston (2013) argues that gay men, Jewishness, and communism are culturally aligned in Western notions of the double agent, none of the factual or fictional older women spies I address in this chapter are double agents.

References

Bennett, Tony and Janet Woollacott (1987), *Bond and Beyond: The Political Career of a Popular Hero*, London: Macmillan.

Besson, Luc, dir. (1990), *La Femme Nikita*, dir. Luc Besson (Gaumont).

Besson, Luc, dir. (2018–2021), *Killing Eve* (BBC).

Boyd, William (2006), *Restless*, London: Bloomsbury.

Burke, David (2008), *The Spy Who Came in From the Co-Op: Melita Norwood and the Ending of the Cold War*, Woodbridge: Boydell Press.

Carlston, Erin G. (2013), *Double Agents: Espionage, Literature, and Liminal Citizens*, New York: Columbia University Press.

Cleto, Fabio (1999), "Introduction: Queering the Camp," in Fabio Cleto (ed.), *Camp: Queer Aesthetics and the Performing Subject: A Reader*, Edinburgh: Edinburgh University Press.

Cobain, Ian (2018), "'Subversive' Civil Servants Secretly Blacklisted under Thatcher," *The Guardian*, 24 July. Available online at: https://www.theguardian.com/uk-news/2018/jul/24/subversive-civil-servants-secretly-blacklisted-under-thatcher (accessed 13 July 2022).

Cunningham, John (2005), "Melita Norwood," *The Guardian*, 28 June. Available online at: https://www.theguardian.com/news/2005/jun/28/guardianobituaries.past (accessed 16 March 2018).

Dalton, Samantha (2012), "Noor Inayat Khan: The Indian Princess Who Spied for Britain," *BBC News*, 8 November. Available online at: https://www.bbc.co.uk/news/uk-20240693 (accessed 16 August 2021).

D'Arcy, Geraint (2014), "'Essentially, another man's woman': Information and Gender in the Novel and Adaptations of John le Carré's *Tinker, Tailor, Soldier, Spy*," *Adaptation*, 7 (3): 275–90.

Evans, Michael (2006), "Le Carré's 'Connie' Dies Aged 99," *The Times*, 3 June: 12.

Falcus, Sarah and Katsura Sako (2014), "Women, Travelling and Later Life," in Imelda Whelehan and Joel Gwynne (eds), *Ageing, Popular Culture and Contemporary Feminism: Harleys and Hormones*, 203–18, Basingstoke and New York: Palgrave Macmillan.

Gill, Rosalind (2016), "Post-postfeminism?: New Feminist Visibilities in Postfeminist Times," *Feminist Media Studies*, 16 (4): 610–30.

Gill, Rosalind and Christina Scharff, eds (2011), *New Femininities: Postfeminism, Neoliberalism and Subjectivity*, London: Palgrave Macmillan.

Gilman, Dorothy (1966), *The Unexpected Mrs Pollifax*, New York: Fawcett Books.

Gray, Frances (1994), *Women and Laughter*, Charlottesville: University Press of Virginia.

Gullette, Margaret Morganroth (2004), *Aged by Culture*, Chicago and London: University of Chicago Press.

Halberstam, Judith (2011), *The Queer Art of Failure*, Durham and London: Duke University Press.

Horn, Eva (2013), *The Secret War: Treason, Espionage, and Modern Fiction*, translated by Geoffrey Winthrop-Young, Evanston: Northwestern University Press.

Kaur, Sanmeet (2020), *Sex and Power 2020*, London: The Fawcett Society. Available online at: https://www.fawcettsociety.org.uk/sex-and-power-2020 (accessed 16 August 2021).

Knightley, Phillip (2003), *The Second Oldest Profession: Spies and Spying in the Twentieth Century*, second edition, London: Pimlico.

Le Carré, John (1974), *Tinker, Tailor, Soldier, Spy*, London: Sceptre.

Le Carré, John (1979), *Smiley's People*, London: Sceptre.

Oldham, Joseph (2013), "'Disappointed Romantics': Troubled Heritage in the BBC's John le Carré Adaptations," *Journal of British Cinema and Television*, 10 (4): 727–45.

Proctor, Tammy M. (2003), *Female Intelligence: Women and Espionage in the First World War*, London and New York: New York University Press.

Reid, Beryl (1984), *So Much Love: An Autobiography*, London: Arrow Books.

Rooney, Jennie (2013), *Red Joan*, London: Vintage.

Rose, David (2001), "Mission Implausible," *The Observer*, 16 September. Available online at: https://www.theguardian.com/books/2001/sep/16/biography.features (accessed 13 July 2022).

Rowe, Jon and Robert Kahn (1987), "Human Ageing: Usual and Successful," *Science*, 237: 143–9.

Sandberg, Linn (2008), "The Old, The Ugly and the Queer: Thinking Old Age in Relation to Queer Theory," *Graduate Journal of Social Science*, 5 (2): 117–39.

Shade, Ruth (2010), "'Take My Mother-in-Law: 'Old Bags,' Comedy and the Sociocultural Construction of the Older Woman," *Comedy Studies*, 1 (1): 71–83.

Shildrick, Margrit (2015), "Living On; Not Getting Better," *Feminist Review*, 111: 10–24.

Sisman, Adam (2015a), "Le Carré the MI6 Spy Who Came In From the Cold War," *The Mail on Sunday*, 17 October. Available online at: http://www.dailymail.co.uk/news/article-3277217/Le-Carr-MI6-spy-came-Cold-War-botched-mission-contempt-handlers-led-reluctant-secret-agent-create-George-Smiley.html (accessed 18 March 2018).

Sisman, Adam (2015b), *John le Carré: The Biography*, London: Bloomsbury Publishing.

Sontag, Susan (1972), "The Double Standard of Ageing," *Saturday Review*, 23 September, 29–38.

The Telegraph (2005), "Melita Norwood," 29 June. Available online at: https://www.telegraph.co.uk/news/obituaries/1492969/Melita-Norwood.html (accessed 16 March 2018).

Travis, Alan (2014), "National Archives: Thatcher Demanded Action to Stop Soviets Funding Miners," *The Guardian*, 3 January. Available online at: https://www.theguardian.com/politics/2014/jan/03/national-archives-thatcher-demanded-action (accessed 13 July 2022).

Wallace, Diana (2011), "Literary Portrayals of Ageing," in Ian Stuart-Hamilton (ed.), *An Introduction to Gerontology*, 389–415, Cambridge: Cambridge University Press.

Warner, Michael (1993), "Introduction," in Michael Warner (ed.), *Fear of a Queer Planet: Queer Politics and Social Theory*, vii–xxxi, Minneapolis and London: University of Minnesota Press.

Wearing, Sadie (2007), "Subjects of Rejuvenation: Ageing in Postfeminist Culture," in Yvonne Tasker and Diane Negra (eds), *Interrogating Postfeminism: Gender and the Politics of Popular Culture*, 277–310, Durham and London: Duke University Press.

Wheelwright, Julie (1992), *The Fatal Lover: Mata Hari and the Myth of Women in Espionage*, London: Collins and Brown.

White, Rosie (2012), "Dorothy Gilman's Mrs Pollifax and Ian Fleming's James Bond: Soft and Hard Spy Fiction," in Robert Lance Snyder (ed.), *Paradoxa 24, Espionage Fiction: The Seduction of Clandestinity*, 73–89, Vashon Island, Washington: Paradoxa.

White, Rosie (2014), "Beryl Reid Says . . . Good Evening: Performing Queer Identity on British Television," *Journal of European Popular Culture*, 5 (2): 165–80.

Woodward, Kathleen (1999), "Introduction," in Kathleen Woodward (ed.), *Figuring Age: Women, Bodies, Generations*, ix–xxix, Bloomington and Indianapolis: Indiana University Press.

Woodward, Kathleen (2006), "Performing Age, Performing Gender," *National Women's Studies Association Journal*, 18 (1): 162–89.

9

"What's the Character?"

Adapting Agency and Gender in
The Little Drummer Girl

Rachel Hoag

The twenty-first century has seen an influx of adaptations of decades-old spy narratives. Films like Tomas Alfredson's *Tinker, Tailor, Soldier, Spy* and the *Jason Bourne* trilogy were critical and commercial successes in the early 2000s, adapting Cold War era narratives from John le Carré and Robert Ludlum, respectively. Increasingly, however, spy narrative adaptations took to the small screen as series, with novels like le Carré's *The Night Manager*, William Boyd's *Restless*, Len Deighton's *The Ipcress File*, and Mick Herron's *Slow Horses* all receiving television adaptations between 2012 and 2022. This chapter explores one such television series, Park Chan-wook's *The Little Drummer Girl*, and how its adaptation transforms the presentation of gender in spy narratives from bygone eras. The adaptive choices of the series arguably imbue Charlie's character with a greater sense of agency than her character in le Carré's novel. Endowing Charlie with greater autonomy mitigates some of the problematic gender dynamics in the novel and allows Park's adaptation to explore the extent to which Charlie, as a female spy, determines her role within the geopolitical landscape of the Arab-Israeli conflict.

As Charlie Ross ponders the "acting" job offered to her by Israeli spymaster Martin Kurtz in the 2018 television adaptation of *The Little Drummer Girl*, she poses a question to Kurtz. "What's the character?" she asks. "A terrorist," replies Kurtz, as if a single label could encapsulate the highly improvisational role he was asking her to play in his operation. In the adaptation's final scene, Charlie is still asking questions about identity, only this time they're more personal. "Who are you? Who am I?" she asks Gadi Becker after seeking him out in Berlin. Her questions reach beyond who her character is and express the extent to which she realizes she has been used as a young, attractive, Western woman by the men on both sides of the operation, as well as expressing her desire to explore her actions within that system and her agency outside it.

Questions about Charlie's character and the degree to which she acts with her own agency are at the heart of John le Carré's 1983 novel and persist into director Park Chan-wook's television adaptation. As a spy recruited purposely for her lack of official belonging to either the Palestinian or the Israeli cause—she is "peacefully unaligned" and part of "the extreme center" as Kurtz puts it in the television adaptation—Charlie's agency is constricted. The Israelis and Palestinians value Charlie's unaligned status because, by being what they are not (Western) she can be whatever they *need* her to be, in this case an empty vessel that they can motivate to achieve their political aims. As an actress and a young, attractive woman, she is ideally suited for the role, and their expectation is that she will fulfill it without exerting her own will upon the operation. Examining three areas of the novel and the adaptation—how Charlie is recruited, how her relationship develops with Gadi, and how she responds after the operation concludes—reveals how both works depict Charlie as confined by stereotypical gender expectations and lacking in meaningful political autonomy. But while the novel maintains Charlie's lack of autonomy throughout, Park's adaptation imbues Charlie with more self-awareness and opportunities to flout these expectations. These adaptation decisions—to maintain or erode Charlie's positioning as an object within the narrative—reflect understandings of political agency appropriate to each narrative's time and relationship to the Israeli-Palestinian conflict. The novel suggests that as with much spy fiction, Charlie's exclusion is a gendered one and that women cannot affect the conflict in a significant way. By carving out a more definite (albeit limited) autonomy for Charlie and recasting the coda at the end of the story, Park's adaptation suggests that in the twenty-first century this lack of agency is not gendered but rather individualized: the Arab-Israeli conflict has grown so intractable that the individual, regardless of gender, cannot affect change. In creating the conditions that lead Charlie to this realization, the adaptation allows her to escape many of the gendered tropes of spy narratives regarding female agency.

Much of the theorization around the agency and ideologies of spies assumes a male spy working in the employ of his own country, and Charlie flouts those conventions. She catches Kurtz's eye specifically because of her gender and because she is neither Palestinian nor Israeli.

According to Kurtz, "if you want to catch a lion, you first must tether the goat" (le Carré 2011: 44). This attitude aligns with critics and scholars who tend to position Charlie as an object rather than a subject in the narrative, an empty vessel or a pawn in the Israelis' fight against Palestinian terrorism.[1] Le Carré's novel is significant because Charlie is a female spy, which naturally leads to consideration of how such a character fits into the tropes of spy novels. As Hepburn notes, within the genre, "in effect, a spy belongs nowhere" (Hepburn 2005: 11), and that perhaps goes doubly for female spies whose roles in these narratives are often more marginalized. Women, like other marginalized groups, "have different relationships to the nation state" than men do and have generally "not been citizens of most nations on equal terms with men" (Carlston 2013: 5). Accordingly, spy narratives often reflect the social view that liminal groups like women and minorities "both lacked the mature rationality necessary to form a true social contract" (Carlston 2013: 37). The genre is prone to binaries wherein men are skilled professionals, while the women are objects or amateurs, primarily concerned with the domestic and emotional realm (White 2007: 93). As objects, female spies in narratives like Fleming's Bond novels are luxurious commodities enjoyed alongside his other expensive tastes (Denning 2014: 109), leading critics like Lassner to decry how cartoonish spies like Bond "perform their gender roles in extremis, equating their glamorous masculinity and femininity with moral righteousness and their monstrous opposition with depravity" (Lassner 2016: 171). Horn argues that the figure of the female spy "[oscillates] between grande dame and prostitute," in turns "seductive and seduced" (Horn 2013: 171). Female spies often fall within a distinct binary of seductresses or secretaries, the latter of which do the silent organizing of intelligence (Horn 2013: 171). While le Carré's work is more realist compared to Fleming's spectacle, White argues that "the women in le Carré's Cold War narratives perform a structural function similar to that of Bond's girls: they are on the periphery of the action and, if not part of the scenery, then an obstacle to the hero's success . . . There is a different mood here, but the power structures are the same" (White 2007: 32). As le Carré's first female protagonist, Charlie invites critical examination of how she reifies or reforms the gendered tropes of spy narratives.

Interpretations of Charlie's character are complicated in part because the critical consensus around the novel is highly contentious as well. The novel's complexity and subject render disparate threads of analysis defensible. Aronoff notes that "none of le Carré's novels have received such contradictory reviews and interpretations as has *The Little Drummer Girl*" (Aronoff 1999: 73). He adds that "part of the controversy derives from the ideological positions of the reviewers," who use the novel as a canvas on which to project their ideological approaches to the Israeli-Palestinian conflict (Aronoff 1999: 73). Aronoff notes that Arab publishers rejected the novel on the claim that it was too pro-Israel, while one Israeli newspaper found it too sympathetic to the Arab cause, another proclaimed the book was pro-Israel because the Israeli characters alone could "see a way out of the confrontation" (Aronoff 1999: 73).) These disparate views arise because le Carré resists lecturing on a solution to the Israeli and Palestinian conflict, maintaining "it was a hard story to come to grips with" (le Carré 2011: xi) and that he was unsurprised that both sides found things to like and to decry about the book:

> I endured, pretty much in silence, the cheap jibe that anyone who criticizes Israel is by definition anti-Semitic. I received some foul letters from American Jewish organizations, but some remarkably moving ones from individual Jews . . . A leading Arab American dismissed it as "the usual stuff about Arabs as terrorists." In the Arab press, the book was praised and damned in the same haphazard way. An important Arab critic declared it anti-Palestinian, on the grounds that, in the novel as in life, the Palestinians lost. (le Carré 2011: xix)

The Little Drummer Girl instead explores the intractable nature of the conflict on a systemic level. The novel "implies that there is no solution" (Aronoff 1999: 79). This aligns with themes from le Carré's other spy novels, which meditate on the toll that political and economic systems exact upon the people charged with propagating those systems. He exposes the rot without suggesting the cure, and indeed no cure is to be found, as le Carré notes that more than a decade after the novel's publication, little had changed: "My sadness is that, with few changes, the story could be played today, tomorrow, or the next day, and Charlie my heroine would still come out of it, as I did myself, torn to pieces by the battle between two people who both have justice on their side" (le Carré 2011: xx).[2] The novel implies an intractable conflict because, at the time of publication in 1983, there was no resolution in sight, a condition which persists well into the twenty-first century.

While the ideological battle lines drawn during the Cold War are largely considered settled, little progress has been made toward a similar settlement in the Israeli-Palestinian conflict. As Burke notes, the book's topicality helped spur its success upon publication in 1983 (Burke 2018: para 3). It was a time in which Palestinian terrorists brought the conflict to the West's doorstep. The Black September attacks on Israelis took place in Europe at the 1972 Olympics, and over the next decade, terrorism occupies a growing part of the global consciousness. Burke notes that in the year prior to *The Little Drummer Girl*'s publication, more than 3,000 acts of terror were executed worldwide, many of them on European soil. Seven months after the novel's publication, a truck bomb detonated outside a US military barracks in Beirut, killing 241 servicemembers. The threat of violence "was woven through politics, journalism, popular culture, and the lives of ordinary people as it is today" (Burke 2018: para 3).

Because the complexity of the conflict positions Charlie between these ideologies, her characterization is highly contested as well. Some scholars, like Aronoff, assign the status of the novel's hero to a completely different (and male) character, Gadi.[3] Arnoff allows that Charlie eventually develops "a level of self-awareness" throughout the novel, although he does not argue that this self-awareness derives from or results in increased agency (Aronoff 1999: 72).[4] A few critics of the novel, like Silver and Beene, allow Charlie more motivation without necessarily allowing her autonomy. Beene notes Charlie's prominence within the "family" of her theater troupe as a motivating pattern of family-finding that she replicates later with the Israelis and Palestinians. Silver's lengthy exploration of Charlie remains the most convincing argument to date for Charlie's eventual autonomy, arguing that she remains an object of contention between the Palestinians and the Israelis until the close of the novel, when she, destroyed by the spy games, develops some agency once she stops spying (Silver 1987: 39). The autonomy that Silver ascribes to Charlie occurs after the novel's end, however, making it hoped for rather than definitive. Furthermore, Silver's contention that she gains agency does not change the fact that Charlie still lacks it throughout the novel. Park's adaptation initially maintains that lack of autonomy but carves out minor ways for Charlie to assert herself. These adaptive choices illustrate Charlie's drive for agency even though she is excluded from meaningful political autonomy.

Charlie occupies a number of liminal spaces as a character that make it difficult to assign her a position within the traditional generic structures of spy fiction. She is a protagonist without agency. She is a woman being run by men. And she is, as Kurtz notes, unaligned, which makes her an aberration in the genre in which most spies are recruited because of their allegiance to one side or the other. Unlike other spies, Charlie's lukewarm politics resists classification as an ideology, putting her at odds with Hepburn's assertion that "ideology produces spies" (Hepburn 2005: xiv). She does, however, experience a similar abrogation of personal identity to serve the purposes of the state that Hepburn's examples demonstrate (Hepburn 2005: xiv). Her neutrality makes her attractive to Kurtz, but in performing both ideologies, Charlie must sublimate herself, ending up in a state shared by many women in spy fiction: "living between visibility and invisibility" (Hepburn 2005: 283). Ultimately, this inability to determine her own visibility renders the novel's Charlie as an object rather than a subject. While she may be a successful agent in many regards, juggling competing loyalties, playing her role, and avoiding detection, she cannot control how and when she makes herself visible to others.

In Charlie's case, it is her lack of ideology that prompts her recruitment. Kurtz wants a puppet, a naïve actress who can improvise using ideas he feeds her. This is possible because Charlie's position is determined by a system that expects women to have no political autonomy. Horn argues that women emerge as spies because they were viewed as "seemingly apolitical" and belonging to the private rather than the public sphere, making them less likely to draw scrutiny (Horn 2013: 170–1). Not only is Charlie ideologically unbound, but she is also an actress, which accompanies its own set of gendered assumptions about her character and abilities. In examining the recruitment of Charlie in the novel and television series, one can see the ways in which Charlie is expected to perform according to gendered stereotypes, particularly as a naïve object, easily swayed and prone to fits of emotion. Her ability to play the role lies at the heart of her recruitment, and both the novel and the series depict this recruitment as a coercive process where Kurtz and the Israelis use gendered assumptions to manipulate Charlie into accepting the part.

The novel uses the two lengthy chapters containing Charlie's interrogation by Kurtz to establish his pattern of manipulation, which Aronoff calls "one of the most effective portrayals of the systematic invasion of a personality ever portrayed in fiction" (Aronoff 1999: 165). Kurtz's interrogation in the novel seems designed to back Charlie into corners, not make her feel free, an effect compounded by the fact that Charlie arrives at the meeting after being essentially kidnapped by Gadi. As part of her recruitment, Kurtz challenges Charlie's biases toward Jews and Israel and the geopolitical context—"When you looked at a map, did you once wish the Arabs would leave *us* alone?"—and makes her feel that "her flip phrases had a schoolroom cheapness. She felt like a fool" (le Carré 2011: 128). Marty responds to Charlie's rant about power and the oppressed by asking Charlie if she can recite Guevara, and she admits she cannot, by extension revealing that her convictions are drawn from canned speeches and cribbed from her boyfriend Al. Gadi attempts to defuse the situation by assuring Kurtz and the team that she could use her "excellent recall" to learn it if necessary (le Carré 2011: 153). But the purpose of the Guevara question is not to expose Charlie's ignorance. Rather, it functions to put her on the defensive and highlight her subjective position: In this room, with these Israelis, she knows the least and controls the least, putting her at the mercy of Kurtz, who insists to his superiors before the recruitment interrogation begins that "A lady who consents to listen is a lady who consents" (le Carré 2011: 131–2). Nothing about the interrogation in the novel is designed to empower Charlie, unlike the audition scene and recruitment process in the adaptation. The novel's aggressive approachment of Charlie illustrates how her consent is taken as a foregone conclusion. Kurtz is not making her an offer; he is already convinced she will join them. The recruitment, therefore, is about evaluating her acting skills and establishing her as an object rather than a subjective player in Kurtz's schemes. When it is over, all parties understand that Kurtz is in control.

The adaptation's version of Charlie's recruitment is more subtly coercive and designed to make her feel empowered without actually granting her any real autonomy. Charlie's status as a naïve object is apparent from her first appearance in Park's adaptation, where Kurtz stages a fake audition to evaluate Charlie's suitability for his mission. This scene is unique to the adaptation and establishes the ways in which Kurtz grants Charlie the illusion of control from the earliest stages of their relationship. Charlie begins her audition confidently but is undercut by the constant interruptions from Kurtz, posing as a director, and Rachel, playing his assistant. They exhort her to be more loving, to smile less widely, and when Charlie pushes back with a curt, "What's that meant to mean?" the pair give her the latitude to create the audition she wants. Charlie thinks she is being given freedom, when in fact she's being led down the precise path plotted by the Israeli team. Their interruptions test the limits of her tolerance and her ability to improvise convincingly. Charlie feels empowered but is instead at the mercy of Kurtz's machinations. He looms, offscreen, as an antagonistic presence. As Charlie grows increasingly exasperated by the directions she is given, the aspect ratio becomes smaller, and the camera draws in close. The viewer feels the camera bearing down on her as she feels less and less free to interpret the scene as she would like because of their interruptions. The framing reminds the viewer of the constraints of Charlie's position and that she is mitigated by and performing for the lens.

When the viewer learns later that Kurtz orchestrated the audition so that he could evaluate Charlie before recruiting her to their cause, the reasons for inserting this scene into the adaptation become clear. The scene emphasizes Charlie's naïveté to Kurtz's manipulations and makes explicit for the viewer the dynamic that Charlie will enter into once she agrees to work with the Israelis. Her reliance upon Kurtz for direction primes her to accept their terms of the relationship, wherein she will be the actress responsible for her performance, which is primarily orchestrated by Kurtz through Gadi. The dynamic for their relationship is set: Charlie must constantly respond to their shifting behavior to suit their needs while being given just enough control to feel empowered and like she has tackled their challenge. By establishing Kurtz as Charlie's director through this audition, Park illustrates for the viewer Charlie's skill as an actress and her conditioning to accept her diminished autonomy when she later becomes more and more involved in the Israeli mission.

The novel and adaptation emphasize Charlie's youthful appearance and acting skills as a way of performing both gender and autonomy. The novel notes that Charlie at 26 years old is "not the prettiest of girls, by any means, though her sexuality shone through" (le Carré 2011: 60). The adaptation emphasizes Charlie's attractiveness through the use of bold-colored dresses that make her stand out. In both versions, she contrasts with a character like Miss Bach, who is older and fits more neatly into the "secretarial" category of spies than the seductress. The novel describes her as a "quiet mannered business lady" who helps create Charlie's cover documents (le Carré 2011: 38) while the adaptation dresses her in conservative knitwear and anonymizes her so much that she is able to reconnoiter apartments without drawing attention. In both versions, she is both competent and aware of the overall operational plan. Comparing Charlie and Miss Bach suggests that youth and attractiveness hold a different value than age and experience. Charlie's appearance makes her ideal bait, but it does not necessarily confer on her the sort of agency Miss Bach has. Miss Bach may be older, graying, and "an old lush" (according to the adaptation), but she is also entrusted to be part of Kurtz's personal team. Charlie's appearance and youthfulness are therefore an asset to Kurtz's operation, but not to her own agency. Kurtz needs her to be able to perform the femininity that she can present but that Miss Bach lacks for the operation to succeed. He needs the beautiful young actress.

Charlie's career as an actress draws attention to the performative function of women in espionage narratives. Horn argues that the female spy "is first of all an actress" who often performs in front of the curtain while the men direct from behind (Horn 2013: 177). Charlie performs two heroines in the narrative: Joan of Arc from Shaw's *Saint Joan* and Rosalind from *As You Like It*. Gadi initially observes Charlie in *Saint Joan*, a play which thematically mirrors Charlie's situation: Joan's entanglement in the clash between competing, male-dominated societal forces, the Catholic Church, and the feudal lords mirrors how Charlie will be similarly caught between and destroyed by the Israelis and Palestinians. Casting Charlie as Rosalind associates her with the character's resilience and quick wit, both of which she needs to work for Kurtz. But Charlie cannot subsume her femininity like these characters do to assert power (Joan) or control over their lives (Rosalind). Kurtz needs her femininity to lure Khalil, so she must perform the part of woman who is beautiful but malleable.

Being an actress places Charlie in the middle of the Israeli-Palestinian conflict, embodied by Kurtz and Khalil. She is positioned as the object of contention between them, which means she cannot exert subjectivity herself. Considering Silver's paradigm where women in spy narratives "function as the third term in a triangle that is predicated on male rivalry and male bonding" (Silver 1987: 14), it is difficult to position Charlie as a subjective agent within this triangle. Female spies in Silver's schematic are almost always the contested object, a goal to be won. In *The Little Drummer Girl*, Kurtz and Khalil function as subjects competing to use Charlie for their aims. She is their object, the "exchangeable product" that both men vie for control over (Silver 1987: 14). If she were not malleable, Charlie would not be such an alluring prize.

Almost from the moment she accepts the mission, Charlie begins to explore ways of asserting her autonomy, whereas in the novel she accepts a teacher-pupil relationship with Gadi. The adaptation recognizes that Charlie's formal introduction to the Israelis is more a hostage situation than courtship, both in the sense that she is abducted after her date with Gadi at the Acropolis and because Kurtz preys on her psychologically, continuing in the Greek villa the manipulation that began at the fake audition. Charlie's relationship with her handler Gadi also begins in coercive fashion, with him deceiving her in Greece about his identity and motives. In the novel, Beene argues, Charlie's choice of Gadi over her sometimes-boyfriend Alastair simply substitutes one form of abuse for another (Beene 1992: 113). Kurtz and Gadi both enact their coercive desire to control Charlie, even if Gadi's abuse is emotional rather than physical. To counter this dynamic, Park's adaptation lets Charlie become aware of her status as object and works to capitalize on her value and exercise some autonomy within the male-dominated spy game. Thus, Charlie ceases to be a naïve object and instead enters a kind of self-aware objectified state.

The television series uses Gadi and Charlie's trip to deliver the car to let Charlie redress the power imbalance she senses between her and her Israeli handlers. Charlie does this in two ways that separate the adaptation from the novel: she insists on revising parts of the "fiction" the Israelis have created for her, and she establishes a system wherein she earns information from Gadi in exchange for every step of the mission she completes. In the novel, Gadi passes the fiction on to Charlie, who is expected to absorb it. Park's adaptation, however, shows Charlie asserting herself upon that narrative early in the trip. As they drive, Gadi outlines her fictional relationship with Michel, including the detail that Michel does not approve of women smoking. Charlie replies, "And I don't approve of men who disapprove of women smoking. Mush . . . I'm still meant to be myself, or a credible version, right?" She continues smoking, having won that round and changed, ever so slightly, the narrative Gadi built for her. That night, Gadi allows Charlie to construct the fiction surrounding Michel and Charlie's first sexual encounter, asking her how Michel is as a lover. "Enthusiastic, but he lacks technique," she replies. This marks a change from the novel, where Gadi continues to control the narrative, telling Charlie that Michel is "a little unimaginative, but his enthusiasm is boundless and his virility impressive" (le Carré 2011: 255). Park's television adaptation allows Charlie to define this sexual relationship in her own terms, giving her a greater stake in the narrative and helping make the fiction more real for later recollection.

Charlie's early insistence on contributing to the fiction gives her a greater stake in the narrative and bolsters Gadi's confidence in her ability to operate independently. The next day, when Charlie emerges from the hotel in heavy makeup, she waves away Gadi's look of apprehension by explaining that Michel loves it. He rewards her assertiveness and act of self-authorship with the keys to the car—she is in the driver's seat and Gadi appears to have accepted her as a co-author of the fiction. As such, Charlie takes control of some small parts of the fiction that Gadi has already built for her. In the larger sense, these interactions also imbue Charlie with a more distinct sense of self than she has in the novel. She knows herself well enough to know the things that she would not compromise on in her fictional relationship with Michel, even if she was head-over-heels in love. During the road trip, Charlie also establishes a system of exchange wherein she gets to ask Gadi one question every time she completes a task for him. She asks for this "so we're even," recognizing that she is risking more than she gains by working for the Israelis. The first question she asks him is, "How much of this is you?" She wants to know where he stops playing the role of Michel and starts being himself, but she pivots to a different question before he can answer. Instead, she poses a more mundane question about his marital status. This exchange demonstrates two things about Charlie's development of limited autonomy in the adaptation. First, she recognizes her value and leverages it for more information. Second, she also understands that knowing some information, like how much of Gadi is real and how much is performance, risks her ability to complete the mission. Charlie understands that the Israelis need her to have a limited perspective of the scope of the operation in order to play her role. She accepts that while finding smaller ways to feel more like a collaborator in the mission, like the system of exchanging actions for answers.

The adaptation appears to give Charlie significant agency, perhaps approaching autonomy, while on the trip.[5] She concocts the plan to fool the border guards through cleverness, disguising her nerves as an attempt to smuggle moonshine into Austria rather than deliver a carful of explosives whereas in the novel she distracts them by flashing cleavage and letting the thigh-high slit on her skirt fall open. While the novel's approach achieves the same practical ends—Charlie manages the border crossing—the adaptation does so in a way that allows Charlie to demonstrate her cunning and her independence rather than playing on her sexuality. This moves Charlie beyond the tropes of "more conventional spy thrillers" that position women "as ornamental sidekicks, villainous or dispensable sex objects" (Lassner 2015:11). She successfully delivers the car, and her conversation with Gadi when they reunite highlights just how much consideration she has earned from him. In the Munich hotel room, he entertains multiple questions from Charlie rather than just one:

> Gadi: Marty says you're a star. He wants to thank you in person tomorrow.
> Charlie: And what about you? Do you want to thank me in person?
> Gadi: You did a good thing today.
> Charlie: I enjoyed it. I loved it. Is that what happens? It gets addictive?
> Gadi: If you're the type.
> Charlie: Are you? Why did you tell me about the explosives when I got in the car?
> Gadi: One question at a time. [Pause] Because you *are* the type.
> Charlie: You said you would try to lie to me as little as possible. You wanted me to say no, didn't you? Is it wrong, Gadi, what we're doing? Or were you trying to help me for another reason?
> Gadi: You should run a bath. You need to relax.

While Gadi entertains her questions, even after invoking his "one question at a time" rule, this conversation also demonstrates the limitations of Charlie's ability to leverage her value in exchange for information and autonomy. Gadi draws back when the questions become personal and again threaten to reveal information about himself that may jeopardize Charlie's ability to view Gadi and Michel as the same entity. Charlie's acuity and ability to operate on her own earn her a greater, but not absolute, degree of transparency from Gadi. He divulges little and rebuffs her clear advances. More significantly, he reintroduces Kurtz into the equation and reminds the viewer that Charlie's autonomy exists within their fiction and does not extend into her relationship with Kurtz. Gadi may have controlled the fiction and allowed Charlie to contribute to it, but Kurtz controls the mission. The narrative is a means to an end for Kurtz, and the details of it matter little so long as it effectively builds a legend for Charlie to use within the larger mission.

The end of Gadi and Charlie's collaboration on the fiction precipitates both characters' realizations of the limits of their autonomy. Charlie is sent back to England to await contact from the Palestinian terror cell, and fades into the background as her handler, watching as the two subjective players in the game, Khalil and Kurtz, consider their next moves. Since neither Charlie nor Gadi occupies a subject position within the narrative, their system of exchange occurs between equals and works only until Kurtz reasserts himself as the architect of the operation, his machinations reimpose themselves on both characters. Charlie returns to England and in the adaptation expresses frustration at feeling like a sitting duck "paddling around all day with no direction, with no idea what might be coming up from the dark" to get her. She expresses awareness that her gender is what renders her an object in the narrative, remarking later in that exchange that, "that's all right. I'm a woman. I'm used to men pissing me about." Within the Israeli operation, Charlie has only been exposed to men in positions of control and women acting in service of those men. Even if operatives like Rose, Rachel, and Ms. Bach receive a high degree of respect and autonomy, they still operate under the purview of Kurtz. It is not until Charlie infiltrates the Palestinian terror organization that she encounters an example of female agency influencing the geopolitical structures of the narrative.

This example of agency takes the form of Fatmeh, Michel and Khalil's sister, whose role in the television series elevates her to a position of authority and subjectivity by making her directly in charge of the terror group. She directs the group, which allows her to influence events on a global scale, whereas Fatmeh in the novel exists as a functionary with the organization. The novel features Fatmeh as a worker in the "revolutionary offices" (le Carré 2011: 51) and as a nurse in the refugee camp. She is working for the cause, but her impact is local and confined to the camp, itself a former prison. The novel boxes her in symbolically and renders her functionally voiceless. When Tayeh brings Charlie to meet her, he notes that Fatmeh speaks no English and that he must interpret for her. Tayeh then uses Fatmeh as a tool to interrogate Charlie and test her authenticity. He inserts his own questions into his translations for Fatmeh, and he scours Charlie's face for signs of falsity. When he is finished and Charlie has passed his test, Tayeh washes his face as Fatmeh "rose and went silently to the basin and fetched a glass of water for him" (le Carré 2011: 423). Fatmeh serves Tayeh in the novel, but the adaptation inverts this dynamic and has Tayeh stand in as the puppet for Fatmeh. He questions Charlie until Fatmeh dismisses him and takes his place, making clear that she is not a servant but rather an autonomous participant in the espionage game on her own terms, leading the refugee camp and directing the attacks that Khalil undertakes. In Park's television adaptation, Fatmeh is a key player within the Palestinian organization, and through her Charlie observes an autonomous woman directing the conflict.

In the absence of Kurtz and Khalil, Fatmeh becomes a compelling rival for Charlie's loyalty. Fatmeh also clearly knows, like Kurtz, the limitations she faces that Charlie does not. Fatmeh notes how people will be drawn to Charlie's "pretty white face and clean passport," much the same way that Kurtz argued that Charlie was necessary to the operation because "a toy goat won't play" if you want to catch a lion. Charlie is drawn to Fatmeh's passionate and authoritative presence. When Fatmeh prepares her to leave, Charlie asserts that she is ready to do whatever Fatmeh says, claiming that for every Israeli attack they will together "strike back again, and again, and again."[6] Through her time with Fatmeh, Charlie sees the ways in which a woman can wield agency within this geopolitical context. Fatmeh appears to operate in the adaptation like the secretary in Horn's conception of female operatives. Whereas the Israelis in the novel possess a decent understanding of Fatmeh's role in the Palestinian group, Kurtz's group in the adaptation is unaware of the depth of her involvement. Kurtz's intense focus on Khalil lets Fatmeh fly under the radar. She may lack the physical freedom to cross borders unquestioned like Charlie, but living in the camp grants her anonymity that she uses to coordinate bombings and arms shipments. Being a woman makes this possible for her; if she were a man, Kurtz likely would have focused his attention on her as he did on her brothers.

Through witnessing Fatmeh's autonomy and reach, Charlie arrives back in England fully aware of the limitations of her own agency as she executes the final act of Kurtz's play. In both narratives, the fake bombing is successful and Kurtz insists on playing Charlie back to Khalil, so that she can use his attraction to her as a way to infiltrate the organization on a long-term basis:

Kurtz: Gadi, this changes everything. We follow her tonight.

Gadi: And take him, but don't kill him.

Kurtz: No . . . we let them run. Deep cover. We will have her by his side as he becomes the leader of his people.

Gadi: That could take years.

Kurtz: No, can't you see, Gadi? Can't you see what a big future he has? We could pull in every contact, every cell.

Gadi: No, you can't do that to her.

Kurtz: Give her the location transmitter, tell her to remove the batteries. If she is in real danger tonight, we will come in, if he is not so loving as she thinks, but otherwise . . . we leave her.

This exchange prompts Gadi to exercise real agency for the first time in the context of the broader mission, not just in his handling of Charlie and the fiction. This also marks the point where the adaptation begins to shift significantly away from the ending of the novel to emphasize Charlie's subjective agency and Gadi's awareness that he, too, is a puppet directed by Kurtz. Gadi listens to Kurtz, then tells Charlie a completely different plan: when she cuts the signal on her transmitter, he says, that will be the signal for the team to take Khalil. Gadi's sabotage of the plan is not part of the novel, and as such represents the strongest statement of Gadi's own agency within the adaptation, and perhaps its most significant alteration of the novel. His actions separate him from Kurtz and save Charlie so that she can forge her own autonomous path, creating a very different ending from the novel. Charlie does not emerge unscathed, but she is much more whole and self-possessed.

The divergent endings of the two narratives make clear that the adaptation's Charlie achieves a kind of personal, if not political, autonomy while her prospects for autonomy in the novel are much more uncertain. Charlie expresses a desire to "go back to where [she] was" (le Carré 2011: 527). This choice does not reflect growth but rather a desire not to change or be changed by what she has done. She returns to acting because Kurtz and the Israeli psychologist "decided that the time had come to throw Charlie back into the water" (le Carré 2011: 531); Charlie flounders in her return to the stage and is relegated to comedies. She cannot handle tragic roles because "she had no stomach any more—and, worse, no understanding for what passed for pain in Western middle class society. Thus comedy became, after all, the better mask for her" (le Carré 2011: 531). She mentally decompensates to the point where she sees Joseph in the audience during her show but cannot be certain that it is him "because the divide between her inner and outer world . . . had virtually ceased to exist" (le Carré 2011: 533). As with her return to the stage, Charlie has no choice in whether Gadi seeks her out. She flees the theater, a site of artifice and artificiality, and he follows her, with the novel ending after this exchange:

> Joseph came towards her down the empty street, walking very tall, and she imagined him breaking into a run in order to beat his own bullets to her, but he didn't. He drew up before her, slightly out of breath, and it was clear that someone had sent him with a message, mostly likely Marty, but perhaps Tayeh. He opened his mouth to deliver it, but she prevented him.
> "I'm dead, Jose. You shot me. Don't you remember?"
> She wanted to add something about the theater of the real, how the bodies didn't get up and walk away. But she lost it somehow. . . . She was leaning on him and she would have fallen if he hadn't been holding her so firmly. Her tears were half blinding her, and she was hearing him from under water. I'm dead, she kept saying. I'm dead, I'm dead. But it seemed that he wanted her dead or alive. Locked together, they set off awkwardly along the pavement, though the town was strange to them. (le Carré 2011: 534)

While critics like Aronoff and Silver have argued that the novel's ending contains the seeds of possibility for Charlie and Gadi to start over together, that optimism elides the clear damage Charlie has suffered while being the contested object between Kurtz and Khalil. Beene contends that the novel suggests "that they may repair the damage their psyches have suffered" and that "hope faintly appears as the two set off together" (Beene 1992: 122). The exchange that precedes that, however, exposes the depth of Charlie's emotional and psychological damage and the power imbalances that still typify the relationship. Charlie must rely upon Gadi for physical support and mental stability. Gadi still steers the relationship. *He* seeks her out after she returns to acting. *He* pursues her when she flees the theater. More troublingly, the text suggests that Gadi may not be removed from the spy game, but rather may be sent with a message from Kurtz, perhaps an offer for another mission. As a result, the novel presents a much more uncertain view of Charlie's autonomy in the end, questioning whether she is making decisions for herself and whether she is free of the Israelis and stable enough to make independent choices.

In the coda to Park's adaptation, Charlie's final actions constitute the full-fledged deployment of the personal autonomy that she exercises incrementally throughout the series. Kurtz's visit to her at the seaside retreat ties up loose threads of the plot while allowing Charlie to exercise her autonomy through her actions. Kurtz rationalizes his continued pursuit of Palestinian terrorists—a new bomber has emerged to replace Khalil, killing fifteen in Amsterdam—by saying, "You cannot stop the devil, only the man performing him." The Amsterdam bombing reveals the flaw in his plan. As le Carré wrote in a reflection on the 9/11 attacks and the relationship between terrorism and counterterrorism: "When it's over, it won't be over" (le Carré 2001: 17). In the novel as in the real world, killing one architect of terror only gives rise to more (and more zealous) recruits to the cause. Kurtz is a participant in a cycle of violence, no matter how much he tries to position himself as a moderating force keeping the more Hawkish echelon of Mossad at bay. Park's adaptation conflates Kurtz's tactics with the Palestinian terrorists so thoroughly that both parties are implicated in the continuation of violence. If Khalil played the devil to the Israelis, then Kurtz is the devil to the Palestinians. More importantly to Charlie, both are willing to sacrifice her, which she acknowledges when Kurtz admits to her that Gadi foiled his plan to feed her back into the Palestinian organization. When Charlie asks why Kurtz had Khalil killed, he replies, "That was not my order. Khalil would have gone on to become so much more than a terrorist," to which Charlie replies, "And Gadi stopped it." She now understands her role as Kurtz's sacrificial lamb, and she rejects his handshake, severing their connection. The scene reinforces this finality by having them depart down opposite staircases. Charlie strides off-screen with her head held high. Kurtz, by comparison, shuffles off slowly to continue his lonely crusade. He has lost Gadi, who he says, "will not speak to me anymore" and Charlie, the only two characters possessing the empathy necessary to understand the other side and perhaps break the cycle of strike and counterstrike so entrenched in the Israeli-Palestinian conflict.

Inserting this final confrontation with Kurtz followed by Charlie's reunion with Gadi allows the adaptation to end with a different tone, one that is "quite different . . . from the original, but moving and effective in its own right" (Hale 2018: C1). When Charlie leaves the Israeli retreat and seeks out Gadi, they are now on equal footing: permanent exiles from the Israeli apparatus. This allows Charlie to seek out Gadi at the end, making her the director of her own action for the final (and also first), definitive time in the series. The seeds of this decisive action are sown at the retreat, where Charlie initially rejects the package sent by Gadi, which contains his coded address, the vodka they drank together, and the scarf she used to signal that she needed him. These items are tokens from a past she no longer wants to be connected to. The adaptation makes it Charlie's choice to pursue a reunion with Gadi. He makes himself available, but for the first time, her choice belongs fully to her without coercive influence from the Israelis. There is no indication that Gadi would have sought her out if she had not come for him. Whereas previously the Israeli men sought her out, now Charlie must take action—typically a man's purview—to reunite with Gadi. She finds him living a quiet, domestic life, tending to his plants and sipping tea in the small courtyard outside his Berlin apartment. He sighs in relief upon seeing her and visibly relaxes. Charlie takes the lead in the conversation. "Who are you? Who am I?" she asks. Gadi responds, "One question at a time" and the series ends.

Charlie's final questions to Gadi may seem like an admission that she is lost, but in fact they represent a self-aware subjectivity not granted to her in the novel. The questions are not an indication that Charlie doesn't know who she is; she is past those existential confusions. Rather, these questions indicate that Charlie has grown beyond being a "manipulated object [who makes] unreflective choices" (Beene 1992: 114). Her identity to this point has been inextricably tied to a lie, her actions orchestrated by others. Park's version of Charlie never attempts a return to the theater, having had her fill of duplicity and living other people's lives. She is done acting for the benefit of others, realizing that the only agency she has is over her own life. Charlie must find a new way forward, a new thing to be that is neither an actress nor a spy. All she can be is herself.

Charlie's example provides the roadmap for Gadi to extricate himself as well. Watching her be destroyed by the opposing forces—Israeli and Palestinian, Kurtz and Khalil—that he could not control foregrounds his inability to resolve the broader conflict. The closure of Charlie's espionage career in Park's adaptation serves as an opening for viewers to consider the ways in which the central geopolitical conflict of the narrative resists definitive conclusions. Whereas the ideological disputes of the Cold War are considered for the most part settled by the end of the twentieth century, the conflict le Carré tackled in *The Little Drummer Girl* shows little sign of resolution almost 40 years after the novel's publication. From 2017-2019, Palestinians fired 2,600 rockets from Gaza into Israel (Frantzman 2021: para. 4), prompting retaliatory attacks by Israel. Palestinians continue to advocate for an autonomous state, while according to the United Nations, more than 700,000 Israelis live in illegal settlements in the West Bank ("Israel Settlement Expansion" 2021: para. 1). The extremes in the conflict remain entrenched, and much like Khalil and Kurtz, unable to "conceive that the other side might have some legitimacy" (Herman 2019: 114). Charlie and Gadi through their experiences can no longer deny the humanity of their opponents. They may not agree with the Palestinian tactics, but they find the Israeli counterterrorism efforts to be equally repulsive. In a mirror of reality, the exodus of moderating and empathetic voices from the discussion means that the positions of the terrorist and the counterterrorist remain incomprehensible to each other. The extremes on both sides control the conversation.

After existing as an object for both sides to contend for, Charlie knows her voice will not sway either side. Her agency still does not extend into the political realm. Instead, she unwittingly recruits a male agent to her perspective. Gadi joins her in rejecting espionage in favor of the private sphere, retreating to the "unguarded domesticity" (Garcia 2018: para. 15) of his flat in Berlin. Reunited there, both can exercise their autonomy, personally but not politically, going forward. The choice to end with Charlie and Gadi united in their withdrawal from the conflict makes sense for an adaptation thirty-five years after the novel's release. With so little progress made in resolving the conflict politically, the best a twenty-first-century adaptation can offer is the chance to retreat on one's own terms, to make one's own choices in determining the future. Charlie's autonomy is incomplete; it does not extend to the political realm, but the adaptation's end makes clear that political autonomy does not extend to most men, either. All one can hope for in the face of such intractable conflict, Park suggests, is the time and space to determine your own, personal future. That is exactly what happens at the close of the series. Gadi holds his door open, inviting Charlie in, but it is Charlie who chooses to cross the threshold, determining for herself where—and who—she wants to be.

Notes

1   In a review for *The New Republic*, David Pryce-Jones characterizes Charlie as a "decoy" whose motivations are "incoherent" and declares that "the willing submission of Charlie to Kurtz and Gadi is an implausibility so enormous and so central that the

story collapses under it" (Pryce-Jones 1983: 28–9). Van Teeffelen's discussion of the Palestinian portrayal in *The Little Drummer Girl* pegs Charlie as a "sympathetic but immature-looking British actress" (Van Teeffelen 2004: 445). In his 1983 review of the novel, Kellman notes that it is the rare literary outing in which its critical reception matched its commercial one—it became an immediate bestseller—but he does not allow for much autonomy for Charlie (Kellman 1983: 906). He considers her an "actress of hazy leftist sympathies and easy virtue" and does not explore her autonomy beyond calling her a victim of Israeli kidnapping (907). In his reading, Charlie is not an actor on this stage, but rather another victim "torn between contradictory world views, between the arms of Khalil and those of Joseph" (Kellman 1983: 911). Aronoff calls Charlie a "fantasist" and notes that by the end of the novel, Charlie wants out rather than to sleep with Khalil, but she cannot extricate herself because of Gadi's persistence, so she remains in an objectified position (50). Emerson chastises le Carré as "not good on sex and love and women" in her review of the novel, which she claims, "reads like a dream" regardless of "the central problem of Charlie" (Emerson 1983: 76). She concludes that Charlie, not motivated by the Israeli's ideology, instead craves a "master/slave relationship" that results in her having "little identity or purpose" (Emerson 1983: 76). To Emerson, Charlie is "a doll the Israeli men animate rather than a person" (Emerson 1983: 76).

2   Park's television adaptation offers a tepid way forward in the sample of Professor Menkel's lecture where she says, "Both peoples are wounded. And both peoples have wounded. It is only through accepting our own faults that we might forgive those faults" in the other side. Such a statement falls short of suggesting a solution, however, and is contentious enough to make her a target for assassination, suggesting that such moderating figures have little chance of success when positioned between the extremities of Kurtz and Khalil.

3   Aronoff assigns the hero's role to Gadi, whom he calls "the first hero in a le Carré novel in which Smiley does not appear to display the development of a skeptical stance" (Aronoff 1999: 69).

4   Perhaps the most prominent review to contest this and argue that Charlie plays an active role in the novel is Broyard's 1983 review for *The New York Times*. Broyard notes in *The Little Drummer Girl* "women now play active, not passive, roles in politics" (Broyard 1983: C29). Broyard's reading elides any discussion of motivation, however, and Charlie's remains murky and driven by Kurtz rather than by her own choices. She is not an ideologue, and without intervention from Kurtz likely would not have felt urged to action on either front beyond her superficial participation in causes.

5   It should be noted that this minimal autonomy does not mean that Charlie entirely avoids being objectified by the camera. Indeed, Park's television adaptation dresses Charlie in a variety of bold outfits, often with daring low cuts and thigh slits, frequently without the benefit of a bra. This visual objectification makes the viewer feel in some way complicit with the objectification she chafes against in the television adaptation. Viewers see her, through the camera, primarily as a product of Israeli (male) authorship insofar as it pertains to her visual presentation. It is only through her actions that her cleverness pushes back against this visual objectification to assert that she can and will contribute to her own narrative. These actions help overcome the fact that complicates how the viewer "gets at the interior of the characters' minds as they listen; they must visibly, physically embody their responses for the camera to record, or they must talk about their reactions" (Hutcheon 2012: 25). Park does externalize Charlie's interiority in a way that makes her thoughts explicit. He inserts a scene where

Charlie recites Palestinian poetry as the camera pans across the faces of the Israeli team listening in through the bug in her apartment. Charlie knows they are listening, and the poetry reflects an interiority that seeks to humanize both herself and the Palestinians: "As for me, I like to be loved as I am, not as a color photo in the paper, or as an idea composed in a poem amid the stags. I hear Leila's faraway scream from the bedroom. Do not leave me a prisoner of rhyme in the tribal nights. Do not leave me to them as news. I am a woman—no more, and no less."

6　If there is a weakness in the television adaptation's narrative, it is that it firmly establishes Charlie's acting abilities early and often. Even in this crucial moment, the viewer feels little risk that Charlie has gone over to the other side. When she makes contact with the Israeli team almost immediately upon her arrival at the airport, any doubt about her allegiance evaporates. This is not a fatal flaw for the narrative, however, since Park's adaptation is less about whether Charlie remains loyal and more about whether Charlie succeeds in extracting herself from opposing forces who are vying for her loyalty yet would sacrifice her without a second thought if necessary.

References

Aronoff, Myron (1999), *The Spy Novels of John le Carré: Balancing Ethics and Politics*, New York: St. Martin's Press.

Beene, LynnDianne (1992), *John le Carré*, New York: Twayne Publishing.

Broyard, Anatole (1983), "Books of the Times: THE LITTLE DRUMMER GIRL. by John le Carré," *The New York Times*, 25 February, Saturday, Late City Final Edition, C29.

Burke, Jason (2018), "Does the Little Drummer Girl Help Us Understand Modern Terrorism?" *The Guardian*, 27 October. Available online: https://www.theguardian.com /tv-and-radio/2018/oct/27/little-drummer-girl-le-carre-modern-terrorism-bbc-drama

Carlston, Erin (2013), *Double Agents: Espionage, Literature, and Liminal Citizens*, New York: Columbia University Press.

Denning, Michael (2014), *Cover Stories: Narrative and Ideology in the British Spy Thriller*, New York: Routledge.

Emerson, Sally (1983), "Recent Fiction," *Illustrated London News*, 1 May: 76.

Frantzman, Seth J. (2021), "What do we know about the Number of Rockets Fired at Israel?" *The Jerusalem Post*, 17 May. Available online: https://www.jpost.com/arab -israeli-conflict/what-do-we-know-about-the-number-of-rockets-fired-at-israel -668339

Garcia, Lawrence (2018), "Shadow Play: Park Chan-Wook's *The Little Drummer Girl*," MUBI Notebook, 05 December. Available online at: https://mubi.com/notebook/posts/ shadow-play-park-Chan-wook-s-the-little-drummer-girl (accessed January 3, 2021).

Hale, Mike (2018), "Loads of Seduction and Some Spycraft," *The New York Times*, 19 November, C1.

Hepburn, Allan (2005), *Intrigue: Espionage and Culture*, New Haven: Yale University Press.

Herman, Peter C. (2019), *Unspeakable: Literature and Terrorism from the Gunpowder Plot to 9/11*, New York: Routledge.

Horn, Eva (2013), *The Secret War: Treason, Espionage, and Modern Fiction*, Evanston: Northwestern University Press.

Hutcheon, Linda (2012), *A Theory of Adaptation*, New York: Taylor & Francis Group.

"Israel Settlement Expansion 'tramples' on Human Rights Law, Experts Contend," *United Nations News*, 3 November 2021. Available online: https://news.un.org/en/story/2021/11/1104792

Kellman, Steven G. (1983), "The Fearful Symmetry of John le Carré," *The Georgia Review*, 37 (4): 905–11.

Lassner, Phyllis (2016), *Espionage and Exile: Fascism and Anti-Fascism in British Spy Fiction and Film*, Edinburgh: Edinburgh University Press.

Le Carré, John (2001), "A War We Cannot Win," *The Nation*, 273 (16): 15–17.

Le Carré, John (2011), *The Little Drummer Girl*, New York: Penguin Publishing Group.

Pryce-Jones, David (1983), "A Demonological Fiction," *The New Republic*, 18 April: 27–30.

Silver, Brenda R. (1987), "Woman as Agent: The Case of le Carré's 'Little Drummer Girl,'" *Contemporary Literature*, 28 (1): 14–40.

Van Teeffelen, Toine (2004), "(Ex)Communicating Palestine: From Best-Selling Terrorist Fiction to Real-Life Personal Accounts," *Studies in the Novel*, 36 (3): 438–58.

White, Rosie (2007), *Violent Femmes: Women as Spies in Popular Culture*, New York: Routledge.

10

"Extolling the Virtues of Alpaca Cloth or Buttons Made of Tagua Nut"

The Influence of Douglas Hayward, Tailoring and James Bond on *The Tailor of Panama*

Llewella Chapman

This chapter focuses on John le Carré's satirical spy thriller, *The Tailor of Panama* (1996), its subsequent film adaptation, and how menswear and tailoring impact on the narrative, plot, and characterization of these texts. *The Tailor of Panama* focuses on Harry Pendel, a British expatriate and former convict living in Panama City, who has since established a successful bespoke tailoring business "Pendel and Braithwaite". However, on meeting and being manipulated by British MI6 agent, Andrew Osnard, his fantasies spiral out of control when he feeds information to Osnard that focus on the "Silent Opposition", leading to a geopolitical invasion of Panama by the United States. Besides tailoring, *The Tailor of Panama* is heavily inspired by Graham Greene's novel *Our Man in Havana* (1958), in that both novels are an ironic take on protagonists, who are recruited by the British Secret Service, as *ineffectual* spies and their double identities. A film adaptation of the novel was released in 2001, directed by John Boorman, and starring Geoffrey Rush as Pendel and Pierce Brosnan as Osnard, who at the time also starred as James Bond. In the novel's acknowledgments, le Carré writes: "Doug Hayward of Mount Street W allowed me my first misty glimpse of Harry Pendel" (le Carré 1996: 360). Hayward was le Carré's personal tailor, and in this chapter, I will analyze the extent that tailoring and the Bond films influence the novel, scripts, and film. As recognized by Gerald Egan, "the predominant focus" on studies of fashion and literature "has been on representations of clothing and dress within literary texts, or on the discourses that occur around these texts. What, we might ask . . . about the author? How did he or she dress?" (Egan 2020: 3). Therefore, this chapter will analyze how these factors shaped le Carré's authorship through his knowledge of tailoring obtained from Hayward, and the subsequent film adaptation.

Unlike Greene's protagonist in *Our Man in Havana*, James Wormold, a vacuum cleaner retailer based in Havana, le Carré elects to focus Pendel's identity and "double cover" on the intrinsic relationship between tailoring, clothing, and spying instead.

The connection between espionage and tailoring is not new, and is exemplified by the suit being coded in literature and cinema as the "armour" of the "gentleman hero," as acknowledged by Jay McInerney, Nick Foulkes, Neil Norman, and Nick Sullivan in their analysis of the Bond character: "the well-tailored suit is to Bond the armour of his profession. And the better the tailoring, the more effective the armour" (Norman 1996: 117). Similarly, Edward Buscombe argues in relation to Cary Grant's portrayal of Roger Thornhill, dressed throughout in a two-piece blue-grey glen check suit, in *North by Northwest* (1959): "Grant is a conspicuous example of what can be achieved in that department by meticulous dressing, and the type of manhood that it implies . . . Grant showed that being genteel, *soigné*, and well-mannered was an equally successful form of masculinity," as opposed to "the kind of aggressive masculinity which the cinema so often promotes, the kind we associate with Clark Gable and Gary Cooper, or more latterly with Mel Gibson or Bruce Willis, the rugged, hirsute, sweaty sort of manhood that spurns a neatly pressed trouser leg or crisp white shirt cuff" (Buscombe 2000: 203). The most recent entry and satirical take on the relationship between espionage and suits is the series of *Kingsman* films (2014, 2017, 2021) adapted from Mark Millar's and Dave Gibbons's comic book series *Kingsman: The Secret Service* (2012–2018), which, as Harry Hart (Colin Firth) puts it in *Kingsman: The Secret Service* (2014): "The suit is the modern gentleman's armour."

However, the wearing of a well-tailored suit as the "armour" of a gentleman hero does not necessarily equate to class. As argued by James Chapman, despite Bond of the novels "having all the trappings of the traditional fictional gentleman hero" (2007: 24), the character is presented by Ian Fleming as "a modern, even classless, hero" (2007: 29). For example, although Bond owns a vintage Bentley and refers to having an "expensive tailor" in *Dr. No* (Fleming 1958: 23), as a secret agent employed by the British Secret Service, Bond is a middle-grade civil servant and is reflective of the rise of the professional society, which Harold Perkin explains "is structured around career hierarchies rather than classes, one in which people find their place according to trained expertise and the service they provide rather than the possession or lack of inherited wealth or acquired capital" (1989: 359). Bond remains classless in the films, although he is assigned a Savile Row tailor in *Dr. No* (1962)—Leiter: "Interesting. Where were you measured for this, bud?" Bond: "My tailor. . . Savile Row"—in part to emphasize the quality of his "armour" to audiences.[1] Arguably, it is the "gentleman hero" form of masculinity that Pendel attempts to embody through his relationship to tailoring and clothing to hide his convict past.

As recognized by Stella Bruzzi, academic discussions of costume "have tended to exclude men and masculine identities, as if an attention to dress is an inherently feminine trait, despite the recent debates around masculinity and the eroticised male image in cinema . . . or some recent psychoanalysis-based studies of men and cultural/social identity," a case that remains true today in relation to tailoring, espionage, and fiction which this chapter will redress (1997: xv). To research this relationship between tailoring and spying in the different versions of *The Tailor of Panama*, I draw upon the three draft scripts penned by Andrew Davies and Boorman for the film that are available in the Andrew Davies papers held by De Montfort University's (UK) special collections (DMUSC), and assess how the costumes worn by Pendel and Osnard in the film contextualize the role of tailored suits in fictional narratives promoting masculinity and espionage.

Douglas Hayward

Born in London's East End, Hayward eschewed his working-class roots when deciding on the job role he wanted to train for—his father cleaned the boilers at the BBC and his mother worked in a bullet factory during the Second World War —becoming a tailor as "he wanted a clean job" (Glenys Roberts 2019). Initially employed by Montague Burton in Shepherd's Bush, it was requested that Hayward work in the back of the shop owing to his Cockney accent and "to work on his act" (Roberts 2019). It was here that Hayward met Richard Burton and Peter Sellers, and also acquired contacts in the film and entertainment industry through Basil Dearden, who was married to Melissa Stribling, the sister of his first wife Diana. On Hayward leaving Montague Burton to work as the "front of house man" for tailor Robbie Stanford, he met Dimitrov Major, who at the time was employed by Stanford as an out-worker. Hayward and Major went on to briefly form their own firm, Major Hayward Bespoke, in which Del Smith explains: "Hayward was the personality; a great networker who could get the clients, and Major was the craftsman who made everything in the workshop" (2019). Hayward left the partnership in order to set up his own bespoke firm in 1967, briefly running it from shirtmaker Frank Foster's premises in Pall Mall, and during this time relied on the famous clients that he had made through his exuberant, witty, and charming personality, before purchasing premises at 95 Mount Street so as to avoid the "military mentality" of Savile Row, and where he remained until his death in 2008.

Besides le Carré, Hayward's notable clientele included Roger Moore, for whom Hayward would tailor the suits for his Bond films *For Your Eyes Only* (1981), *Octopussy* (1983) and *A View to a Kill* (1985), John Barry, Tony Bennett, Michael Caine, Terry Donovan, Clint Eastwood, Mia Farrow, John Gielgud, Rex Harrison, John Osborne, Michael Parkinson, Harold Pinter, Jean Shrimpton, Terence Stamp, Tommy Steele, and Sharon Tate.[2] Hayward's previous film credits include tailoring suits for Laurence Harvey in *The Spy with a Cold Nose* (1966), Stamp in *Modesty Blaise* (1966) in which Hayward appeared in a cameo role, Noël Coward in *Boom!* (1968), Stephen Boyd in *Assignment K* (1968) and Caine in *The Italian Job* (1969). Hayward was named as the costume designer for *The Reckoning* (1970) and credited as costuming the men for *Dominique* (1980).

Hayward outlined his approach to tailoring bespoke suits:

> The basics of a suit you don't mess about with: single-breasted, with two or three buttons, side vents, straight jacket pockets with flaps (no one has waistcoats any more, thank God). You make it simple and you make it well. There's no great secret to it, you bring your taste to it and, of course, the way you actually cut the suit. Tailoring is the same everywhere, it's just how you interpret the rules . . . I've always thought that if you line up ten of my suits, no one should be able to tell who the tailor is, except me. If you go to Anderson & Sheppard, or Huntsman, or any Savile

Row tailor, you can tell them from thirty yards. They are very elegant, beautifully made, but they have a particular style. (Jones 1998: 420)

However, as Moore put it: "You can always spot a Hayward" ("Douglas Hayward" 2008: 21). Regarding Hayward's principle toward tailoring Moore's suits for his Bond films, Hayward wanted to

> keep them as classic as possible, as I believe people will be watching Bond films in twenty years' time . . . keep noticeable details, such as turn-back cuffs, to a minimum. Fred Astaire could walk down the street today in a suit that was made for him in the 1930s and look fabulous. I have always borne that in mind when making clothes for films and I don't think I have ever done work for a film I am now embarrassed by. (Roger Moore with Gareth Owen 2012: 125)

On Hayward's charisma, which was oft cited as the reason behind the tailor's success, and how he came to be le Carré's inspiration for Pendel, Terry O' Neill referred to Hayward as "the buddha of Mount Street," explaining: "You wouldn't believe the number of people who go to him for advice. He's probably the best-loved man in London," and Hayward himself admitted: "I suppose women talk to their hairdresser and men talk to their tailor. If you give them the chance all their worries will come flying out" ("Douglas Hayward" 2008, 21). As Hayward's daughter, Polly Westmacott-Hayward, put it: "On the grounds that you hear all sorts of things whilst you're measuring someone's inner leg, *The Tailor of Panama* is the perfect spy scenario" (2019). This tendency to reveal information to one's tailor is not dissimilar to the role of the spy in espionage narratives, in that they obtain information and draw confidence by presenting themselves as an impassive and blank screen to which people inadvertently project their thoughts and feelings, a technique used by both George Smiley and the Soviet spy chief Karla in le Carré's *Tinker, Tailor, Soldier, Spy* (1974) (Mark Fisher 2011: 37–42).

Douglas Hayward as Harry Pendel in
The Tailor of Panama (1996)

In le Carré's full acknowledgment to Hayward, he outlined:

> Doug, if you ever drop by to be measured for a suit, is likely to receive you sitting in an armchair beside the front door. There's a cosy old sofa to sit on, and a coffee table strewn with books and magazines. No portrait of the great Arthur Braithwaite hangs, alas, on his wall, neither does he tolerate much in the way of chit-chat in his fitting room, where the mood is brisk and businesslike. But if you close your eyes one quiet summer's evening in his shop, you may just hear the distant echo of Harry Pendel's voice extolling the virtues of alpaca cloth or buttons made of tagua nut. (1996: 360)

The novel begins with Osnard entering Pendel and Braithwaite to demand Pendel measure him for a suit, and alludes immediately to Pendel's different personas: "When he barged in, Pendel was one person. By the time he barged out again Pendel was another" (le Carré 1996: 1). The first reference to the process of tailoring is on Pendel visiting his bank manager, Ramón Rudd, to discuss his failed investment in a rice farm:

> Rudd's jacket was pinching him under his armpits. They stood at the big window face-to-face while he folded his arms across his chest, then lowered them to his sides, then linked his hands behind his back while Pendel tentatively tugged with his fingertips at the seams, waiting like a doctor to know what hurt. "It's only a tad, Ramón, if its anything at all," he pronounced at last. "I'm not unpicking the sleeves unnecessarily because it's bad for the jacket. But if you drop it in next time we'll see." (le Carré 1996: 9)

On being named as le Carré's inspiration behind his lead character Pendel, the tailor remarked: "I'm flattered if I have helped with the book. David Cornwell took me out for a couple of lunches and he checked a lot of details about tailoring with me," although he denied he was the character in real life: "But I am not Pendel, even if he thinks I am. The atmosphere of my shop is very accurate and that's all I think he used" (Nigel Reynolds 1996: 3). In the novel, le Carré describes the atmosphere through the eyes of Osnard:

> The curved mahogany staircase leading to the gents' boutique on the upper gallery: my goodness me the dear old staircase . . . The foulards, dressing gowns, monogrammed house slippers: yes, yes, I remember you well . . . The library steps artfully converted to a tie-rack: who'd have thought *that's* what they'd do with it? The wooden punkahs swinging lazily from the moulded ceiling, the bolts of cloth, the counter with its turn-of-the-century shears and brass rule set along one edge: old chums, every one . . . And finally the scuffed leather porter's chair, authenticated by local legend as Braithwaite's very own. And Pendel himself sitting in it, beaming with benign authority upon his new account. (1996: 25. Emphasis in original)

This echoes both Caine's and Moore's reminiscences regarding the atmosphere on visiting Hayward's shop, as well as echoing Fleming's description of opulent surroundings in his novels, for example, Blades gentlemen's club in *Moonraker* (1955), seen through the eyes of Bond.[3] Besides Bond and tailoring, it is over the course of Osnard persuading Pendel to spy for him on behalf of the British government that Osnard comes to codename Pendel "Buchan," which le Carré used in reference to John Buchan, author of *The Thirty-Nine Steps* (1915).

On a tailor being deployed as a spy, Hayward opined:

> Yes, I suppose a tailor might make a very good spy . . . In a way you do hear a lot of gossip, lots of incidental things about business and so on. You do know things because in a way a tailor is rather anonymous and customers say things in front of you as if you were not there. You get into a position with a tailor when it is very

difficult to be formal when you're standing there in your underpants. (Reynolds 1996: 3)

This is reflected when Pendel explains to Osnard, "Andy, if I told you that the walls of my fitting room hear more confessions than a priest in a penitentiary, I'd still be underselling them" (le Carré 1996: 56). An example of not overhearing information in the novel includes Pendel making a visit to the President of Panama, of which Osnard has requested that Pendel discover the reason for the president's "missing hours" in Paris, Tokyo, and Hong Kong, and where the president mistakenly refers to Pendel as Braithwaite:

> The great spy is kneeling, pinning the presidential left trouser leg, but his wits do not desert him. "And if I might enquire of His Excellency with respect whether we were able to relax during our highly triumphant Far Eastern tour at all, sir?" . . . And still no phone rings, nothing disturbs the blessed truce while the Keeper of the Keys to Global Power considers his reply. "Too tight," he announces. "You make me too tight, Mr Braithwaite. Why won't you let your President breathe you tailors?" (le Carré 1996: 118)

Pendel goes on to exaggerate this conversation when relaying it to Osnard, telling him that the president engaged in secret talks with the Japanese, and possibly offers a Bondian reference when embellishing the cut of the president's suits: "The president wishes a special pocket inside the left breast of all his suits, to be added in total confidence. I'm to get the length of barrel from Marco" (le Carré 1996:121). For example, Anthony Sinclair cut the suits for Sean Connery's Bond larger so they might accommodate a gun prop yet ensure the line and drape of the suit remained clean.[4]

On the other tailors credited by le Carré, Dennis Wilkinson, a fourth-generation tailor who worked for the family business L. G. Wilkinson based in St George Street, London, was named as the inspiration behind Pendel's love of classical music (*The Mikado* and Mozart in particular), with the author explaining "when he cuts [suits], [Wilkinson] likes nothing better than to turn his key upon the world and play his favourite classics" (le Carré 1996: 360). Similarly to Hayward, Wilkinson also insisted that his advice was confined to the processes of tailoring, rather than inspiring any characters who appear in the novel (Reynolds 1996: 3). Another name credited by le Carré was Alex Rudelhof, manager of the gentleman's outfitter, Mr. Alex, based on Heath Street in Hampstead, of which le Carré lived locally. Rudelhof "admitted" le Carré "to the intimate mysteries of measuring" (le Carré 1996: 360).

Tailoring the Novel: Andrew Davies's and John Boorman's Script Adaptations (1998–2000)

In the "Production Notes" for the film, Boorman explained that when Columbia Pictures first mooted an adaptation of le Carré's novel to him, he was presented with a draft script penned by the author himself: "I met le Carré and got on with him enormously well—he's wise and funny and a great raconteur, I shaped the script from the book and le Carré's script" (Columbia Pictures 2001: 3). However, Boorman's statement denies the contribution of Andrew Davies, whose film scriptwriting credits included *Circle of Friends* (1995) and *Bridget Jones's Diary* (2001) prior to *The Tailor of Panama*, and whose work was an obvious influence on Boorman's script (Davies would also receive a scriptwriting credit for the film, along with Boorman and le Carré).

Davies's first draft script was completed in January 1998. On its title page, Davies scrawls in a spidery hand: "Open with Harry, playful Sean Connery titles" demonstrating his intention to inject Bond references into his adaptation (1998). This is, in part, based on le Carré's playful and subtle reference to Bond when Nigel Stormont, Head of Chancery at the British Embassy considers Osnard's name: "Mister Andrew *Osnard*—was that some sort of bird?" in reference to Fleming electing to name Bond after the author of *Birds of the West Indies* (1936) (le Carré 1996: 101. Emphasis in original). Davies's mention of Connery is a suggestion made after the completion of his draft script, as it differs from the first scene that is written to introduce the viewer to Osnard first instead. Osnard is described as brooding "like a rather louche young hawk . . . a flop of hair, intelligent eyes, mouth all appetite," and Davies suggests that the character wears a "dark suit, not too well pressed, but carried off with style" (1998: 1). Later, Osnard is further described as having "the utter confidence of an upper-class Englishman though (like many younger examples of the breed) his diction is slovenly and slightly [Thames] 'Estuary'" (1998: 9). We are introduced to Pendel in his tailoring workshop after Osnard enters San Jose Church:

INT. HARRY'S SHOP. DAY.

Harry Pendel is a tailor, an artist and a dreamer. Solidly built in shirt sleeves, measuring tape draped over his shoulders. He is about to start cutting a new suit. The rich cloth, the chalk line a mere indication. He picks up his sheers. Pauses a second, as if in prayer or dedication. The choir—we've been hearing the church music—pause for a moment. Marta, Harry's manageress, stands by like an acolyte . . . Two of Harry's assistants, sitting cross-legged in the traditional style, pause too in their hand-sewing, their needles suspended in the air.

Then Harry cuts, with the firmness and accuracy of a surgeon. The sound of it in the silence—then the joyful music of the choir again, Harry smiles, the sewing tailors carry on with their work. (1998: 1–2)

On Osnard entering Pendel's premises and being measured for a suit, Davies directly borrows lines from le Carré's novel regarding the size of Osnard's waist:

"What's the damage?" Osnard asked.
"Let's say a modest thirty-six plus, sir."

"Plus what?"

"Plus lunch, put it that way, sir," said Pendel, and won a much needed laugh. (le Carré 1996: 39–40)[5]

Davies further tweaks text from le Carré in this scene, including a moment where, on measuring Osnard's inside leg, Pendel quips: "And we dress right—or left? Most of my gentlemen favour left these days—I don't <u>think</u> it's political!" (1998: 14. Emphasis in original).[6]

In a reference toward tailoring and geopolitics, and possibly Bond in Davies's script, Pendel furiously reacts when his friend, Mickie Abraxas, questions: "Why do you make this shit, Harry? Why can't you make suits like Armani?" to which Pendel replies:

> Why can't I make suits like Armani? You think Armani could make a suit like Harry Pendel? OK! Get out, fuck off, go down the road, buy an Armani, save yourself a thousand dollars! See if I care! Here you get Savile Row bespoke tailoring with four hundred years tradition behind it, there you have an Italian gents outfitter, if you can't understand the difference, save your money! The whole country is going down the plughole, nobody cares! Someone has to stand up and be counted, someone has to say "here I am and this is what I stand for—impeccable standards and old-fashioned integrity," And if you don't like it, you can go down the road! But let me tell you something, gentlemen! When you've gone down the road, it's all over! It's curtains! And I'm not just talking about Panama! I'm talking about the whole human race! (1998: 93)

This is adapted directly from the novel; however, Pendel's speech to Mickey is less about geopolitics and more about the quality of a Pendel and Braithwaite-tailored suit over Armani, and Pendel later echoes Hayward's belief that a suit should be anonymous: "If somebody *notices* a suit of mine, I'm embarrassed because there must be something wrong with it" (le Carré 1996: 245. Emphasis in original). Davies adapts this speech to demonstrate the British perception of superiority through the quality of Savile Row bespoke tailoring over Italian made-to-measure suits—and thus by extension, the rest of the world—and it also perhaps reflects the British press's reaction when it was announced that Brosnan was to play James Bond, for which Brosnan wore an Armani suit to the press launch in 1994.[7]

Davies's script differs mainly from the novel in the ending afforded to Pendel and Osnard. In the novel, Osnard absconds from Panama with the money that Sandy Luxmore, Osnard's superior in London, provided him to fund the uprising of the "Silent Opposition", Pendel and his wife Louisa are not reconciled, with Pendel leaving their home to experience the sacking of the city that he caused: "And certainly in the place that he was headed for, nobody would ever again ask him to improve on life's appearance, neither would they mistake his dreaming for their terrible reality" (le Carré 1996: 358). Instead, Davies elected for Pendel to shoot Osnard:

> OSNARD
>   Fuck. That was a surprise.
>   What d'you do that for? Stupid cunt.
> HARRY
>   I always knew you weren't a gentleman. (Davies 1998: 132)

Davies also adapts the ending where Pendel remains with his wife, Louisa, after Pendel takes the British government's money brought to Panama by Luxmore to pay his debts from the rice farm, although they remain on bad terms: "She looks at him. She can't bear it. She turns away and walks down the hill after the kids. He stands there, rich, guilty" (Davies 1998: 135).

Boorman came to rewrite elements of Davies script, with a fifth draft being completed in March 2000 having been revised throughout February. Adopting the Bondian trope of a pre-title sequence, the script begins with a US Airforce attack plane flying toward Panama with the co-pilot asking "Why are we bombing Panama again?" to which the pilot replies "It's got a canal" (Boorman 2000b: X1). Boorman then elects to begin with Pendel in his shop instead, as Davies had scribbled on the front of his version:

> [Pendel] is conducting a private consultation for a newcomer. His panelled walls bear photographs of the Queen of England and the Duke of Edinburgh, the Panamanian President in a cutaway suit, and distinguished customers—we might recognise Sean Connery and Jack Nicholson . . .
>
>> HARRY
>> The way I see it, we all have a dream of ourselves that we could be more than we are. Well, Pendel and Braithwaite are here to help you realise your dream, in the Savile Row tradition. This one, now [shows customer a "fine blue-mid cloth"].
>> CUSTOMER
>> ["a thick set man with a bald head"]
>> Yes. I guess this is kinda. . .
>> HARRY
>> I thought you'd like that one. (whispers). Mr Connery's choice. ["The customer's eyes widen in awe"]. Matter of fact, as soon as you came in, I thought who does he remind me of? And that's it. In the build, too. Golfer's shoulders. (2000b: 2A)

The description of Osnard is also tweaked slightly from Davies's, as having "the confidence and addiction of an upper-class Englishman" (Boorman 2000a: 14). Boorman further develops Davies's ideas and makes his version more explicit in its geopolitics, particularly in jest against the Bond films. For example:

> INT. PENTAGON. CONFERENCE ROOM.
>> GENERAL MORECOMBE
>> (banter) How's the Empire, Scotty?
>> LUXMORE
>> Ever shrinking, but still far flung.
>> GENERAL MORECOMBE
>> That's what I like about spying. Size doesn't matter. Little guys, big guys. Same with countries. You can be the world's only superpower, or you can be a has-been little island with nothing to lose but its illusions. Long as you've got a few secrets to put on the table, nobody gives a shit. (2000b: 94)

On replacing the pre-title sequence that originally included the US Airforce with scenes set in the MI6 building at the beginning of his revised "production draft" dated September 22, 2000, Boorman explained that he wrote it following the casting of Brosnan, and both the director and actor were concerned about the liability of casting "Bond" as Osnard, with Boorman musing "a liability or an asset? A bit of both I suppose. We're reconstructing the Bond myth really, so that scene is a steer for the audience. It's skewered to him being an absolute shit." (Chanty 2001: 81) The "M" sequence begins with Osnard, "a spy in his 40s," in Luxmore's office being informed that he will be sent to Panama: "Best I could do, Andrew. In the circumstances. Given your sins. They were baying for blood. I pleaded with them, 'put his long service, his fine brain in the balance against the gambling debts, the blown cover and the wives, the wives . . .'" (Boorman 2000c: 1). Osnard is then sent on a flight to Panama, with Boorman directing that the "main titles proceed as before" (Boorman 2000c: 2). Later, Stormont questions: "Not the Osnard drummed out of Madrid? The foreign minister's wife, wasn't it?," to which Osnard replies: "Not his wife. Mistress. There are some things I wouldn't do for England. In the line of duty, incidentally," making a wry comment with particular regard to both Moore's and Brosnan's performances as Bond (Boorman 2000c: 32A).

Regarding the ending, of which Boorman retained Davies's idea of Pendel shooting Osnard in the fifth draft screenplay dated March 2000, Boorman explained that it had to be changed because American preview audiences did not appreciate it: "We had a disastrous preview. Studios think in slogans: me directing Pierce in a le Carré thriller. They talk themselves into thinking it's a quasi-Bond film, and that's how they recruit the preview audience" (Chanty 2001: 81). So instead, Boorman rewrote the scenes to ensure Osnard's survival, absconding from Panama with the money and diplomatic immunity, similarly to the way le Carré ended his novel, though Boorman wrote it in keeping with the other Bondian references introduced in the scripts:

INT. LEARJET. DAWN.
Osnard has the moneybags strapped into the seat next to him. An attractive stewardess hands him a sandwich in a plastic bag.
STEWARDESS
    Breakfast.
Their eyes meet. Her smile goes beyond the call of duty.
OSNARD
    There's two ways we can handle this my dear . . . (Boorman 2000d: 5)

Boorman also adapts Pendel's ending, with Pendel telling the truth to Louisa about his past before cooking breakfast pancakes for his children.

Tailoring the Film Adaptation (2001)

Maeve Paterson was employed as the costume designer, Susan O'Conner-Cave as the wardrobe supervisor, Mark Holmes as the wardrobe master, and Carol Graham as the wardrobe assistant on the film. Rush's and Brosnan's attire was sourced from

Angels Costumiers, London.[8] Boorman explained that for the set of Pendel's shop they recreated Hayward's in Ardmore Studios, Ireland. However, the tailoring workshop was filmed on location in Panama, although it is unclear where this was as Boorman only alludes to "a tailor's shop we found in Panama City" (Boorman 2001).

Rush spoke of how he attempted to get into the role of Pendel by training with a tailor in Sydney, Australia, and one in Panama City:

> I said to John Boorman that I'd have to learn how to tailor. I hate cut-aways to someone else's hands . . . That sort of stuff also helps you to get into the mental state of the character. So I knuckled down . . . to learn how to chalk and cut up jackets. On the first tailoring demo I was chewing up the cloth and the chalk was going everywhere. Not a jacket you'd want to wear. ("Hot tickets" 2001: 9)

Although he does not name who he trained with, it could have been the family-run La Fortuna Bespoke Tailoring firm in Panama, established in 1951 and referred to as "the home of El Sastre de Panamá", of whom the master tailor at the time of the film's production was José Abadi ("About us" 2022). Members of the cast including Rush, Brosnan, and Jamie Lee Curtis (Louisa) visited La Fortuna's premises during filming to purchase personal bespoke items ("Memories of le Carré" 2011). It is not certain whether La Fortuna's workshop doubled as Pendel's in the film.

Rush's tailoring training comes to the fore in the film during two scenes in particular. The first is during the film's title credits when the audience sees Pendel "striking up" (marking) suit fabric with chalk, which Boorman has revealed was shot in one take (Boorman 2001). He sped up the take in the film in order to demonstrate the full process to the audience as well as to emphasize Rush's skill. The other scene involves Pendel measuring Osnard in the fitting room, which Boorman deliberately made smaller than would be "typical" in a tailoring shop because he "wanted to force the actors into an enforced intimacy" (Boorman 2001). During the scene, Pendel measures Osnard in the "correct" order, with Boorman commenting admiringly: "[Rush's] patter [and] jargon here is very accurate," acknowledging that this was adapted directly from le Carré's novel which was in turn inspired by Hayward (2001).

Regarding his casting in the role of Osnard, Brosnan also referenced the tailoring theme of the material, explaining that for his performance: "I have my work cut out for me. The role has embroidery of character that is so layered compared to the style of a Bond movie. In many respects it's a hundred miles from Bond yet they are of the same cloth. There's a great moral ambiguity to this character" ("Movie weaves its spell in Panama" 2000: 18). Brosnan's comments regarding the "layered" character of Osnard likely refers to the character not acting on behalf of "Queen and country," as exemplified by his portrayal of Bond, but rather Osnard working for own personal gain and pleasure.

Throughout the film, Osnard is deliberately costumed in ill-fitting suits, and creased casual clothes, which work to highlight the character's "anti-hero" status in that he does not wear a well-tailored suit as the "armour" of his profession—synonymous with the British Secret Service and the gentleman hero—but whose clothes reflect Osnard's rebellious and disruptive nature instead. Boorman explained: "In costuming Pierce, I

Figure 7 Osnard's "sloppy," ill-fitting suit.

wanted to get away from his Bond look and so we put him in all kinds of sloppy, casual clothes," although he admitted "but whatever you put on him looks elegant. I mean, it's almost impossible to make him look bad" (2001). Nevertheless, the costume team succeeded in the brief to make Osnard look "sloppy". In the pre-title scenes, we first view Osnard in Luxmore's office, wearing an ill-fitting dark grey two-piece suit made from a woven blend that is thrown into sharp relief when compared against Luxmore's attire, a three-piece chalk stripe navy blue silk-blend suit, blue-and-white striped shirt and maroon red tie with polka dots (Figure 7). Osnard's suit is deliberately cut to make Brosnan's physique look larger, with the waist and skirt of the jacket cut smaller to achieve this, and is reflective of le Carré's description of Osnard in the novel, of having a thirty-eight-inch waist, having a "heavy body" (1996: 38), being "well cushioned" and "generously built" (1996: 166). The jacket has wide, dropped shoulders, notched lapels, a two-button fastening, and flapped patch pockets. The trousers are flat-fronted, and beneath the jacket Osnard wears a blue cotton shirt that is loosely fastened with a badly knotted dark grey satin tie that includes a black dot pattern—the only time in the film when Osnard wears one.

In contrast, Pendel initially appears immaculately dressed until the scenes that occur during his daughter's birthday party to which Osnard has been invited by Louisa. Following this, Pendel's attire begins to disintegrate, reflecting the wilder lies he tells as he becomes further embroiled in Osnard's plot. We first view Pendel exiting his shop in the pre-title sequence wearing a three-piece cream linen suit (Figure 8), reminiscent of 1930s suit styles, something which Boorman was keen to evoke: "A *Casablanca* without the heroes" (Boorman 2001). The single-breasted jacket is cut straight, and includes wide padded shoulders, peaked lapels with a long gorge, two straight flapped pockets, one flapped ticket pocket, and a long, narrow skirt. A beige silk pocket handkerchief with dark polka dots is worn in the welted breast pocket. It has an ivory three-button fastening and the cuffs are fastened with four. At the rear there is a single vent. The waistcoat includes two welt pockets, five buttons of which four are fastened with the last unfastened at a wide cutaway notch and a cream silk back lining. The trousers are cut high-rise with a front pleat and plain hems. The shirt worn beneath the waistcoat is made from off-white cotton and has a moderate spread collar that is fastened with a silk tie that has light beige and grey horizontal striping that is separated by thin red and charcoal stripes between them. Along with the suit, Pendel wears a cream Panama hat with a dark taupe grosgrain ribbon and tan and cream blucher shoes.

It is this suit that Pendel wears in the final scenes of the film, and which becomes more disheveled and filthier after he discovers the body of Mickey, confronts Osnard and reveals the truth to Louisa at the end of the film, meaning that the suit works to develop the narrative and reflect the loss that Pendel experiences after his lies catch up with him, almost destroying the life he built in Panama in the process. As part of this, when Pendel attempts to convince Stormont that he lied to Osnard and to ask the American Air Force to abandon its raiding of the city, Stormont dismisses him and questions: "I'm sorry, but aren't you that tailoring fellow?" Boorman elucidated: "I think the way that Nigel dismisses [Pendel] emphasises the still lingering British class system"; "Here's the gentleman, and here's the tailor" (Boorman 2001).

A good example of the contrasting wardrobes for Pendel and Osnard comes when the pair meet one another for the first time in Pendel and Braithwaite (Figure 9). In this scene, Pendel wears a light grey silk-blend three-piece suit, of which the single-breasted

Figure 8 Pendel's immaculately-tailored, "*Casablanca*" suit.

Figure 9 The contrasting attire worn by Pendel and Osnard to reflect their personalities.

jacket is tailored with straight and padded shoulders, notched lapels, and is cut with a similar slim silhouette as with the cream three-piece suit. It has two flapped patch pockets on the hip, a welted breast pocket, is fastened with three buttons and four cuff buttons, and has a single vent at the rear. Again, the trousers are high-rise with a single pleat and plain hems. The waistcoat has notched lapels, a six-button fastening (with the last remaining unfastened), two welted breast pockets, two welted hip pockets and a dark grey silk lining. Pendel wears a white cotton shirt beneath the waistcoat with a spread collar, fastened with a light blue silk tie with green and white square pin dots, and French cuffs. By way of comparison, Osnard wears a grey basketweave jacket made from a wool/linen blend with wide, dropped shoulders, notched lapels, a three-button fastening made from horn, a welt breast pocket, two patch pockets and a single vent. Beneath the jacket, Osnard wears a creased and unfastened, loose-fitting and short-sleeved cream shirt with an open collar, and light grey linen trousers that are flat-fronted and plain hemmed.

Reviewing *The Tailor of Panama*

The American and British trade press and critics were also inspired to use tailoring and Bond quips when reviewing the film. Steven Gaydos believed that its "greatest achievement" was "a total deconstruction of the Bond hero" by Brosnan, referring to his portrayal as "The Spy Who Fucked Me" (2001: 6). *The Guardian* noted that Brosnan appeared to be "having the time of his life" with the opportunity to play the antithesis of Bond: "Bond's amiable 'sexist dinosaur' is here a man who blurts out, 'Look at those fucking tits!' . . . Brosnan's presence is the movie's subversive little masterstroke, and we can forget those sneaking suspicions we may once have had about his thespian limitations. He's nasty!" (2001: 16). Grace Bradberry felt that *The Tailor of Panama* was "not an off-the-peg spy yarn" and "could confuse audiences expecting a James Bond-style caper when what they really get is as much a sly parody of the serious spy film as anything else" (2001: 21). On Brosnan, Bradberry believed that he performed Osnard as "Bond's dissolute twin, and he certainly shows the sleazy flipside to 007's suavity". *Entertainment Weekly* stated of the film: "In a world full of off-the-rack thrillers, it's fine boutique quality." J. Hoberman opined that "*Tailor* is a cut above last season's best studio offerings. The performances are well turned out. The morality is stylishly grey. The attitude is almost fashionable. The Bond analogy is a joke that never stops giving, or surfacing," although the ending was a "late change and a poor fit" (2001: 115). Tom Chanty praised Boorman in that he had "fashioned a deft, dapper and quintessentially English comedy playing on our aggrandised post-colonial self image" (Chanty 2001: 81). Alexander Walker believed of Brosnan's and Rush's performances: "They take each other's measure with the finesse of a Savile Row fitting room" (2001: 29). Andrew O' Hagen felt that *The Tailor of Panama* was "well worth a look, though, not least for Brosnan's deliciously nasty subversion of his 007 persona," and Anthony Quinn referred to the actor's performance as "a sort of Hyde to 007's Jekyll." (O' Hagen 2001: 25; Quinn 2001: 10).

Not everyone, however, was keen on the film. Derek Malcolm concurred with Hoberman in that the end of the film "hints at what is wrong with this quick-paced, but undistinguished John Boorman version," and that "Brosnan can't seem to muster more than a very gentle parody of his 007 persona that it must have been thought that he was too charming a rogue to kill . . . [Brosnan] seems just too suave for the le Carré equasion" (2001: 38). Malcolm did, however, believe that the script was one of the film's strengths. Nicholas Barber drew upon tailoring quips to explain that "Boorman appears to be stitching together two separate films, each cut from a different cloth," namely contemporary politics and a "Cold War shaggy-dog story." (2001: 2) Philip Kerr complained of that the "supposed Savile Row excellence of the tailoring" strained all credulity: "Pendel's suits look as if they were cut with the same cheese knife that was used to edit the film. I have seen better suits worn on Martin Bell," though admitted that "Brosnan is rather good . . . playing a satisfyingly nastier James Bond" (2001: 48).[9]

Conclusion

This chapter has outlined the various influences of both Hayward and Bond on the different versions of *The Tailor of Panama* produced from novel to film. As Hayward concurred, both the tailoring shop in the novel and the film was inspired by the design of his own premises on Mount Street, and in the film, viewers receive a sense of the atmosphere that has been reflected upon by clients of Hayward. However, there are also small elements included in Pendel's characterization and dialogue that hint toward Hayward being part of le Carré's inspiration. For example, when Pendel tells Osnard that alpaca cloth "is in my fairly informed judgement the finest lightweight in the world bar none. Ever was and ever shall be, if you'll pardon me," and this has been adapted by Davies and Boorman in their scripts and Boorman's final film (le Carré 1996: 28). Furthermore, Rush's Pendel slips into the character's native Cockney accent when admitting his lies and embellishments to Louisa at the end of the film, an accent that Hayward retained throughout his tailoring career despite having been ordered to "work on his act" on first working for Montague Burton (Roberts 2019).

In relation to the influence of Bond, the references are more subtle in le Carré's novel, for example, the mention of Osnard's surname referencing a bird, a reference to the inspiration for Fleming naming his gentleman spy-hero "James Bond", Davies develops the Bondian references in his script, and Boorman goes further owing to the casting of Brosnan as Osnard, with both the pre-title sequence and the film's ending being re-written late in the production process. The pre-title sequence was included to provide an ironic scene where Brosnan's Osnard is presented in character and costume as the antithesis of Brosnan's Bond, as well as a twist on the perception promoted in other films relating to spying and suits in that they exemplify the "gentleman hero". The film's ending was changed owing to American preview audiences believing that there were to view a "quasi" Bond film where "Bond"/Osnard is shot by Pendel at the end of the film, although Boorman has subsequently argued that Pendel's shooting of Osnard was changed as that would not fit with the "gentlemanliness" of Pendel's characterization and Rush's portrayal. This is reflected by Pendel, who in the scripts and film is initially positioned as the "gentleman hero" with his "armour" of well-tailored suits, against Osnard's slovenly dressed "anti-hero" character. Pendel's suits slowly come to disintegrate following his "tailored" storytelling, with Pendel revealing to Louisa who questions why he would "do something like this?" in Boorman's draft script: "I don't know. It was a game. Tell a story, flesh it out a bit. Like tailoring" (Boorman 1999: 119).

Acknowledgments

I would like to thank David Millns, archives assistant at De Montfort University, and staff at the British Film Institute's Reuben Library for their help and assistance with my research for this chapter. I would also like to thank Glenys Roberts, Polly Westmacott-Hayward, and Del Smith for discussing Douglas Hayward with me.

Notes

1   Although, of course, no Savile Row tailor has to date been employed to create any of the suits worn by the Bond actors in the films (Llewella Chapman 2022: 10–11).
2   For a close analysis of the suits Hayward tailored for Moore's Bond films, see Chapman (2022).
3   For Fleming's description of Blades, see *Moonraker* (1955, 2009: 38–48). Caine and Moore visited Hayward's workshop to reminisce on their experiences in the BBC documentary *British Style Genius: A Cut Above—The Tailored Look* (2008). An excerpt of the documentary can be viewed here: https://www.youtube.com/watch?v=np -myoje0_8 (accessed January 23, 2022).
4   Sinclair explained the cut of Connery's Bond suits to the American *ABC News* network following the release of *Dr. No* in 1962 (*Inside Dr. No* 2000).
5   In Davies's script, the measurement is changed to "a very credible thirty two plus" (1998: 14).
6   This is a reference to the rise in popularity of the Labour Party in the UK, in which they were elected for Government in 1997.
7   See Chapman (2022: 211–13).
8   One of Rush's suits that he wore in the film was sold at a ScreenUsed auction with an "Angels" costume label attached, http://www.screenused.com/?sectionID=item-detail &subsectionID=index.cfm&item_id=5207 (accessed via the Internet Archive, January 20, 2022). Whether any items were sourced from La Fortuna remains unknown.
9   Kerr is ironically referring to the former British Member of Parliament, Martin Bell, who was sometimes referred to as "the man in the white suit," and who would often wear an over-large, ill-fitting, and crumpled off-white suit.

References

"About us" (n.d.), La Fortuna. Available online: https://www.lafortunapanama.com/about -us (accessed January 25, 2022).

Barber, N. (2001), "Culture," *Independent on Sunday*, 22 April: 2.

Boorman, J. (1999), *The Tailor of Panama* third draft script, 15 November.

Boorman, J. (2000a), *The Tailor of Panama* fifth draft script, 15 February [white]. [DMUSC; Papers of Andrew Davies; D/061/A/056/A/02].

Boorman, J. (2000b), *The Tailor of Panama* fifth draft script, 29 February [pink]. [DMUSC; Papers of Andrew Davies; D/061/A/056/A/02].

Boorman, J. (2000c), *The Tailor of Panama* production draft, 22 September. [DMUSC; Papers of Andrew Davies; D/061/A/056/A/03].

Boorman, J. (2000d), *The Tailor of Panama* fourth revised reshoot pages, 3 October. [DMUSC; Papers of Andrew Davies; D/061/A/056/A/03].

Boorman, J. (2001), "Commentary," *The Tailor of Panama* [Film] Dir. John Boorman, Ireland/USA: Merlin Films/Columbia Pictures.

Bradberry, G. (2001), "Unofficial Secrets Act," *The Times* (Section 2), 2 April: 21.

British Style Genius: A Cut Above—The Tailored Look (2008), [TV programme] BBC2, 14 October.

Bruzzi, S. (1997), *Undressing Cinema: Clothing and Identity in the Movies*, Abingdon and New York: Routledge.

Buscombe, E. (2000), "Cary Grant," in S. Bruzzi and P. Church Gibson (eds), *Fashion Cultures: Theories, Exploration and Analysis*, 201–4, London and New York: Routledge.

Le Carré, J. (1974), *Tinker, Tailor, Soldier, Spy*, London: Hodder & Stoughton.

Le Carré, J. (1996; 2017), *The Tailor of Panama*, London: Penguin Classics.

Chanty, T. (2001), "Tailormade: Boorman and le Carré Are Well Suited," *Time Out*, 18–25 April: 81.

Chapman, J. (2007), *Licence to Thrill: A Cultural History of the James Bond Films*, 2nd edn, London and New York: I.B. Tauris.

Chapman, L. (2022), *Fashioning James Bond: Costume, Gender and Identity in the World of 007*, London: Bloomsbury.

Columbia Pictures (2001), "Production Notes," December: 3.

Davies, A. (1998), *The Tailor of Panama* first draft script, January. [DMUSC, Papers of Andrew Davies; D/061/A/056/A/01-01].

"Douglas Hayward" (2008), *Daily Telegraph*, 30 April: 21.

Dr. No (1962), [Film] Dir. Terence Young, UK: Eon Productions.

Egan, G., ed. (2020), *Fashion and Authorship: Literary Production and Cultural Style from the Eighteenth to Twenty-First Century*, Switzerland: Palgrave Macmillan.

Fisher, M. (2011), "The Smiley Factor," *Film Quarterly*, 65 (2): 37–42.

Fleming, I. (1955; 2009), *Moonraker*, London: Penguin Books.

Fleming, I. (1958; 2009), *Dr. No*, London: Penguin Books.

Gaydos, S. (2001), "*Tailor* Pops Seams of Spy Genre," *Variety*, 19–25 February: 6.

Greene, G. (1958), *Our Man in Havana*, London: Heinemann.

Guardian (2001), G2, 2 April: 16.

Hoberman, J. (2001), "Sound Investitures," *Village Voice*, 3 April: 115.

"Hot Tickets" (2001), "Geoffrey Rush on. . . *The Tailor of Panama*," *Evening Standard*, 19 April: 9.

Inside Dr. No (2000), [Documentary] Dir. John Cork, USA: MGM Home Entertainment.

Jones, D. (1998), "Bespoke Buddha," *The Sunday Times*, 19 April: 420.

Kerr, P. (2001), "Tailored to Fit," *New Statesman*, 30 April: 48.

Kingsman: The Secret Service (2014), [Film] Dir. Matthew Vaughn, UK/USA: Marv Films/ Twentieth Century Fox Film Corporation.

Malcolm, D. (2001), "Brosnan Far Too Suave by Half," *Screen International*, 16 February: 38.

McInerney, J., N. Foulkes, N. Norman and N. Sullivan (1996), *Dressed to Kill: James Bond the Suited Hero*, Paris and New York: Flammarion.

"Memories of le Carré and the *Tailor of Panama*" (2011), *Newsroom Panama*, 6 September. Available online: https://www.newsroompanama.com/entertainment/memories-of-le -carre-and-the-tailor-of-panama (accessed 25 January 2022).

Moore, R. with G. Owen (2012), *Bond on Bond: The Ultimate Book on over 50 years of 007*, London: Michael O'Mara Books.

"Movie Weaves Its Spell in Panama" (2000), *Asian Age*, 18 March: 18.

North by Northwest (1959), [Film] Dir. Alfred Hitchcock, USA: Metro-Goldwyn-Mayer.

O' Hagen, A. (2001), *Daily Telegraph*, 20 April: 25.

Perkin, H. (1989), *The Rise of the Professional Society: England Since 1880*, London: Routledge.

Quinn, A. (2001), *Independent Review*, 20 April: 10.

Reynolds, N. (1996), "Two Tailors Cut Out to be le Carré Characters," *Daily Telegraph*, 11 October: 3.

Roberts, G. (2019), "Telephone Interview with Author," 8 November.

Smith, D. (2019), "In-Person Interview with Author," 14 November.

The Tailor of Panama (2001), [Film] Dir. John Boorman, Ireland/USA: Merlin Films/ Columbia Pictures.

Walker, A. (2001), "Dressed Down Bond," *Evening Standard*, 19 April: 29.

Westmacott-Hayward, P. (2019), "Telephone Interview with Author," 7 November.

11

Darling Men, Lover Boys, and Rogues

Connie Sachs, Molly Doran, and the Precarity of Institutional Memory in John le Carré's *Tinker, Tailor, Soldier, Spy* and Mick Herron's *Dead Lions*

Paul Lohneis

Introduction

This chapter explores the representation of Connie Sachs and Molly Doran in relation to their narrative function using discourses around paradigms of domesticity and motherhood, common associations with disability, and how these together might articulate formulations of abjection theory, in particular, those posited by Julia Kristeva (1982). The focus on women as custodians of family memory and other gender stereotyping, as well as the so-called "affective charge" of disability,[1] reframe these narratives with implications beyond the usual tropes of reductive genre storytelling. George Smiley and Jackson Lamb, the respective protagonists of these novels, navigate estranged and difficult relationships to access the arcane information held by Sachs and Doran. These women are gatekeepers to a secret but contested past, and in different ways also its personal construction. Both appear to have been emotionally and physically affected in the course of their work. The question as to whether their gender and somatic representation are significant as expressions of abjection is key, but also how it might correspond to the idea of the grand narrative, or inversely, the notion of the archive as a flawed symbol of intellectual freedom and a postmodernist metaphor for truth.

Following conventions in the spy novel, as well as in other genres, the archive is also a means to hide or obscure the truth, and in these novels is pitted against the recollections of the analyst or archivist, in this case Sachs and Doran, as the only true authoritative voice. Both characters could also be construed as the embodiment of historical narratives that deploy transgressive paradigms of matriarchy and disability to articulate mythologies of national character, in particular exemplifying moral certainty, resilience, or fortitude in a time of crisis. Sachs and Doran are instrumental in burnishing these versions of the past by couching them in their own nostalgic recollections. Their representation, however, poses questions as to whether this also operates in other ways, and becomes a means to bracket off aspects of history that are perhaps less palatable; difficult histories that might challenge a universalizing master narrative.[2] Connie Sachs "has a spurious logic, part inspiration, part intellectual opportunism, born of a wonderful mind which had never grown up" (le Carré 1999a: 115), and Molly Doran is "the keeper of overlooked history" (Herron 2013: 253). Although both are seen as paragons of competence, their characterization suggests that there is an underlying fragility to institutional memory, one that their respective male protagonists ultimately must control and remediate. Toby Manning (2018) has argued, in relation to Smiley (but equally this could be said of Lamb), that the function of the protagonist in this regard "repairs the breach and compact[s] the fictional ground, embedding the dominant ideology in a restabilized Cold-War consensus" (Manning 2018: 2); in effect, Smiley and Lamb must enact a paternalist exercise to curate and reinforce an enduring historical version of the past that extends beyond the text.

Smiley and Lamb rely on a small number of supporting characters to help them win the day. Foremost among these is Smiley's protégé, Peter Guillam, and in the case of Lamb, a larger interchangeable group that, among others, includes Catherine Standish, Louisa Guy, Roderick Ho, and River Cartwright. Connie Sachs is a serial character in four of the Smiley novels, and features most prominently in the Karla Trilogy: *Tinker, Tailor, Soldier, Spy* (1974), *The Honourable Schoolboy* (1977), and *Smiley's People* (1979). In a later novel, *A Legacy of Spies* (2017), she is used to provide context to the events of *The Spy Who Came in From the Cold* (1963). Sachs is "the unchallenged wunderkind of research into Soviet and Satellite intelligence agencies" (le Carré 2017: 208), conceived as a brilliant but eccentric intelligence analyst who has previously worked with Smiley at the Circus. Molly Doran, on the other hand, makes only brief appearances in all but one of the seven Lamb novels to date: *Dead Lions* (2013), *Real Tigers* (2016), *Spook Street* (2017), *London Rules* (2018), *Joe Country* (2019), and *Slough House* (2021). She is also the protagonist in "The Last Dead Letter," included in a short story collection, *Dolphin Junction* (2021). Doran has lost her legs in a previous espionage operation "way back at the dawn of time" (Herron 2017: 117), one in which Lamb is intimated to have been involved. She is now in a wheelchair, an archivist who presides over "Records" (Herron 2013: 252), an analogue collection of intelligence files in the basement of MI5 headquarters, known as the Park. Following Propp, Sachs and Doran could be described as characters whose double morphological meaning has been assimilated into a single function, which locates them at a shifting intersection between the categories of "donor" and "helper" in his scheme of narrative "Dramatis Personae."[3] Both characters conform to a similar genre typology: a helpmeet with privileged access to secret or special knowledge, whose principal narrative impact is as an intercessor between the protagonist and the truth. The access to this knowledge, and its interpretation expands the protagonist's partial view, which then later contributes to his eventual omniscient understanding and resolution of the case.[4]

As a corollary to the occluded nature of the past in these novels, Sachs's and Doran's representation as women who are older, stubborn, eccentric, physically disabled, and marginalized, plays on traditional gender stereotyping that situates truth as subjective and unknowable unless it is somehow controlled or managed. The liminal nature of this typology might also be seen as a potential threat to the status quo, one that sits outside "culture's hegemony" and could, at any moment, usurp the authority of the protagonist, or indeed the author himself.[5] In addition, tropes of disability in genre crime fictions that have conventionalized disabled but "cognitively exceptional investigators," as Ria Cheyne (2017) puts it, do little in these particular texts "to trouble reductive beliefs about disabled people."[6] Do they instead work to compound stereotypes in these authors' search for a memorable character, exacerbated also to some degree by their seriality? Their disabilities, for instance, become a recognizable adjunct to each of their appearances. Clare Parody (2011) propounds a theory that relates to the "transmedia franchise character" as a site to develop "brand markers." These are stock traits and motifs designed to promote audience familiarity that make a character more commercially amenable or "extensible" across different texts,[7] but also inevitably become a means to perpetuate dead metaphors and reinforce negative stereotyping. Sachs, for instance, is characterized in terms of her physical size and her memory, but also her pet dogs, her alcoholism, and her arthritis. Doran appears in a motorized wheelchair, her legs missing below the knee. She is heavily made up like a "doll," with "a face powdered to clownish white" (Herron 2013: 252), has an acerbic wit, and is usually found in the basement of the Park.[8] Are disability tropes, in this case, simply devices designed to further emphasize the difficulties associated with close reading and the precarious nature of truth? Does the character's material otherness also raise questions about the depiction of Sachs and Doran in relation to their narrative function, particularly as it evokes the notion of the "monster-woman" and its association with "intransigent female autonomy" (Gilbert, Gubar 2004: 841)? In their role as custodians of secret knowledge, these characters are proximate to an institutional archive, whether in its physical form or recreated through their own exceptional powers of anamnesis. This recalls a domestic paradigm of motherhood associated with oral histories, where, in this case, as women in the Intelligence Service they become the "prime keepers" of spy-familial memory.[9] If the Circus and the Park can be equated to home, then the peripatetic circumstances of the displaced protagonist (Smiley is variously retired, a "caretaker" chief, etc., and Lamb is exiled to Slough House) transform Sachs and Doran into "objects of memory," matriarchal authority figures, who are sought out and consulted as oracular sources of institutional history.[10] In functional terms, this is usually to provide exposition and consolidate backstory while also creating a deductive foil for the protagonist. As the embodiment of an institutional past, however, do these characters somehow contribute to the erosion of epistemological authority, or further, become a somatic expression of its abjection? Sachs and Doran appear to connote a different perspective to the officially held version of the past, even when it is absent,[11] and one that is particularly associated with trauma and the retelling of "difficult history."[12] As personal stakeholders themselves, these voices conflict with accepted institutional lore. They resist the teleological, and undercut the quasi-religious, universalizing master narratives of English exceptionalism that form the backdrop to these novels.

All Her Gorgeous Boys

Manning suggests that le Carré uses "a mythic register that can invest institutions with emotion—nostalgia, reverence, regret—that blends the personal with the political" (Manning 2018: 8). Le Carré's figuration of the past in Oxford, and in particular, Smiley's visit to Connie Sachs is a good example of this, which illustrates how the personal and the political in these texts are inexorably intertwined. Smiley's recollections, inflected by Proustian memories of his own time as a student "passing the Bodleian he vaguely thought: I worked there. Seeing the house of his old tutor in Parks Road . . . and hearing Tom Tower strike the evening six" (le Carré 1999a: 110), all work to establish an emotional connection with an Edenic, prelapsarian vision of England.[13] This is not just a relationship to his own past, organized by hierarchies of class and sexual politics, but also an ideological proving ground for other characters at the Circus, notably all male, and their recruitment as spies. Sachs already occupies an ancillary role in this economy because she is a woman. She has not followed the same formative path or been recruited in the same way as her male counterparts. "Her brothers were dons, Smiley remembered; her father was a professor of something. Control had met her at bridge and invented a job for her" (le Carré 1999a: 115). Sachs's intellectual credentials are measured not necessarily by her own academic attainment, but through those of her immediate male relatives. Her appointment to the Circus appears casual by comparison; a lesser process of selection based on her social standing, her aptitude for games like bridge, pastimes like the Times crossword, "her only recreation" (le Carré 1999b: 74), and a memory "as compendious as her body" (le Carré 1999a: 115).

Geraint D'Arcy (2014) describes Sachs as an "inside-outsider" because, although she belongs to the right social class, she is a woman in a man's world, and in order to remain on a comparable footing must trade on her memory and intellect.[14] For instance, in *A Legacy of Spies*, Guillam describes Sachs as a "brisk, chubby little body, bluestocking, born into the clover, and impatient of lesser minds like mine" (le Carré 2017: 208). Her role as an analyst in the Circus is frequently patronized in this way, with the use of pejorative terms like, "bluestocking," for instance, and is repeatedly juxtaposed or compared with references to her body and aspects of her disability, as if these were a necessary contingency. Sachs is politically relegated to a precarious position, first as a woman, and then as an older, disabled woman: intellectually brilliant but "castrated" and dismissible.[15] She is snared in this symbiotic opposition, "where the only thing a man could give her was time" (le Carré 1999a: 116). In this case, it is Circus "time," dispensed and controlled by Smiley. In narrative terms, Sachs becomes a functional prop for Smiley, supplying him with "difficult" information that might endanger the reputation of the Circus, while at the same time, making an emotional injunction to preserve it. In *Tinker, Tailor,* this contradictory position gives Sachs a moral authority, but demonstrates her limited agency, because she is the only member of the Circus who understands "the absurdity of the situation where there is a 'mole' working to destroy an institution that is already fatally flawed because of its adherence to outmoded class structures and sexual politics" (D'Arcy 2014: 280). At Oxford, to reach Sachs's house, Smiley makes "detours all the way," and eventually simply heads, "north" (le Carré 1999a: 111), reflecting perhaps both her dislocation and liminal status, because by living where she does, she remains in thrall to his earlier sentimental journey across the city, and all that this represents.

The sense of pilgrimage surrounding Smiley's visit; that he appears to have "walked all the way from London" (le Carré 1999a: 113), underlines the heightened atmosphere of their encounter, but in the context of his own recruitment as a spy at Oxford also lends it greater significance.[16] In a later visit to Sachs, which again conflates the sacred and secular, Oxford becomes a shrine to English exceptionalism; elevated to an "academic Jerusalem" (le Carré 1979: 214). Smiley metaphorically retraces his steps, and through Sachs's arcane knowledge, reappraises the official, elliptical version of the past, with its inevitable ramification for the future. In *Tinker, Tailor*, her premonition that Smiley's investigation is a revisionist exercise that will upset the accepted history; "making our time into nothing" (le Carré 1999a: 129), in effect comes true. It leads to the exposure of Haydon as a traitor, but also ties this to a broader narrative of national decline: "Poor loves. Trained to Empire, trained to rule the waves. All gone. All taken away. Bye-bye world" (le Carré 1999a: 125). Sachs is ostracized from the Circus when her suspicions are aroused by Polyakov, a Russian Cultural Attaché in London, and she is sacked for "losing her sense of proportion" (le Carré 1999a: 114). She is evidently badly affected by her arthritis and is now the landlady of a boarding house in Oxford. Smiley seeks information from her to corroborate a story that Polyakov might be "running an English mole" (le Carré 1999a: 126). When Smiley arrives, Sachs is tutoring a student called "Jingle," one of her so-called "dunderheads" (le Carré 1999a: 111). The scene affects an idealized paradigm of domesticity and motherhood: Sachs at home with her surrogate child toasting bread in front of the hearth. Her recollections are framed by Smiley's references to her "passion for family trees," and her "grandmother's glow of enchanted reminiscence" (le Carré 1999a: 115). The domestic tableau and her maternality are quickly displaced by a more enigmatic figure; someone who is sexually and politically outcast, similar perhaps to a fairy-tale witch, but one who displays an asexual-libidinal ambiguity that could be associated with both motherhood, and a supernatural "anti-mother" who threatens the status quo.[17] Sachs personates her anecdotes using a *galère* of voices and a satirical xenolalia to mimic former colleagues at the Circus. These are interspersed with sudden bouts of weeping, and the whole scene takes on an air of ecstatic theater. Sachs's impersonations, her inability to stay still due to arthritic pain, and her meditative digressions suggest altered states of consciousness that anticipate her shamanic impulse to predict the future. Smiley's offerings of sherry and platitudes become oblations, evoking quasi-religious rituals of purity and catharsis, engendering her "enchanted reminiscence" that later causes the Circus operation "Witchcraft" to unravel.

As a metaphor for the Circus, allusions to a fallen Arthurian Camelot, tie the fairy-tale trope to an abiding mythology that puts chivalric England at its center. Sachs might bear comparison to versions of Morgan le Fay in the Arthurian canon; in some stories a benevolent enchantress with the capacity for curative prophecy, and in others, an evil witch who threatens to destroy Camelot. The slippery nature of Sachs's representation makes more sense in this cultural context, and perhaps partially explains the negative stereotyping, if one considers that it is rooted in a patriarchal, imaginary past located both as a creation myth and a moral fable. Le Carré has described the Circus as "a vessel into which one has put all sorts of English attitudes both social and individual," and "a perfect metaphor for our time" (le Carré, in Bragg 1977). Arthurian romance situates England, and *ergo* the Circus, at the heart of a mythical origin story of Judeo-Christian culture, transposed here by Sachs, with the authority of her surrogate maternity, to manage a new crisis of national identity and to reconstruct it around her own personal experience. This is, on the one hand, a rose-tinted version of the past that centers on notions of martial honor and a "Just War,"[18] but also a domestic one inhabited by "all her gorgeous boys" (le Carré 1999a: 127). Sachs leverages the Second World War as a nostalgic touchstone of common experience, symbolized by the mementoes kept in a scuffed attaché case under her bed: "a good time," when "Englishmen could be proud" (le Carré 1999a: 129), and exemplified by Haydon, "the golden boy" (le Carré 1999a: 127). Once Sachs is exiled to "the real world" (le Carré 1999a: 114), Smiley compels her to readdress this mythology, remediating Polyakov, for instance, from a romantic, "fairy-tale hero" (le Carré 1999a: 121), into her unrequited lover, Aleks, "a six-cylinder Karla-trained hood" (le Carré 1999a: 123).

In *The Honourable Schoolboy*, Smiley calls on Sachs to reconstruct the past in the absence of institutional history. Sachs is rehabilitated and invited back to the Circus because the official record is missing or unreliable, due to Haydon's "traitorous trepidations" (le Carré 1999b: 4). She is still regarded with contempt for the secular reality she represents, in particular by Martindale, Smiley's arch critic, who decries Sachs as "that mangy old Russian researcher. . . the don woman from Oxford, against all reason, calling her a mother when she wasn't" (le Carré 1999b: 58). Once back at the Circus, Sachs reclaims her maternal function as "Queen Bee" (103, 178, 179), and "Mother Russia" (74, 392). Her other characterizing motifs also follow her; she is a "Don woman" (58, 570), though only, "some sort of academic" (74), "mangy" (58),[19] crippled (74, 181, 412, 570), and now "her extravagant shape" has suddenly "acquired a prim discipline" (le Carré 1999b: 302). Under Smiley, "the caretaker chief" (le Carré 1999b: 3), her return to the Circus is temporary, and as a potential threat to the stability of the institution, she must reside in its, "nether regions" (le Carré 1999b: 81). In *Smiley's People*, the circumstances of another meeting with Sachs are similar to those in *Tinker, Tailor*, as again Smiley seeks information about an old case, which this time leads to the defection of his nemesis, Karla. Sachs is now even further away from Smiley's "academic Jerusalem" than before. She lives in a "dacha" (le Carré 1979: 215), a single-room cabin in the woods, together with various domestic animals and her lover, Hilary. Sachs has again taken on the role of an ostracized "anti-mother," her lesbian sexuality here reinforcing her otherness and tying it to Smiley's recollection of Hilary's instability and mental breakdown at the Circus.

Smiley notices that Sachs has, "voices for everybody, . . . even for herself" (le Carré 1979: 222), and this encounter invites comparison with another folkloric witch; this time one more reminiscent of "Baba Yaga." The various references to Russia and the domestic circumstances in which the meeting takes place situate truth as both universal and subjective at the same time, and given Sachs's proximity to death, perhaps even more precarious than before.[20] Baba Yaga brings together the emergent themes in this chapter, particularly in relation to the duality of Sachs's representation, which as I have described, articulates a liminal ambiguity, an opposition that oscillates between paradigms of domesticity and motherhood, and those that threaten its destruction.

This conflict must be held at bay to protect the political status quo. In this case, Sachs is ostracized from the Circus, and like her cognate Baba Yaga, literally lives in the woods. Through rituals of purification and initiation, Baba Yaga also represents a means of magical transformation, with all the concomitant associations this has with Judeo-Christian ritual, but most significantly, where loss or sacrifice becomes gain.[21] In *Tinker, Tailor*, Smiley suffers "currents of alarm and anger and disgust" (le Carré 1999a: 130), after consulting with Sachs, because he now understands how his investigation might impugn the collective reputation of the Circus. This corresponds to the route Sachs herself must navigate between a sacred mythology of exceptional Englishness, the universalizing master narrative she so desperately clings to, and a far less rosy secular imperative to deliver the actual truth. It is here perhaps, that Kristeva's conceptions of abjection might be useful to interrogate Sachs's representation and the ambiguity of her narrative function. For Kristeva, abjection is both a state and a process; a polarity that creates an unbearable tension in relation to its subject, what she describes as "a vortex of summons and repulsion" (1982: 1). In simple terms, it concerns the restoration of stability, in which fear of the other becomes central to its formulation. If these characters are both a representation of institutional history and its abjection, then to achieve equilibrium or stability in this case, Sachs and Doran can only "hover[s] at the boundary of what is assimilable, thinkable" (Kristeva 1982: 18), or they must be expelled completely. The latter would defeat their narrative purpose, so instead their agency is proscribed in various ways; relegated as older, disabled, women, and hidden from view, but still accessible to the protagonist.

Holding the Candle

In much the same way that Connie Sachs fondly greets Smiley in *Tinker, Tailor*, Molly Doran in *Dead Lions* appears equally elated to see Lamb, apparently for the first time in fifteen years. As in the case of Sachs and Smiley, there is a personal history between Doran and Lamb that quickly demonstrates her lack of agency, an emotional response similar to Stockholm syndrome, revealed in her submission to Lamb in her subaltern role. Doran is the solitary occupant of Archive Level at the Park, and appears to exercise some autonomy, for instance, by overriding an official injunction and not allowing internal security, known as "the Dogs," on to "her floor" (Herron 2013: 253). She remains, however, in a "sunless cellar" (2013: 259), hidden from view, in a subterranean archive that appears to be the extent of her jurisdiction. Doran spends more of her time at the Park than not, working the nightshift so as not "to frighten the youngsters" (2013: 253), and her representation is comparable to Sachs's, because, although Doran is still part of the organization, her situation suggests both sequestered confinement and abandonment. As an ostracized figure, she is only called upon to respond to unofficial inquiries about histories that have been effectively discarded already. This becomes more pronounced by the distinction between the un-digitized past in Doran's archive, and "the Beast," her collective name for the Park's digital databases. It is an opposition that plays on the notion of Doran's claims to possession of a "sole bank of reliable memory" (Herron 2018: 198), and framed in terms of moral panics about the security and resilience of digital infrastructure: ". . . when they crashed—which they were bound to, sooner or later—there'd be no telling them apart anyway. Just one dark screen after another. And she'd be the one holding the candle" (Herron 2013: 255). D'Arcy suggests that Sachs is "the personification of an archive and consequently her exile from the Circus becomes an economic strategy in the pursuit of information" (2014: 11). In Doran's case, this is more nuanced; here "information" is located in a hierarchy, prioritized, according to its accessibility (or digital vulnerability), and limited to the analogue files in her archive. The institutional "strategy" to keep it at arm's length, however, remains the same, but now is managed by doubly protecting it, consigning it to an internal exile, and literally burying it in the basement of the Park.

Doran describes herself as "there to tick all the boxes. Age, disability, gender" (Herron 2021: 197), and this knowing set of criteria against which she ironically scores her employability status, are inevitably the stereotypical signifiers for her marginalization. As a consequence, she becomes, "a creature of the dark" (Herron 2018: 216), "the old bat with the wheels" (Herron 2016: 205), with, "absences below the knees" (Herron 2013: 287), whose face is "a thick white mask of powder" (Herron 2016: 94). The "near-silent" wheels of her wheelchair that occasion her sudden appearance (Herron 2021: 117), and its cherry-color and velvet upholstery lend Doran an air of the Gothic and evoke conventions found more readily in the horror genre. Her disability and her ghoulish appearance become her principal motifs, as does her isolation. Doran's depiction here again invites comparison to Sachs, as the archetypal fairy-tale witch. As somatic expressions of institutional memory, these representations evince a rejection of difficult histories. But in Manichean terms: exemplified by the moral simplicity of the fairy tale, or indeed the generic horror story. These characters are ostracized because they represent something terrifying, or as Lamb jokingly downplays it: "you cripples make us normal people uncomfortable" (Herron 2016: 195). In effect, Doran and Sachs represent a secular, postmodernist threat that potentially challenges a sacred, normative master narrative. Both suffer exclusion but are retained by the protagonist despite the threat they might pose to this status quo: Smiley re-employs Sachs in *The Honourable Schoolboy*, while Lamb engineers the reversal of Doran's forced dismissal in *London Rules*. This is perhaps a concession to their core narrative function but also highlights the "inside-outsider" ambiguity that is necessary in the restoration of reputational stability in these texts, and how in each case, this is managed. In *Dead Lions*, for instance, Lamb's consultation with Doran becomes just such an exercise: essentially a ritual in institutional catharsis. It leads to the exposure of Nikolai Katinsky as Alexander Popov, a Russian sleeper agent, motivated by revenge for the historical destruction of a Soviet closed town, ZT/53235, which is indirectly caused by the discovery of a British spy. The Katinsky narrative challenges the official version of the past. Once he kills himself, the reputational threat recedes, and by exposing his real identity, Doran's role in, "purifying the abject" (Kristeva 1982: 17), is complete; this iteration of the exceptionalist ideal is once again restored.

Doran demonstrates her commitment to the institutional family by guarding "her fiefdom like a lioness its kill" (Herron 2016: 194). She lectures "baby spooks" annually in a "one-off class," presumably a catechism as to how the institutional past should be managed, which is known "to reduce the intake's hardest customer to a bubbling jelly"

(Herron 2017: 118). This invokes another aspect of her surrogate maternality, where tough love is channeled in a reimagining of spy-familial history. Doran fills the gaps in the archival record by fictionalizing them, replacing her defective knowledge with nostalgia. In "The Last Dead Letter," Doran eulogizes Dominic Cross, a former spy based in Berlin, in an exchange of information with Lamb: "illuminating one of the mysteries that haunted her archive" (Herron 2021: 191). Doran trades Lamb's illicit access to Park records for his own secret knowledge of the past. This encounter between the two characters takes place at St Leonards, the "Spooks' Chapel" (189), where former spies are memorialized under their false identity or cover name. St Leonards symbolizes the liminal tension of abjection, a recalibration of institutional memory, in which sacred ideals meet the expiation of secular truths to propagate benign "legends" and reaffirm a numinous mythology. As Service "legends" themselves, both Doran and Lamb have also become part of this narrative of exception.[22] This recalls *Dead Lions*, and Doran's realization that Alexander Popov is not a legend, but flesh-and-blood Nicolai Katinsky, a "Bogeyman" (2013: 259), because he threatens to upset a previously accepted version of the past unless he is remade somehow or expunged from the record entirely.

Conclusion

The allusion to the representation of masculinity in the title "Darling Men, Lover Boys and Rogues" and how this reflects the position of Sachs and Doran, particularly in light of their disability, are illustrated principally by their relationship with the protagonist in each case. This tends to be a conventional one centered on masculine power, but in this reading, the dichotomy between these women's benign maternity and political/sexual otherness is made more complex. As protagonists, Smiley and Lamb are not conventional in physical terms, insofar as they are both overweight and "at best middle-aged" (le Carré 1999a: 20). They are objects of affection but are seen as flawed by both women, which casts them as lovable rogues to be mothered, and also, perhaps without contradiction, as potential lovers, though this characterization never impinges on their authority as protagonists. What is implicit, however, is a key comparison around the notion of mobility. Both women are largely trapped by their disability, whereas the men, despite their somatic representation, are always on the move and free to act as they see fit.

The representations of Sachs and Doran suggest that the heuristic recovery of hard-to-get-at information is more than just a convention in these texts. As serial characters they reinforce genre stereotyping, in order to suggest, perhaps, that the truth is itself problematical and difficult, with the aspersion that any formal historical account is somehow unreliable precisely because it excludes politically unpalatable, but nevertheless important, subjective experiences like theirs. The embodiment of difficult history, inflected through these characters' gender, age, and disability, might well typify "freakish females in male-authored texts" (Gilbert Gubar 2004: 842), but also become sources of abjection located at the boundary of what is "assimilable" (Kristeva 1982: 18), and as such, must be carefully managed if a male-centric status quo is to prevail. Paradigms of domesticity and motherhood become a useful counterpoint to Sachs's and Doran's function as narrators of crisis, because it also articulates their redemptive double role to reformulate difficult histories as cautionary tales or myths that ultimately affirm this status quo and its transcendent grand narratives.

Notes

1   Cheyne (2017).
2   What Jean-Francois Lyotard describes as "localised representations of restricted domains."
3   Propp (1968: 66–70).
4   Christopher Booker describes this as "seeing whole" and suggests that in many cases this can be attributed in narrative terms to the "feminine value," an opposition to the "power of darkness" centred on the ego. The "feminine value" has "the ability to see whole, making connection, the healing of division and life": 257.
5   Paraphrasing Sherry Otner in *The Madwoman in the Attic*, Gilbert and Gubar (2004: 841).
6   See various references in *Disability in Genre Fiction*, Cheyne (2017).
7   A theorising of "the franchise character as extensible, designed to anticipate, sustain and generate serial development and representation across multiple texts." Parody (2011).
8   Connie Sachs in *Tinker, Tailor, Soldier, Spy*: "Her arthritic fingers were turned downward as if they had all been broken in the same accident, and her arm was stiff." (113); "a rocking chair that relieved certain pains: she could sit nowhere for long" (121).
9   Gillis suggests that "women became the prime keepers of family memories, but in the absence of home they also became objects of memory" (125).
10   In *A Legacy of Spies*: "You climb the five scruffy steps to the doorway of the Victorian eyesore that we variously call HO, the Office or just the Circus. And you're home": Guillam returning from "some god-forsaken outpost of empire" (13).
11   In *The Honourable Schoolboy* the record is missing or unreliable. See Smiley's interview with Sam (82–3).
12   See Rose (2016).
13   See James Chapman (2018: 203–22).
14   See D'Arcy (2014).
15   See Mulvey (1989).
16   See Chapter 1: "A Brief History of George Smiley" in *Call for the Dead* (1961).
17   See Szachowicz-Sempruch (2019).
18   See the notions of a "Just War": conceptions of muscular Christianity, most notably celebrated in the chivalric romances of the late Medieval period and the promotion of chivalric values during the Crusades in Keen (1984).
19   In *The Honourable Schoolboy* this is also used to describe her dog: "She has brought Trot, her mangy brown mongrel, with her. He lies misshapenly across her vast lap." (395).
20   Propp makes reference to Baba Yaga in his *Folktale* (7). In another essay he describes her as "Mistress of the Forest," and how she is transformed from a mother and mistress of the beasts into a witch. Propp uses Baba Yaga as an example to show how folktales are historically derived from religion. In some texts Baba Yaga is both "donor" and "villain" at the same time, appearing in both roles as sisters. For more see Johns.
21   Ibid.
22   See *Spook Street*: "Molly Doran wasn't quite a Service legend, but she was heading that way" (118).

References

Bragg, Melvin (1977), *The Lively Arts: In Conversation with John le Carré*, BBC, 2 September: 25.

Chapman, James (2018), "James Bond and the End of Empire," in *James Bond Uncovered*, edited by J. Strong, London: Palgrave Macmillan.

Cheyne, R. (2017), "Disability in Genre Fiction," in *The Cambridge Companion to Literature and Disability*, edited by C. Barker and S. Murray, 185–98, Cambridge: Cambridge University Press.

D'Arcy, G. (2014), "'Essentially, another man's woman': Information and Gender in the Novel and Adaptations of John le Carré's *Tinker, Tailor, Soldier, Spy*," *Adaptation*, 7 (3): 275–90.

Gilbert, Sandra and Susan Gubar (2004), "The Madwoman in the Attic," in *Literary Theory: An Anthology*, edited by Julie Rivkin and Michael Ryan, 2nd edn, London: Blackwell Publishing Ltd.

Herron, Mick (2013), *Dead Lions*, Kindle edition, London: John Murray.

Herron, Mick (2016), *Real Tigers*, Kindle edition, London: John Murray.

Herron, Mick (2017), *Spook Street*, Kindle edition, London: John Murray.

Herron, Mick (2018), *London Rules*, Kindle edition, London: John Murray.

Herron, Mick (2021a), *Dolphin Junction*, Kindle edition, London: John Murray.

Herron, Mick (2021b), *Slough House*, Kindle edition, London: John Murray.

Johns, Andreas (2004), *Baba Yaga: The Ambiguous Mother and Witch of the Russian Folktale*, Oxford: Peter Lang.

Keen, Maurice (1984), *Chivalry*, Yale University Press.

Kristeva, Julia (1982), *Powers of Horror*, New York: Columbia University Press.

Le Carré, John (1979), *Smiley's People*, London: Hodder & Stoughton.

Le Carré, John (1999a), *Tinker, Tailor, Soldier, Spy*, [1974] London: Sceptre.

Le Carré, John (1999b), *The Honourable Schoolboy*, [1977], London: Sceptre.

Le Carré, John (2011), *The Spy Who Came in from the Cold*, [1963], London: Penguin Classics.

Le Carré, John (2012), *Call for the Dead*, [1961], London: Penguin Classics.

Le Carré, John (2017), *A Legacy of Spies*, London: Penguin.

Manning, Toby (2018), *John le Carré and the Cold War*, London: Bloomsbury Academic.

Mulvey, Laura (1989), *Visual and Other Pleasures: Language, Discourse, Society*, London: Palgrave Macmillan.

Parody, P. (2011), "PhD Thesis: A Theory of the Transmedia Franchise Character," University of Liverpool, September 2011.

Propp, Vladimir (1968), *The Morphology of the Folktale*, 2nd edn, Austin: University of Texas Press.

Rose, Julie (2016), *Interpreting Difficult History at Museums and Historical Sites*, London: Rowman & Littlefield.

Szachowicz-Sempruch, Justyna (2019), "The Witch Figure in Nineteenth and Twentieth-Century Literature," in *The Routledge History of Witchcraft*, edited by J. Dillinger, London: Routledge.

Coda

Stella Rimington: *Open Secret* and the "Mission to Inform"[1]

Ann Rea

Stella Rimington caused a public furor[2] when she published her autobiography, *Open Secret*, in 2001, just three days after the 9/11 attacks in the United States, which she observes in the Preface to the 2002 edition to justify the work of the Secret Intelligence Services. Rimington, with the authority of many years of working in the Services and becoming MI5's first woman Director-General, asserts the public need for the Intelligence Services more than ever in a time of *jihad*, even before the era of "Wikileaks" and the release of classified documents to the general public.[3] She observes,

> Understandably, unless faced with clear evidence of a present danger, British governments of whatever political colour will lean towards providing maximum civil liberty. To behave differently is to let terrorism win its war against democracy before the shot is fired. But after an event such as September 11th, we see the balance begin to swing gradually the other way, to give more emphasis to our safety than our civil liberties. (Rimington [2001] 2002: xvii)

While many of us might expect cover-ups and inadequate public information, Rimington implicitly believes in the rightness and justice of the Intelligence Services[4] to which she gave her professional life, and that greater public knowledge of this work would benefit the public *and* the Service. Her autobiography and indeed her spy novels are written to serve this clearly defined mimetic purpose. Rimington began publishing spy novels in 2004, with her series of novels featuring Liz Carlyle: *At Risk* (2004); *Secret Asset* (2006); *Illegal Action* (2007); *Dead Line* (2008); *Present Danger* (2009); *Rip Tide* (2011); *The Geneva Trap* (2012); *Close Call* (2014); *Breaking Cover* (2016); *The Moscow Sleepers* (2018); and finally *The Devil's Bargain*, which features Manon Tyler (2022). These novels variously focus on Rimington's areas of expertise and experience: the Middle East and jihad; Northern Ireland, where she worked on counterterrorism; Russia's threat to oligarchs living in Britain and efforts to sow political distrust and anti-NATO sentiments in Europe. Rimington lays claim to no *literary* ambitions in these novels, but instead aims to be informative. As she notes, the nature of terrorism in Britain meant that the work of MI5 would come to the attention of the public, "if only through trials in the courts" (Rimington [2001] 200: 253). She argues, "If their [the public's] entire knowledge of MI5 was based on James Bond films or John le Carré novels, or even on the sort of reporting which was at that time common in the press, they might think not a word we said could be trusted" (Rimington [2001] 2002: 253). She perceived that, "the task was to raise the level of the debate about security matters. It was a mission to inform, using my high public profile as a way of doing it" (Rimington [2001] 2002: 253).

This use of the word "mission" contrasts sharply with the popular concept of spy missions, with their gadgets and explosions, but according to Rimington, the necessity to inform the British public about the Intelligence Service arose from the very existence of fiction by Ian Fleming and John le Carré who, she claims,

> had done their jobs too well. They had convinced us all that the world of intelligence was full of intrigue and excitement involving men like Alec Guinness and Sean Connery. When a middle-aged woman popped up as the only representative they had ever been told about, looking as someone said to me "as if you could have been a teacher," no-one knew how to react. Their readers thought MI5 was just like spy stories; that it had not changed since the days of Vernon Kell before the First World War. Not surprisingly, they did not know things had moved on. By saying nothing at all about ourselves and what we did, we had allowed the myths to continue. The semi-covert handling of the announcement of my appointment had merely made things worse. (Rimington [2001] 2002: 243–4)[5]

Against this background of glamour and thrills, Rimington sought to defend the work and the secrecy of the Intelligence Services even before WikiLeaks and Edward Snowden and the ubiquity of information on the internet led to advocacy for greater public availability of the information. Rimington herself knew secrecy was often necessary, and in *Breaking Cover* (2016) she portrays Liz Carlyle striving for a compromise between secrecy and openness, as a Communications officer takes on the task of informing the public about this balance, where we read, "As Liz saw it, there was a necessary amount of secrecy about the intelligence services and people—but there was also *un*necessary secrecy, which could be positively harmful to effectiveness in the modern world" Rimington 2016: 16). In *Open Secret* Rimington asserts,

> Intelligence and security services are vital to democracies, and to be effective they must be able to conduct their operational activities in secret. When I first joined MI5 in 1969, that was taken to mean that practically nothing could be said in public about the Service, about what it did, where its offices were, the people who worked there. Over the years that has gradually changed. Thinking has moved on, and it will move on further, with developments in the law and in the arrangements for oversight of the secret services. [. . .] But it is clearly still true that revelations about specific operations, details of sources of information, human or technical, or about the precise way in which intelligence is gathered are damaging and risk undermining the effectiveness of the intelligence machinery and eroding the confidence of the human sources of information, who often provide the best intelligence and risk their lives to do so. (Rimington [2001] 2002: 244)

When she agreed to give a Dimbleby Lecture on BBC in 2006, Rimington felt that "it was a seminal occasion in terms of our [MI5's] relationship with the British public" (Rimington [2001] 2002: 257). The publicity her gender attracted, when she became Director-General of MI5, made her determined to exploit this public's awareness to further the goal of openness. Much of the media attention to her appointment was personal:[6] journalists frequently commented on her clothes and other aspects of her appearance, scrutiny that women in public life often experience. Rimington's autobiography also describes the familiar domestic struggles of a professional woman with children, distinguishing them from memoirs of men in similar roles. And men in positions such as the Director-General of MI5 contend less with the conflict between publicity and privacy that Rimington describes. But the coincidence of her sensational appointment with the Service's efforts toward greater openness, which she supported and would further, contributed to public interest in her appointment.

Openness versus secrecy lies at the heart of the autobiography, as the title emphasizes. In her role as Director-General from 1992 until she retired in 1996, Rimington sought to inform the public about the Service's defense against terrorism as well as the Cold War, and then increasingly against Russia's growing hostility to the West. Rimington observes that when she joined the British intelligence community in 1969, the "shadows [of the Cambridge spies] hung heavily over us," by which she meant not just Burgess, Maclean, and Philby, but by then the "very recently uncovered and not at that time publicly known, Anthony Blunt, the Keeper of the Queen's Pictures and spy for the Soviet Union" (Rimington [2001] 2002: 99). The result of these traumatic scandals, which appears repeatedly in the essays in this volume, was as Rimington asserts, "an old-fashioned, inward-looking organization, cut off from modernizing influences and afraid and unwilling to change" (Rimington [2001] 2002: 99). The uncontrolled publicity provided by Peter Wright's *Spycatcher,* released in 1987 in Australia, under a gag order in Britain but smuggled into the country, provided Rimington's main headache as director of counterespionage.[7] Wright alluded to the existence of a Russian mole in MI5, which would become a central preoccupation of spy fiction and of the Service. The double agency of traitors within the Intelligence Services was the nightmare from which MI5 could not awake, from the early 1950s until Margaret Thatcher exploited it by outing Sir Anthony Blunt in November 1979,[8] after a cover-up of fifteen years. Considerable discredit to the Service resulted from the duplicity of some members of the Intelligence Services and their Establishment ties.

As some of the studies in this volume of the fiction from the 1960s assert, the period after the 1950s exposures coincided with the rise of a meritocracy, one from which Rimington herself would benefit. Erin Carlston explains the shift, after Burgess-Maclean, toward "anti-intellectualism and the new right," which was opposed to "the intellectual, Eton-educated, aesthete cabal that allegedly controlled British foreign policy" and what the *Daily Mirror* described as, "the Old School Tie brigade" that gave way to "a transformed Conservative party identified more with the nonconformist petty bourgeoisie than with the aristocratic or upper-middle-class Anglican establishment" (Carlston 2013: 211). Rimington herself observed this transition from inside MI5 and comments on it frequently in the novels when her protagonist, Liz Carlyle, observes the few remnants of this cabal among her colleagues in MI5 and

Counterterrorism. The fiction, at least, suggests that these Establishment figures are now no more powerful than any other officer and that by the 2010s their numbers steadily diminish.

Early in *Open Secret*, Rimington describes her initial experience of MI5 in Leconsfield House where the Service maintained its Registry, containing its files of information. As both Rosie White and Paul Lohneis argue in this collection of essays, women maintained this store of information, and Rimington describes the "Registry ladies" who did the work of "file making, storing and the indexes." Mick Herron's Molly Doran (Lohneis) presides over the Service's archives, as Lohneis explores, and as Rosie White argues, women in espionage often did the work of the "invisible functionary, the secretary and silent organizer" to whom Eva Horn refers (Horn 2013: 171).[9] Rimington moved through the ranks from the lowliest positions, to become a "professional" within the service, rising to its highest position—Director-General. But she reveals that even by the 1980s, "MI5 still seemed to me a male-dominated, old-fashioned organization, which was going to take years to change" (Rimington [2001] 2002: 171). She observes that in her earliest years, "Many of the men had come into MI5 from a first career in the Colonial Service," many of them lacking in motivation, and she notes that "The nearest the women got to the sharp end of things [. . .] was as support officers to the men who were running the agents" (Rimington [2001] 2002: 101, 102). Rimington's appointment as the first woman Directory-General of MI5 "did not mark the opening of the floodgates; it was not followed immediately by a great surge upwards of female graduates," and only when women in the service objected to the discriminatory recruiting and promotion policies she notes, "The men in charge were genuinely surprised," resulting in some policy changes in recruitment and promotion, if not yet to the "taboos on what the women could do" (Rimington [2001] 2002: 124). In the novels, Liz Carlyle still observes vestiges of gender discrimination, although she carries similar prestige to her author. Indeed Rimington commented in an interview, "I take some pleasure, I must say, in putting things in Liz's mouth that I might quite have liked to have said—but probably never did—when I was in her position." Rosie White writes that "the fictional spy is [. . .] a fantasy of agency for the subject in an increasingly confused and confusing world" and Liz Carlyle certainly performs this function for readers, perhaps especially women (White 2007: 6). For Rimington herself, Carlyle seems to serve as a slightly more glamourous, but nevertheless pragmatically plausible avatar. Rimington showed in her fiction that terrorism grew as a threat, with jihadi terrorism within Britain, as well as, potentially rogue IRA terrorists, and attacks on Russian oligarchs who denounce Putin's regime.[10]

Her prominence and professional prestige were unusual, nevertheless, and she acknowledges that women were still underrepresented in the upper levels of the service. Rimington attributes much of this sexual discrimination to the recruiting practices which depended, still, on Oxbridge Dons suggesting to undergraduates that they might consider a different type of work, and certainly did not improve diversity. A Security Commission enquiry into "management practices and style" in 1985 observed the Service's "closed culture [and] remote management," of which, Rimington contends, "None of those who had the responsibility in those days had any relevant training or experience. What's more, because of the closed and secretive culture of the time, they were isolated from contact with thinking that was going on elsewhere" (Rimington [2001] 2002: 178).

Essays in this volume refer to the prevalence of "Establishment" men working in the British Intelligence Services (White, Chapman, Lohneis, Rea) and Rimington's fiction contains references to men wearing various old school ties that Liz Carlyle initially misreads, and then learns to recognize, largely as warning signs of arrogance and paternalism. The novels' American CIA character, Andy Bokus notices that Geoffrey Fane wears a "tie sporting the discreet stripes by which Englishmen communicate with each other," suggesting a prevailing semiotics of the public-school tie (Rimington 2008: 45). Liz learns to read the signs of American preparatory school ties too, noting that their stripes run the opposite way from those on British ties, especially in *Dead Line* (2008). The mutual mistrust between the British and American "cousins" becomes cultural confusion when Miles Brookhaven confides to Liz that Andy Bokus carried "a hell of a chip on those big shoulders of his, in spite, Miles says, of the 'myth [. . .] that it's a classless society'" (Rimington 2008: 196–7). Liz's reaction is that "[s]he wasn't going to pretend to understand the intricacies of American society," but this detail suggests that both the American and British services are riven by surprisingly similar class distinctions (Rimington 2008: 197). In *Dead Line* (2008) American Brookhaven observes that Bokus, who went to a state university, "can remember the days when half the staff went to Yale. A bit like your services and Oxbridge" (Rimington 2008: 197). Liz says, "It changed here a long time ago," and thinks, "And a good thing too" (Rimington 2008: 197). Bokus thinks of Brookhaven as "preppy" and as an "Ivy Leaguer," and shows class insecurity and resentment that make him unreliable (Rimington 2008: 222). Bokus was reluctant to admit his mistake in trusting Kollek, the rogue "agent" who seeks to blow up delegates to a Middle East peace conference to gain revenge for his father's death. Rimington, therefore, depicts *American* class resentment as problematic, with the British Service as largely having overcome its structure built upon privilege.

Rimington began to publish espionage fiction in 2004 and remains the most notable woman publishing spy fiction today. Her motivation for doing so is very different from that of other writers in this study and her concern is to offer a realistic portrayal of the Service like the one that her autobiography establishes. Written before she began writing fiction, her autobiography makes no mention of the novels, of course, but Rimington's Counterterrorism and then MI5 agent protagonist, Liz Carlyle, resembles Rimington herself, which is amusing when we consider that many of the men in the novels are secretly in love with Liz! Like many of fiction's spies, Liz contends with the loneliness that her work creates, with long hours and the need for secrecy, and even danger, impeding intimate relationships,[11] a common concern of spy fiction that makes a human claim on the reader's sympathies. In spite of these romantic tendencies, Liz is a proven stoic, and values the colleagues who have proven to be trustworthy, guarding herself against those who have let her down by impulsive decisions or disloyalty.

The fiction also engages with the complexities of the "special relationship"— Britain's close diplomatic ties with the United States—largely in the depiction of a variety of American CIA agents working in London, whose dependability Carlyle must gauge. *Present Danger* (2009), set in Northern Ireland, shows that MI5's role in counterterrorism arose from the IRA campaign that began in 1969. *Open Secret* portrays the IRA threat as one toward British security personnel in Great Britain, not to citizens of Northern Ireland, perhaps attributable to the division of labor between the police in Northern Ireland and the Intelligence Services. But still, Rimington's reference to "the emergence of a serious threat of terrorism on our own doorsteps" reveals that she considered Northern Ireland as being outside the UK (Rimington [2001] 2002: 106). *Present Danger*'s Liz Carlyle works in Belfast for several months, and the surprisingly accurate and warm portrayal of the city doubtless stemmed from Rimington's own experience there. The novels depict both counterterrorism and counterespionage, MI5's concern after the end of the Cold War. The end of the Cold War, rather remarkably with hindsight, led to the British Service advising former communist leaders in how to reconcile intelligence with democracy. The autobiography's chapter entitled "End of the KGB" shows an optimism ultimately belied by subsequent trends in some former communist countries. Nevertheless, Rimington's fiction displays her awareness of Russia's growing totalitarianism and the overspill of its domestic intrigues on to British soil in *Illegal Action* and *Breaking Cover*. The end of the Cold War created the public perception the need for MI5 had also ended and she observes, "We felt a need to explain ourselves and to justify our existence in a way that we had never felt before" (Rimington [2001] 2002: 229). The remit of the novel of espionage, in her hands, often becomes the portrayal of counterterrorism and counterespionage.

Rimington's—and Liz Carlyle's—story of MI5 marks the impressive progress of the author herself, from the lowly "invisible functionary, the secretary and silent organizer" that recurs in the chapters in this volume, to Director-General, and a category of feminine power above and beyond the old categories in the fiction (Horn 2013: 171). Depiction of Liz Carlyle celebrates, for Rimington, the excitement of what she was able to experience, as well as the knowledge she acquired. Rimington's mimesis—her realistic portrayal of the work of the Secret Intelligence Services—serves a very clear and consciously articulated purpose for her. "This is what work in the intelligence services is like," she is effectively telling us. She employs the simplest form of literary representation then—"this is what it like," or verisimilitude—as a direct relationship between the portrayal and the thing portrayed. Robert Snyder objects to Stella Rimington's mimetic portrayal, asserting the superiority of the highly self-reflexive diegesis in novels by, for example, le Carré and Eric Ambler. But the Liz Carlyle novels strive for something different: a realistic portrayal of a senior woman spy with true agency, albeit working within the confines of the Service, at the highest level in her profession. The stereotypes surrounding women spies, voiced by observers of both Liz Carlyle and Rimington herself, lead to comparisons with Fleming's Rosa Kleb, notably not the Mata Hari or lowly official of Horn's definition. Even Rimington evokes Fleming's caricature of the woman spy, when Liz's colleague Dave Armstrong compares Liz's "pointed plum-coloured," kitten-heeled shoes to Rosa Kleb's sensible brogues with the stiletto blade in the toe (Rimington 2004: 3). Liz, we are encouraged to see, is instead a heterosexual woman who wears frivolous shoes on occasion, but is nevertheless competent, professional, and pragmatic, even if she is engaged on no mission to kill. We cannot dismiss Liz's professional prestige by saying that it is unrealistic, since her own literary creator, Rimington herself, rose even further in the SIS, from the lowest to the highest ranks.

Notes

1 Rimington ([2001] 2002: 253).
2 See Robert Lance Snyder's chapter about Rimington in *The Art of Indirection in British Espionage Fiction: A Critical Study of Six Novelists* (2011), in particular, the opening pages in which Snyder discusses the "chorus of male denunciation" of her publication of *Open Secret*.
3 Rimington's 2016 novel, *Breaking Cover* features two Russian illegals, under other nationalities, who, the Service assumes, "were targeting the anti-surveillance lobby, probably trawling through internet chat rooms, looking for people to approach" (Rimington 2016: 324).
4 An example of this can be seen when Rimington talks about the Gibraltar incident, in which IRA terrorists planned and would imminently carry out a bombing attack on a British military source. The shooting of the terrorists before they had planted the bomb provides an example of an intelligence operation making a judgment about the level of risk presented by a terrorist threat. Rimington's autobiography evinces an absolute faith that the legal system's investigations into the incident would have thoroughly and correctly explored the justification and appropriateness of the shootings. She notes the stages of investigation, from the inquests up to the European Court of Human Rights, which judged that the killings were not justified to defend the safety of others. Rimington objected to the television program *Death on the Rock,* which, she posits, "make no attempt to give honest consideration to the difficulties of balancing the risks in operational situations," which she attributes to "their enthusiasm to prove that the state is a fault" (Rimington [2001] 2002: 210).
5 Points of overlap between spy fiction and the direct, lived experience of espionage work are the focus of *The Great Game: The Myth and Reality of Espionage*, by Frederick Porter Hitz. Written by former Inspector General of the American Central Intelligence Agency, Hitz's book is blurbed as "show[ing] the remarkable degree to which truth is stranger than fiction" even as he examines spy fiction with a lens that highlights where it departs from verisimilitude.
   We should remember too, John le Carré's 1989 introduction to *The Spy who Came in from the Cold*, which recounts le Carré's own experience as an agent in Berlin, when he observed the erection of the Berlin Wall. Rimington must have been aware of le Carré's own experience as an agent in the Intelligence Services.
6 In their efforts to characterise Rimington, the media applied various reductive stereotypes of women to her, labelling her as "Housewife Superspy," "Queen of All Our Secrets," and "Woman of Mystery" (Rimington [2001] 2002: 244). She adds, "Later on I became a hard-eyed manipulator of Whitehall. Even later still I was repackaged as 'M', Ian Fleming's Head of MI6" (Rimington [2001] 2002: 244).
7 Rimington attributes Wright's publication of the book to his resentment about what he perceived as the unfair way in which his pension was calculated. She emphasizes that his entitlement had been reviewed several times, both inside and outside the Service.
8 BBC ON THIS DAY | 16 | 1979: Blunt revealed as "fourth man."
9 This section of Rimington's autobiography clearly influenced Ian McEwan's writing of *Sweet Tooth,* (2012) whose protagonist, Serena, works in MI5's Registry.
10 *Illegal Action* (2007), the third book featuring Liz Carlyle, revolves around a scheme by the Russian government to silence a wealthy oligarch living in London and appears

to have been written in reaction to the poisoning in London of Alexander Litvinenko, a former KGB officer and dissident living in London.

11   Robert Lance Snyder, in his chapter on Rimington in *The Art of Indirection in British Espionage Fiction: A Critical Study of Six Novelists* (2011), objects to the novels' references to Liz's romantic life which, he argues, turn the novels onto "romantic fiction" (Snyder 2011: 165).

References

Carlston, Erin G. (2013), *Double Agents: Espionage, Literature, and Liminal Citizens*, New York: Columbia University Press.

"For Former MI5 Head, Real Life Inspires Spy Novels," *NPR*, July 21, 2008, 12:54 PM ET, Heard on Morning Edition.

Horn, Eva (2013), *The Secret War: Treason, Espionage, and Modern Fiction*, Evanston: Northwestern University Press.

Rimington, Stella ([2001] 2002), *Open Secret: The Autobiography of the Former Director-General of MI5*, London: Arrow Books.

Rimington, Stella (2004), *At Risk*, New York: Vintage Crime.

Rimington, Stella (2007), *Illegal Action*, New York: Vintage Crime.

Rimington, Stella (2008), *Dead Line*, New York: Vintage.

Rimington, Stella (2009), *Present Danger*, London: Quercus.

Rimington, Stella (2016), *Breaking Cover*, London: Bloomsbury.

Snyder, Robert Lance (2011), *The Art of Indirection in British Espionage Fiction: A Critical Study of Six Novelists*, Jefferson: McFarland and Company.

White, Rosie (2007), *Violent Femmes: Women as Spies in Popular Culture*, London: Routledge.

Index

Printed in Great Britain
by Amazon

56b53aa9-e234-4eda-bc4f-921d9230acfeR01